S. C. Porter

ALSO BY E. ANNIE PROULX

Heart Songs and Other Stories

Postcards

The Shipping News

E. Annie Proulx

ACCORDION CRIMES

Scribner

SCRIBNER
1230 Avenue of the Americas
New York, NY 10020

Designed by Jenny Dossin
Set in Adobe Garamond

Manufactured in the United States of America
1   3   5   7   9   10   8   6   4   2

Library of Congress Cataloging-in-Publication Data
Proulx, Annie.
Accordion crimes / E. Annie Proulx.
p.   cm.
I. Title.
PS3566.R697A63   1996
813'.54—dc20   96-16299
CIP

ISBN 0-684-19548-8
0-684-83311-5 (signed edition)

ACKNOWLEDGMENTS

I wrote *Accordion Crimes* during two years of disruption and uprooting that included the deaths of my mother and several relatives and friends, a move in stages from Vermont to Wyoming with books incarcerated in boxes for eight months, constant travel, a broken wrist, a publisher takeover. I never would have finished this book without the help of many interested and kindhearted people who aided with accordion source material, lore, lists of books, clippings, photographs, postcards, tapes and CDs, introductions to accordion-music scholars and accordion musicians. To all listed below my truly grateful thanks, but especially to Liz Darhansoff, coolheaded, who many times calmed my anxiety that the book could not stand another interruption, to Barbara Grossman who helped get it under way, and to Nan Graham who gave me lunch, time and a long leash.

Thanks for a 1992 Guggenheim Fellowship which helped with research for *The Shipping News* and *Accordion Crimes,* and is still helping another, now in progress. The Ucross Foundation of Wyoming provided a quiet island (literally, thanks to a spring flood) where sections of this book were written. Special thanks to Elizabeth Guheen and Raymond Plank for a hundred kindnesses.

Thanks to Patricia A. Jasper, director of Texas Folklife Resources, for permission to listen to the Resource Center's collection of taped interviews with Texas accordion musicians and for introducing me to the southeast Texas music scene from Antoine's in Austin to the Continental in Houston, and thanks to Rick Hernandez, Texas Commission on the Arts, who put me in touch with her. Thanks to Jane Beck of the Vermont Folklife Center for several useful suggestions. Huge thanks to musician-scholars Lisa Ornstein and Nick Hawes of the Acadian Archives at the University of Maine in Fort Kent. Lisa's deep knowledge of Québec music, her kind introductions to Marcel Messervier and Raynald Ouellette, accordion virtuosi of Montmagny, and her translation help were invaluable. To Raynald Ouellette, not only an internationally renowned musician but a maker of fine accordions and organizer of the *Carrefour mondiale,* thanks for his remarks on the history of the accordion and its manufacture. To Marcel Messervier, whose fine accordions and extraordinary musicianship are legendary, thanks for an hour in his workshop and for his comments on his life as an accordion musician. Thanks to Jerry Minar of New Prague, Minnesota, for his help with the elusive Chemnitzer concertina, better known locally as the German-style concertina. Thanks to Joel Cowan, witty and peripatetic editor of *Concertina and Squeezebox.* Thanks to Bob Snope, accordion repairman at the Button Box in Amherst, Massachusetts, for his patient and thorough explanations of all facets of accordion lore, for his suggestions, and for reading the manuscript for accordion errors. Thanks to Rhea Coté Robbins of the Centre Franco-Américain, University of Maine at Orono, and to Vermonter Martha Pellerin of the trio Jeter le Pont, for their comments on Franco-Americans and Franco-American music. Thanks to Bart Schneider, musician and editor of *Hungry Mind Review,* for winging the odd accordion book my way. Thanks to Pat Fisken of the Paddock Music Library, Dartmouth College; to Judith Gray, folklife specialist, Edwin Mathias of the Recorded Sound Reference Center, and Robin Sheets, reference librarian of the Music Division, all at the Library of Congress. Thanks to Laura Hohnhold of *Outside* magazine for the occasional Chicago accordion tidbit. Thanks for the gimlet eye of Christopher Potter at Fourth Estate who picked up errors in fact and nuance. Thanks to Jim Cady of Cady and Hoar for clarifying a detail of a character's business dealings. Thanks to my German editor Gerald J. Trageiser at Luchterhand Literaturverlag, who caught errors both subtle and gross. Thanks to Barry Ancelet at the University of Southwestern Louisiana for his invaluable suggestions.

Thanks to long-playing help from my son Jonathan Lang, sound engineer, and my daughter-in-law, blues singer Gail Lang, for instruction books, esoteric articles on current innovations in the accordion world, tapes of wizard accordion musicians, and advice on ancient speakers. To my son Morgan Lang, student of ethnomusicology, who first told me about the Chinese sheng, ancestor of the free-reed instruments, and widened my musical experience in every dimension, thanks. Thanks to my son Gillis Lang for San Diego accordion clips and witty puns, and to my daughter, Muffy Clarkson, who eased my heart and provided English muffins in extraordinary variety. Thanks to my father, George N. Proulx, for his true story of a punishing teacher who put male students under her desk.

To Joel Conarroe, thanks for the photograph of Uncle Dick in knickers with an accordion on his knee; thanks to Claire Van Vliet for the personalized paper accordion toaster by Cece Bell; thanks to Jon Fox for the miniature accordion (and case) that does everything but play. To Dan

Williams, thanks for hard-to-find records, tapes and CDs, and dittodit-toditto to Robert Warner for extraordinary accordion ephemera. Thanks to Bobby Doberstein for advice and help with everything from ski routes to stuck garage doors. Thanks to Kimble Mead for the Hawaiian Cow-boy (and many other) tapes, and to the Breakfast Club who showed me real-life collectors in full frenzy. Thanks to Laurent and Pascale Gaudin who brought me back hard-to-find musette recordings from France, and thanks to Tom Watkin, fellow enthusiast and companion tripper to Montmagny's annual weekend *de l'accordéon*. Thanks to the Tattered Cover Bookstore in Denver, especially Dotty Ambler, for books, help and quick service beyond all normal expectations. Finally, thanks to strong Gillian Blake in New York who carried bags of books from the Museum of Television and Radio back to my hotel for me.

My dad came over with a button accordion in a gunny sack, that's about all he had.

RAY MAKI,
liner notes, *Accordions in the Cutover*

Without the presence of black people in America, European-Americans would not be "white"—they would be only Irish, Italians, Poles, Welsh, and others engaged in class, ethnic, and gender struggles over resources and identity.

CORNEL WEST, *Race Matters*

Caminante, no hay camino,
Se hace camino al andar.

Traveler, there is no path,
Paths are made by walking.

ANTONIO MACHADO

The green accordion travels from hand to hand over a hundred-year period, plays the music of many different ethnic groups. Necessarily, historic personages mingle and converse with invented characters. In some cases invented characters have been placed in real events; in others, real events have been slightly or greatly fictionalized. The story of the fictional accordion maker is set into a fictionalized account, based on March 1891 articles in the New Orleans paper the *Daily Picayune,* of the real 1891 lynchings of eleven Italians in New Orleans. Throughout the book appear real newspaper advertisements, radio spiels, posters, song titles, scraps of verse, labels on common objects and lists of organizations; mixed in with them are fictional and invented advertisements, spiels, posters, song titles, verses, labels, objects and lists. No characters are based on living, real-life persons. The accordions are what you might expect.

The Accordion Maker

A TWO-ROW BUTTON ACCORDION

The instrument

It was as if his eye were an ear and a crackle went through it each time he shot a look at the accordion. The instrument rested on the bench, lacquer gleaming like wet sap. Rivulets of light washed mother-of-pearl, the nineteen polished bone buttons, winked a pair of small oval mirrors rimmed in black paint, eyes seeking eyes, seeking the poisonous stare of anyone who possessed *malocchio,* eager to reflect the bitter glance back at the glancer.

He had cut the grille with a jeweler's saw from a sheet of brass, worked a design of peacocks and olive leaves. The hasps and escutcheons that fastened the bellows frames to the case ends, the brass screws, the zinc reed plate, the delicate axle, the reeds themselves, of steel, and the aged Circassian walnut for the case, he had purchased all of these. But he had constructed and fashioned the rest: the V-shaped wire springs with their curled eyes that lay under the keys and returned them to position in the wake of stamping fingers, the buttons, the palette rods. The trenched bellows, the leather valves and gaskets, the skived kidskin gussets, the palette covers, all of these were from a kid whose throat he had cut, whose hide he had tanned with ash lime, brains and tallow. The bellows had eighteen folds. The wood parts, of obdurate walnut to resist damp and warpage, he had sawed and sanded and fitted, inhaling the mephitic dust. The case, once glued up, rested for six weeks before he proceeded. He was not interested in making ordinary accordions. He had his theory, his idea of the fine instrument; with the proof of this one he planned to make his fortune in La Merica.

He set the fourths and then the fifths with a tuning fork and his naked ear, catching an aching but pleasurable dissonance. His sense of pitch was sure, he heard harmonies in the groan of hinges. The button action was quick, the subtle clacking like the rattle of dice in a gambler's hand. From a distance the voice of the instrument sounded hoarse and crying, reminding listeners of the brutalities of love, of various hungers. The notes fell, biting and sharp; it seemed the tooth that bit was hollowed with pain.

The world is a staircase

The accordion maker was hairy and muscular, a swell of black hair rising above a handsome face, an ear like a pastry circle. His irises were an amber color: in his youth he suffered the name "Chicken Eye." When he was twenty he had defied his blacksmith father and left the village to work in the north in the accordion factories of Castelfidardo. His father cursed him and they never spoke again.

He returned to the village when Alba, his betrothed, sent news of the opportunity to rent a plot of land with a handkerchief vineyard and miniature house. He was glad to leave the city for he was embroiled in a dangerous affair with a married woman. His hairiness drew women's attention. From time to time in their marriage his wife accused him of infidelities, and there were several. Accordions and hair drew women, could he help this? She knew it—his gift for music had attracted her powerfully, his silky pelt, the hair curling from the throat of his shirt.

He took chills easily, shivered when the sun passed behind a cloud. His wife was warm and it was possible to stand close to her and feel the heat that radiated from her as from a little stove. Her hands seized children, plates, chicken feathers, goats' teats with the same hot grasp.

The rented vines, *Calabrese, Negro d'Avola, Spagnolo,* made a harsh wine without name, sold as a blending wine to foreigners. It was the local custom to hold the fermenting must on the skins for a week, the source of the wine's rough character and purple-black color. Swallowed straight down, it raked mouth and throat and, as other astringent liquids, was reputed to have beneficial medicinal qualities. The foreign buyers paid very little for it, but as it was the only possible source of cash income, the growers could not protest. The lack of land, money and goods, the boil of people, produced an atmosphere of scheming and connivance, of sleight of hand, of oaths of collusion, of brute force. What other way through life?

Besides the vineyard the accordion maker and his wife rented five old olive trees and a fig espaliered against the wall, and their lives were concerned with children, goats, hoeing and pruning, lugging panniers of grapes. At night the poverty of the place sounded in the whistle of wind through the dry grapestalks and the rub of moaning branches. Their hold on the plot of land weakened as the landlord, who lived in Palermo in a house with a copper roof, increased the rent one year and again the next.

The accordion maker's shop was at the end of the garden—a hut that once housed sick goats with a floor space no larger than a double bed.

On a shelf he had pots of lacquer, a box of flake shellac, various glues and sizings, squares of mother-of-pearl, two corked vials the size of a little finger containing bronze paint. Here were files, scrapers, his chisels—one a flake of chert he had unearthed from the soil—and gouges, taps, dies, metal tongues and hooks, tweezers and lengths of spring-steel wire, calipers and rules, nippers, punches and clamps, many of these tools stolen from the factory in Castelfidardo—how else to gain possession of these necessary things? With a rigger's brush of a few sable hairs he painted scrolls and keys, flourishing triple borders bristling with bronze thorns. He sold the instruments to a dealer in the market town who, like the wine merchants, paid him almost nothing, enough to feed magpies, perhaps.

As the accordion maker gained mastery over his craft he began to imagine a life not possible in the malicious village, but likely enough in the distant place that rose and set in his thoughts: La Merica. He thought of a new life, fresh and unused, of money hanging in the future like pears hidden in high leaves. He whispered and murmured at night to his wife. She answered, "never."

"Listen," he said aloud furiously, waking the baby, "you know what your brother wrote." That bracket-faced fool Alessandro had sent a letter, spotted with red sauce and grimy fingerprints, that said come, come and change your destiny, turn suffering into silver and joy.

"The world is a staircase," hissed the accordion maker in the darkness. "Some go up and some come down. We must ascend." She refused to agree, put her hands over her ears and moaned when he announced a departure date, later pointed up her chin and rolled her eyes like a poisoned horse when he brought home the trunk with metal corners.

The General's paralysis

The accordion maker's posture, suggestive of hidden violence and challenge, caught the eye of other men. He stood with the left foot planted, the right cocked suggestively, his shoes black broken things. His character betrayed his appearance; he seemed *louche* and aggressive, but was not. He disliked grappling with problems. He depended on his wife to comb through difficulties. He produced the vaulting idea, the optimistic hope, she ordered the way in everything—until now.

How many wake in the night, stretch out a hand to the sleeping mate and encounter a corpse? In the evening the accordion maker's wife had wept a little, lamented the looming journey, but there was nothing, nothing that gave a sign paralysis would come in a few hours to crouch

above her ribs and thrust shims into her joints, stiffen her tongue, freeze
her brain and fix her eyes. The accordion maker's fingers trembled up
the rigid torso, the stone arm, the hard neck. He believed she was a dead
woman. He lit the lamp, cried her name, slapped her marble shoulders.
Yet her heart beat, sending the blood pounding through the pipes of
veins until her rib-harp vibrated and this encouraged him to believe the
affliction was a temporary fit that would ease when daylight came, but
it did not.

As days passed it became clear that this paralysis was an evil put on her
by some choleric force, the will of an enemy that she never leave the village, for she had been a healthy woman, her only defects an occasional
seizure dating from childhood and a clouded eye, injured by a hurtling
almond as she danced at her wedding supper. She was never ill, up from
childbed within a day, running her household with authority. Her strong
contralto voice was made for command. Her father had called her "the
General" when she was a child. Such a person has enemies.

The accordion maker was ready to throw himself from a cliff or rush
into the wilderness, only let someone say what he should do. He
appealed to his mother-in-law.

The mother of the paralyzed woman folded her arms. It was as
though a powerful dwarf with a basso voice spoke from within the
baggy yellow skin. "Go. Three years. Make money and return. We will
care for her. It is better that the man goes alone first." The wet olive eyes
shifted.

The old father nodded a little to show the good sense in this advice.
Their oldest son, Alessandro, had emigrated to New York two years earlier and sent them letters stuffed with money, letters describing his
handsome clothes, his position, his fine new bathtub (the bathtub in
which he was fatally attacked a few years later by a Bohemian, lunatic
with rage because Alessandro had kicked his son for making a noise on
the stair; even then the old parents denied that their family was cursed).

The accordion maker's daughters, sniveling because they could not
go on the ship to La Merica, were parceled out with aunts. Silvano, the
only boy—conceived on a Sunday—was eleven, old enough to stand a
day's work; he would be the one to accompany the father. The girls
looked at him with hatred.

Another who suffered from these events was the frozen woman's
younger sister, a child herself, whose task it became to funnel gruel
through the stiff lips, to ease the stinking cloths from beneath her sister's dribbling vents, to roll the wasting body with its raw bedsores to
new positions, to drip clear water into the dry, unseeing eyes.

The helpful young man

The father and son left in the dimming starlight of morning, descending the steep path with jumping steps, away from the rigid woman and her relatives' restless eyes, the resentful girls, past the stone in the shape of a beehive that marked the limit of the village. The accordion maker carried the trunk, his tools and the instrument on his back in a kind of harness made from knotted rope. The boy, Silvano, bent under a rolled-up sheepskin and a grey blanket, a canvas bag stuffed with cheese and loaves of bread. The village was out of sight forever in less than seventy steps.

They walked for two days, took a ferry across glittering, white-stippled water, then trudged on to a railway station. During this journey the father hardly spoke, thinking first, with tears marring his view, that his wife had been the cloth of his shirt, the saliva in his mouth, then recasting the situation in the harsh male proverb—the best cold meat in a man's house is a dead wife. Unfortunately his wife was neither quick nor dead. The boy, gangling, humiliated by his father's silence, no longer asked questions but, as they approached villages, filled his pockets with fingerstones to pelt snarling dogs.

It seemed Sicily was pouring out as cornmeal from a ripped sack. The railway station swarmed with people shouting, gesticulating, dragging valises and wooden boxes this way and that, crowding from the door of the station onto the platform, itself a crush of relatives embracing and clenching each other's shoulders, a storm of heaving cloth, the women's head scarves folded in triangles and knotted under their chins, brilliant geometries against the mass of black backs.

The father and son boarded the train and waited for it to move in the company of buzzing flies and passengers struggling on and off. They sweltered in their woolen suits. On the platform the people seemed mad. Women cried and threw their arms up in the air; men pummeled the shoulders and upper arms of departing sons; children howled and clung to receding skirts with grips that tore fabric; babies wrenched their mothers' hair. The conductors, the train officials, shouted, pushed back the unticketed. Down the length of the train passengers leaned out the open windows, crushing and kissing hands for the last time, their mouths contorted by grief.

The accordion maker and Silvano sat unspeaking, their eyes casting over the scene. When the train started, a cry went up as those on the platform watched the cars glide away from them, saw dear faces already changed into the unknowable masks of strangers.

An aging man, corpse-thin in a rusty suit, broke from the crowd and ran alongside the train. The hooks of his eyes caught Silvano. Strangers often stared at the boy, taking in his big cheeks and sagging eyes, an uncommon face for a child, something Spanish or Moorish in those red-rimmed eyes. The man shouted something, repeated it, shouting and running as the train gathered speed; he ran with spidery legs over the rough ground beside the track, and as the track curved and the train drew away, the boy looked back and saw the man still running, far behind the train, and at last on all fours, motionless in the locomotive's falling smoke.

"What did he say?" demanded the father.

"He said to tell Silvano—I thought he meant me—this other Silvano to send him money. He said he would die if he couldn't get away."

The accordion maker ground his teeth, crossed himself. It twisted his spine that a stranger would call his son's name and ask for money. But the one on his left, a strong young man who had just boarded the train, an ugly fellow with a gap between his front teeth and a flattened nose, pulled his sleeve.

"I know that one! *Pazzo, pazzo!* That crazy one comes to the platform every day, chases the train crying for someone to tell his brother to send him money to come to New York! *Pazzo!* He has no brother! His brother died a hundred years ago, crushed by the hooves of a horse in La Merica! And you, you are going there?"

The accordion maker felt the pleasure of a direct question; the urge to confide warmed him.

"To New York. My wife and children, all of us were going, yet two months ago, think of it, only two months, my wife became a wooden plank, transfixed by an evil illness, and now only the boy and I go. She is not dead, she lives, yet cannot move. It was our plan to go to La Merica, start a small music store for instruments and repair. I am an accordion maker, also a little of a musician, you know, I can play for weddings, saints' days. I know a hundred songs. An accordion maker knows how to make the instrument show its voice. But constructing the accordion is my destiny. I understand the instrument, I have a feeling for it. Also I can repair other kinds—a cracked violin, mandolins, a torn drum."

He opened the case to show the instrument's sleek lacquer, the polished buttons. He sounded a flourishing chord, sprinkled a few drops of notes to illustrate the superiority of the tone to this young man, not to play, because the grave condition of his wife made that unseemly. It seemed he had to behave as a widower. He returned it to the goatskin case slowly, tied it closed.

"Very nice! A very beautiful instrument! I have cousins who play, but they have nothing so fine as this. One of them, Emilio, was wounded last year by a man so engorged with jealousy that he later perished from apoplexy. Perhaps you will do well in New York! Perhaps not. New York attracts Italians from the north, stuck-up *Liguri*. The place is full of them! Many musicians there, many accordion makers! There is already an enormous music store on Mulberry Street where they sell piano rolls, everything, books, gramophones, mandolins, sheet music! In New York the winters are savage, the flesh freezes on the bone, there is snow! Winds of a ferocity not to be imagined! There, in old buildings, Sicilians live as close as straws in a bundle! New York? Everything is cold, noise and rush! I have stayed in New York for a year! Unbearable! It was in New York that the crazy one's brother was dragged to his death by a horse, a horse maddened to fury by arctic temperatures! You should do what I am doing— I am going to Louisiana, to New Orleans! The climate is as soft as baby's flesh! The soil, blacker than the pupil of the eye, of incredible fertility! Sicilians are there in every kind of work! The shrimp and oyster boats! Tremendous opportunity! No music store such as you describe! The place cries out for one! The people of this city love music! The Gulf is a cornucopia—shrimp of such a size a man can hold only two in his cupped palm, oysters as large as cakes and as sweet as honey, fish of every kind, and a rich nut, the pecan, which grows wild everywhere! The fruit boats give work at once! You can quickly earn enough to make your music store! Think of it! You get off the ship, walk down the dock and get a job in two minutes carrying boxes of oranges! The man hiring you speaks Sicilian, he understands you! Before you sleep on your first night in La Merica you have earned money, more money than you'd see in a week, in a month, in Sicily! But maybe you have relatives waiting for you in New York, perhaps you have cousins and many brothers, perhaps you have *connections* who will help you battle the immense music store on Mulberry Street? Perhaps you already have enough money to open your own music store at once?" He lit a cigar, offered one to the accordion maker who took it with effusive thanks.

No, no, they had no one, he said, rejecting the detested brother-in-law, Alessandro, with his face like dirty clothes. He did not want to see him, that Antichrist. After all, that one was not blood of his blood. No, he said to the young man; his son was not particularly musical, but he was strong and good in mathematics. Whether boats or music stores, he would be useful. The accordion maker leaned forward, asked, what more of Nov' Orlenza, of Luigiana? Were the inhabitants truly inclined toward music? The aromatic smoke formed a cloud around their heads.

Greenhorn, thought the young man. One more among thousands and thousands and thousands. He did not count himself.

All the way to Palermo, the train jerking down the long incline to the sea, the young man amused himself by extolling the delights of Louisiana, inventing musicians who, for lack of competent repairs, played broken husks of instruments, were forced to sing *a cappella* because there were no accordions to accompany them, until the accordion maker did not know how he could have considered New York's wolflike cold and crowded tenements, a New York inhabited by the braggart Alessandro— who, alone of all people on earth, persisted in calling him "Chicken Eye"—when a city of desperate musicians awaited him. In Nov' Orlenza he would work at anything, unload bananas, juggle lemons, skin cats, to put every scudo—*penny*—aside. In his pocket he had the name of a boardinghouse and a map drawn by the young man on the train who had already sailed on another, swifter ship—so many ships left Palermo for America. The young man had sworn he would meet their ship in Nov' Orlenza, help them find their way. The map was only if they missed each other.

And so the accordion maker veered onto a fatal course.

The land of alligators

At Palermo he hesitated. The ship passage to New Orleans was more expensive than that to New York. He had planned to use the savings from not purchasing passage for the paralyzed wife and the daughters to give him a little sum toward the music store. Yet he bought the tickets, forty American dollars each, for he conducted his life as everyone does—by guessing at the future.

The Palermo wharf boiled with immigrants. The accordion maker and Silvano stood apart, the trunk between the man's feet, the instrument on his back. Already he dreamed of himself in the whitewashed shop, his tools on the table before him, looking over a list of orders for accordions. In the background he imagined a vague woman, perhaps the paralyzed one restored to action, perhaps a milk-skinned *americana*.

Silvano was repulsed by the moil on the wharf. It was as though some great spatula had scraped through Italy and deposited this crust of humans on the edge of the oily harbor, the squirming crowd a thousand times greater than at the train station. Everywhere were people standing and bending, a man wrapped in a dirty blanket and dozing on the stones, with his head on a suitcase and a knife in his lax hand, crying children, women folding dark coats, anxiously retying cords around scarred cases, men seated on baskets of possessions and gnawing heels of bread, old women in black, scarves knotted under their bristly chins, and running boys, clothes flapping, insane with excitement. He did not join them, only watched.

Hour after hour the noisy, dragging mass shuffled up the gangplank onto the ship lugging bundles and portmanteaus, parcels and canvas telescope bags. The line of people hitched along the deck to a table where a pockmarked official counted off groups of eight, families sundered, strangers joined, all the same to him, gave the tallest man in each group a numbered ticket that signified their place at mess call. These eight, familiar or unknown to one another, were bound together by this meal ticket over thousands of miles of water. In the accordion maker's group was a disagreeable old woman with a face like a half-moon, and her two jabbering nephews.

The accordion maker and Silvano descended three levels to the men's quarters, long tiers of berths like wooden shelves in a warehouse. They had the top boards, a slot where they slept and stowed everything: the trunk and the accordion, the rolled-up sheepskin and the grey blanket. Oil lamps cast a phlegmy glow, shadows that swayed like hanging men, cast an uneasy, twitching light that raised doubts and encouraged a belief in demons. They had seen the steady calm of electric lights in Palermo.

(The smell of kerosene, bilge, metal, marine paint, the stink of anxious men, of dirty clothes and human grease, mixed with the briny flavor of the sea, etched Silvano's sensibilities, a familiar effluvia later on the Texas shrimp boats, and not even the rank stench of crude oil and gas in his roustabout days in the early decades of the new century erased it. For a while he worked on the tank farm fire crews, shooting cannonballs into fiery storage tanks to release the oil into the circular ditches around each of them before it exploded. He went on to Spindletop, Oklahoma's Glenn Pool, caught a glimpse of Pete Gruber, the King of Oil, in his million-dollar rattlesnake suit, worked down the Golden Lane from Tampico to Potrero to Lake Maracaibo in Venezuela where his game ended as he crouched in the jungle trying to relieve himself and a hostile Indian's arrow pierced his throat.)

The accordion maker warned Silvano that the passage would be rough, would cause incessant vomiting, but as they drew away from Palermo, from Sicily, from Europe, into the waters of the globe, they entered a zone of fair weather. Day after day sunlight gilded the waves, the sea was calm, without whitecaps or crested waves, numberless oily swells casting off rags of foam. At night this watery lace glowed and shimmered a luminous green. The ship hissed through the sea and Silvano stared into a sky so deeply colored that he saw swarms of larvae, the gestation of stars or wind, crawling in the purple depths. Each morning the passengers emerged from the ship's depths like weevils from a stump and spread out in the sunshine, the women sewing and working lace, the men at some handwork, declaring their plans, walking around and around to prevent costive gripe. Nearly everyone ate on deck, avoided the reeking messroom. The ship's slop metamorphosed into something good as dried tomatoes, garlic, sausages, hard cheese, came out of suitcases. The accordion maker took the calm sea as a sign that his fortune had turned, lit a cigar and enjoyed it, played his accordion in the evenings. Already a few women had smiled at him, one asked him if he knew "*L'Atlantico*," humming the wavelike melody. He told her he wished to learn it if she would be his teacher.

Stories of New Orleans began to trickle from the crew members and passengers who had been there or read letters from earlier travelers: a scimitar-shaped city fitted in the curve of the great river where moss hung from trees like masculine beards, where the tea-colored water of the bayous harbored alligators and ebon people nonchalantly strolled the streets, where the dead lay aboveground in marble beds and men walked holding pistols. A sailor taught Silvano the words "*ais crima,*" a kind of rare and delicious frozen confection achieved with a difficult machine and much labor.

The young man on the train had said their language would be easily understood in New Orleans, but in their mess call the old woman who had lived in New Orleans, whose son and family had died of some pestilence, who had gone back to Sicily to fetch her two nephews and was now returning with them, warned them to cast away their Sicilian dialect, to speak Italian instead and quickly learn American.

"Italians say Sicilians speak thieves' language in order to plot murder in their open faces. Americans believe Sicilians and Italians are the same and hate them both, curse them as sacks of evil. If you wish success you must master the American language."

Words to break the teeth, thought the accordion maker. She looked at him as if she read his thinking. "I see in your face that you will not learn it."

"And you?" he retorted. "You speak it fluently, no doubt?"

"I have learned many words," she said. "From my son and his children. Now I will learn from my nephews. In America the natural order of the world is reversed and the old learn from children. Prepare yourself, accordion maker."

On the last days of the voyage, as they rounded the tip of Florida and entered the Gulf of Mexico, the musky scent of land came to them.

They had crossed some invisible bar, were no longer departing but arriving. The accordion maker brought his instrument on deck and played, sang in the high, strangling style of the village.

> *Now we arrive in La Merica—*
> *Farewell to our childhood homes.*
> *Here we begin our true lives.*
> *Here we find money and respect,*
> *Fine houses and linen shirts.*
> *Here we become princes.*

A member of the crew sang a comic American song—"Where, Oh, Where Has My Little Dog Gone?"—but the accordion maker scorned to try it and countered with "*Sicilia Mia.*" His strong posture, his hairiness, his desperate voice and the accordion's suggestive breathing drew a circle of women and girls around him. Still, he believed in a hell where sinners sat astraddle the heated wards of giant keys and served as clappers in white-hot bells.

They coasted into the delta, breathed its odor of mud and wood smoke under sunset clouds, gold curls combed out of the west, or the powdered stamens of a broad-throated flower. In the dusk they could see flickering lights in the side channels, sometimes hear a gruesome roar—the alligators, said a deckhand; no, a cow bogged in mud, said the woman with the nephews. The immigrants crowded the rail as the quivering ship moved into the Mississippi River, within the pincer of land. Silvano stood next to his father. A red moon crawled out of the east. On the shore the boy heard a horse snort. Hours before New Orleans the odor of the city reached them—a fetid stink of cesspools and the smell of burning sugar.

A demon in the backhouse

Nothing went as the accordion maker anticipated. The young man from the train was not at the dock. They waited hours for him while the other passengers disappeared into the teeming streets.

"True friends are as rare as white flies," said the accordion maker bitterly. Silvano gaped at the black men and especially the women, whose heads were wrapped in turbans as though they concealed emeralds and rubies and chains of gold beneath the winded cloth. They puzzled their way along through the noisy, thronged streets with the young man's map and found Decatur Street, but there was no number sixteen there, only charred timbers among rampant fireweed, a gap in the row of frowsty tenements. The accordion maker forced his courage, spoke to an approaching man who looked Sicilian; at least his hair appeared Sicilian.

"Excuse me, I seek a boardinghouse, number sixteen, but it seems there is no building here—" The man did not answer, spat to his right as he passed. Silvano saw the punishment for not knowing American. The man must be an American—one who despised Sicilians.

The accordion maker, unnerved, said to Silvano, "a cursed fool, let him dine on weeds made bitter by the piss of drunkards." They dragged their bundles and the trunk back to the wharf. There was the ship they had left only hours ago. Silvano recognized the faces of crew members. They returned his stare with disinterest. One shouted something ribald in American. Silvano experienced the helpless rage of the prisoner of language. His father seemed not to notice.

The employment office described by the young man on the train was a blue shack at the end of the wharf. A dozen men, both white and black, leaned against pilings and boxes and spit tobacco, smoked cigars, staring at them as they approached. Inside the shack a dog with an iron collar lay under the chair and a man with a swollen, bruised nose who called himself Graspo—Grapestalk—spoke to them in language they could understand, but he was suspicious and insolent, demanding their papers, asking their names, the name of their village, parents' names, the name of the wife's family, who did they know and why had they come here? The accordion maker showed the map, told of the young man on the train who had given the address of the boardinghouse, described the charred timbers, said he knew no one, wanted work on the boats or docks.

"What was the name of this man on the train?" But of course the accordion maker did not know. After a time Graspo softened, although his tone was still lofty and condescending.

"It is not as easy as you think, *contadino,* there are many things involved in working here, many people of strength against each other. There is sometimes trouble, the times are difficult. The Sicilians suffer very much. We must look out for one another. But I can tell you the name of a boardinghouse in Little Palermo, number four Mirage Street, cheap and well located for work. Perhaps I can get you something on the fruit boats, you and the boy. You will see that the Irish and the black men have the best of it, those who are screwmen. The humble Italian—for here Sicilians are regarded as Italians and you must swallow that as well—must be content to be a longshoreman." He cleared his throat and spat. "For you the cost is three dollars, for the boy two, and the address of the boardinghouse is free. Yes, you pay to me. I'm the *bosso.*

That is how it works in America, *Signor' Emigrante Siciliano.* You must pay to be paid. You know nothing, no one, you pay for an education. I offer you this education for a modest sum."

What choice had he? None, none. He paid the money, turning his back to Graspo while he pried the strange coins from the kidskin money belt, stained now with sweat. Graspo told the accordion maker to go to the boardinghouse and make an arrangement, come back in the morning for the shape-up; if fortune was with them there would be work. The accordion maker nodded, nodded, nodded and smiled.

"They will ask you at the boardinghouse what work you have. Show them this paper and tell them you work for Signor Banana. Ah-ha."

They found the boardinghouse in Little Palermo, a noisome district as bad as any Sicilian slum, except that black people lived here as well as Sicilians and Italians. Mirage Street was lined with decayed French mansions shedding flerried slates like dandruff, the fine rooms chopped into cubbies, thin strips of deal bisecting plaster cherubs, a ballroom partitioned into twenty mean kennels. Number four was a filthy brick pile obscured by crisscrossed lines of grey laundry and belted around and around with sagging balconies. Somewhere a dog barked.

(Years later in the oil fields it was not the horrible event that Silvano remembered but this relentless barking by an unseen animal that went on day and night. An American dog. In Sicily someone would have killed it for its disobedience.)

The courtyard was knee-deep in refuse, smashed bed frames, scrap wood, great drifts of oyster shells, suitcase handles and bloody rags, holed cooking pots and tin cans, broken crockery, chamber pots half filled with green-scummed water, weather-stiffened hames, a legless horsehair sofa furred with mold. In a corner of the courtyard was a reeking *baccausa* which served the scores who lived in the building. When the accordion maker entered this outhouse he turned away, retching; the mound of excrement protruded from the hole. In the corner was a smeared stick to push it down a little. He noticed later that some of the residents squatted in the courtyard like dogs to relieve their bowels, and in this wasteland children played.

"Listen," he told Silvano. "Do not go there. There is a demon in that backhouse. Find another place. How do I know where? Anyway, it is better to hold it in as much as possible to get the most good from the food I buy for you." So began Silvano's lifelong suffering with constipation and griping bowels.

They climbed splintered stairs to the top floor, away from the leaning banister.

"Here is high living, my friend," said the landlord in a laughing voice. The room was hardly bigger than a closet and filthy. There were two plank beds, over each a long shelf, one partly filled with the belongings of a man with whom they must share this space. A deaf man who would be no trouble, the landlord said. Silvano would sleep on the floor on the sheep-skin. The accordion maker touched the broken plaster, kicked at the loose floorboards. From a nearby room they heard cries of abuse, a slap, another, muffled shrieks and blows. But Silvano was delighted with the window, two clear panes above an amber wave of stained glass. They could take turns, he said, looking out over the rooftops at the creamy river where boats growled up and down. Flies buzzed at this window and the sill was buried an inch beneath their husks.

But when he ran down the dark, groaning stairs three boys cornered him on a landing. The one with the dull face and crooked mouth he counted least dangerous, but while the others danced and jabbed at him, that one sidled behind, interlaced his fingers and raised his joined hands to bring Silvano crashing to his knees with a double-handed chop to the back of the neck. Silvano rolled between Dull-Face's legs, reached up and twisted the tender flesh inside the thigh despite three kicks in the face that scraped his cheek across the gritty floor. A door on the landing flung open and cold greasy water flew at them; there was a tinny rattle and a cascade of spoons and forks as the three attackers leaped down the stairs, shouting back curses.

Sugarcane

The landlord, crippled and obese, possessing only one foot and half blind, skin as grey and slick as the bottom of a boat, hands and arms crisscrossed with cane-cut scars, took the first week's money from them. He called himself Cannamele, Sugarcane, from the old days when he worked on the sugar plantations, before he crushed his foot in the grinder. The stiff point of a cane leaf had ruined his eye.

"But look, once my hands were strong enough to squeeze water from stones." He made a clenching gesture. When he heard the name of their village he shook with emotion; for he said he had been born two villages away. He begged them for news of many people. But none of the names he presented was familiar and after a quarter of an hour it was clear that Cannamele had mistaken their village for another. Yet a certain cordial-ity, a connection, had been established. Cannamele felt it necessary to explain how things were.

Here in Little Palermo, he said, the Americans never came. All the

dialects and regions of Italy and Sicily were crushed together here, people from the mountains and the rich plains below Etna, from northern
Italy, from Rome, even from Milano, but those haughty ones moved
out as soon as they could. He told the accordion maker that the backhouse was supposed to be emptied once a month by black men who
dug out the stinking shit and carted it away in their "aggravation wagons," but they had not come for a long time, no one knew why. Perhaps
they would come tomorrow. So, Graspo had promised him work?
Graspo was of the Mantrangas, stevedores at war with rival *padroni,* the
Provenzanos, in a rough squabble over who would control the hiring of
labor to work the fruit boats. The Irish and the black men, the cotton
screwmen, had the highest-paid work; Sicilians and Italians had to take
what was left, the longshoreman jobs, but at least they were better off
than the roustabouts, all black men—wild, roving river hogs covered
with pale scars. And as for those black ones, if the accordion maker had
eyes, he could see for himself most were wretched and ragged and their
so-called freedom was a mockery. Yet on New Orleans docks they had
certain rights which often worked against Sicilians and Italians; there
the black screwmen were as good as anyone and better than immigrants. The crafty Americans knew well how to play each against the
other. The other occupant of their room, the deaf man called Nove—
Nine—because his little finger had been chewed off in a fight, was a
stevedore. As for "Signor Banana," he was the esteemed and wealthy
Frank Archivi, born in New Orleans of poor Sicilian parents, an American by birth, and who knows, if not galvanized by the madness of grief
when he was twenty, he might have become a boatman or an organ
grinder instead of the owner of a shipping line, a man who controlled
the rich fruit-import business.

"Think of it, after one week of marriage his bride died of a shrimp
which she inhaled while laughing—never laugh when you eat shrimp—
and Archivi, the crazed one, eyes as red as lanterns, came to her tomb at
night and removed her stinking corpse, dragging it through the streets
and kissing the rotting lips until he collapsed. He lay in a fever for a
month and when he came to his senses he was as cold as a glacier, interested only in money. And now Archivi, Archivi is bananas and fruits
from Latin America, lemons and oranges from Italy. Archivi is deals and
ingenuity, and that hard work that makes a fortune, a fortune that
grows and swells. If you would see Archivi, look at the carts of the street
vendors. He owns ships, warehouses, thousands work for him, he
moves in the high circles of New Orleans society, he is an important
man in politics. He shook the hand of John D. Rockefeller. He is a

Rockefeller of fruit. Every piece of fruit that comes to these docks is controlled by Archivi. He turned his grief and madness to money." The accordion maker listened greedily.

"He is brave and agile, he fought the Reconstructionists. You would do well to study him, *americanizzarti,* to Americanize yourself as he has done. When the black men tried to muscle the Sicilians away from the dock work, he led an army of longshoremen against them. I saw this. It was bloody and he won, I can tell you that, he won. You have a knife? Good. You must get a pistol as well. It is necessary. In New Orleans you defend yourself every day."

Archivi, he said, moved confidently in the Americans' world.

"But don't bother to play your accordion for him. He has refined tastes in music, he prefers concerts and the opera. On the other hand, rejoice. There are many musicians working the docks. New Orleans is the queen of music, the queen of commerce." He sang a few contorted lines of some song the accordion maker had never heard, a limping, crooked song.

"I plan to open a music store," confided the accordion maker. "I will be the Archivi of accordions." Cannamele shrugged and smiled; every man had his fantasy. He had thought himself that he would start a bank, first for Sicilians, but later . . .

It was true, the fruit vendors in their stained clothes who spread through the city each day displayed on their carts an extraordinary variety of fruits; Silvano counted twenty kinds in the distance between the boardinghouse and the wharf: ox-heart cherries with juice like blood, yellow peaches, orange silky persimmons, barrows of pears, Panama oranges, strawberries the size and shape of Christ's heart. The lemon barrows lit up dark streets. Once, moved by his hungry stare, a vendor gave him an overripe banana, the skin black, and, inside, the faintly alcoholic mush of decaying pulp.

"Hey, *scugnizzo,* your mother must have craved these fruits when she carried you. You are fortunate you do not have a great banana-shaped birthmark on your face." (Four years later this barrowman moved to St. Louis and started a successful macaroni factory, American Pasta, and died a thousandaire.) Silvano did in fact have a birthmark but it was on his belly and in the shape of a frying pan, the cause of his perpetual hunger.

Bananas

Graspo started them unloading bananas, great green claws of fruit as heavy as stone, of brutal weight even for the accordion maker's muscular and broad shoulders. For twelve hours' labor the pay was a dollar and a half. Silvano tottered twenty feet with a hand of bananas, then went to his knees. He did not have the legs to bear such weight. Graspo put him at fifty cents a day to pick up loose bananas from broken bunches, crush the hairy tarantulas and little snakes that fell from the clusters of fruit. Silvano darted fearfully at them with his cudgel.

The docks and levees stretched for miles along the river in a stink of brackish water, spice, smoke, musty cotton. Gangs of men, black or white, stacked bales of cotton into great piles like unfinished pyramids, others rolled the bales over and over toward the ships whose funnels stretched into the hazed distance like a forest of branchless trees. Two and two, men piled sawed lumber, raw cities waiting to be nailed onto the prairies upriver, teams of four black men double-cut tree trunks into squared timbers. Downriver the shrimp boats unloaded baskets of glittering crustaceans. In the cavernous warehouses men shifted more cotton, barrels of molasses and sugar, tobacco, rice, cottonseed cakes, fruits; they sweated in the cotton yards where the great bales were compressed into five-hundred-pound cubes. Everywhere men carried boxes, rolled barrels, stacked firewood for the voracious steamboats, each swallowing five hundred cords of wood between New Orleans and Keokuk. A gang of men rolling barrels sang:

Roll'm! Roll'm! Roll'm!
All I wants is my regular right!
Two square meal and my rest at night!
Roll! Roll'm, boy! Roll!

The din of commerce sounded in a hellish roar made up of the clatter of hooves and the hollow mumble of wheel rims on plank, the scream of whistles and huffing of engines, hissing steam boilers and hammering and rumbling, shouting foremen and the musical call and response of work gangs and the sellers of gumbo and paper cones of crawfish and sticky clotted pralines, the creaking of the timber wagons and the low cries of the ship provisioners' cartmen urging their animals forward, all blended into a loud, narcotic drone.

Of all of these, the swaggering screwmen were the kings of the docks, earned six dollars a day. In gangs of five they threw down their half-smoked cigars and descended into ships' holds with their jackscrews, waited for the longshoremen to winch up the bales of cotton from the dock and lower them down into the hold, one at a time. The screwmen seized the bales, stacked them high and tight, forced them into impossibly cramped spaces, odd crannies and corners, through the use of boards and their expanding jackscrews, until the ship nearly split; yet the cargo was perfectly balanced, the ship unsinkable.

In the late afternoon one day the word flew from man to man: a board had snapped under pressure and shot a splinter into the throat of a black screwman named Treasure. The accordion maker heard cries from an adjacent ship, joined the gathering crowd. He moved slowly, watching, saw a limp body raised from the hold, carried away, the blood pattering on the deck, the ramp, the dock.

"Move a d'banan', sonamagogna!" shouted the foreman, driving the Sicilians back to the fruit.

Apollo's lyre

On Saturday night, while Silvano gawped through the mosquito-stitched streets, listening to the American jabber and making up his mind to steal a sweet, drawn this way and that by the cries of vendors of pots and pans, clothes, lemonade, "*gelati, gelati,*" candies and kitchen implements, but stopping before a man who sold enchanting toy cats of spotted tin that squeaked when their sides were pressed, the accordion maker went with Cannamele, first to Viget's Oyster Saloon, hot and smoky, where Cannamele swallowed four dozen with lime juice, then to a barrelhouse in the next street packed with ruffians where they drank union beer, ate the stale eggs and firefanged cheese and vinegary pigs' feet, and the accordion maker wished for the harsh village *rosso.* But both of them blackened many bottles' eyes and the accordion maker treated himself to a two-for-a-nickel cigar from a box of fat Rajah torpedoes. A bowlegged Italian sang "*Scrivenno a Mamma*" in a weeping voice, stopped singing and blubbered.

"He who saves, saves for dogs," cried Cannamele, signaling for American whiskey.

"Heart's-ease, you grape-jumper," shouted an Irishman.

In and out went Cannamele through the scores of dives, tonks and jooks and barrelhouse joints that lined these streets, the accordion maker lurching after him through the musical din of drums and ringing banjos, shouters, pianos clinking away, squealing fiddles and trumpets and other brass snorting and wailing from every interior, and sometimes a string quartet sawing crazily. On the streets children watched and fought for discarded stogie butts, black street musicians and white played for coins, singing improvised songs of insult at those who failed to toss a whirling coin.

Bow-leg
Curl-shoe
Stingy one
Bad luck on you.

An apron of sound lapped out of each dive. Inside, chairs scraped on the floor, loud music and talk tangled with roaring laughter, there was endless traffic toward and from the back where little rooms lined the hall and young black girls took customers until their flesh was raw, the rasp of matches, the slap of cards and the clink of bottles on glass, the clack of glasses on tables, the creak of table legs on the floor, the thudding feet of dancers doing the slow drag, the itch, the squat, the grind. Dice doctors with their loaded ivories, drinkers and cockers with feathers stuck to the bloody soles of their boots crowded the rooms, and the street din entered with each customer. And often there was a *faito,* with grunts and snorts and curses and smack of flesh on flesh, a scream, then a tenor roaring *"O dolce baci . . ."*

The accordion maker had a pistol now and carried it in the waist-band of his trousers. Silvano had a staghorn-handled knife with three blades and threatened with it when the gangs closed around him. He had stolen it from a lolling drunk, practiced his first American sentence on a one-eyed dog scavenging for orts.

"Get outta, I killa you."

The accordion maker disliked the music that the black men played, confused music, the melody, if there was one, deliberately hidden in braided skeins of rhythm. He was contemptuous of their instruments—a horn, a broken piano, a fiddle, the wiry curls of its strings twisting out of the neck like morning glory vines, the banjo. He recognized one of the players from the docks, as black as a horse's hoof, a man with an eye patch and a latticework of scars from the corner of his eye to his jaw that made his face rigid and expressionless on one side. They called him Pollo— what, "Chicken"? thought the accordion maker, but it seemed the creature's name was Apollo, someone's sardonic joke— flailing at a—what was it?—a corrugated surface, somehow familiar, set in a gaudily painted wooden frame, a thing that made a raspy, scratching sound like a treeful of cicadas, and singing *"shootin don't make it, no, no, no."* It was a quarter of an hour before he recognized the object—a washboard, a thing women used to rub the dirt from wet clothes—and saw the metal thimbles on the man's fingers. Pollo put away the rub-board and pulled a pair of spoons from his back pocket, making a clatter like heavy castanets. And the other one, Fish Man, scraping a knife

over his guitar strings to make a wobbling shrill. What wandering
imprecision! What kitchen music! And the words, the accordion maker
could not catch one, but understood the singer's salacious tone and low,
hot laugh. Fish Man twirled his old guitar with a scarred back, sang:

> *On my table there a blood dish,*
> *Dish with drop a blood,*
> *Somebody butcher my old cow,*
> *Tell me it really good,*
> *It really good—*
> *I don't have to milk her no more.*

Soon enough the accordion maker was distracted when Cannamele,
cock-a-hoop, shoved a black woman against him, a dirty puzzle with
running eyes, put his wet mouth to the accordion maker's ear and said
she would change his luck.

"The man who holds back risks tuberculosis and worse. The bodily
system weakens. Go ahead, mine some coal." (Although the accordion
maker contracted syphilis from these adventures, he never knew it.)

In a Sicilian village, the right eye of a woman no longer paralyzed
itched with great ferocity.

A strange instrument

In the weeks that followed, the accordion maker recognized many
dockworkers among the musicians of the barrelhouses. There were no
accordions to be heard until a band of gypsies camped outside the city
on a bit of high ground with their tinkers' tools, horses and fortunes;
two of the men played accordions. They stayed a week, another week, a
month, mending pots and pans. Sometimes at night passersby heard
their private music, a slow, sad wailing, saw the shimmer of sequined
bodies dancing. He went to their camp one evening with Cannamele
to hear what was to be heard. The music was boisterous and wailing at
the same time and five or six men danced a fight with sticks. He was
interested in their accordions but could not make the men understand
that he wished to examine one. Their language was incomprehensible
and they turned away as soon as money changed hands. True outsiders,
he thought, people without even a home, lost in the wild world. One
day they were gone, leaving trampled earth.

"Moon men," said Cannamele, winking his bad eye.

At first the accordion maker was afraid to bring his instrument into the sweating, dangerous dives where men fought and bled and over-turned the tables. He played it only in the room he shared with Silvano and Nove, forty years old and half deaf, who came in many nights streaming blood from knife fights, would wake from midsleep and shout hoarsely, "listen! Somebody knocking!" But the knocking was in his head and in a few minutes he would lie down and sleep again in his rumpled, stained clothes.

The accordion maker found his own music calming and beautiful after the wailing, thumping, rattling music of the joints. That slangy music was not suited to the accordion, although its morbid voice might fit the style, but it was impossible to loosen and bend the notes. An accordion would have to play the drone, to be satisfied with the back of the music rather than the front.

He got up the courage to bring it to one of the barrelhouses. It was noisy enough as usual. He sat off by himself—the bartender complained of his "Italian perfume," the smell of garlic—and after a while, when the piano man left for the whorehouse, began to play. No one noticed until he lifted his high, strangling voice and a silence fell, heads turned toward this sound. He sang an ancient grape harvest song that had stamping and shouts. But after two or three songs the din of the place rose again, call-ing, laughing, talking, shouting, drowning him out. Only the Sicilians pressed closer, hungry to hear the lost music that brought with it the scent of thyme and the tinkle of goat bells, and they called out for certain melodies that made them contort their faces with grief.

Late in the evening Pollo came toward him, forcing his way through the crowd, smiling around his blond cigar. Up close he was the strange red-black color of furniture, of a mahogany table. He said something, pointing at the accordion.

"He want to know what you call it," said Cannamele and answered in a loud voice as if speaking to a deaf man: "Accordion. Accordion."

The black man said something more, reached for the accordion, looked at it, hoisted it, feeling its lightness, held it to his body as he had seen the accordion maker do and squeezed the bellows gently. *Anh. Onh. Anh. Onh.* He said something. Cannamele laughed.

"He say it sound like his woman."

Pollo bent over the instrument, pressing the buttons and getting it, getting the feel of it and its sound, and in a few minutes, foot beating, the accordion huffing in an unaccustomed way between bursts of words and *um-hm* sounds, a rough little song came out. Cannamele screamed with pleasure.

"He's the man, the singing is the man, and he's doing it to a woman and the accordion is the woman!" The accordion maker blushed as the instrument moaned against the black man's voice.

> *How you like*—Anh
> *My sweet corn, baby*—Onh
> *Plenty buttah*—Anh
> Anh—*make you crazy*—Onh.

He handed the accordion back, grinning violently.

The next day the accordion maker saw the black man, Pollo, sitting on a bollard, graceful, smoking a long blond cigar, on his feet St. Louis flats, heelless shoes with mirrors pasted on the toes, a dreaming expression on his face, but alert enough to spy the accordion maker, catch his eye and make squeezing motions as though playing an accordion or pressing a fat woman's breasts.

The first order

By early October the cotton crop poured onto the docks and the levees swarmed with workers loading night and day. The accordion maker was making and saving money—despite his excursions with Cannamele. One morning when he and Silvano came out of the boardinghouse Pollo was in the street waiting for him. He said something, a question the accordion maker did not get. Silvano understood, could already mangle his way along in American.

"He wants to buy your accordion. He will give you ten dollars!"

The accordion maker smiled pityingly. "Tell him it is not for sale. It is my showing accordion. But tell him I can make one similar in every way. Tell him the cost is thirty dollars, not ten. Tell him it will take four months' time." He had figured out what he must charge.

Pollo spoke, ticking off items on his long, pale-fronted fingers. He was describing or listing. Silvano translated.

"He wants it red—this green is not good for him. He wants his name, Apollo, on it, here. And on the folding part paint a picture, the *Alice Adams* with a head of steam up."

"Tell him nothing could be simpler. But on Saturday he must give me five dollars as surety and for the materials." He was excited. His success was beginning.

That night he set up a tiny worktable in the corner of their room, sat on a box which he kept under the bed when he was not working on the instrument, rose before daylight to glue and fit, saw and sand; he worked a few minutes at night as long as he could afford the candle, could stay awake, and worked all day Sunday—for he did not go to mass in this godless new country—was drawn into the spell of precise craftsmanship as another might be charmed by words or incantations. He was fortunate to have the room—many slept on the streets and docks and every morning lifeless forms were carried away, throats slit and pockets turned inside out, even young children. All around him were men who had to piss in the nettles.

For weeks he stopped going to the saloons except on Saturday night, despite the allure of the music and the black women, but reduced his life to work, the accordion, a little sleep. He was getting the Italian look—thin and ragged, eyes very hard and watchful.

A shooting

On a November night Cannamele came up to his room and said, "listen, you work like a fool. You will develop a brain fever."

"I am making a success."

Cannamele shook his head. "A Sicilian cannot make a success here," he said. "It is not possible unless you know certain men and do certain things. This is the truth. If you come out you will ease your mind. Look at you, half crazy. Besides, I will buy the beer."

"One hour only. To look for new customers."

The landlord leaned on the bar in the Golden Dagger, listening to the crying music. The accordion maker had his instrument and sat in a corner trying to fit minor chords like long moans to a scraping fiddle and a rattling tambourine, when the doors burst open and police beat into the room, kicking and striking with their batons.

"All Italians, hands up, over there, get up you dirty dago bastards, move, MOVE!"

The accordion maker stared uncomprehendingly like a fool until he was dragged from his chair, the accordion falling to the floor. He cursed and reached for it and was jerked back, hands closed on him. His frightened eye fell on the black man, Pollo, crouched in the back near the hall door. Their eyes caught. The black man nodded and looked away, slid into the darkness of the hall.

Silvano, in the street outside, was taken when he ran toward his father. Pressing the prisoners against the wall of the building, the Americans battered them with a volley of incomprehensible questions. The accordion maker's silence and shrugging infuriated them, and when they found his pistol and Silvano's knife they herded them into a line of men tied ankle and wrist with a long connecting rope, slapped and kicked them along the streets and away to the pound, to the Parish Prison, to cells packed with Sicilians and Italians.

The crime was serious. Someone had shot the chief of police. The American Patriotic League screamed *Italians! Catholics!*—another vicious example of ceaseless warfare on the docks between Italian gangs, between the Irish and the Italians and the blacks, a mix of languages and colors, hatreds and competition of such ferocity that the spray of blood and interruption of labor stained the name of New Orleans. The Americans, who usually held themselves above the dirty business of foreigners and black men fighting for mean jobs, flared with outrage, ordered the police into the streets.

"Tell them," the accordion maker begged a man in the cell who spoke American, "tell them they have made a mistake. I have done nothing." His jacket was crusted with some white substance.

"Do you suggest that I did?"

"No, no, but—"

Many were released in the next weeks, including Cannamele, but not the accordion maker, whom they accused of deliberate conspiratorial silence, of suspicious skulking, of murder with the confiscated pistol, nor Silvano, because he also was silent, and silence meant complicity. Dozens of Sicilians and Italians wept and prayed in the cells as the month ground through December. They were in a zone of uncertainty. The accordion maker was in an agony of frustration.

"Ah," he cried, "how I regret coming to this place." And when he sent a message to Cannamele to get his accordion from Pollo and keep it, word came back that Pollo was upriver working on the wood boats, that he had been thrown off the *Alice Adams,* that he had taken the accordion with him.

On Christmas Eve an elderly black woman, sent by someone unknown, brought the prisoners oranges and an "old lady's face," *faccia da vecchia,* the baked crust spread with sardines and cheese and onion. Someone whispered, *Archivi.*

"This is the land of justice," said the accordion maker, confident again, swallowing his sliver of the delicacy. "They will soon realize their mistake and release us."

But another prisoner, a short muscular man built like a crate, sneered.

"The Americans treat us like cheap shoes. They buy cheap, they walk long and hard, when the shoes are worn out they throw them aside and get others. Shiploads of these shoes come every day. You speak of justice and your stupid accordion, but you are a shoe. A cheap shoe. *Sfortunato.* An unlucky man."

Yes, thought Silvano.

An evil dream

One night there was an uproar as the guards brought in another, dragged him down the corridor to a cell at the end.

"*Oh Gesù, Gesù,*" whispered Polizzi.

"What? Who is it?" They had seen the prisoner, his smeared face, his torn clothes, for only a few seconds.

"*Oh Gesù, Gesù.*"

A whisper started, grew to a murmur. "Archivi. Archivi."

Flies clustered in the corner of the ceiling, like nailheads.

"Look," said someone. "Even the flies are afraid and dare not fly for fear they will be accused."

Archivi shouted from his cell. "This filthy America is fraud and deceit. My fortune is lost. America is a place of lies and bitter disappointment. It promises everything but eats you alive. I shook the hand of John D. Rockefeller, yet it means nothing." He spoke in American.

A sarcastic voice added, "*chi non ci vuole stare, se ne vada*"—if you don't like it here, go somewhere else.

A few nights later the accordion maker had a waking dream of raw meat, of the wet kid carcasses he remembered from village butcherings, of basins of red flesh marbled with fat, of glistening bones with maroon shreds of tissue clinging to the joints, of dark gobbets dropped randomly on a great flight of stairs.

The rat king

Just as Pinse's left foot touched the garnet runner of the top stair, the *ching* of the breakfast room bell sounded. He had come in very late, hours past midnight, after a week away at the Robinsonville levee break. He had no doubt; it had been dynamited by the malcontents he had fired from the timber contract; foreigners, all of them, observed creeping and slinking for the better part of a week. And as soon as the levee breached they'd disappeared. The damage was local, hard on the Yazoo Valley, but in the long run the silt deposit would improve the bottomland. He knew one thing; he'd rather have niggers than dago socialist rabble screaming for weekly paydays and threatening strikes and blowing up levees in revenge when they did not get what they wanted. His eyes burned. The staircase wound as did a chambered nautilus, and he walked down quickly, one hand on the banister—taking pleasure in the mild centrifugal force of the descent, the flash of his passage in silvered mirrors—stepped into the foyer, glancing at the seascape, a study of icebergs in some northern sea, hanging against the brown paper, looked through the archway at the hall stand with its coats like headless bodies, taking satisfaction in the carved chair, the electroplated card receiver with the head of Hadrian staring at the beaded doorknob. He noted the sweep of herled feathers in a jardiniere—that was new—felt the usual irritation at his squabby reflection in the hall-stand mirror. He yawned.

A Boston fern on an octagonal plant table colored the breakfast room with a greenish light reflected by the mirrored sideboard; he glanced at his wife's orchids in the fogged Wardian case, sighed and stretched and yawned. There was the faint bitter smell of damp tea leaves from an early sweeping. A cloth embroidered with trumpet vine covered the table, on the walnut sideboard, carved with dead hares and pheasants, waited a silver cover, the coffeepot over a pale flame, his grandmother's cut-glass decanter. More than any other room this one expressed his wife's vivid pleasure, pitched fever high as the tuberculosis advanced, in exotic blooms, marble and mirrors, crystal, silver and green, velvet. More than that—she had been ill for months with nervous prostration after a terrifying incident as they walked out of the house at dusk, she leaning on his arm, and an owl swooped on the decorative bird adorning her hat, the striking talons laying open her scalp to the bone, blood everywhere, and he smelling the hot, louse-ridden feathers as the bird beat upward, carrying away the hat. The children's Astley-Cooper chairs, for straight posture, stood against the wall; the boys and the girl all slumped.

He tipped the coffeepot, releasing the aroma of chicory and dark-roasted Martinique, blew on the black liquid. Too hot. He set the cup down, took his glass of anisette between thumb and forefinger, swallowed a drop or two. In the oval wall glass his reflection swallowed as well. The smell of levee mud and brackish water lingered. He drank the coffee. His temples were pounding. Again the anisette and the coffee. His *Times-Picayune* was not on the table. No telling how much of the trial he'd missed. He'd followed it avidly until he was called away to the damaged levee. He rang the bell.

"Where is the paper?" He said it even though he saw it on the tray she carried.

"Just come, sah. They late this morning."

He shook it open—nothing on the front page but the trial: ah, gone to the jury yesterday—jabbed appreciatively at his stuffed oxtail, disliked by the rest of the household, and began to eat, the tines of the fork seeking out truffle moons.

The fork stopped in midair, sank again to the gold-rimmed plate. He brought the paper's details closer to his eyes. He had thought the headline read "Nine Guilty," but, unbelievably, it was "None Guilty"!

Unspeakable.

They had tampered with the jury. Yes, New Orleans was drenched in blood these years, the loathsome Italians murdering each other, that was all right, they could kill each other until the last one dropped, but they were assassinating the innocent and upright as well, and all out of a depraved greed for the banana trade, *the banana trade!*, he thought of a ridiculous music hall song he had heard in London, "I Sella da Banan'"—a festering foreign corruption was rotting Louisiana's heart. The Black Hand had killed Captain Hennessy. It was known, known. All of these Mafias and Camorras. The endless labor problems of the docks, strikes and the threats of screwmen. All of it tied to the city's eternal problem of letting white men and niggers work together— nowhere but in New Orleans—half and half, snarling trade in knots with their insane rules, encouraging miscegenation and rebellion. White men? Foreigners. Irish and Italians. Socialists. They were dirty, diseased and dangerous incendiaries who did not know their place. Why in the name of God had the businessmen ever encouraged the Italians to come, what had made them think they could replace the shiftless blacks? Oh, the Italians worked well enough at first, but they were greedy and cagey, their first thought to push to the forefront. At least niggers knew their place, knew what could happen. Now look at that greasy dago Archivi, who had leeched his way to the throat of the city's commerce, who had been received in Pinse's own house, who had looked at his wife's orchids, had praised them and simpered over them. Treat the Italians well and see what happens. They were dangerous. They went too far. Give an inch and they would seize the city.

And barely any action taken until private citizens forced the authorities to arrest and bring the Italians to trial—naive belief in justice. Now that trust in the law had been cynically betrayed. *None Guilty!* This slippery call of acquittal and mistrial was the final mocking proof of corruption in high places, proof of Italian fixing and fiddling, of crooked foreigner-loving lawyers and perverted law. It was vomiting cowardice, unendurable to men of honor.

His racing eyes devoured the page, the sketches of the courtroom, the faces of the Italian assassins—especially that whinging, buck-toothed, chinless and craven poltroon Politz, Polizzi, whatever his name was, he who had been carried bodily, weeping and fainting, from the courtroom during trial, he with the lying, hard-faced mistress, he who had confessed, Polizzi, declared a mistrial? And in the right-hand columns, there were the portraits of that other set of criminals, the jurors, headed by the Jew jeweler, Jacob M. Seligman, smirking as he told the reporter, "we had a reasonable doubt." The home address and place of business of each juryman was given. Good! They would know where to find them. And here was the bearing question; the reporter asked juror William Yochum, a weak-faced little rat: "Did you hear of any of the persons having been approached before the trial?" No, he had heard of no such thing, the lying, slithering vole.

Approached? Of course the jurors were approached, approached and embraced, their palms clasped in golden Italian handshakes, their shoulders enwrapped by the oily arms of the moneymen of the Black Hand and, he didn't doubt, of Hebrew Jewish bankers behind the whole scheme.

He tore the pages as he turned to the editorials. "AT THE FEET OF CLAY. Elsewhere we print an advertisement . . . a mass meeting at the foot of the Clay statue . . . expressed object of the meeting . . . what it is intended to do . . . doubtless murdered by Italians, but not by the Italians as a race . . . Let us have no race prejudice . . ." Rubbish, rubbish. He searched for the advertisement, missed it, went back and found it at the bottom of the editorial page itself where his hand had obscured it.

> MASS MEETING! All good citizens are
> invited to attend a mass meeting on
> Saturday, March 14, at 10 o'clock a.m.,
> at Clay statue, to take steps to remedy
> the failure of justice in the Hennessy
> case. Come prepared for action.

Come prepared for action. It could be no clearer. And below were the alphabetically ordered names of prominent men, though not, of course, his own. He had no wish to see the name Pinse on the same roster as certain men. His eyes lingered on, returned to the place where the inky show of his name would have fallen. The clock chimed the quarter hour. The streets would be jammed. He stood up, thrusting the chair back. The air would clear his headache. The half-eaten oxtail lay on his plate.

In the hall he put on his derby, glancing at himself in the mirror, and fumbled through the sticks in the umbrella stand until he found the staff he had bought in England years before on a walking tour of the Lake District. Why had he not purchased the ebony walking stick with the lead-weighted head he'd seen in London? *Come prepared for action.* He shook the staff, knocking askew a box of stereopticon photographs, sending to the floor the novel scene of two black men hanging an alligator from a limb, a rope knotted around its neck, the men grinning and straining against the weight. He had his revolver.

Halfway down the drive, stubbing the staff so vigorously that the ferrule dug at the crushed oyster shell, he heard Joppo running behind him. The stableman hauled up, panting and jerking his head.

"What is it? I can't delay now."

"Sah, sah, we got a king back of the stable, big rat king, sah, swear to Jesus real big."

"Ah!" He had seen only one in his life, years before, down in the family's cotton warehouse on the docks, a horror of a thing. "How big?" He loathed rats and vermin; had been a child in the years of the yellow fever plague, when thousands of people died, when his mother died, and they fired the cannons day and night until his head ached from the sound, they burned barrels of tar in the streets to drive out the pestilence spread by fetid vapors, scuttling creatures and foreigners, the invisible seeds of disease spraying out from their loose mouths. Even now the memory of the relentless booming induced a hopeless mood and migraine headache that sent him to the sofa in his darkened study for days. He remembered the corpses stacked on the wharf, from a distance resembling goods ready for shipment. Yes, a shipment to hell, his grandfather had called it, and the rain streaming down the window glass while in the yellow streets the dead carts rolled.

Joppo held up both hands twice—twenty.

"Some a them dead, some a them rotten meat."

He strode quickly across the grass toward the stable, Joppo lumbering after him and describing the rat king, who had discovered it, how they jabbed and dragged it out from under the floor with a yam fork, the supposed weight and mass.

There was a crowd behind the stable, his stable hands, the cook twisting her apron, some of Colonel Sawday's darkies coming through the gap in the hedge, falling back when they saw him.

They had it out ten or twelve feet from the wall, a circle of rats perhaps three feet across, the animals facing outward, their tails gripped and twisted in an inextricable tangle from which none could escape. Several of the rats were dead, others showing bright blood on them from the yam fork's action, and a few gnashing their brown teeth defiantly. He counted them, ticking each on the head with his stick: eighteen. Close enough to twenty. A filthy sight, this rotting clutch; terrible that it had been squealing and scrabbling under his stable floor.

"Better club them." He hurried away to the street, hearing the clicking teeth and stick thumps.

At the feet of Clay

Where Canal and Royal converged, hundreds of men carrying sticks and clubs, some with pistols or rifles, crowded around the statue of Clay. Three men stood on the base of the statue itself, above the crushing people, above the sea of bobbing derbies and slouch hats that gave the effect of a choppy black lake.

He saw the face of Biles, known to him, a face resembling that of a deer, with his forward snout and fawn-colored muttonchops. Biles raised his stick.

"Pinse! Wondered if I'd see you here, sir. Didn't see your name in the paper."

"No. Not in the same list as— I've been up at the levee break."

"This is truly something, isn't it?"

"They mean business."

"Oh yes. It was all arranged last night. There are some who see we've got to stop this tumult, this labor nightmare. Pinse, recall the screwmen's strike last year. My sister had five thousand bales of cotton on the dock, not an inch of warehouse room, and the ships riding high and empty. Then the rain. Did you ever see rain like it? Never. And not a bastard would touch a bale. She lost fifteen dollars a bale."

Pinse snorted into his linen handkerchief. His nose felt swollen inside and his temples throbbed. "I've been saying it for years. The dominant American class must assert itself or lose everything. We're overrun by the mongrels of Europe. I tell you, this flood of immigrants—I've heard it said in some quarters that the Pope is behind it, that it is a secret and massive effort to seize this country for Catholicism. My wife is Catholic, but I begin to wonder if there is not some truth in the statement."

"You should have seen it last night in Dagotown—a parade with twenty saints, flags flying, singing and music, candles, a parade. They were all drunk. They think they have got away with it, you see."

Men shouted and gestured, pushed a way through the crowd, the shifting glint of rifle and shotgun barrels. The three men on the platform before bronze-visaged Clay waited to speak, their glances casting over the crowd. One raised his hands for silence. He began, his voice growing louder as he described the treachery of the jury, the evil machinations of the Italians. ". . . was a noble man. No one in this country knew more about the Italian desperado than he, no one was braver than he in the face of threats from the dago Camorra."

Biles sniggered in Pinse's ear, "nor readier to hold out his hand for dago money." His black buckeyes shone.

"Will every man here follow me and see the murder of a brave man vindicated?"

A thick-bellied man dressed in a rumpled black suit, his face contorted with passion, climbed halfway onto the base of the statue and screamed, "hang the dagos! Hang the dirty murdering dagos!"

"Who is that?" asked Pinse.

"I don't know. The rabble turn out for these things."

The three came down and began to make their way toward Congo Square and the Parish Prison. The crowd surged forward with a sound like a great engine. Whores leaned from half-opened windows above the street. Near Congo Square a wash of ragged blacks filtered into the crowd. Somewhere sticks were rattling and a man scraped at a fiddle.

"You gonna see a different dance than the 'Hog Face'! Come on, niggers!"

At the prison the mob washed up against the steel main door in subsiding waves, cursing their puny crowbars and sledgehammers. For a few minutes indecision ran around the edges of the crowd.

"There's a wood door at Treme Street," shouted someone. At once the mass of people, black and white, sucked back from the main door and flowed like some viscous human lava toward Treme Street, seizing railroad ties from a work site as they went.

Ten or twelve men rushed at the Treme Street door with a squared tie, the crowd shouting HAH with each lunge. HAH HAH HAH.

A rush

The jailer fixed his eyes on Frank Archivi, his whiskey breath tiding in and out. "They are coming. The door can't hold. Hide. Anyplace you can in the prison—best chance is the women's section, upstairs!"

"For the love of Christ, man, give us some guns!" Archivi's face was the color of cold bacon grease.

"I cannot."

The planks tore from the hinges.

Some of them raced up the stairs into the women's section. Silvano darted into an empty cell and crawled under the mattress. He lay flat against the raw boards. His ears pounded, his back tried to arch. He was rigid with fear, could not control his bladder.

In the street an immense black man came toward the oak door carrying a boulder. He crashed it against the lock plate. A tremendous shout went up as the metal burst and the door sprang open. The mob surged up the stairs, Pinse not far from the front clenching his walking stick.

A guard shouted to them, voice cracking with excitement. "Third floor. They are up on the women's floor."

A hundred men thundered up, the stairs creaking and groaning under their thudding feet, and before them the prisoners fled down the back stairs and out into the yard. The gate was locked. Beyond was the street. They could look into the street, jammed with men. The delighted Americans, roaring with triumph, poured into the yard and the Sicilians, their arms linked, crowding together, shrank into a corner. The accordion maker saw the approaching men with searing clarity, a loose thread on a coat, mud-spattered trouser legs, a logging chain in a big hand, the red shine of the engorged faces, a man with one blue and one yellow eye. Even then he hoped to be saved. He was innocent!

Pinse held his revolver loosely in his hand, had lost the staff in the rush up the stairs, so crowded it had been, looked at the Sicilians knotted in the corner, their wicked eyes glittering, some of them pleading and praying—the cowards! He thought of the rat king, fired. Others fired.

A barrage of bullets and shot of every caliber and weight tore the Sicilians. The accordion maker reared twice and fell back.

A headache cure

At the Treme Street door the crowd had Polizzi, limp and bloody, spittle cascading down his receding chin, but still breathing. They tossed him high into the air, into the hands of other men who seized him and tossed him like a chip above their heads for the length of a block, a game to throw him high, a feat of strength to catch him, until on the corner of St. Ann Street someone strung a rope from the lamppost and put the noose around his neck.

A voice shouted, "twis' a hang-knot thirteen time or it be bad luck!" Up, up the limp form, raised by shouts and cheers as well as hemp. The body rotated, then, miraculously, the legs of the hanging man jerked, the scrawny arms lifted and the hands seized the rope; a revived Polizzi began climbing up the rope, hand over hand, toward the lamp bracket. There was a thrilled gasp.

"My god!" shouted Biles. Someone in the crowd shot, then many men in sudden laughter, betting who could shoot out an eye, take off the end of Polizzi's long nose. The arms dangled loose forever.

"That's enough for me," said Biles. "I haven't the stomach for this kind of thing. But something had to be done." He retched, apologized.

"Come," said Pinse, taking his friend's elbow and steering him toward a street they both knew well. "You need something. Our duty is done." His headache seemed a little better.

At the Cotton Guild's bar he said, "two sazeracs" to Cooper, and when the heavy tumblers came, both swallowed the golden drink as though it were water, and Biles snapped his fingers for two more, turned to Pinse, offered him a Havana *oscuro* from his leather case and took one for himself. He wet the head of the cigar in his red mouth and with the nail of the little finger on his right hand, grown especially long for this chore, slit the wrapper and took the burning match proffered by Cooper.

"We are setting up a new company to handle the trade," said Biles. "With a gentleman you know well. Your name was mentioned. We think of calling it Hemisphere Fruit."

Inspection

The crowds surged through the prison inspecting the dead men, kicking the bloodied Archivi who held an Indian club in his stiffening hand, snatched up from somewhere in the last minutes.

A guard discovered Silvano under the mattress and, with his fingers knotted in Silvano's hair, half dragged him down to the hall where the corpses of the Italians had been arranged in a display like a butcher's cutlets. Outside in the street celebratory music erupted, a horn and a harmonica full of spit on which someone played fast sucking chords, shouting between pulls on the reeds—*eeh!* chord *hanh!* chord *eehh!* chord—and the same scraping fiddle, the rattling drum. Silvano's damaged father—*sfortunato!*—lay on his back, bloody head propped against the wall so that his chin rested on his sternum. His arms, in their lacerated coat sleeves, stretched along his sides as though he lay at attention. The trousers rode up on his shins and the feet pointed outward, the soles of the shoes worn through. The guard watched the boy's distorted face, seemed eased by Silvano's wretchedness and pushed him along to the war-den's office where a roomful of Americans pressed in, demanding answers from him, shouting questions in his face, asking for details of how the accordion maker had murdered the chief. One after another knocked him off the chair. A man seized his ears and jerked him to his feet.

"Tell us how he lay in wait and shot." They cuffed and mauled, someone pressed a lighted cigar against his lip. Suddenly they rushed away when someone said "rum," and the guard wordlessly thrust Silvano out the door and into the street.

(Decades later the great-grandson of this guard, intelligent and handsome, enrolled as a medical student; he served as a donor of sperm at the medical center's in vitro fertilization program and was the maker of more than seventy children reared by other men. He accepted no money for his contribution.)

Bob Joe

He crouched on the wharf afraid to move, mosquitoes whining around him under a sky like black paint, ribbons of distant lightning curling from it. His throat was raw with suppressed weeping. A shrill tinnitus rang in his left ear. Hopelessness filled him as a chord of organ music fills a hall. A whistle sounded from a dark recess, a kind of zipping flourish as though someone were blowing a carnival prize whistle, and he folded his arms over his head, believing the Americans were coming again, would kill him this time. He waited for them to advance with their pistols and ropes but no one came. The whistler was silent and rain began, hard drops like thrown coins, then a pelting tropical downpour as warm as blood. He got up and stumbled toward the black bulk of the warehouses. The cobbles streamed. He counted his mother rigid with paralysis, his unlucky father dead, the impossibly distant village, his lost sisters and aunts, himself stranded penniless in this wild hostile world. He despised his father for being dead. A hardness began to form in his chest, a red stone of hatred, not for Americans but for the foolish, weak Sicilian father who had failed to learn American ways and let himself be killed. He made his way downriver in the shadow of warehouses, passing the steamboats and freighters, the flat-bottomed wood boats, moving toward the stink of fish and bilge.

A few shrimp boats were tied up at the dock, others moored a hundred feet out in the river. Someone was whistling the same three notes over and over, a rough Sicilian voice said something about being sick, two drunk American voices cursed each other. One boat was silent except for the sound of snoring, a choking snort followed by a gurgle.

The name on the stern was American: *Texas Star.* He dropped onto the deck of this boat and curled up behind the stacks of reeking baskets, pulled his shirt over his head against the mosquitoes. "Bob Joe," he said quietly in American, burning with hatred for Sicilians. "My name are Bob Joe. I work for you, please."

Upriver

A hundred miles up the river, Pollo sat on the deck of a wood boat tied up for the night, half watching for a steamer and ready to call out "wood—ho, wood—ho" to any passing fireman running low on fuel, all the while squeezing the green accordion and singing,

> *I think I heared the* Alice *when she blowed,*
> *I think I heared the* Alice *when she blowed,*
> *She blow just like a trumpet when I git on board.*

Fish Man slid the blade of his bowie knife against his guitar strings making silvery, underwater notes, slapping a little at mosquitoes, but thinking, yeah, why we on this wood scow instead a the *Alice Adams* is Pollo make trouble and I git it when he git it. The light of the flickering fire they had built on shore reflected in the red metal eyes of the accordion.

"You playin like a fool," said Pollo. Fish Man said nothing and hummed.

But in the ashy light before dawn Fish Man crept to Pollo and slid five inches of string-honed steel between his ribs. He cut the charm bag with its gold coin from around his neck and eased the thrashing body over the side. Under a sky the tender violet of the oyster's inner shell, he cast off and began to pole upstream against the sluggish current, taking the accordion along for the ride.

The Goat Gland Operation

A CLUB STYLE ACCORDION

Prank

The town was settled and abandoned twice, burned out the first time, then emptied by cholera and a bad winter a few years before the three Germans arrived and planted corn along the Little Runt River. It was a fluke that this rich cut of prairie lay fallow, for the good land of the midwest had been claimed and worked for a generation.

The day the three Germans—a Württemberger, a Saxon and a Königsberger who became Germans in America—arrived, they found four or five ramshackle deal buildings, fifty feet of boardwalk and a clogged public water pump downhill from the saloon's outhouse. The withering heat of summer and the scouring prairie wind had popped the nails in the siding until the clapboards curled, bristling with rusty points.

They arrived, one by one, unknown to each other, on a late spring day in 1893. Ludwig Messermacher, the son of German-Russian emigrants who had shifted from the steppes to Kaliningrad to North Dakota, tied his spot-rumped horse to a flimsy rail—a horse traded, though he did not know it, first from a Nez Percé named Bill Roy up in the Palouse country to an itinerant dentist and elixir stumpman, to a Montana holdup artist, to an Indian agent for the Rosebud reservation, to a succession of ranchers and farmers, never staying with any of them long because of his crowhop habit which Messermacher calmed out of him. (The grandfather of Bill Roy had shot from the back of this horse's great-grandsire and, using a bow of laminated mountain-sheep horn, had killed a female bison and her flank-running calf with a single arrow.)

Messermacher was the first to walk along the warped boardwalk, peering into buildings through the broken windows. Meager and hard of frame, he understood farming and carpentry. His swarthy face was dished as though a cow had stepped on it when he was a child, and his lipless mouth, thatched by a mustard-colored mustache, was framed in curved ice-tong lines. A beard of darker color, like an unraveled braid, hung from his chin. He had traveled along the river, the banks choked with sandbar willows and, beyond, wild rye and switch grass. He slept under the cottonwoods, making a small fire with the deadwood that littered the ground, sometimes turning over arrowheads with his sturdy German shoe. Everything he owned he carried in two grain sacks.

An hour later Hans Beutle arrived, driving a springy buckboard, clicking his tongue and singing to his bay mare. The flesh of his face fell straight away from high cheekbones. A low sagittal crest suspended his eyebrows just above the pale irises giving an expression of peculiar intensity to his face. The blunt nose, the round ears, and stiff hair the color of ironstone were not memorable, but the mouth, with its twist, the lips pouting a little as though ready to begin kissing, and his skim milk–and–gravel voice, high-pitched and raw, drew attention. He was broad and very strong, with thick-wristed hands. He had been a miller's apprentice in Bavaria with musical abilities, but after a quarrel with the miller that left the man choking and smothering inside a quarter-filled sack of flour, Beutle fled to America promising to send for his wife, Gerti, and baby Percy Claude. He was never sure later whether he had been fortunate or unfortunate to find a job playing the cornet with an Italian marching band for a salary of twenty dollars a month. In Chicago the bandleader broke a tooth on a fragment of butternut shell in a piece of divinity fudge given him by a country girl in a stained dress. The tooth throbbed. The bandleader tried to lance the swollen gum with his case knife and set a galloping septicemia in action. He died in a dirty room owing the rent; the musicians were on their own. Beutle was sick of the jolting train rides and sweaty crowds, sick of Italian music and emotion. He saw a railroad advertisement for free land on the Little Runt River. As long as they were giving away quarter sections to anybody who proved up a claim, count him for one. The farm life was a good life, they said.

The third German, William Loats, arrived at sundown, pumping along on a shrieking bicycle and gnawing a heel of bread. The afternoon light streamed out of the west and lit the street like a stage. He slowed and stopped at the end of the grass-grown street, saw two men drawing lines in the dirt with sticks. The air quivered. Suddenly the other two straightened and looked at him.

He had come as a child from the old country to his uncle's farm on the north shore of Lake Huron where, from the highest field, one could see the smoke of steamers churning west. The language of the uncle's house was English.

Loats was clever and thrifty, as thin as a hoe handle, had a stone-shaped head with a frizz of dark crimpy hair, puffed cheeks and small cross-eyes. He was easygoing, the kind of man who would never shout at a horse. The uncle's twelve sons denied the possibility that a portion of the farm could ever come to him, and finally he had struck out for himself, fired up by the advertisement in his uncle's farm paper for free homestead land. He took passage on the *Vigorous,* a passenger-freight steamer bound down the Great Lakes for Chicago. The steamer was loaded with barrels of sugar and three hundred passengers—a family of Courte d'Oreilles Indians, a gang of young Polish laborers in high spirits heading for the meat-packing plants, two Norwegian clergymen, Irish railworkers and three families of white-blond Russians on their way to the Dakotas. They stopped at St. Ignace to take on more passengers. The wind was coming up. White petals from a nearby orchard in flower drifted onto the dark water and the deck. Dutch immigrants clumped on board in their wooden shoes, headed for utopia in Indiana; they found places on the overcrowded deck—more of them were left on the dock, calling out messages to be passed on to their relatives.

An hour and a half after midnight, under a full, cold moon, the *Vigorous* struck an uncharted reef and broke apart. The bow sank quickly, but the stern floated on, filled with fire that set the sugar barrels ablaze. The moonlight shone on the rolling waves and the wet faces of the drowning passengers, who cried out in six languages. Loats kicked to shore in the company of a young Dutch woman, both clinging to the headboard of the captain's pine bed. As the headboard dipped and plunged, Loats imagined a life-saving machine, a right-angled wooden frame with an inflated rubber cushion for buoyancy, a rear propeller driven by a hand crank, another under the feet driven by pedals; and there would be a mast with a little sail, a whistle hanging from a lanyard, a signal flag, and even a lantern. But how could one light the lantern? He puzzled at it until the waves swept them into the sandy surf. He helped the woman, reeling and choking, toward a green house with smoke streaming from the chimney. All along the wet sand lay the wooden shoes of drowned Dutchmen and from the woods a bear emerged, head up into the wind, lured by the smell of burning sugar.

A coincidence

Messermacher and Beutle beckoned Loats to them. Now the three stood on the warped boardwalk speaking a mixture of German and American, sizing each other up, discovering similarities, exclaiming over the strange coincidence that had brought them to this tall grass on the same day. They were all of an age, twenty-eight, their birthdays within weeks of each other.

"Like brothers!"

"The Indivisible Three!"

"Aller guten Dinge sind drei!"

Beutle's laugh came from a chest like a stuffed mattress. "Not like those fellers was going up in the mountains to look for gold, two prospectors, friends and comrades forever. Before they go they get provisions and everything they need at the trading post. There's no women in the mountains so at the store they buy these love boards. It's a pine board with a knothole, a piece of fur nailed on." He winked. "So a year later, down from the mountains comes only one prospector. 'Where's the other feller?' the trader asks him. He says—" When he finished the story Messermacher laughed but Loats drew the side of his mouth down.

They built a camp near the river in a clump of bur oak, and after the sunset blaze burned down into coals they smoked the Western Bee cigars Loats passed around, talking until the leaves of the trees disappeared in the darkness, until one by one sleep stifled their voices.

In the morning they waded through grasses, bluestem and Indian grass, needle grass and foxtail barley studded with bird-foot violets, wild strawberry blossom and multiflora rosebuds, prairie clover, whitetop and larkspur, until they were soaked to the thighs with dew, their pants legs caked with yolk-colored pollen and their strides releasing the green perfume of crushed stems. They veered around a huge swale of slough grass, for the saw-toothed blades cut like knives.

"But it's good feed," said Loats. "Twist it up, you can burn it." Messermacher was anxious to find clay—a good clay pit, he said, and he would show them how to make the best house in the world. They stumbled over bison bones, cast their eyes across the prairie, over the iridescent, undulating sea. They pointed to islands and archipelagos of bur oaks, a stand of black walnut, to the cottonwoods, elm and green ash on the riverbank. Loats pulled up a spindly plant with a cluster of creamy flowers. "Not this! Poisons your stock. Death camas. My uncle had this plant." He looked for others but did not find one.

"This here is *Tiefland*," said Messermacher.

Fate had dropped them in a wreath of birdsong to hear the meadowlark's gurgling double notes, the prairie blackbird's rusty cries, *kiss-he, kiss-he,* the dickcissel's *jup jup jup clip clip,* husky trillings and clear pensive notes, quavers and sliding whistles, sweet warbles, rattles, purrs and buzzes and the fragrant air shot through with lazuli buntings as a length of silk may show metallic threads. When they found a bank of slick blue clay along the Little Runt, Messermacher said some higher power had directed the event, and he took off his broken hat. He dropped his beard on his chest and said a prayer.

Loats suggested they name the settlement Trio.

"*Nein, nein,* no," said Beutle, holding up his hands, sinewy and cal-lused. "It's these *Pranken,* these paws, that will build our farms and the town. Let the name show the work of our hands." He was the most emotional of the three, the most volatile, the most sensual. A minor chord could make him weep. He was self-educated, owned a number of books, was never without facts and explanations.

"*So* call it *Pranken,* then," Messermacher said, his dark face twitching at the idea, but when they filed the papers at the county seat, the word was written down as Prank.

"If we called it *Hände,*" said Loats, "it would of turned into Hand, a not bad name. But Prank? A joke. Your life place becomes a joke because language mixes up!" And every year thereafter he petitioned to change the name of the town, suggesting in turn Snowball, Corn, Par-adise, Red Pear, Dew, Buggywhip and Brighteye. (Later his suggestions were bitter: Forget It, Roughtown, Hell, Wrong, Stink.)

A polka in the lumber office

They had no time. Ground had to be broken; it was late in the season. The three Germans drove themselves without mercy, sleeping in their clothes, eating in their sleep, crawling out in the darkness before dawn when the only sign of the approaching day was the fresh odor of moist earth. They staggered in dirt-stiffened overalls to hitch the horses, plow and harrow and plant corn and wheat and drive the birds from the swollen, germinating kernels. Messermacher used one of his grain-sack traveling bags to make a seeder, filling it a quarter full with winter wheat seed, then folding and strapping it across his breast so the bag gaped, and steadily he cast the seed in an even fan. A little wheat, yes, said Beutle, who had read somewhere that corn was the destiny of the place, civilization was built on corn. Loats nodded. Then came a rush to throw up temporary sod hovels.

"I don't get my woman here pretty soon, you fellers better sleep with the axe handy by," said Beutle, rubbing his groin and moaning in mock agony. Their faces were sundark, with startling white foreheads marking hat lines, their bodies supple and strong in the crusted overalls, their eyesight keen and expectations brilliant. They worked with demoniac energy. Everything seemed possible.

They made trip after trip to Keokuk, first to fetch their women and children, then a milk cow and seven pounds of coffee for Messer-macher, then lumber for the houses and barns, southern pine shipped up from Louisiana on the Kansas City Southern. Back and forth they went in Beutle's wagon hauling the resiny yellow boards to Prank and going for more.

"You want your nails to stay clinched, yellow pine'll never let go," said Messermacher who had knowledge of wood and joinery.

Loats ordered a dozen bald-cypress boards but wouldn't say why until they pried it from him that it was for a casket.

"It don't ever rot, stays sweet and solid a hundred years. Believe in looking ahead."

"That's right! No telling what the price of coffin wood will be next year," said Beutle. "And you already twenty-eight years of age."

In the lumberyard office Beutle counted out the money. His eye went around the familiar room, taking in the stained deal boards, the dusty clock, the counter polished black by the action of coat sleeves, the finger-marked safe with its painted gilt flourishes. On the safe stood a green button accordion, furred in dust.

"You play that instrument?" he asked the clerk. An American.

"Nah. Something Mr. Bailey got off a nigger last year come through here off the boats and hungry. He couldn't play it neither with a broken arm. I reckon Mr. Bailey felt sorry for him, give him something for it, two bits and goodbye, keep moving along."

Beutle picked it up, gave it a tentative squeeze, then filled the office with a loud and pumping polka. The dust flew from it as he worked the bellows. The other two Germans stood with their faces ajar.

"Hans," said Messermacher. "This is marvelous. That you can do this. This music gives me happiness."

"Not bad," said Beutle. "Nice tone, quick buttons. How much wants Mr. Bailey for this thing?"

"I dunno. He's not here now." The clerk made up his mind to try the instrument as soon as the Germans had gone. It couldn't be difficult if Germans could play it.

"You ask him. I got to come back in September, get more lumber. You tell him he want to sell it, I buy it. If it ain't too much money, like the old feller with a nickel in his pocket said to the whore."

New houses and women

They spent the summer cultivating and hammering, raising frames and fencing, pacing off new fields for corn and oats and hay. All three of them were as hard and corded as hickory rails. The sown fields grew maniacally. In one plot Gerti planted some black seeds, the size and shape of squash seeds, given out by the land office, a new thing to try, watermelon, they called it.

"*Raus! Raus!*" shouted Beutle to his children in the black morning of each shortening day, pulling them from the rustling tick stuffed with wild grass and setting them to chores and labor. The women—except Gerti—sweated and strained, pressed bricks of clay, grass and manure from wooden molds, fed the stock and worked in the fields, keeping track of the little children by the bells pinned to their clothes, while the men hammered until they were striking by feel, blind in the darkness, packing the clay bricks, *batser,* between the vertical studs as Messermacher said, "like this, like so." Gerti worked with the men, brandishing a hammer and singing.

When the watermelons were as large as a child's head, the women boiled them, but they collapsed into a tasteless green mush that no one could eat, not the children, not the cow. In mid-August the second cutting of hay was stacked and Loats sowed rye seed between his corn rows to plow under in the spring. The others laughed; with such rich loam it was a waste of time.

By the end of September they were out of the sod huts and into the small, good houses with their smooth exteriors of clay, thick walls, and central chimneys of the same hard bricks. Over the winter Messermacher's wife stenciled a design of red flowers with pointed petals along the walls near the ceiling, very much admired by a finger-cut Indian woman who appeared one morning with a basket of snakeroot for barter. The earthen huts were renamed barns, and next year, said Messermacher, they'd enlarge the houses, build better barns. Gerti and the children walked through the long grass feeling for bison bones with their bare feet (a man came in a wagon at the end of the summer and paid cash for the bones which were shipped east and ground into fertilizer), ate wild rose hips for the fleeting taste of sweetness. Beutle's oldest son, Wid, had a gift for finding grassy meadowlark nests.

The green accordion

"Look now. Four months since we walked on the naked land. Now is three farms started."

Before they started harvesting the corn Beutle went back to the Keokuk lumberyard for henhouse studding. The accordion was still on the safe.

"Well, how much does Mr. Bailey want for it?"

The clerk pulled a sour face. "Mr. Bailey don't want nothing for it.

Mr. Bailey is gathered to his maker. See that lumber you got on your wagon? That fell on him. That and more. Bad stacking. That's his brains and blood on it. You look at the ends. It stove his head in, crushed him like a bug. His own fault. He'd get anybody to stack them boards; bums, eyties, polacks, krauts, hunkies. He goes out there, pulls at a board on the top to start loading up some gink's wagon, the whole thing come down on him. He give one scream you could sharpen your axe on. Took me over a hour to get the pile off'n him. So I guess it's up to me to name a price on that damn squeezebox. I don't know what you Germans see in it. Sounds like Mr. Bailey when the boards come at him. One dollar. In cash."

A memorial photograph

Beutle played the accordion in the new house still smelling of the southern pinewoods, the resinous odor evoking the hissing sound of wind in the needles, the buzz of cicadas.

"Look at it. It's a pretty color." He stretched the green accordion out on his knee, pulled long chords from it. "A good voice." His saccharine tenor soared, the old German songs flowered in the kitchen, the children played under the table slipping straws beneath Beutle's tapping toe and the women wiped tears away.

"Yes, it's a nice little accordion," Beutle said loftily, firing up his curved pipe. "But I would rather have a good German Hohner. It would be stronger." Messermacher thumped the laundry tub and Loats buzzed at a paper and comb until his lips numbed.

"Now we got everything," said Loats.

"No," said Beutle, treading on the finger beneath his toe. "A tuba we need. And a *Bierstube.* I miss that place, the chairs and little tables with the red-check cloths under the trees, the little birds hopping around for crumbs, everyone peaceful with a stein of fine lager—oh how I miss Herr Gründig's lager, he made it like a fine wine—a little music sometimes, an accordion playing this"—and he drew out a few bars of "*Schöne Mähderin*"—"the children sitting quiet, and how I remember the old ladies knitting with their little glass in front of them. There is nothing like this in America, there is no place to go. Everybody stays home and works. Americans understand nothing of how to live, only to get and get and get. Now we make our own *Bierstube,* eh? I make a place down by the river under the willow trees, and on Sunday afternoon when it's nice we go there and pretend to ourselves we are in a place of warmth and convivial feelings. The children can play at waiters."

"Um," said fiddle-faced Clarissa Loats. "And shall I be one of the old ladies knitting with the little glass before her, or like a demented one, carrying cakes and cheese and sausage from the house back and forth?"

"A woman's work is a woman's work," said Beutle. "First carry, then knit and drink."

Loats's uncle had belonged to a *Turnverein,* and the nephew, impressed with the old man's wiry strength, persuaded the others to do exercises. Every morning at daybreak the three Germans arose in their separate houses, emptied their bladders, then performed three knee bends, toe touchings, and finally they flung their arms outward, forward, and to one side. Messermacher was exceptional with his homemade Indian clubs; Loats could walk on his hands. Then each went to table and drank a quart of home-brewed beer—Beutle smoked a cigar as well— while the woman of the house clattered the cover off the milk crock and salt pork crackled in the frying pan.

"We got it good," said Beutle.

But in November one of Loats's children fell sick with second summer complaint and convulsions that worsened into brain fever, and Beutle's vaunted doctor book, *Praktischer Führer zur Gesundheit,* was useless; after a week the boy died. Loats and Messermacher dug a grave a little way out on the prairie, and Beutle, tears streaming down his face, swore to fence the plot in the spring. He played "The Dead March" twice through on the accordion and the women sobbed. It was only the beginning of the unending illnesses and accidents that seemed to afflict the Germans. Over the years the children sickened of diphtheria, spinal fever, typhoid, cholera, malaria, measles, whooping cough, tuberculosis and pneumonia as well as lightning strikes, injuries, snakebites and frostbite. When Beutle's youngest son died of complications following measles, Gerti sent Beutle riding after the itinerant photographer who had passed by a few days earlier so they might have a memorial photograph. She quickly dressed the dead child in his older brother's trousers and a black winter coat and, while he was still pliable, arranged the small body on a chair in a sitting position and in his hands placed the wooden horse Beutle had carved. Because the corpse would not stay upright, Beutle had to tie him in place with a rope blackened in soot that it might not show. The photographer arrived, they carried chair and child into the brilliant sunlight. There was still no fence around the plot and this time Beutle played "The Dead March" once. That was enough. The lives of children were in precarious balance; it was better not to love them too much.

The Rawhide & Hog Lard

In 1900 there were thirty farms around Prank, new families impelled west by private failures, drifting in from drought-ruined Kansas and Nebraska, some stragglers from the east who had failed to get decent land in the Oklahoma land run the year before, a few ruined by the Depression and looking for a new start, some ex-cattlemen brought to their knees by the terrible blizzards of '86 and '87, still hoping to get back to where they had been, and most of them flying high on the idea of the new century, sensing a chance at momentous things. Some seasons the corn grew like nothing any of them had ever seen or dreamed, jerking up out of the purple-black loam as they watched, and in the hot silence of a windless summer day, standing among the rows they could hear the screak of stalk growth, the force of life.

But drought came as well, baking the crops to a total loss, and hellish grasshoppers in whirring clouds that clung so thickly to the barbwire fences that the strands appeared to be made of frayed hawser, hawser that writhed and moved. Black walls of cloud sucked themselves into the roaring tunnels of tornadoes, hurricane winds burst out of nowhere and blew down barns and houses, cast horses into gullies. Men were frozen as they staggered across the prairie in bitter ground blizzards, horses died in the traces, a woman bent against the screaming wind and gripping her husband's hand as they struggled to the house fell and lost her hold. He could not find her until the next morning, her icy corpse blown up against the side of the barn, and would have rolled to the Missouri had the barn not caught her. Long savage droughts were broken by torrential downpours that gullied the powdery soil and washed out the dying crops. Hail as large as teacups, misshapen like baroque pearls, pounded cornfields into pulp and bruised the stock. Children drowned in the Little Runt, were lost in the forests of corn.

The long-awaited railroad line came in, the thirty-mile Rolla & Highrod, derisively called the Rawhide & Hog Lard for its improvisational operation—the company used rendered lard instead of expensive bearing oil for engine lubrication, dipped water by hand from the Little Runt River rather than put up water towers—but it was a connecting route to the Chicago markets and prosperity. So read the railroad's posters and handbills. Beutle despised the Irish bogmen who laid the track with their "Irish spoons," those pointed shovels, but their money spent as well as any, and for a year the Beutles boarded four of the dirty, praying whiskey drinkers.

"Oh the dirty Irish," said Gerti who had brought a bowl of potato gruel to a shack where four children lay deathly sick with smallpox. The mother had offered her a cup of coffee and, when Gerti nodded reluctantly, went into a filthy kitchen alcove. After a minute Gerti glanced in and saw the wretched woman licking clean the inside rim of a cup while on the stove a pan of long-boiled coffee gave off the odor of a burning rag.

Beutle sold the black walnut grove for railroad ties and congratulated himself on making a good dollar. Some of the Irish stayed to mine the limestone discovered beneath the town, and some of them drifted out west, following the railroads, dropping out now and then to become ranch hands, land agents, clerks in the new government offices.

"Those dirty Catholics," said Beutle. "They are all criminals, they commit any crime because they can go to confession, a few prayers and *zack!* all is wiped clean. There was an Irishman stole five chickens from his neighbor, he goes to confession and says, 'Father, I stole some chickens.' 'How many?' says the priest. 'Five, Father, but let's say ten and I'll get the rest on the way home.'"

Gerti kneaded dough for twenty loaves of bread each week, her great enlarged hands like articulated hooks, the muscular arms so overdeveloped in the forearm they seemed deformed. After a restless cow she was milking in the yard shifted against the wash platform and sent the heavy tub of water onto her shoulder, the right one drew up permanently. Despite this crookedness and her sufferings from inflammatory rheumatism, she worked in the fields, cursing housework, and every morning she braided her hair and the hair of her daughters to form a coronet although the fashion in town was for a bun of hair the size of a young cabbage drawn up at the top of the head. She combed out the rippled hair with her fine comb, parted it into two long hanks which she braided swiftly and tautly, working in a strip of cloth near the end of each braid. She wound the finished braids around the head, and where they met at the nape of the neck she tied the strips and hid them in the hair. The flat double braids made a glinting crown of hair on the young daughters; hers was dun, streaked with grey. At night the braids were undone—who could sleep on ropes of hair?—to cascade down in crimpy hot waves. And when several times each year the girls came home from school—never sit next to the Irish, she warned them—with head lice, she washed their hair in kerosene, combed the reeking strands with a fine-tooth nit comb, and when they itched and writhed with worms, she dosed them with Dr. Lug's Vermifuge, a tarry substance with the reek of scorched cowhorn.

A second rail line came in, a double track laid by Chinese laborers who spoke an incomprehensible jabber, running south to Kansas City and north to Minneapolis. The railroad built a station, manned it with a stationmaster, a telegraph operator, a freight manager. The waiting room featured a ten-foot bench of perforated plywood that spelled out an immense motto, VISIT THE SICK. Buck Thorne, the stationmaster, had been an engineer until he lost one leg in a derailment. He made a joke of referring to himself as a steam locomotive. When he went home for lunch he put on his dome casing, limped along on his flat-wheel wooden leg, side rods working, headed into his roundhouse to fire up and take on coal and water. Saturday night he drank whiskey until he was in a roaring state and declared himself to be thoroughly oiled.

The Kansas City train made its first run on the Fourth of July. Prank celebrated success.

The three Germans stood in the front row on the raw plank platform. Each held a homemade American flag tied to a sapling pole. Behind them children held tiny paper flags the size of stamps on toothpicks between their thumbs and forefingers. On the other side of the tracks, in the hog holding pens, pigs stood on their hind legs, front feet hooked on the fence, watching the crowd.

"Vork hard and good fortune got to come," Beutle orated, his accent thickening. "Ve got miles a corn shows vat good, hard vork does, and now ve got the railroads opening up the country"—sweating and stuttering with the honor of it, the Irish sniggering at his clumsy speech. The train from Kansas City hissed and groaned, the whistle screamed a raw, hoarse cry, the tone modified by a block of wood engineer Ozro Gare had jammed against the reed in the whistle to make a distinctive call, the three Germans leaned their flags against the station wall, and Beutle took up the green accordion from the baggage cart and crashed into the new Sousa piece, "The Westward March," even though the new line ran north and south. Loats came in on his tarnished tuba with powerful blats and snarls, and Messermacher rang a bar of iron, a section of rail with a piercing clangor, in honor of the railroad. The children imitated the squealing pigs and all bellowed "The Battle Hymn of the Republic."

With a breathy shriek the train pulled away, the crowd cheering, waving at the caboose until it was out of sight. Five or six boys laid their ears against the rail to hear the receding steely song. The men set up trestle tables on the platform and the women brought out the pans of chicken and dumplings, washtubs of rolls, bread pans of butter, pickled beets. The German women had brought the most food: an enormous pink ham and red sausages cooked in beer lying beside each other in dozens in the pan, smoked pork ribs with sauerkraut seasoned with pepper and wild juniper berries, radishes and sour cream, an onion pie fifteen inches across, pickled pork with apples and pears, head cheese.

Twenty ripe watermelons cooled in tubs of ice had come up on the train, and there were prune pies, Gerti's *Apfelkiachle* and twelve pound cakes with honey glaze. One of the Irish children bit into a second piece of cake and screamed with pain when a yellow jacket feeding on the sweet glaze stung his tongue. Girls stood at intervals along the table flapping away flies with willow branches and dishcloths.

" 'Member how we cooked them melons the first year?" said Clarissa Loats, laughing her thin ha-ha. Loats twirled his Indian clubs and Beutle crept up to the station loft and threw handfuls of peppermint candies from the open window. Off to the side an Irishman played a mournful pipe and another did a clog dance on the platform until the planks sent up gouts of dust, but it was the Germans everyone watched. In the cooling evening the crowd moved to the new schoolhouse where the desks were all cleared away for a dance.

"Jesus Christ! Now dance!" shouted Beutle, starting off with comic German songs—"*Die Ankunft der Grünhörner,*" "*Auf der Alm da steht 'ne Kuh,*" and the great favorite, "*Herr Loats, was ist mit deiner Tuba los?*"—until the Irish had enough of it and shouted for jigs and reels that the Germans could not play, and the Americans wanted "Old Uncle Ned" and "Arkansas Traveler." The three Germans played until midnight, the tireless Beutle pumping out accordion polkas and the tuba honking and a fine spray of sweat, caught in the gaslight's white rays, flying from couples spinning the tight corner turn. At midnight someone tolled a bell, an Irishman fired a shotgun into the sky and the three Germans performed their most astonishing feat.

They brought two anvils from Loats's wagon and set one on the ground upside down. Beutle packed the hole with gunpowder and sprinkled a little around the margin and out to the edge to serve as a fuse, then placed the second anvil, top down, over the charged hole. Messermacher set off the gunpowder with a red-hot poker. A terrific barrage of explosions, the anvils banging, jolted the station, the pigs squealed in terror, and Prank shouted itself hoarse.

Sunday

The population of Prank passed six hundred. Farm roads from the hinterlands knotted beside the tracks. O'Rourke's Comestibles and Merchandise installed a nickelodeon theater in the back room and Beutle, on a Saturday trip into town, cranked installments of *The Great Train Robbery* through the apparatus.

"It is something to see, all right, but nothing at all compared to a good

German play." A troupe of gypsies came by, selling willow chairs for porch sitting, and Beutle bought two, thinking of his *Bierstube* down beside the river, crabbing at the price. But when, at the end of the day, he carried the chairs down to the picnic spot, he found the willows hacked to the ground and fire circles where the *Roma* had camped. "Jesus Christ, I bought my own trees." (And when the next year the same or another caravan camped down along the river, he drove them away at shotgun point, becoming impatient when one of their wagons mired in the wet earth, and laughing that he would get them going, aimed at the black-skirted behind of an old woman throwing her weight against the wheel. She fell shrieking, and Beutle's children began to cry.

"Shut up! She ain't hurt—foreigners is animals, they don't feel no pain. She pretends, to make you sorry for them." He spat and shouted "*raus, raus!*" until they pulled out onto the road, the woman hauled into one of the wagons.)

On Sundays the three Germans stayed home drinking beer, smoking homegrown tobacco, eating and playing music—in fine weather down by the river in the place Beutle had cleared, outfitted with a few benches and small plank tables and the gypsy chairs. (After all, the willows had grown up again.) It was very agreeable there in hot weather, with the sound of the river slipping along and the songs of meadowlarks thrown into the yellow afternoon light. They had no taste for the Yankee version, a day of gloom and bleak prayers.

"You know why the Puritans left England for America?" Beutle set the green accordion on a chair and reached for the beer pitcher. "Jesus Christ, like the feller says, it was so they could carry on their religion in freedom and in their own way and force others to do the same." He made a tremendous fart and the children screamed with laughter.

A trip to Chicago

In town they began to say that the children of the three Germans looked remarkably similar—perhaps the families were closer than anyone suspected. Stories about Beutle had circulated for years, and if it hadn't been for his accordion and his aggressive, half-laughing character, he might have been roughed up some dark night.

"Jesus Christ! Somebody wants to make trouble with me, *den rauch ich in der Pfeife!* I smoke him in my pipe!"

On one memorable trip to Chicago to sell the hogs—six cents a pound!—the noble German white hog—Beutle said he intended to give the beat-up little green accordion to Messermacher. He'd teach him how to play it. It was not a bad little instrument. Himself, he was buying a new one, a Hohner, a German instrument by a firm that made excellent harmonicas. It had a few helper buttons that gave him some sharps and flats. Then they'd get up an accordion band, a German accordion band if they had another instrument. Loats suffered from the motion of the train and went to stand on the platform in the cold rushing air, breathing in the sulfur stink of burning coal.

"Germans invented the accordion," Beutle explained to Messermacher. "A thousand things they invented, but accordions most of all. Because Germans think, Germans have brains. There was this feller, a musician, a German violinist, he ends up playing in the court orchestra in Russia, not Catherine the Great but around that time, he plays the violin. But because he's a German, Jesus Christ, he notices things, he notices when he hangs up his bow on a nail back in his room she makes a nice little tone. From this he invents the nail violin, very beautiful tones, I have heard it. A circle of wood with nails sticking out, you run the bow on the nails and *ooo aaa ooo aaa,* a beautiful tune. One day this feller gets a strange thing from China, somebody gives it to him because interested in things he is—naturally, he is a German—and he sees a round bowl with some bamboo pipes sticking out, and on the bowl a mouthpiece. He blows on it. It's a fine sound. This thing the Jesus Christ Chinese put reeds inside the pipes, same as in the accordion, little reeds stuck on one end with wax, the other end can vibrate like this." He trembled his hand at Messermacher. "The German violin player learns the playing of this instrument, *die liebliche Chinesenorgel,* and from this he passes to other Germans the idea of the accordion— the free reed. That's how it begins. Later comes the bellows."

In Chicago Beutle drank imported Bavarian beer and smoked a twisted Spanish cigar at a beer hall, ate plates of kraut and wurst, sang drinking songs until midnight, fornicated with prostitutes, and bought a new instrument with some of his hog money, and for his wife a perforated cardboard motto, *God Bless Our Home,* and a selection of colored threads for working it. Loats thought of yellow pencils and sheets of coarse paper for the children and chose a tape measure holder in the shape of a hen and a bottle of THANKS A MILLION tonic for his wife who was already somewhat broken in health. He ate a plate of Chicago sausages of a strange bronze color and a flavor like kerosene. Messermacher ordered a rocking chair and one of the new bedsprings for a total of six dollars, bought a box of oranges for his children and from time to time took the cover off to inhale the fragrance.

On the train back to Prank, the new accordion changing laps, teasing their fingers, they talked about the power of music over men. "Listen to the sound of this, how strong and clear." For the new accordion had good steel reeds and a bright and aggressive German tone, though it was difficult to play because of the extra buttons. Beutle had looked at a washing machine, a copper Maytag with a handle for the woman to crank until the clothes were clean, and a wringer, but did not buy it, got instead a windup phonograph and several Edison discs, including one featuring an accordion player named Kimmel playing a selection of German waltzes and Irish jigs and reels. He burned to get home and hear it.

"You got to think a musical instrument is human or, anyway, alive," said Beutle. "You take a fiddle now, we say it has a neck, and in the human neck what do you find? Vocal cords like strings, where the sound comes from. Now, the accordion, we have here an instrument that breathes! It breathes, it lives. Jesus Christ! Even so without a neck. Lungs it's got. And the piano? The keys are fingers, answering your fingers. The trumpet, the cornet, is a nose. That you blow. Here's a good one I heard. See, a feller goes to Chicago to sell his hogs and he gets a high price. His pocketbook is full, he can't hardly close it. He's afraid of thieves. But he don't want to go back to the farm without some fun. So he finds this place full of women, hard-looking women with arms like sailors. Still, that's all he can find so he says to himself, 'OK, I be careful.' The woman asks him one dollar. 'OK,' he says, 'I give you two dollars if—' "

"Look out!" said Loats in a strangled voice, lunging for the window to vomit Chicago sausage.

Beutle's lust

At first Beutle denounced the playing of Kimmel as fakery. "It's two accordions. No one can play this music." Then he said of course it was one musician—a German—a genius of the accordion although too fond of Irish jigs.

The three Germans made good loud farmers' music and the way to dance to it was to stamp.

"If you play like those Germans play, when you grow up you'll be fit for nothing at all but to blow a train whistle, like Quint Flint," sneered an Irish pipe player to his son who had tried once to play with the Germans but had been drowned out. Quint Flint, a train engineer, blew "Polly Put the Kettle On" when he approached his home station.

When traveling bands came through Prank, Beutle trailed after the leader, introduced himself as a former traveling musician. "You have heard of Tonio's Golden Touring Band? *Ach,* years ago, different towns.

I used to play with them. Now I'm a farmer. Well, maybe you got some instruments you want to get rid of, they're maybe a little broken. I could buy them if they're not too much, fix them up. Something for us out here on the lone prairie for music." And so the Germans gained saxophones and drums, harmonicas, glockenspiels, and Beutle taught the children to play them. Messermacher's son, little Karl, learned several instruments quickly, could play "The Camptown Races" on the accordion, the penny whistle and the harmonica at seven years of age.

In town they said, "get the three Germans for the dance," and then they'd laugh, and someone would say something about Beutle and Gerti. "The Three Germans" became the name of their band even when half a dozen of the kids were playing with them. They played music for dances with a beat thumped out by Beutle's right foot, as steady and solid as the tick of a wound clock. They sat around the hard-coal heater, a great thing after burning twisted slough grass for so many winters, Lotte squeaking the violin, the accordions huffing, little Wid working a set of foot chimes, and Percy Claude ringing the banjo, so bright and clever in its sound that the old dog sat up and howled whenever he took it from the nail on the wall.

The Beutles were lusty, there was no doubt, and not just because they had nine children living—many in Prank had a dozen and more—but because Beutle didn't have the decency to control himself until the privacy of the night and the bedcovers. The Railway Express man, Mulkens, drove out with a shipment of young apple stock for him and stumbled on a scene in the woodshed with Gerti bent over the chopping block and Beutle going at it "like a starved hog at the slop bucket." He whipped his horse into a gallop on the way back to town, eager to tell what he'd seen, right down to red blemishes on Beutle's buttocks that were maybe not pimples but the mark of some awful disease. Or maybe even bite marks! German beasts. The postman told of an envelope addressed to Beutle that had somehow come unglued and revealed indecent photographs of women, one in a black union suit with cut-out circles from which the breasts protruded.

In autumn, trying to get the corn shocked, the three worked together in each other's fields, especially when their boys were too young to be useful. Once when they were working at Beutle's place, Gerti drove up at noon with the dinner pails and jugs of vinegared water. The day was warm. Beutle was working close to the noon spot, waiting for Gerti, Loats thought, probably famished. Loats and Messermacher walked down the field, unstrapping the husking pins from their right hands (for Beutle husked his corn in the field), raising and lowering their heads to get the kinks out of their necks. They saw Beutle and Gerti crawl under the wagon.

"Look, Beutle is gettin into the shade," said Messermacher enviously.

"Gettin into more than the shade," Loats said, squinting at the white flash of Beutle's buttocks. They walked down to the wagon.

"*So,* you don't care who's seeing this?" said Loats, tearing at the cold pork with his yellow teeth. He crouched down and stared under the wagon, hoping to embarrass Beutle.

"Look good, Willy," said Beutle, breathing deep and rocking deeper, "you learn how to do it and Jesus Christ, I don't have to come your place Sunday afternoon."

"*Animalisch!*" said Loats.

"*Leck mich am Arsch!*"

"So what, people don't blink their eye if the dogs do it, or the bull mounts the cow," Gerti said to Clarissa. "Tell me the difference. We're the same like them. A natural urge. *Sowieso,* I can't stop him. He has to do it three times a day or die." She was a little past forty, her upper lip already pleating up in fine wrinkles. She craved a little money of her own but Beutle was tight with the purse. She always had a new scheme: butter from the cow—but it was a terrible lot of work and brought only five cents a pound—and when she tried to raise turkeys, first a hailstorm killed seventeen, then the hawks took them.

"The difference is we are Christians and animals are not," said Clarissa. And she thought, Three times a day! *Wahnsinn!* The man was a maniac, a living curiosity.

He was a maniac. As Beutle got older his desires deepened and Gerti's waned. Nothing halted or slowed his sexual drive. He was like the locomotive roaring down the straightaway twenty miles to the east that the train men called "the old board plank." In 1910 a road company of Irving Berlin's *The Girl and the Wizard* came through Prank. Beutle was crazy about it, adopted as his own the naughty song "Oh, How That German Could Love."

The hen's nest

The three Germans joined the German-American Historical Society in Kringel, a heavily German town thirty miles north. The society met once a month to promote pride in *Kultur* through guest speakers, concerts and singing evenings. Beutle enjoyed the long drive. The size of the country still made him giddy, and even after a drenching rain, the horse steaming as it trotted, he tossed off his slicker, pulled the fresh air into his nose and looked at the washed sky, the rolling cloud drawing away, while he perfected the phrases in the speech he was to give: "Germans gave much to America. The American Revolution would have failed if Germans didn't help out. The Republican Party come about from the interest of German Americans. And never forget that Abraham Lincoln was descended from a German immigrant named Linkhorn. America needs Germans to fulfill its destiny."

But down in Prank the Railway Express man said, better drown them all—they can't never fit this country, the Dutchies, those squareheads, those sourkrauts.

Beutle took a German paper that came weekly by mail and, when he was done reading it and clipping out the interesting advertisements, passed it on to Loats and Messermacher. It was from this paper he had learned of Linkhorn and from it ordered a perforated cardboard portrait of the dead president for Gerti to work up in colored wools. She dyed the wool strands for the face with ironweed, giving Lincoln a yellow complexion that changed slowly to a greenish brown over the winter. She was sewing the hem of a pinafore. A sewing machine—if she only had one.

"It's the Germans making this country great," agreed Loats. "Here's the dirty Irish in Prank, there's not one can read a signpost or sign his name."

Messermacher was the richest of the three, although he had trouble with his eyes, sensitive to the windblown dust he lived in, and he dosed them with Dr. Jackson's Eye Water. Two of his sons worked with him on his farm, the other three farmed adjacent or nearby sections, and one son, Karl, lived in town and worked for the railroad as a telegraph operator. Messermacher bought one of the new wireless check-row corn planters but it fouled and skipped when it passed over dead furrows. He modified it, wrote a letter to the manufacturer, and when the representative came out, gave him such an impressive demonstration that the company paid him one hundred dollars and an annual royalty for the invention for years. Until the war they used his photograph in their advertisements: *Farmer L. Messermacher says "This planter won't go wrong. Simple enough so a boy can run it."*

Loats's hogs were famous in Chicago; a few were fattened for the table of the governor and for the Century Club in Chicago. He had skill with wheat and hogs but thought the best thing on his farm was a twenty-acre orchard of sour cherry trees, each tree a phosphorescent globe of white netting as the fruit ripened.

Yet there was something strange. Although they were all successful farmers, the farms showplaces of thrift and good management, although they played music for every dance, the Germans were disliked in Prank. The children (called cabbageheads in school) and women were friendless except for each other's company. Part of it was because Clarissa was a fanatic housekeeper who scrubbed the exteriors of house and barn and whose snow-white floors dazzled, and few women wanted such a perfectionist for a friend; part because the three Germans were freethinkers, self-confessed agnostics who bragged that there was not a bible among them. And part of it was because in spite of locust, drought, hail, flood, tornado, summer frost and untimely thaw, the three always made a decent crop while men around them lost everything. In the flood the Little Runt rose over Beutle's low field, but when the water receded, dozens of fine fish were stranded in the wet, enriched furrows. He had only to gather them. The gossip flourished, juicy tales of German lubricity and incest. Most of the whispers routed back to Beutle and his insatiable appetites.

"Nah. The reason we don't play them dances so much now," said Beutle, "is the people hereabouts wants coon songs. Ragtime. The saxophone. They wants the piana accordion; the button accordion ain't good enough for them anymore. You see?"

By the time there were grandchildren around—the oldest son, Percy Claude, and his wife had built near the main house and the other boys had houses on the section—Gerti didn't want to be caught accommodating Beutle. At their age, she told him. Grey hair and all. Her big belly and his hairy hams like a bear. She pushed him away more frequently. Behavior that had been exciting when he was young was repellent in a slack-skinned man with grey hair. The situation got more complicated when she walked into the henhouse and there he was with the hired girl, he sitting in a hen's nest and the girl straddling him, her knickers on a nail. He winked at his wife as if to say, you won't and she will. There were straws in his hair.

She dodged away as though she had been sluiced with a bucket of icy water, a freezing despair running over her. She ran for her kitchen, moaning, heavy breasts swinging, the great haunches pumping her along. In the kitchen she leaned against the cold stove, put her forehead to the chrome edge of the warming oven and sobbed with grief and insult until her nose swelled. She stumbled to the knife drawer in the dresser and took out the black-handled carving knife, IXL stamped on the blade, and without reflection drew it across her throat. The heat of her own blood soaking her shirtwaist brought her to her senses. To kill herself over a man in a hen's nest! Never!

She got to the wavery-glassed mirror over the sink and looked. The blood was seeping, not jetting, though the cut gaped half an inch wide; the good layer of fat had saved her. Stanching the wound with a snowy dish towel, she got needle and thread from her sewing box and went back to the mirror and sewed up the lips of the wound with a steady hand. The thread was blue. She wrapped a clean rag around her neck. She had a mind to sew something else up as well.

Now Beutle was a dirty old thing to her. She killed every hen that had witnessed her humiliation, screamed at the hired girl until she ran home bawling, and he couldn't say a thing. She dumped floor sweepings into his tobacco box, stirring to mix in the clots of dirt. She thought often of putting a little rat poison in his coffee, yet did not.

But he'd get in the buggy after lunch and go somewhere.

"Goin over to see Loats," he'd say, and she guessed he was after Loats's daughter Polly who was still at home, a dried-up old maid at twenty-six who had almost died of consumption and then gained on the illness, and maybe not as dried-up as all that; she must have some juice.

She said something to Clarissa who kept her eyes open and sure enough, one day she saw Beutle following Polly into the apple trees. Clarissa ran to Loats and asked him to get the shotgun and use it.

"For what? He's just walking along behind her, you say."

"You know Beutle. You know what he's up to."

"You say he was following her. If she was in the lead, it don't sound like he's forcing nothing at all."

"She don't know what she's doing. She's innocent, I tell you."

"Going on thirty, maybe not so innocent as you suppose."

"You ought to beat the stuffings out of him, but I see you don't do a thing."

No, Loats wouldn't do a thing. If Beutle was having fun with Polly, he was doing something no one else had done. Loats believed the three Germans were bound by fate, and fate was the strongest force in life. And though once he'd trusted that common fate had removed them from the pinched seasons of the old country and directed all three of them toward rich and fruitful lives, fate began to turn its hand against them when the Serbs shot the Archduke Ferdinand in Sarajevo. It was as though ancient European enmities had sought them out from over the sea, slinking along behind each of them, just out of sight, had burrowed under the grass, waiting, as a pestilence waits until the right moment, then had risen up, eager and poisonous.

The war

Hatred came on slowly, like chill air rolling down a slope at sunset.

" 'Hyphenism'—what is this 'hyphenism' business?" said Loats, smoothing out Beutle's paper. They sat at the oak table in Loats's over-heated kitchen, the wife pressing shirts near the stove where the heavy irons heated, Beutle firing up his black pipe with lunty puffs. On the scrubbed table stood a vinegar cruet, a celluloid baby rattle and a stoneware jar of gleaming forks and knives.

"This is Roosevelt's horse, he is riding it hard. He don't like hyphens! Jesus Christ! He is concerned about German hyphen Americans. See here, down here. He says, 'some Americans need hyphens in their names because only part of them have come over. But when the whole man has come over, heart and thought and all, the hyphen drops of its own weight out of his name.' And what else drops? Jesus, Jesus and Christ, a beautiful language, Bach, Handel, Mozart, Schiller drops, Goethe drops, Kant and Hegel, Wagner, Wagner drops. Schubert, he drops. The accordion drops. And beer drops. Instead we get crazy dried-up American women yelling for the vote and the goddamn dried-up Americans and their dried-up American ideas about Prohibition. They don't see the Germans are the best, the hardest-working people in America. They don't see that everything that is good in America come from the Germans."

"Not the electric irons," said Loats's wife—the new wife, Pernilla—Clarissa had finally died of tremors and weakness. "I heard in town Mrs. O'Grain got a iron runs from the electric cord. She don't have to heat it on the stove, roast to death. That's what I want with my egg money, one of them irons."

"Jesus Christ," said Beutle, "you got to have electricity first. Where you going to plug it, up your hole? The iron ain't no good by itself." (Six months later, when he discovered the appliance was made by Rowenta, a German firm, he told Loats he ought to buy one.)

In the autumn of 1916, Beutle, furious at the crooked reporting of the American newspapers, subscribed to a second paper, *Fatherland,* which he read with vitriolic relish. He donated three dollars to a German war relief fund and as a token received a ring decorated with a replica of the Iron Cross and the inscription *To show my loyalty to the old Fatherland, I brought it gold in time of trouble for this piece of iron.*

"Well," said Loats, "don't pass this damn paper along to me anymore, Hans. I don't like it no more. Anyway I got one of them crystal sets. They are broadcasting the war news." (Although he sat with the earphones on his head, adjusting the cat's whisker by the hour, he heard nothing.)

"Oho!" said Beutle. "Listen, my friend, the crystal set will be as bad as the American newspapers and everything you read in an American newspaper favors the English and condemns the Germans. That's Wilson's famous neutrality! *Fatherland* only corrects this unfair reporting of the news. The lies and unjust accounts of the *Lusitania*? You can't deny their lies. *Fatherland* tells you right here about this crazy American newspaper that named what happened to the *Lusitania* as 'the worst crime since the crucifixion of Christ.' Jesus Christ, they don't admit the ship was loaded with munitions. You have to read *this* paper to discover the truth! And look here, American news too—in New Jersey a man is poisoned by his wife through pancakes."

"I guess I give up the hyphen, Hans. I don't care if they drop a thousand bombs on the Kaiser's head. I don't feel so German now. My children, they're born here, this is their country. I should keep hanging on to the old place that never did anything but drive me away? I just want America to stay out of it, this war, I want to work my farm and sit down to a good dinner and sleep good at night." And it was true that Loats's daughter Daisy had borrowed a copy of Walt Whitman's *I Hear America Singing* from the teacher and read it aloud after supper.

Beutle hawked and spit at this perfidy, ordered four new gramophone records from Columbia's Patriotic German Music selection: *"Hipp, Hipp, Hurrah," "Die Wacht am Rhein," "Wir Müssen Siegen"* and *"Deutschland, Deutschland über Alles,"* sung by a rich-toned male quartet. But this was not enough. He joined the German-American Alliance and his buggy showed up at every rally. He wrote, in his rusty German, a repetitive four-page pamphlet titled "The German Hog in America," listing the names of outstanding noble German white hogs, many of them his own. Two evenings a week, after supper, he took his accordion down to the saloons in Prank and tried to explain reasonably to the men he knew that as a person of German extraction he was loyal both to his motherland, Germany, and to his bride, America. He tried to persuade them with German music.

"And this is terrible beer. Jesus Christ! You come out my farm and try *my* beer, German beer, one time."

The bartender rolled his cold American eyes away from Beutle, turned his shoulder. He spoke to a customer at the end of the bar.

"They come right up to you and tell you they're better."

"Hang the Irish and shoot the hyphenates," said the customer, sniggering. The next day a sign without a single flyspeck hung over the bar:

GERMANS NOT WELCOME. GET THE HELL BACK TO DUTCHLAND. The bartender pointed to it. Beutle read it, made a face as if while swallowing a cup of vinegar he'd witnessed a flying cow, farted and walked out. He went to the new movie palace down the street to see long-faced William S. Hart and Louise Glaum in a shoot-'em-up, *The Aryan*. The intertitle flashed on the screen while the Irish piano player rattled out a march. "*Oft written in letters of blood, deep carved in the face of destiny, that all men may read, runs the code of the Aryan race: our women shall be guarded.*" He thought of guarding Gerti from harm and snorted.

Misfortunes

Anti-German fever flared. In April 1918 they heard that in Illinois some miners, like fifty cats with a single mouse, played with German immigrant Robert Prager for two days, a young man, naive and confused, who knew little English. They stripped him raw, prodded him up and down the muddy streets forcing him to kiss the American flag again and again, to sing "The Star-Spangled Banner," which he could not do, to sing "We'll Fight for the Red, White and Blue," which he managed, stumbling over the words, letting him go, losing him, capturing him again from the grinning police, grilling and questioning, more flag-kissing and singing, calling for tar and feathers but finding rope and, drunk and inept and deadly, hauling the wretched man up into the air by his neck until at last he strangled. A rain of black moths fluttered from the tree, agitated by the dying man's commotion.

In May, Karl, Messermacher's son who was the telegraph operator, fell panting into the kitchen at broad noon, his clothes torn and his face bloody, his celluloid collar hanging in a jagged arc, left arm hanging useless, wrenched so badly he was never able to raise it above his shoulder again.

"They come right in the telegraph office and pulled me out, said I was a German spy sending messages to the kaiser. Gonna string me up," he gasped. "Like Prager. They had the rope, they was going to do it. I seen Jack Cary in the crowd, my god, he was in school with me! I got away, I don't know how, just fell down and crawled between their legs and got up and run so hard as I could. I come up over the horse path through Uncle Hans's corn."

He would not stay, let his mother arrange a white linen sling for his arm, then hid under a pile of sacks in the back of Loats's cart, nothing to hear but the clap and thump of hooves as the horses trotted and the sound of his heart. At the railroad station in Kringel he telegraphed the front office. They told him to take the next train to Chicago and ride in the baggage car.

Beutle persisted in going into Prank, said nothing about Karl or Prager or the Kaiser or American news reports, but joked at the feed store that maybe he would hire Farmerettes to help him with the corn harvest, earnest young girls in bloomers and smocks to help the farm labor shortage. He had seen a dozen of the pretty things marching around the square in Prank. There was a sullen silence. O'Grain spit on the floor and Beutle spit near O'Grain's foot.

In the evening, while they sat forking up the potatoes, a rock smashed through the window and hit the enamel kettle on the stove.

"Chipped it good," swore Beutle. The rock was wrapped in a page torn from the Reverend Newell Dwight Hillis's lubricious and pornographic tales of German atrocities in Belgium. A sentence was underlined in heavy pencil: "German blood is poisoned blood."

"Don't that look like O'Grain's underlining? Don't it? Jesus Christ, that paddy son-of-a-bitch. You know why an Irish is like a fart? Both is noisy, both you can't put back where they come from, and both stinks."

They set his fields on fire. A hundred acres of smoking wheat. Beutle walked into the blackened field, the fine char flying up with each step, and he was coal black and coughing before he'd gone a hundred feet. He went defiantly into town on Saturday and was stoned by a gang of boys and young men who shouted "heinie!" and "fucken dirty Dutchman!" and "baby raper!" at him.

"I bought Liberty Bonds!" he shouted back at them. "We got a boy Over There. My boy Wid Beutle, born here, right here in Prank." The horse, hit by stones, shied and reared, and set off for home at a gallop. Beutle's hat flew away and he was struck in the mouth by a rock that cracked a good German tooth, which Loats had to extract later in the week with his villainous dental pliers, wrecking a kitchen chair in the doing. Beutle sat spitting blood and sweating, occasionally hissing "*rauch ich in der Pfeife!*" But that evening Gerti relented and let him mount her again, even though the smell of blood from his mouth reminded her of the day she found him in the hen's nest, even though she had embroidered over the motto *God Bless Our Home* with a motto of her own choosing: *God Damn Our Adulterer.* Beutle had never noticed it.

A run of evil events occurred. Messermacher's youngest son was killed when he fell from the top of a haystack, a distance of sixteen feet; a broken neck, but at least he didn't suffer, didn't die an ironic death, as did Wid Beutle, far off in the old country, in Germany, dead in Germany, shot in the groin, his roaring blood freezing in a black pool below his buttocks in the bitter December of 1917. (Sixty years later an anonymous photograph of the dead son's mud-caked boots and stiff, putteed legs appeared on the dust jacket of an Australian history of the Great War.) Loats befriended an itinerant violinist who stayed with them for a week, eating like an ogre, then stole all the ready money in the household and crept away before dawn.

"Must of been a gypsy," said Beutle.

Then Loats collapsed one forenoon because his ill-fitting spring truss pressed on his femoral artery so severely he was dizzy all the time. Without the truss, his groin rupture bulged halfway down his thigh and showed obscenely in his pants. He went, groaning, to Kringle to consult the druggist in his back room and purchased another mechanical device which was painful in a different way and for a while gave the illusion of relief. The new pain he blamed on the druggist, a Greek marblehead.

Night cares

The summer after the war ended, a mysterious event harmed Beutle's twin granddaughters, Florella and Zena, eleven years old. In the afternoon, the mother saw them playing with three of the Messermacher girls under the cherry trees where the hens scratched for insects and kept secret nests. At suppertime Gerti called from the back steps, "*Essen! Kommt!*" For Percy Claude and his family and whatever hired men— there were no more hired girls—ate with Gerti and Beutle. But the children did not come to the table, even when Beutle himself shouted impatiently.

"Let them do without, then. They're over at Messermacher's stuffing their faces." After dinner Percy Claude and his wife went to Messermacher's with the wagon, found Messermacher's family still at table eating bread with molasses, but no twins.

They had played Bachelor's Kitchen in the orchard, said Thomalina, the oldest of the three girls, then they had played Rivers, twisting through the orchard and colliding on the way to the hog pen that was the ocean. At last they played Black Spider, and Florella was a horsefly, Zena a dragonfly and Thomalina a mayfly. Greenie was both mother and nurse because there weren't enough of them to play the game properly, and Ribbons was the black spider. Now Ribbons spoke, the adults scowling at her.

"I caught the horsefly, that's Florella, and I put her in the grass, and then I went back and got Zena and put her in the grass with the horsefly, and I went back and caught Thomalina and got her and took her to the grass, but the flies were gone, they were gone. We thought they changed the game to Hide-and-Seek, and we looked, but after a while we couldn't find them and then we got mad and went home."

"So you didn't see nobody?"

"No."

"You did! I can tell by the way you bite on your finger. Who did you see?"

Greenie started to cry.

"In the lane. Two big bears were running away."

"There isn't no bears here!"

"Or like dogs. With short tails, and they looked at me and went in a hole in the ground!" There was terrific shouting from Messermacher and they all walked to the lane in the twilight and searched for tracks (none), the hole (none), and made the girls reenact the scene. Messermacher whipped his daughters to make them reveal everything they had seen, to force them to recant the story of the bear-dogs, but Gerti shuddered, remembered an evening, ten years ago at least, when she came up the lane in the same thick twilight after searching for a broody hen's nest in the grass and saw sitting on the wheel of the hay rake an immense black man who shot plumes of smoke out of both nostrils before vanishing into the air with a sound like the burst swim bladder of a fish.

The three Germans combed the property into the night, their lanterns bobbing in the dark fields like boats on the swelling sea. There was nothing, no sign. But before dawn Beutle heard a wagon rattling on the road, heard it stop, then rattle away. He went out and there in the sallow morning the two girls limped up the lane, their hair matted with leaves, their dresses torn and stained. They were barefoot, their knickers gone, blood on their thighs, and not a word of what happened could be pried from them. They swore, crying hysterically, that they did not know what had happened. One moment they were playing in the orchard, the next they were shivering on the dark road. Among themselves Beutle and Loats and Messermacher believed the worst, that the Americans had come from town, chloroformed and raped the girls in revenge for Belgium.

It was too much for Pernilla who, six months after marrying Loats, went down with some internal gripping pains that no elixir subdued (Loats was unlucky in wives). She shouted that Beutle, the grandfather, had harmed the children himself, everyone knew in what manner. Then she fell silent. After weeks of not speaking, her mind took a turn. She went outside to the fields with a potato fork and dug wild holes, hurling stalks and earth, moving farther away across the field until she was a tiny dot against the dark soil. No one saw her return and go into the barn where she went straight to Beutle and began to choke him with steely fingers.

"Jesus Christ, the woman's a maniac! And the fools give women the vote."

The doctor at the state hospital wrote down the particulars, had her photographed in her apathetic state. "It is unlikely there will be an improvement," he said carelessly, a little bored with female insanity. Half the women in the state seemed out of their minds.

"I wish *I* could go crazy," said Gerti, visiting Pernilla and looking around at the beige-painted walls. "To be mental, in a nice room like this with all the time in the world and no worries of life, just a warm bed and all your dinner brought to you—why, it sounds good to me. You are getting a rest from it all. They say you see movies here. The only other way to get a rest in this life is to die."

But after a month Pernilla was home again, though convinced that the Americans came out from town at night and poisoned the well. These thoughts followed a parade she had seen in Prank, as she sat and waited for Loats in the worn buckboard, conscious of her dusty bunned-up hair, her dowdy dress and cracked shoes, her aged and crazy face. The parade featured W.C.T.U. women marching around the courthouse, well-dressed American women, many with bobbed hair, in their pale linen dresses and white shoes with straps across the instep, holding placards: DRINK IS THE CURSE OF THE IMMIGRANT and TRUE BLUE AMERICANS FOR PROHIBITION and SPIRITS WILL KILL THE AMERICAN SPIRIT. Loats would hear her get up at night, making her haptic way through the dark rooms, peering through the windows into the night for the telltale lanterns of the Americans. She left notes on the table: *don't drink the Wasser.* In the daytime she said, "I'd like to sleep but sleep don't come" and "what's the use to work so hard on a farm? Mr. Loats buys more land so's he can raise more hogs to buy more land. Pretty soon he owns the whole world." There were times she enjoyed eating paper, a shred or thin page of the bible rolled in a pancake with sour cream, liked it because it made a kind of resistance in the mouth, a pleasant and lasting chewiness under the teeth. Even the bitter taste of the ink she liked. One evening as she stood at the stove cooking potato cakes she became very stiff and still, the spatula clenched in her unmoving hand. The smell of scorch rose from the griddle. Loats pulled his face out of his farm paper.

"What are you doing, burning them up?" For a moment longer the woman did not move, and then she slapped her own face with the greasy

spatula, seized the boiling kettle and poured it over the hot metal of the
stove. A hissing cloud of steam enveloped her, she was tearing at the stove
lid with one hand and pouring boiling water with the other. Clarissa's
daughter Jen shrieked, "Pernilla, you fool stepmother!" and Loats cursed
and sprang at her, wrenching the kettle from her seared hand.

Gerti came over in the evening carrying a lemon extract cake. "I
wouldn't go crazy if I was you," she whispered to the sweating woman,
"not even for the nice room. I wouldn't give them the satisfaction.
What's the point?"

Pernilla was all right the next day, her burned hands wrapped in
greasy bandage.

After the Wall Street explosion in 1920 and the high feeling against
immigrants, the three Germans and their families drew into themselves,
never went into Prank, taking the long road instead to Kringel where
Germans outnumbered Irish. On a Sunday Beutle sometimes got out
the two-row Hohner and played a line or two of some song or another,
but the music of the three Germans was finished.

Karl makes good

Prank touched the borders of their farms. There was a feeling, in the dry
years after the war, as after a summer storm that fails to cool or refresh
the air, of continuing sullen humidity and irritating heat, of another,
more powerful storm building below the horizon. The old world was
dead and gone, replaced by a feverish anxiety for something, anything,
new. New roads were going in everywhere, and an army expedition
came through, driving coast to coast to show the country how bad the
roads were, how something had to be done. John O'Cleary converted
the old schoolhouse at the crossroads into a gasoline station, selling Fisk
tires and Mobiloil and Standard Oil gasoline, "guaranteed to test the
best—no kerosene oil or other injurious substance."

Karl Messermacher came down from Chicago, wearing plus fours
and driving an automobile. He brought magazines and papers: *True
Confessions, Reader's Digest,* the funny papers, with Tillie the Toiler and
the Katzenjammer Kids, which Beutle stuffed into the stove as a mockery of Germans. Karl laughed about the way they'd pulled him out of
the telegraph office five years earlier.

"By god, the company give me an office and a promotion and a telephone because of that. I'd probably still be down in Prank banging the
key—or hanged—if not for Jack Cary. I hear *he* got a lungful of mustard gas and is down at his mother's place coughing his guts out. I'll

stop by and thank the son-of-a-bitch before I go back." Karl's voice was mocking. He showed off his argyle sweater, talked about the color movie he'd seen, *The Toll of the Sea,* passed around a packet of the new invention, potato chips, invited his female cousins out behind the barn to smoke Murad cigarettes, showing them crazy dance steps, cavorting and twisting until he slipped on duck turd and stained the knee of his white flannel trousers.

Before he slipped, his cousin Lulu said, "Karl, you look like an American college man."

"Call me Charlie," he said. "I changed my name—Charlie Sharp. That's me. Listen," he said. "I'm no German. I was born right here in Ioway. Listen," he said, "there was seven copycats sitting on a fence. One jumped off. How many was left?"

"Six?" said Lulu.

"Girlie," said Karl, shaking his head and laughing, "you are a hick from the sticks, girlie. Come on, I'll take you girlies to the show."

They walked into the Palace after the movie had started, on the screen an automobile factory and in front of it an enormous black kettle. Into one side of the kettle danced clots of immigrants in old-country costumes, singing in foreign tongues and kicking their legs, and out the other side marched a row of Americans in suits, whistling "The Star-Spangled Banner."

"This movie stinks," whispered Charlie Sharp. "Come on, we'll get some hot dogs and something that will curl your hair."

Beutle said he'd gone far beyond dropping the hyphen and Karl countered by laughing, saying that accordion music was old-country junk.

Messermacher was enraged by the cigarettes. "If God wanted humans to smoke them things he would of put a chimney in the top of your head. A man smokes a pipe or a cigar." He pronounced the potato chips not fit to feed hogs.

The three old Germans and their wives stayed close to home, but the children and grandchildren went into Prank. The malevolent, sniffing nose of public hatred was scenting new dangers—Reds, Jews, Catholics, other foreigners, not just Germans. When a klezmer band arrived in town in a rackety De Soto, the sheriff told them to keep traveling, no Jew agitators wanted in Prank and he didn't care what kind of music they played on their dirty accordions, Prank had had enough of accordions, get out, and the same for any goddamn gypsies with their swift and pilfering fingers, the only kind of music Prank wanted to hear was "The Old Rugged Cross" and "My Country 'Tis of Thee," although his daughter sang "I'm in Love Again" and accompanied herself on the ukulele.

No one yelled "beer, brats and bellies" when Percy Claude and his second, obviously pregnant wife, Greenie, the seventeen-year-old daughter of Messermacher, came into the drugstore. Two of Messermacher's other girls married Americans from Minneapolis, both streetcar conductors, and moved to the city. Another daughter, Ribbons, got work as a hired girl for the limestone mine manager's wife and quit after a year to marry the new express agent, became Mrs. Flanahan, bridging the Irish ditch. Loats's sons Felix and Edgar bought a Ford model T truck and started a feed store business. Felix (children believed he had been named for the cartoon cat) was crazy for driving after years of walking along the side of the hot roads and getting the dust blown in his face by American youths speeding past. He wouldn't be passed, would veer and block any other driver who tried it. Both married American girls and no German was spoken in their houses.

(Twenty years later, in 1944, hunting in a field that had once been part of his father's farm, Felix saw a balloon drifting across the Little Runt and ran toward it. There was something suspended from the ropes. He reached up as it glided smoothly down and grasped the Japanese bomb. After the funeral—a complete right hand, a mangled leg and an ear—government men came to the family and swore them to silence to prevent panic and public fear.)

Beutle argued with Percy Claude and refused to get a tractor, still held out against the radio. Messermacher, who had the most money, ordered indoor plumbing from Kringel and burned his outhouse in a pillar of smoking stench, then surprised all of them in the autumn of 1924 by selling the farm and moving to Coma, Texas, to grow cotton. In Coma, one side of the town was German and the other populated with Czechs from Bohemia. Messermacher changed the family name to Sharp, following Karl's example, for Charlie Sharp found life easier than had Karl Messermacher.

Packing up for the move to Texas, one of the daughters came upon the green accordion.

"What to do with this? It's that old accordion *Vati* got from Uncle Beutle. It still plays OK." She squeezed out chords, played the first line of "Yes, Sir, That's My Baby."

"Oh, put it in the brown trunk. If Willy gives up the ukulele, maybe—or maybe one of the grandkids will take it up." The mother dropped it into the bottom of the trunk and on top of it came a sewing basket, the coffee grinder, a worn buffalo robe, a set of wool carders.

Beutle cursed Messermacher for a traitor, leaving the good land they had found together and made into fine farms.

Dr. Squam's goat gland treatment

In the spring of 1929 Loats was the first to die, a complication of his rupture, and was buried in his bald-cypress box. The farm was subdivided among his five surviving children and his grandchildren who sold it off in lots and parcels. Small houses and garages dotted the great fields. A month later word came from Texas that Messermacher had dropped dead at his mailbox, the new Sears catalog open on his breast at the pages showing a selection of women's hair nets. To Beutle, his old friend and neighbor, he left Radio stock valued at two thousand dollars and going up like a rocket.

Charlie Sharp had gotten the old man into the market. Beutle, excited by his windfall and the idea of a quick fortune through the big bull market, got through to Charlie on the feed store telephone and asked his advice. Should he put money into more stocks? Which ones?

"Radio Corporation of America. What *Vati* had. Radio's going to the top. General Motors, Montgomery Ward, the market's the thing, a sure thing. Uncle Hans, everybody in America can be rich. It was a little stormy last winter, the market, but she's steady and climbing again. The country is rock solid." His voice lowered deeply. "I'm telling you something. I'm worth a quarter of a million now, Uncle Hans. I started out buying a little Studebaker stock, but now I'm really doing good. Not bad, anyway, for an Ioway farm boy, hey?" He gave Beutle a quick spiel about buying on margin and offered to act as Hans's broker.

Beutle, dazzled by the proof, after thirty-odd years of experience to the contrary, that in America prosperity was for the taking after all, put a mortgage on the farm and, through Charlie, bought a hundred shares of Radio at 120½. "If you'd bought last week, Uncle Hans, you'd of got it at ninety-four! It's going up fast. There's no limit. The sky is the limit."

Under the thrall of Radio stock and his swelling fortune, Beutle gave in and bought an expensive Freed-Eiseman Neutrodyne five-tube receiver with a Prest-O-Lite ninety-amp battery, two forty-five-volt batteries, an earphone plug, an antenna set, vacuum tubes and a round loudspeaker that leaned against the wall like an abandoned discus and blasted out *The A & P Gypsy Hour*. Percy Claude said, "if you got electric out here, you could skip all them batteries and get a plug-in. You could of got a Crossley Pup for ten dollars, what you spend for all this, fifty? Sixty?"

With his fortune sure, Beutle began to worry about fate. "All three the same age, all three the same life, now Loats and Messermacher die, they are gone, like that, one, two, and I am three, I am next. I will go soon. The same age, all sixty-four, and they're in *dem Grab*." For the first time since boyhood he felt a slackening of desire. Gerti leaned into the potato barrel presenting her rump and singing "The Best Things in Life Are Free," and he thought of his tombstone.

But he was still sitting down to dinner, still lighting his pipe, still waking up in the morning, so he knew he had truly outlived them, the other two Germans, and the only thing he had done differently in life, the activity that had clearly preserved his vigor and strength, was good honest lust. It would keep him alive and interested until the age of one hundred.

"Jesus Christ, I told them!"

Yet his fires were cooling, and this was real and dangerous. He forced himself to grapple with Gerti once a day, but the effort left him wringing wet and depressed. He spoke sharply, commanded his sons as though they were still children—he knew they were waiting for him to join Loats and Messermacher, especially was Percy Claude watching his father with wolf's eyes. An answer came to Beutle out of the radio.

He was devoted to KFKB, Kansas First, Kansas Best, out of Topeka, when he could get it, listened to *Concertina Roundup, The Happy Hillbillies, Cowboy Carl and His Little Guitar,* a few times picked up the *WLS Barn Dance* out in Chicago, but usually got only the Cedar Rapids station with *Coon Sanders' Nighthawks.* He didn't much care for the hot jazz fox trots, said "Muskrat Ramble" was more like Mess Pants Scramble. Sometimes he'd get out the Hohner—the little green accordion would have been better, maybe—and play along with the musicians on *Concertina Roundup* though they were usually a bunch of wacky Swedes making sounds like corks pulled out of bottles, like pissing cows. (Only once did he hear a virtuoso playing Bach's Prelude no. 1 in C on a superb Wheatstone concertina, but so many listeners complained that the experiment was never repeated.) He listened to Dr. Squam's crackling, nasal voice.

"*Friends, this here's Dr. Squam, talking plain talk to you again. Now I want to say a few words to the men out there, so if there's ladies listening, you might just as well go upstairs and get at that mending you put off, for this is men's business. But before you go, take a double spoonful of my number fifty-five tonic treatment and number fifty-nine, for there may be a big change in your life coming soon.*

"*Now, men, when a man reaches a certain age, and you know what I mean, you men who are suffering, he begins to lose interest, his spirit droops, certain glands begin to wither and all the spring goes out of his step. If this sounds like someone you know, pay close attention. Until now there was no hope for such a man, even if he was in good health and otherwise strong and able. But now there is a chance. Dr. Squam has developed a four-phase compound operation that rejuvenates depleted sex organs by directing a new blood supply to the affected area—giving a real kick to the old starter. Listen to what this Texas oilman has to say."*

A slow drawl came out of the rayon speaker fabric, then the announcer's voice, in subdued excitement:

"If you want to know more about how this miraculous procedure can once more give YOU the energy and drive of a boy of eighteen, write to Dr. Squam at this address . . ."

Beutle knew he'd sell some of the stock Messermacher had left him, he'd have the operation on Messermacher's nickel. "Turn over in his grave laughing if he knew. And the hell with writing Squam. Claude! Percy Claude, come on in here, I want you to take me to the station."

He caught the afternoon train to Topeka. Two days later, in mid-August, he lay on a table in an operating room while Dr. Squam made an incision in his scrotum and skillfully implanted sections of goat gland in his testicles. During the procedure a radio played a selection of waltzes and polkas broadcast from the doctor's radio station behind the hospital. When he heard that Beutle played the accordion, Dr. Squam reduced the charge for the operation to a flat seven hundred dollars.

The devil's hot day

The train back to Prank was intensely hot, plowing through a prairie scorcher, a stifling blanket of heat, the hazed air as thick as glue, the corn shriveling before his eyes and a pall of dust coating the margins of every road. The scratchy plush seat in the coach heated up. His swollen testicles began to throb and inside an hour the pressure of the straining cloth of his trousers on his privates was unbearable. He tried to walk up and down the aisle, but spraddled so obscenely the eyes of every passenger fastened on him. By the time the train reached Prank he had collapsed, nearly insensible, his ears ringing. When he looked through his fevered eyes the sky was upside down, birds skittering across it like insects on a glass floor. The conductor dragged him off at Prank and turned him over to Percy Claude who waited, dumb and stolid, in the shade of the station overhang, red arms dangling.

"There's something wrong with the old boy, Percy Claude. Walks like he's got a corncob up his ass. I was you, I'd get the doctor to him."

Dr. Diltard Cude, a spindle-shanked man who held a nice packet of American Telephone and Telegraph stock, came out to the house, took a look at the testicular stitchery, the angry streaks shooting up from the old man's groin and down into his black thigh, said infection, gangrene, nothing to do but take him home, make him as comfortable as possible in this goldarned heat, set a block of ice in a tray and set a fan so's it blows over the ice onto him, then nothing to do but wait for the end. Percy Claude didn't bother to say they couldn't run a fan without the electric.

For thirty hours Beutle lay on the sofa, unable to open his eyes. He felt someone come into the room. There was a great tingling all over his body, a burning and buzzing. He tried to move but could not. He wanted to cry out "*der Teufel!*" but his throat stifled his voice. Yet he was not afraid, but intensely interested, for he heard the wheezing notes of "*Deutschland, Deutschland*" and thought that at least there was German accordion music where he was going.

His name was misspelled on his tombstone as Hans Buttel. That's how everyone spelled it and Percy Claude let it stay that way.

Charlie Sharp's misfire

On the third of September, Radio, split and split again, went for an adjusted price of 505; Beutle's remaining hundred shares were worth more than fifty thousand dollars. Percy Claude straightened up, walked around outside for an hour, then came in and sat down next to Greenie and told her how it was.

"You know *Vater* Hans left some stock. He'd got in on some stock through Charlie, Charlie Sharp. It's quite a bit."

"How much is it?" She lit one of the cigarettes she'd started smoking and blew a plume of smoke from her powdered nostrils.

"Oh, quite a bit." He didn't like to see a woman smoke but said nothing. She'd had her hair bobbed—butchered, he thought—big wads of straight hair chopped off at the earlobes. And she must be doing something to her chest; she was flatter somehow.

"Enough so's we could leave this damn farm and move to Des Moines? There's no reason to stay out here. I thought about living in Des Moines so bad."

"Now, don't sound like some crazy Flaming Mame. You're not think-ing about *Mutti.*"

"Oh, she'll be happy in town—there's other old ladies around, there's stuff to do, go to the movies, learn to play mah-jongg. She can get a nice

Colorinse, primp up a little. Oh god, tell me, Percy Claude, tell me we can move to Des Moines. I'm sick of washing clothes in that damn old boiler and cleaning out them stinking kerosene lamps. We're the only ones in Prank don't have electricity."

"I don't say yes and I don't say no. There's plenty got to be done." But he called up Charlie on the feed store phone and told him he wanted to sell the stock.

"Jesus, Percy Claude! *Not now! Not now!* She's climbing! That stock splits again, you'll double your money. If I was you I wouldn't sell at all, I'd buy more stock, diversify a little. I had my eye on this here Rotary Oil."

"No, I guess I want to sell it. Thinking of putting the farm on the market, too, and moving to Des Moines."

"Listen, if you're going to move, move to Chicago. You can't believe this here city. It's a pretty important city; pretty big men here who pretty damn near run the country right from this here heartland. It's not the millionaires back east who make the world go around. Hey, can you get *Roxy's Gang* down there on the radio? Al Jolson was on the other night. I'm telling you, he's a hot number."

"No. We don't get it. I guess I'll sell."

"Percy Claude, it's your funeral. Just remember what I told you when it goes through the roof."

"I made up my mind."

"Check and double check, Percy Claude."

By the end of the month the market was crashing and sliding, but Percy Claude smiled to himself. He went out to the mailbox every day to see if the check from Charlie was there. Finally he called Charlie up on the feed store phone to ask if he'd sent the check registered mail, but there wasn't any answer on the other end, just the burring ring again and again until the operator came on the line and told him to hang up. They heard the news the hard way, the second week in October, from Loats's daughter who had had a letter from the Sharps down in Texas. Charlie Sharp up in Chicago had lost everything in the crash, including Percy Claude's inherited and unsold Radio stock, and had shot himself in the face. He wasn't dead but his nose and mouth and teeth and lower jaw were blown away, just two crazy little blue eyes staring out of the raw, scabbing flesh. He was a horror to see and they had him down in Texas in a dim back room. Couldn't speak and had to be fed with a funnel.

"You know what, Percy Claude," said Rona Sharp on the phone after she told him that was correct, it was a sad thing, tragic, but there was maybe a bright side because Charlie had found Jesus, and wasn't this a clear connection? "They give you a big box of free tomatoes down here when you fill up your car with gasoline. You ought to move down here."

In a private deal Percy Claude sold the farm to a couple from Ohio, but their bank failed before he could cash the check. They had the deed and he had a no-good check. He had less than Beutle had started with forty years earlier.

"I'm going down to Texas and kill Charlie Sharp," he said to Greenie. But instead they went to Des Moines, where, after three weeks of looking, Greenie got a job working in the five-and-ten and he was assigned to a CCC work gang building roads.

(But wasn't it their son Rawley, born a few years later in the back of a car at a drive-in, who pieced together his grandfather's farm and more, ended up with three thousand acres in production, owned a golf course, a farm machinery dealership, a tile and culvert business and an interest in a cheese factory while receiving twenty thousand dollars a year in government farm subsidies? Wasn't it Rawley who gave money to start the Prank Farm Pioneer Museum and who moved heaven and earth, hired private investigators, to find the old green accordion his grandfather played? Weren't they still searching in 1985 when Rawley and his wife, Evelyn, celebrated their twenty-fifth wedding anniversary with an autumn trip to Yellowstone Park where Rawley, in the West Thumb Geyser Basin, dropped a roll of film, trod on it, lost his balance and fell headlong into a seething hot spring, and despite eyes parboiled blind and the knowledge of impending death, clambered out—leaving the skin of his hands like red gloves on the stony edge—only to fall into another, hotter pool? You bet.)

Spider, Bite Me

A LITTLE ONE-ROW BUTTON ACCORDION

Don't like your look

That great accordion player who was also a busboy, Abelardo Relámpago Salazar, rolled over in bed one May morning in 1946 shortly after
sunrise in Hornet, Texas, and sensed that he was dying, perhaps even
dead. (A few years later when he was truly dying and in this same bed,
he felt violently alive.) The sensation was not unpleasant, though mixed
with regret. Through his eyelashes he saw bedposts of solid gold, a
diaphanous wing quivering at the window. Celestial music washed over
him, a voice of a melting quality he had never heard while he was alive.

Listening, he returned to life and recognized the sun as the source of
the gilded bedposts, knew the seraphic wing was a wavering curtain. The
music was coming from his accordion, not the four-stop, three-row button Majestic in white pearl with his initials, *AR,* set out in tiny cut-glass
gems, but the special one, the little nineteen-button green accordion with
its rare voice. Not to be touched by anyone but him! Still, he listened,
despite the disagreeable sensation of a swollen bladder, the stoking oven
of the coming day. It was the voice of his overgrown, lanky daughter, a
voice that he never heard, except thick humming as she drizzled and
drabbed around the house. He had not even known she could play the
accordion beyond a few strung-together chords, although she had been
his child for fourteen years, although he had seen her a hundred times
fooling with her brothers' small Lido model. When was he ever home
long enough to know his children? It was the sons who were the musicians. His anger burned because perhaps it was the daughter who was
exceptional. That wonderful voice coming from the high part of the nose,
plaintive and quavering, all the ache of life in it. And he thought of his
oldest son, Crescencio, poor dead Chencho, without wit or musical
sense, like a timid dog that was afraid to come forward. What a total
waste! It must have been the devil, not God, who sent that music into his
dream. The same devil who deceived men over the age of the earth by
concealing fossils in perverse places. He was furious as well because she
was mauling the treasure of his life.

He shouted from the bed, "Félida. Come in here!" Put the pillow over the top of his head so she might not see his hair undone. Heard the scrabbling and the huff of the accordion. She came into the room with her head turned away. Her hands empty.

"Where is the green accordion now?"

"In the case. In the front room."

"Never touch it again. Never open that case. Do you hear me?"

"Yes." She turned her sullen face away, slouched to the kitchen.

"I don't like your look!" he shouted.

He considered his daughter's music. How well she sang! He had heard her but he had not heard her. Well, and how had she learned the accordion? No doubt from watching, from listening to him, from admiration of her father. It might be a novelty to let her come with him to one of his engagements, introduce his daughter, let them see how the whole Relámpago family—except Chencho, of course—had been richly gifted by God. But even as he imagined the handsome picture it would make, himself in his dark pants and jacket, the white shirt and white shoes, and Félida in the beautiful lace-edged pink dress Adina was sewing for the girl's *quinceañera*—*ay,* how much that would cost!—and how he would let Félida step forward and release her astonishingly beautiful voice, move over Lydia Mendoza, here comes another *gloria de Tejas,* the future was crouching at a dark side road on the path of events.

A bus went by and filled the room with a roar like a bomb blast echoing in a sewer. He got up, lit a cigarette, felt a pain in his right thigh, held his hair up with his right hand, squinting. How could he run back and forth all day at work and then stand half the night playing music? And the usual business with his *agringada* wife. It seemed to him that few people had to bear what he did. Or could bear it as bravely.

But he was up now, and, as always, the music started in his mind, a kind of bitter, lopsided polka that resembled "*La Bella Italiana*" the way Bruno Villareal played it. All his life he had enjoyed this private music, sometimes sad little phrases that belonged to no known *ranchera* or waltz, sometimes note-for-note repetitions of *huapangos* or polkas he himself played or had heard another play. Sometimes fresh inventions, new music never heard before, an inner musician working all night as he slept.

His little dressing table behind the door held the apparatus for the elaborate arrangement of the long hanks of hair to disguise the bald top. The back and sides were very long, and now, in the mirror of the early morning, he looked like an ancient prophet with the mange. He swept up the long locks with a wooden comb, placing each strand artfully, secured them with bobby pins. Working on his hair quieted his nerves and he sang, "*Can this be you, my little moon, who walks past my door . . .*" He achieved a hirsute look but a stranger glancing at the upsweep some-times—for a moment—took him for a woman. And strangers did see him, for he worked in a restaurant, the Blue Dove—never a waiter, always the one who carried the dishes. The Blue Dove was in Boogie, the town to the south where they once had lived in the ancient house of the Relámpagos. In his own kitchen he heard the clink of the pan as Félida heated the milk for his *café con leche,* from the radio the last chorus of "Route 66," Bobby Troup, and the newscaster saying something about the coal mine strike and federal troops, something about Communists, the same old song, and he was glad when Félida shut it off. He had to hurry now.

He was short, with a full-jawed, fleshy face. Small eyes sunk deep in the sockets, sooty eyebrows arched (he smoothed them with a little spit on his finger), and above them like a panel, the broad forehead the color of fruitwood. The shortness of his neck destroyed any hope of elegance. His arms were muscular and thick, the better, he said, to clasp his accor-dion close; his hands ended in powerful but tapering fingers that moved swiftly. His trunk was not slender, the legs short and heavy, thickly furred, as was his broad chest. *Weight* came to Adina's mind at the sight of his naked thighs.

A restless man, emphatic, his face changing with every sentence, ideas and thoughts bursting from him. Because he had no past he invented one. He made the most common events into stories, minor incidents swelling with drama as his voice pumped them up. *Dios,* said the waiters and his embarrassed children, he talks too much, they must have vaccinated him with a Victrola needle when he was a baby.

Yet he had never been able to describe certain moments in his life: the feeling when two voices paired like a set of birds twisting in close flight and the listener shuddered with pleasure. Or when music jetted from the instruments as blood from an arterial wound, blood in which the dancers stamped while grasping partners' slippery hands, shouting from raw throats.

His own voice pitched excitedly from highs to lows with strong pauses for effects, sound effects. He sang when he wasn't talking, mak-ing up music and words on the spot: "*My beautiful Adina sleeping, black hair on the white pillow, the moon's silver cords binding you to my bed.*" Although his feet were not small, he liked smart shoes and bought them whenever he could, but always the cheap ones that hardly lasted a month before the leather cracked and the heels fell off. When he drank he felt hopeless, he was cast with his music into caves of bat guano and bones gnawed by wild animals.

Abandoned at birth,
Alone in this world without mother or father,
I labored to live.
I wished for beauty
but found only ugliness and scorn—

His job was a stupid job and for that reason he liked it, took a morbid pleasure in unobtrusively sliding the white plates smeared with sauces and cheese off the tablecloth and into the Bakelite tub, bearing away bowls of stained lettuce leaves floating in juices, cigarette butts crushed into fat.

At night he entered his other world and, accordion against his breast and his powerful voice controlling the movements and thoughts of two hundred people, he was invincible; at the restaurant he was subservient, not only to the demands of the occupation but to some cringing inner self. His day began at seven in the morning with empty coffee cups and the crumbs of sweet cakes and ended at six after the first wave of dinner plates. He knew all the day waiters; there were seven. All but one of them respected his dual nature, perhaps cursing him in the passageway to the kitchen where he shoved the tubs of dirty dishes through a window to the sinks, mocking his slowness, clumsiness, stupidity; but in the evenings and on the weekends the same men screamed with joy as they stood in the cascade of his music, touched his sleeve and spoke his name as if he were a saint. They would kiss his feet if they knew what made his music so vigorous, if they knew the green accordion's secret— or perhaps would shove him into the great hot oven in envy.

The Relámpagos

Before the war, before they moved to Hornet in 1936, the family had lived in a certain adobe house near the river. There were a dozen straggling houses, poor and isolated. The train tracks curved in from the west and disappeared. The sons spent their first years playing with tires, dirt, sticks, crushed cans, bottles. Relámpagos had been in this place centuries before there was Texas. They had been American citizens since 1848 and still the Anglo Texans said "Mexicans."

"Blood is thicker than river water," said Abelardo.

In the generation before, Abelardo's mother—not really his mother for he had been an abandoned child, a naked baby wrapped in a soiled shirt and left on the church floor in 1906—was a wordless bent woman of children and tortillas and soil, weeding her chickpeas and squash, tomatillos, chiles, beans and corn.

The old man—not really his father—was a field-worker, always far away, in the Rio Grande valley, in Colorado, Indiana, California, Oregon, and in the Texas cotton. An invisible man (as Abelardo himself became invisible to his children), working, working, away in the north, sending small amounts of money home, sometimes returning for a few months, a crooked-backed man with great scarred hands and a drawn, toothless mouth. That poor man a machine for working, the bruised hands crooked for seizing and pulling, for lifting boxes and baskets, for grasping. The arms hung uncomfortably when work stopped. He was made for work, eyes squinted shut, the face empty of the luxury of reflection, mouth a hole, stubbled cheeks, a filthy baseball cap, wearing a cast-off shirt until it rotted away. If he had beauty in his life, no one knew it.

One day this secondhand father disappeared. The woman heard a long time later that he had drowned in a town to the north, swept away with others in a wall of water that filled streets nine feet deep with yellow liquid, a flood that would have frightened Noah, the cataclysmic result of the most ferocious cascade of rain ever known to fall—thirty-six inches in a single thunderous night.

Abelardo's early life was bound by the music he made with sticks, dried chickpeas in a can, a bit of sheet metal and his own reedy voice; and by the small river that flowed, when it held water, away to the Rio Grande, deep and full with distant runoff, or nothing more than a silty film on the gravel, bordered by cottonwoods and willows thick with spring-loaded birds, huge flights of white-winged doves jamming and fanning the air in September and the guns going off all around, *POUM, poum;* and in the spring, going north, going to the shuddering north, the upwelling broad-winged hawks. He dimly remembered standing beside someone, a man, not his father, in the tangled fragrance of guajillo, black mimosa, huisache, in the cedar elms and the ebonies, watching a dark blue snake twine among the tiny leaves. He had almost seen the dappled ocelot the man was pointing at, as though a piece of earth cast with spots of light had pulled itself up and flowed into the thicket. In the damp soil of the riverbank he once found the imprint of an entire bird but for the head, the wings pressed down and out, the individual feathers of the flattened tail distinct, an impression as clear as the cast of an archaeopteryx in ancient mud. Some larger bird had stood on this bird's back, gripping the head with secateur beak, and at last had carried it away.

He was not a Relámpago by birth or heritage or blood but by informal adoption, yet he became heir to all the Relámpagos had owned, for the eleven other children died early or disappeared. Water was their fate. He saw Elena drown. They were getting water from the river, three or four of the true Relámpagos striving and pushing on the crumbling bank, then a splash and a cry. He saw her flailing hands, her streaming head rise above the muddy current for a moment and then truly disappear. He ran home behind the others, the water sloshing out of the can against his bare leg, the wire bail cutting into his hand.

Victor was the last of the true Relámpagos, and he died at age nineteen in an irrigation ditch, the water rosy with his blood. And the brutal joke was repeated: yes, it is well known that all Texas Rangers have Mexican blood. On their boots.

The inheritance was more or less nothing, a crumbling adobe house of three rooms and a patch of yard the size of a blanket. Yet they lived in it until somehow it was proved the property of a big cotton grower, an American who felt compassion for Abelardo and gave him fifty dollars to erase any notions that he might own the fingernail of land.

Pairs of bulldozers arrived, dragging chains between them, plunging into the branchy maze, macerating the tiny leaves and the white wood of cracked limbs, scraping the thicket into mounds for the burning, life burned, sending up smoke for days. Afterward long, flat fields of cotton, the only relieving color the hooped backs of laborers and the overseer's yellow truck, the air saturated with the smell of chemical fertilizers and insecticides. Yet for the rest of his life he woke in the morning expecting the smell of the river, and from beyond it the imagined perfume of that beautiful and tragic country where perhaps he had been born.

The Crash Creek dance

He met Adina Rojas in 1924 at a dance. He was eighteen, ragged, his single possession the little green accordion he had bought a month earlier in a Texas cotton town after staring at it for weeks through a barbershop window seeing how the color of the bellows was fading in the strong sun and the broken thumb strap curled. It needed many repairs. He bought it for five dollars without hearing a note from it. Something about the instrument appealed to him through the fly-spotted glass and even then he was impetuous. A button stuck, the corner blocks under the bass grille had fallen off, the wax was cracked so that the reed plates rattled, the leather check valves were dry and curled, the gaskets had shrunk. He took the instrument apart carefully, learned to repair it by observation and by asking others. So he discovered the correct mixture of beeswax and rosin, where to purchase fine kidskin for new valves, and worked on it until it was sound and he could join his voice to its distinctive, bitter music.

Adina was five years older than he and dark, strong and willful, still

unmarried. In later life he had only to draw out the first chord of "*Mi
Querida Reynosa*" to evoke again the evening of that dance, although it
was not at Reynosa but in Crash Creek. Adina's face was powdered
white, the white dots of her navy rayon dress shifting giddily as she
moved with him, and he for once not playing; he had put his accordion
in Beltrán Dinger's hands, for Beltrán played well, and he came straight
to Adina and danced a polka in the new style, with his weight back on
his heels, stiff-legged, each step as if it were necessary to free the foot
from the floor, strong and manly movement—none of that Czech hopping, that exhausting *de brinquito* jump step—and the room of dancers
circling counterclockwise, circling the rough floor, the smell of perfume
and hair oil, Adina's wet hands glued to his. After that one dance he
returned to the musicians but watched the polka-dot dress jealously. He
sang the wrenching "*Destino, Destino*" directly to her, his fingers flying
over the buttons, carrying the dancers through the intricate music,
making them shout "*ye-ye-ye-JAI!*" Even two drunks fighting outside
the door came in to listen.

Adina remembered the dance well enough but regarded it as the
beginning of her troubles. Later she preferred to tell her daughter
lugubrious stories of how she had made her own soap and washed
clothes in an outdoor kettle when they lived in the house of the Relámpagos. Because they could not afford a clothesline, she hung the clothes
on the barbwire fence, old barbwire, oxidized deep red, a tangle of
mends and wrappings and metal thorns, so their garments were marked
with bars of rust though Abelardo always had enough money for cigarette papers and tobacco.

"In the Depression it was a dangerous time," she told her daughter.
"The Americans deported thousands of people to Mexico, not only *los
mojados* but many born here, American citizens, yet they were arrested
and forced to go, no matter how they protested, no matter what docu-
ments they waved. So we held our breaths. We could listen in that time
to Pedro González, very early in the morning, what wonderful music, *Los
Madrugadores,* from Los Angeles. I was half in love with him—what a
wonderful voice that man had. And he fought injustice. He would speak
out through a *corrido* of his own composition when Mexican Americans
were treated in an evil manner by the *americanos.* And they arrested him
one day on some false excuse that he had raped a woman singer. He sat
in the courtroom smoking a cigar and smiling and that was his downfall,
that smile, which they saw as insolent. They sent him to prison, to San
Quentin, for many years and never was his voice heard again."

"Not true," said Abelardo from the other room. "They deported him when the war started. He broadcasts to this day from Mexico. He lives in Tijuana. If you were not so passionately addicted to American soap operas you could hear him any day you wished."

She paid no attention. "And during the war we heard *La Hora de Victoria* and *La Hora del Soldado,* two very patriotic programs."

"I played on both many times. 'Anchors Aweigh,' everything like that. Doing the taco circuit. And there was that crazy German used to hang around the studios; he was everywhere we went, trying to get on the air to sing 'God Bless America' in German."

"Yes," she said. "I remember you wanted to be a fingerprint man then, not an accordion player. You cut a coupon in a magazine and sent away for a kit, you studied strange facts, the number of hairs on a brunette woman's head, you'd say some big figure."

"Correct. One hundred and ten thousand. Blond ones got one hundred fifty thousand hairs. That's counting the whole body, even on the arms and face. That old German! '*Herr scheutz Amerika! Land* something-something.' How's that for a memory?"

During those years in the Relámpago house she had cooked on an outdoor fire, stumbling over hundreds of broken clay pigeons, she told Félida in a ferocious voice. Nearby lived a crazy Anglo with six fingers on each hand who practiced shooting his .22 pistol every day, his targets old roller-skating trophies—suggestively formed couples whose nakedness showed through their chrome garments. The heads and arms were the first parts shot away. Every day she had the fear of being wounded or her children killed by this crazy man's bullets. It was she, she said, who had smoothed the mud each year when they replastered the adobe house, the side of her bare, callused hand sweeping the roughness to a fine matte finish, and on one memorable occasion a bullet had struck the wall a fraction of an inch from the tip of her longest finger.

"We were very scared. But what could we do? Somehow we lived, but it was a miracle none of us was killed. Or wounded. When the war started he went and we never saw him again. And for a year I saved up pennies and nickels to buy a nice aluminum teakettle with a whistle, for four dollars and something, but at the store they told me there was no more aluminum left to make kettles, all went to airplanes. All we had was a radio, and how we listened to it!"

"*You* listened to it," Abelardo said. "I would not listen to that junk, those fortune-tellers, Abra and Dad Rango, and that Texas tap dancer you thought was so good, somebody went to the station one time, they wanted to see how he could do those things, those fancy steps, and all it was was a drummer tapping on the rim of his drum with the sticks."

She whispered to her daughter that she did not much care for Abelardo's music, preferred the more elegant sounds of the *orquesta* if she had a choice. Always she presented herself as struggling along a churned road carrying an enormous sack of problems like steel boxes that cut into her back while Abelardo capered ahead playing his accordion.

The finest thing about her was the thick, glossy hair, luxuriant and rich, and her mouth, very full and beautifully cut. She kept from her face every expression except fatigue and bitterness. When she was miserable she had a habit of grasping her hair in both hands and pulling, the raven waves shifting, releasing her warm woman's scent. She was humorless; to her, life was difficult and demanding. The great dark eyes were often remote. She was tall, taller than Abelardo, her ankles and feet slender. All of the children had small feet except poor Crescencio who might have been born from a knot of bloody feathers instead of her flesh. After the birth of Félida her body expanded, great sheets of fat thickened her thighs and belly. The bed sagged on her side, and Abelardo rolled helplessly into the trough. Both his arms could not encircle her enormous waist. She wore dresses without sleeves, loose rayon tents manufactured of orange, electric blue or pink cloth sewn with such weak thread the seams opened in the first washing.

And what of the old house of the Relámpagos? She had hated that house and all it stood for, longed to leave it for San Antonio and the famous opportunities. In later years Félida asked many times, 'tell about the *casa* of the Relámpagos,' for Adina made it like a story of a dangerous place from which they had barely escaped.

There had been, she said in her serrated voice, a living room with brown walls, and the floor covered with an old manure-colored rug. There was the outhouse, which smelled very bad. Of course, a shrine in the corner with statues and pictures of lesser saints—Santa Escolástica who protects children from convulsions, San Peregrino who looks after those with cancer. On a table with turned legs the color of dried blood, a lace cloth worked by some dead Relámpago whose delirious fancies took the form of triangles, a photograph of an unknown wearing dark pants and vest, and an improbable pair of cowboy boots. The frame of this picture was decorated with glued-on toothpicks. There was a box of kitchen matches, a tall bottle of medicinal elixir and two brass ashtrays. On the wall, a net bag for letters and postcards, a calendar showing a Swiss village in the snow. There was a chromo of blood-dappled Jesus in a stamped metal frame that formed a cross at every corner.

Félida wanted to go find the old adobe house, to see the place everyone but she remembered. Abelardo shook his head, said sternly that the house was gone, swallowed up by the valley irrigation project, the whittled plot of land absorbed into Anglo cotton fields. In short, nothing of the Relámpagos remained except their name, carried by people not of their blood.

Hornet

Two of the three sons, Chris and Baby, were as close as fingernails and flesh. Chris rushed at life, greedy for food and opportunity. Baby's blood ran hot, his body temperature, his hands, hotter than anyone's, as if he ran a perpetual fever. To touch him was to sweat. The oldest son, Chencho, was amiable but withdrawn, as if he were measuring the distances between the planets. Félida, that little something, was the youngest. Looking at her only living daughter, Adina said, "you poor little thing, without a sister for a friend. I will have to be your friend." She tried to make the child her special confidante, warned her against the traps of life and the fate of women.

Hornet was never her goal. After the house of the Relámpagos was bulldozed, they started out for San Antonio where Adina believed there were better chances. The borrowed truck traveled six dusty miles north through mesquite, which showed through the dirty windshield like scratches on the landscape, and into the outskirts of Hornet where it broke down. Abelardo and the boys—Crescencio who was eleven then and almost as strong as a man, and Baby and Chris—all pushed it to the garage, Adina carrying Félida in her arms and walking alongside. Inside the garage were two musicians Abelardo knew, a guitar and a *bajo sexto,* standing near the pay phone, swearing a little, telling him they had been waiting for the accordion player, had just learned that *hijo de la chingada,* that fool had fallen from the rail of the bridge and broken his pelvis on the dry stones of the riverbed. No one knew why he had been walking on the rail.

"*Borracho,*" said the *bajo sexto.*

"*Loco,*" added the guitar, already working out a line or two of a *corrido* about the idiot.

As soon as Abelardo dug his accordion out from the boxes of cooking pots and sheets—it was not the Majestic that he played in those days, but the little green two-row—as soon as Adina found his good shoes and rubbed them to a gloss, as soon as he changed into his blue gabardine trousers and a white shirt, they left for the engagement, an anniversary barbecue to the north of Hornet. At noon the next day when Abelardo reentered the garage, hung over and filthy from sleeping under a bush, he discovered that his wife had moved into an old trailer on the edge of the barrio. The trip to San Antonio was canceled.

"How is it you make this enormous decision without consulting your husband? Have you grown a set of balls overnight, is that it? Let me see," reaching for the hem of her dress.

"Get away! Who makes the decisions when you're away at work, gone for months and months, or nights in a row? You think I hold my breath? When the boy was hurt in the tire you were in Michigan, there was no one but me to take the responsibility. You leave me sitting in a broken car while you go to a fiesta, what should I do, hold my breath and die?"

He tried to get his job back at the Blue Dove (though it would mean traveling six miles back and forth) but the wife of the Anglo manager told him to get his ass out of there. No job for somebody who quits one day and comes back two days later. And so, because he had children who had to eat, and because there were no jobs, he went into the fields again for the next two years, up to the Lubbock onion fields, his red eyes tearing constantly, the reek of onions fixed in his clothes and skin, and across his knuckles ingrained lines of dirt like a map of starbursts; his mind, like a man turning a coin in his pocket, never stopped working over the injustice of a musician ruining his hands with field labor.

"Look around," said Adina harshly, "it's all women raising the families. The men are far away playing the accordion."

What a relief and pleasure when the Blue Dove changed hands in 1938 and the new owner personally requested his services again.

The trailer

That trailer Adina had found in Hornet was at the southwest edge of the barrio on a dirt street. To the east the barrio thickened into a maze, to the south lay an immense pasture containing seventy paint horses in powerful colors, to the west, the dirty copper smelter and, beyond, low, gullied hills, ash-colored sagebrush alive with ticks, a vague long sky like a cloth, and, all around, billions of small stones. Although the trailer was at the end of the street, it was connected to the sewer line, not like the oozing and stinking *colonia* to the east where people lived in packing crates and scrap-metal lean-tos.

It was a worn trailer but larger than the old Relámpago house, with three cubby bedrooms, a living room, the kitchen; on the front, a set of foldout steps, a pair of propane tanks like double bombs. Just beyond the trailer was the bus turnaround, a bulldozed circle where the drivers got out and relieved themselves against the tires. Why was it, asked Félida, that both men and dogs had to piss against something? And got a slap for the immodest question. The black exhaust of twenty buses a day billowed against the front of the trailer, accompanied by the squeal of brakes, shifting gears.

Abelardo made up a little song:

> *O you filthy bus,*
> *I was dreaming of love and riches,*
> *I was dreaming of happiness*
> *When you* brrrt! *like ten elephants,*
> *Like a smokestack blowing up,*
> *When you gnashed your gears*
> *And destroyed my fragile reverie.*

The sons added sound effects, squirting air through their lips until their mouths were numb. Adina said she was disgusted. But for years this song made them laugh and it was the first song Baby and Chris learned.

Down the street stood a wreck of an old tamale stand, the remnant of a failed franchise from the 1920s in the shape of a giant tamale, the stucco sloughing off, faded signs drooping: HAMBURGERS AS YOU LIKE'M. *TAMALE PIE.* But in a year the old tamale stand was gone, replaced with a little store and in the back a barber's chair where Señor García cut the hair of men and boys, and all around them the space was filled with houses and trailers. The city flooded around them like water coming over the riverbank.

In this trailer in Hornet, Adina stood with her hands on her hips and told her children, "find a way to better yourselves. Get a control over your own life. Not be like—you know, only working, drinking, working, drinking—and playing the accordion." But Abelardo, resting on the bed, heard her.

"You disgust me," he shouted but did not get up. To himself he muttered, "here comes the business of the money." Adina turned the radio knob to an American-language station and said, "*¿por qué* you kids don't talk American? No more Spanish. From now on American at home too, not just school. If you talk Spanish you'll end up in the fields. Talk American and get an education you get a good job. You're Americans, no? Then be an American and get some money." For her part, she had given them a start with American names: Baby, Chris, Betty. All except the bewildered, smiling Crescencio, named after his drowned grandfather, Crescencio, already defeated by his name, and poor little Roselia who had died in her crib, only a week old.

"How stupid," Abelardo had muttered at each birth, insisting on other names as well, Rogelio, Tomás and Félida. The daughter went by two names, answering to Betty from the mother's mouth, Félida from the father's.

"Yes," said his wife, "what a spiteful man. Why not names of Indians, then? Why not do them a favor? Go ahead, put them as low as you can get! Make their lives truly easy!"

The irony was that she looked more *indio* than anyone, looked a real *oaxaqueña*. Yet her family had come into the Rio Grande valley hundreds of years before, owned land along the same calm river as had the vanished Relámpagos.

"Yes, my family of important landowners." Bitterly. When she was a child her family still visited relatives in Mexico. She remembered two long journeys to Oaxaca but believed it didn't matter, that was in her childhood, the abandoned past that everyone knows and loses and tries to forget. That cloying, smothering family of hers with its fits and hysteric tantrums and her mother's morbid belief in dreams.

Most sharply she retained a memory of great distances, being crowded into bus seats with her younger sisters, very strict in keeping them quiet and well behaved. When she thought of Mexico at all, she thought of it as the country of the senses, of moving colors, even the dust saturated with aromas and flavors. How drab and yellow Texas seemed when they returned, abandoning once more the vanilla beans, the musty olive-colored river, mineral dust and horses, the sanguinary and intestined odor of butchered pigs, the tiny drops of oil that stood on the surface of epazote leaves. She saw herself clenching stems, the green violence of cilantro on her hands. The sadness of the musky soil under the squash leaves where the cat slept, the smell of white cotton garments drying in the sun, of candles and kerosene and incense, of rotting oranges and sugar and frying oil and crushed sage, the roasting coffee beans and the deep little pots of chocolate, the cinnamon-and-almond scent of the female relatives, the odor of corn ground against the stone.

But over the years the visits became infrequent. The Mexican relatives commented unpleasantly about the Texas children's debased Spanish and impolite ways; they held an image of these little *norteños* running as mongrel dog packs up in *Tejas*. When Adina married Abelardo she turned her back on her Mexican relatives. "They don't mean nothing to me now because I am *tejana,* my children are Texans also, Americans." But that deep past was caught unconsciously in her cooking, in the food she prepared and the smoky, sweet dishes she relished: *pasilla* chiles, Oaxacan *mole coloradito,* the spicy pork *picadillo,* the seven *moles,* the black and the deep red and the green—dark in flavor, slightly charred, faintly sweet. Ancient flavors and tastes. Not forgotten.

Almost the very week they moved into the trailer Adina's headaches and fevers began. She had always been healthy but now she became something of an invalid. The fevers would come again and again at any time of the year, oppress her for months, then mysteriously disappear. Although she went to the clinic many times, the annoyed doctors said there was nothing wrong with her. She lay curled up, grey and hot, great circles under her eyes, unable to sleep, ears ringing, consumed by thirst.

"I have not had a night's sleep since we came here," she wept to Félida. "I have the luck of a dancing dog." There was a high-pitched ringing in her ears, a dizziness and deafness to the affairs of the world that was almost like happiness. In the turnaround the buses roared like beasts; she could smell the exhaust, the dust and hot metal. The heat of the air, of her body. Her eyes swam in tears, she could not see well. When she looked up at night the moon seemed covered in thick foam. The walls, the faces of her husband and children, were distorted. She was consumed by fatigue. And lying there in the dozy world of fever, she could not escape the sounds of the accordion.

On and on it played, as though it played Abelardo, as though it were the animate force and he the instrument. Sometimes there were other accordions in the hands of his *conjunto* friends, she could hear a strong voice calling out "*¡sí, señor!*" in the midst of the music. Abelardo knew a thousand songs and he played them all during her fevers. Against her, she thought, against her. That voice, so sad and quavering in public song, so hard and dictatorial in the home.

Lessons

From the time of the flood when old Relámpago disappeared, Abelardo had worked. In his life he spent three months at school. He learned to read as a grown man during the war from closely watching his own children struggle with their American schoolwork. Chencho turned eighteen in 1943 and was drafted at once, sent to the Pacific. Abelardo, sick with worry for this clumsy son, needed to know. He practiced on billboards and road signs and posters, then newspapers, not letting his wife know until he was fluent and then brought home week-old copies of *La Opinión* and the *Los Angeles Times*. He sat at the kitchen table with his legs crossed and took up the *Times,* read a few paragraphs aloud, then snapped open *La Opinión* and, in a very easy voice, read a few sentences about Frank Sinatra whose "*música ha invadido el mundo en estos últimos años*—like a tidal wave, no?" When Adina exclaimed in astonishment, he replied, "it is not entirely difficult. I am a cornucopia of brains." His interest extended beyond the war news to miscellany, such things as the workings of the human digestive system, mysterious tides, the habits of kangaroos.

Somewhere he found a large anatomical chart showing the structure of the ear and this he taped onto the kitchen wall near the photographs of great accordion players. So there loomed over every meal the pale orange pinna resembling some extinct mollusk, the curving tunnel of the auditory canal, the eardrum shaped like a Japanese fan, and beyond it the curious tiny bones of the middle ear, the hammer, the anvil and the stirrup. The eye swept along, unable to escape, to the snail of the cochlea—a whirlpool, a hurricane seen from a cloud, a jelly roll, spinning tops, a fallen strip of orange peel. Not on the chart were the interlacing pathways connecting the music to the cerebral cortex.

Abelardo had hundreds of records, his own recordings of the 1930s, a few with Decca, then with Stella, then with Bell, then Decca again. "In those days I sang in Spanish; those men with the record company said to me, 'we can't tell what you are singing, so don't sing anything dirty.' So of course I sang all the filthy ones."

There was a photograph showing him in a strained position, his right leg stretched out behind him, the left bent slightly at the knee, his torso rearing sharply back and the accordion stretched across his chest like a radiator grille. He was handsome and young, his hair thick.

"You know how much we got paid for those sessions? I thought I was lucky if I got ten dollars. Who can guess how much money the record companies made off us? Hundreds of thousands of millions of dollars." He had old recordings of Lydia Mendoza, of the great accordion players, the records of Bruno Villareal, half blind, a little tin cup wired to the side of his accordion, playing in 1928, "the first recording with the accordion as the star," Pedro Rocha and Lupe Martínez, Los Hermanos San Miguel, dozens of Santiago Jiménez discs. He made a ceremony of putting on the records, made his children sit respectfully.

"Listen, listen, there's the *tololoche* that you don't hardly hear no more. And you get how flowing the accordion notes are, the music very smooth and flowing, like water. That is Sonny playing. How smooth, even though he was a drunk, he drank so much his liver rotted off and there was only the hook where it used to hang inside him. But so smooth. Now it's different, ¿*no?* Now everybody plays very staccato.

That started with the war. You should have seen me then when I started out, I was a crazy man getting people to look in the paper for me, to see if any advertisements for recording sessions was in there. Or go by Señor Chávez's *farmacia*. Señor Chávez made little miniature models of accordions, not to play, but for toys for his grandchildren. He was a kind of talent scout for one of the companies. They put an ad in the paper and you went up to a hotel room or something. Somebody listens to you and if they like you, tell you to come at such and such a time to a place where they had a studio set up at. Ten or twenty people standing in the hall waiting for a turn. Just one take, that was it. It was raw. They gave you maybe a dollar or five dollars. Nothing else, not even when a thousand people bought that record."

He would make them listen to all those old labels: Okeh, Vocalion, Bluebird, Decca, Ideal, Falcon, Azteca, especially the Ideals made in the garage of Armando Marroquín up in Alice. He had played on many of the recordings of the Hernández sisters, Carmen *y* Laura, sitting in Carmen's kitchen in the tangle of wires and microphones. "Here's one—oh *Dios*, what a nightmare! 1931 and what do we sing? 'The Star-Spangle Banner,' to show we are American, the Congress just made this song the national anthem. Is there anybody alive who can sing this awful song?" The children swung their legs.

Between the music and the crops he had done all right, he said, but when the Depression started, everything became impossible and it was then that his possession of the Relámpago place was disproved, and soon after they had moved to Hornet.

He was crazy about the movies, and years later could still frighten his children with the plot of *White Zombie*, which he had watched seven times.

"Movies! You know those old movies—old silent movies—always had Mexicans for the bad guys? The Mexican wears everything black, he has a big hat, he has very dark skin and bulging white eyes. He rages, he is uncontrollable, cruel, he smiles as he stabs, he is attracted to gambling and murder. Then they finally make a movie with a Mexican for the good guy and who do you think they get to play the good Mexican? Paul Muni, all covered with makeup!"

After they arrived in Hornet, for a month he had a job sweeping up hair on the floor of a barbershop; everyone was on relief and there was only a little work in the cotton when you could get it. One day he amused himself by making a strange siren from a pierced metal disk that rotated when he turned a crank and worked a pump with his foot so that it jetted air against the whirling plate. The contrivance made a loud moaning call, but in a few days it broke. Really, said Adina, he had too many children to indulge in such fantastic play.

Each year Adina bought colored school photographs of the sons. Parents chose the sizes they wanted or could afford—a strip of tiny faces the size of postage stamps, or a life-size portrait in a cardboard mat. Adina always chose the small—but not the smallest—wallet size. The Hornet school was segregated, a school for "Mexicans," no matter how many generations you had been in Texas. The Relámpago boys hated the stinking place. The teachers were Anglos, most of them from the north at their first jobs. The lessons were in American. There was an expensive rule: a penny fine for every Spanish word uttered.

"You are in the United States where we speak English," said the principal in morning assembly, stepping to the edge of the stage to lead them in the Pledge of Allegiance.

"I don't got no penny," Chris whispered to his teacher.

"Ten years old, still in the third grade and you talk like a baby. You must say 'I do not have a penny,'" said Miss Raider. "So, since you cannot pay the fine your punishment will be to write on the board five hundred times 'I will speak English.'"

Baby kept his mouth closed, listened. When he finally said something the American words came out clearly enough.

Everyone had to sit straight up when Miss Raider entered the room and say in dragging unison "Good morning, Miss Raider." The crimes of whispering, lateness, coughing or sneezing, foot scuffling, sighing, fidgeting, were punished with "jail"—sheets of black paper taped to the floor on which miscreants stood at attention for one, two hours, forbidden to move or speak. A failure to produce homework, a sullen manner, brought smarting whacks with a folded leather strap.

"Hold out your hand," said Miss Raider before striking.

Crescencio cut his name in the top of his desk, a great curling *C* and fine flourishes like a bower around the entire name. Mrs. Pervil cried, "under the desk," her voice a flail of barbwire. She pointed.

Crescencio went slowly to the front of the room and stood near the desk.

"Get in under there!" He crouched, crept into the dark kneehole. At the bottom of the front panel there was a gap of five inches and in that space the class could see the heels of the crouching Crescencio, his torn sneakers.

"The rest of you open your histories to page forty-one and read the selection 'The Brave Men of the Alamo.'" Mrs. Pervil sat down and drew her chair forward. Her knees filled the space, pressed against

Crescencio's forehead. Her pointed shoes jabbed his knees. Her legs and thighs blocked out the light, invested the kneehole with a horrible intimacy. Suddenly the knees sprang outward, the thighs opened with a faint fleshy sound. The cheesy stench of Mrs. Pervil's unwashed private parts filled the dark space. Crescencio experienced humiliation, claustrophobia, burning rage, sexual excitement, impotence, feelings of injustice, subservience and powerlessness.

The next day he looked for work, found it in an umbrella factory jamming ferrules onto shafts and never returned to school. On Sunday morning Mrs. Pervil's husband discovered all the tires on his new Chevrolet sedan stabbed flat. It happened time and again despite a locked garage and a diabolical arrangement of rigged trip wires and bells, happened until the husband had used up his ration stamps and was forced to buy inferior tires at astronomical prices on the black market. Mr. Pervil blamed "the goddamn Bullsheviks." No one suspected chubby Crescencio, shambling, sadly smiling Chencho with his defeated shoulders. The slashings stopped when he was drafted in 1943 and sent to the Solomon Islands with his squad of Mexican Americans from Texas. One or two of them made it back home. Abelardo ordered and paid for an elaborate stone memorial, but the fateful name "Crescencio" cut in the top of his old desk preserved his memory for Baby and Chris.

Inside the tire

The two younger brothers were so similar in appearance and manner no one outside the family could tell them apart when they were little children. They seemed to be twins, although Baby was a year older. After the accident with the tire, they were so different they did not even resemble brothers. It happened when they were very young, when they still lived at the house of the Relámpagos.

Baby told Chris to climb inside the old truck tire he strained to hold upright. Chris was small and his body curved to fit the hollow inside the tire. Before he had even settled into place Baby pushed the tire down the rubbled hillside with a railroad track at the bottom. He saw the mistake at once. He had expected it to roll smoothly, a wonderful ride, but the tire leaped, sprang into the air every time it hit a rock, Baby running far behind, hands out and arms trying to extend a hundred feet. Beyond the railroad tracks the tire wearied, spun around like a half-dollar on a bar and collapsed.

Baby ran up to the tire, panting, crying. Chris spilled out. He looked dead. With a scream of despair Adina heard at the house Baby picked up a rock and bashed it against his own forehead. And again. So both of them went to the hospital.

Chris had a strange laugh after his recovery, the laugh of a large man enjoying a funny movie, a laugh he had copied from an X-ray technician with a circle of hair like a brown beret. This technician came to see him in the hospital ward on Saturdays bringing a chocolate bar which he broke into small pieces, inserting them into Chris's mouth with his right hand while his left hand frisked under the covers, plucking and rubbing at flesh not covered by bandages and plaster. When Chris walked again he walked differently, one leg slightly shorter than the other and he disguised it by rising on the balls of his feet with each step, a buoyant, agile walk that seemed to seek shortcut paths.

He was destined for injury. When he was fourteen and leaning against the passenger door of a borrowed car on the way to a dance with his father and four others, all of them singing Valerio Longoria's *ranchera* "*El Rosalito,*" a tremendous song of the time, the wonderful *nueva onda* sound, rough and exciting, the worn-out door latch gave way and the door opened. He fell out at fifty miles an hour, the flesh scraped away to the bone, suffered a broken shoulder and arm, a concussion, those things. But once again he recovered.

The best thing to come from this accident was the visit of Valerio Longoria himself—the smooth pompadour, the crouching eyebrows— to Chris in the hospital, joking but serious—"since you were singing my song when it happened I feel a responsibility—"

"That Valerio," said Abelardo admiringly, "he's the real thing, *la gran cosa.*"

The polar bear

At the school in Hornet there was a teacher, Miss Wing, from Chicago, who spoke with great precision and smiled at everything. "Many people have hobbies. Tomorrow I want everyone to bring samples of their hobbies to class. Each boy or girl will tell about their hobby, such as stamp collecting or matchbook collecting. My brother collected matchbooks, which is a very, very interesting hobby."

Most children brought a single matchbook the next day. Angelita brought a lone wooden match, the blue and red tip grimed from her pocket. Even this Miss Wing praised.

The Relámpago brothers brought their accordions. They played the bus song (without singing the words), waited for the teacher to smile. Her white face dipped in disgust.

"The accordion is not a good instrument. It is a rather *stupid* instrument. Polacks play it. Tomorrow I'll bring in some *good* music for you to listen to."

At recess they whispered, what is a polack? Angelita knew.

"A white bear that lives on the ice."

Baby imagined white bears in a row playing their silvery accordions. And the mystery deepened when, on the radio one night, he heard "*I'm a polack, you pretty little poppy . . .*"

"What is a polack? Is it a white bear?"

"Amapola! Amapola! The name of a beautiful young girl!"

Miss Wing brought a record player in a beige case, set it on her desk, pulled at the black cord that was too short to reach the outlet. The big boys had to push her desk toward the wall, the metal-shod legs shrieking over the floorboards. The felt-covered turntable went around and around. She slid a black lustrous disc from its paper sleeve, held it by the edges, and placed it on the moving turntable. Just watching it go around felt good. She lowered the arm. The room was filled with the Boston Pops Orchestra playing "The Syncopated Clock."

But this good music had no effect on the Relámpago boys. In the Relámpago house the accordion was everything. In 1942, at fourteen and fifteen, playing matching accordions in the style associated with their father and singing in harmony two of their father's best-known compositions, the polka "*La Enchilada Completa*" and the *ranchera* "*Es un Pájaro,*" they won a talent contest in McAllen. Already they were playing with Abelardo for dances. They sang searing duets of remarkable feeling. There is no harmony like the matched voices that escape from the throats of those who are blood relatives, the shape and structure of the vocal apparatus similar, like two accordion reeds filed to sound almost the same yet fractionally different. The prize was two hundred dollars and an appearance on a border station beaming its programs as far away as Canada.

Abelardo was elated. "Now you'll see, they'll come, the record companies, wanting to record you. It'll begin for you." Abelardo's waiter friend Berto drove them in his fourthhand Ford. They crossed the border and arrived at the station an hour before the scheduled time of noon. The boys sat silent, clutching their instruments while Abelardo buttonholed everyone—the man with a tray of coffee, a technician festooned with odd tools, an engineer on his way down the hall, a cowboy singer, half drunk and with his fly unzipped, coming from the men's room.

"Look," the American manager said a little insolently, "we've got a little reschedule change here. Go out, get some lunch, come back with the kids at two o'clock this afternoon. We moved the talent program to two o'clock."

In the room beyond, Baby heard a stuttering male voice say to someone, "wha-wha-wha-wha-wha-wha-what's the difference between a Mexican and a bucket of shit?"

Outside, the wind gusted hard and the sky was green-black in the south. Papers and tumbleweed rolled in streamers of dust. They went to the car.

"He said come back at two," Abelardo explained to Berto. "They changed the time."

"But I have to be at the restaurant at two. My shift starts at two. You know this."

"All right. Drop us downtown, we'll swallow something, get a taxi back here and then we will wait in the town until your shift is over."

"It's over at eleven, you know this, and an hour to get here, you'll be sitting around for a long, long time."

"Ah, we'll make friends, play some music, have a good time, see a movie."

"Only one of my headlights work." A gust of wind swept dust into the car. "All right, get in, get in."

As Berto backed to turn around in the gravel parking lot, wind rocked the car and the first drops of rain hit the windshield, large and far apart. There was a tremendous crack and a groaning sound. Baby said, the tower's falling. It was falling, the immense, two-hundred-foot tower was gathering speed as it descended on the station and parking lot. Berto gunned the accelerator and they zigzagged crazily backward, watching the tower hit, the roof of the station buckle, the top twenty feet of the tower smash down on the parked cars and the space they had occupied only seconds earlier. Flying shingles and bits of wood were hitting the ground, the big plywood letter *W* crashed and bounced.

"Let's get out of here," said Berto.

"Go," said Abelardo. "If we stay they will blame it on us."

After that, nothing happened for Baby and Chris. Their fame was confined to the Hornet barrio—"*los dos hermanos* Relámpago who won the contest." There was nothing to do but keep playing with Abelardo at the weekend dances and fiestas and *quinceañeras,* their little moons reflecting his brilliant glare. They had no style of their own.

Missionaries

After the move to Hornet, Adina had stopped going to mass and confession. In a year or two she was putting plates of food in front of two

Yahweh's Wonder missionaries, listening to their stories of doom and salvation, their descriptions of the wilderness of the soul, and later rephrasing these accounts for Abelardo and the children. This religious husband and wife, Darren and Clarice Leak, both blond with white lips and transparent eyes, brought their children with them when they visited (Clarice descended from Rudman Snorl, a member of the missionary party sent to wean the Cayuse Indians from their addiction to breeding and racing fine horseflesh, dying there in the antimissionary uprising of the infuriated Cayuse). The children sat obediently in the hot old car parked close to the trailer for the strip of shade, the windows rolled down to give a little air. They were forbidden to get out, talk to or even look at the Relámpago children. Lorraine was the youngest, then Lassie, and Lana the oldest, an albino child who covered her weeping eyes with her hand against the strong light. They sat very still with their faces to the front of the car, yet their eyes devoured every movement of the Relámpagos who moved about in their line of vision, showing how well they could run or wrestle. Chris stood directly in front of the car and moved his arms and legs in humorous positions, rewarded sometimes by rigid smiles.

A hot day, the parents inside praying with Adina, and in the car Lorraine whined and rocked back and forth.

"No sir!" hissed Lana. "You can't, you have to wait!" But at last they opened the car door a crack on the side away from the trailer, allowed the child to slip out, pull down her ragged underpants and squat. Chris stared at the jetting water, had to pull out his own instrument and piss before them as if to show that the Relámpagos, at least this one, could make a more pronounced display.

Abelardo despised the Leaks, thought them stupid, fanatic and dangerous. He pointed out to Adina that Clarice, listening to the ever-on radio while Darren droned about the Lord this and the Lord that, had written down the name of the station offering "an autographed painting of Jesus Christ, framed in hand-tooled gold-tone finish, for only five dollars."

Bending twigs

Abelardo wanted his sons to die for the accordion. He played to each of them when they were still babies, choosing the last hour of light for the most impressionable time, for who has not heard music at the end of the day, the quarter-light infused by somber harmonies that say everything that has ever been said? A listening child never forgets the scent of the uprushing darkness, the gleam of a white shirt as someone approaches.

He bought each of his sons two-row diatonic models similar in style to the old green accordion. "I don't bother with those little ten-button ones," he said. "Let the kids start out right." But, rushed and pressed, he was impatient in teaching them, made them sit on the wooden chairs under the signed photographs of his accordionist friends, Narcisco Martínez, Ramón Ayala, Rubén Naranjo, Juan Villareal, Valerio Longoria, in a row on the wall. Crescencio had no interest in the accordion. Abelardo said to his face, very sadly, "Crescencio, you are stupid, truly stupid." He gave up on him and concentrated on the younger sons. (Yet Chencho was a wonderful dancer—not to this music, but to big-band swing on the radio, a real jitterbug, spinning and twirling the girl and lifting her up above his head.)

"The accordion is an important instrument. It can even save lives. Last spring a man played the accordion to calm the frightened passengers in a shipwreck in the fog in New York. Now listen and see, this is how I play this," he would say. "Now you try it," executing a quivering bellows shake, fast arpeggios, tricky dissonances, but he had no time to show them slowly and carefully. He was out of the house again, working or playing for a dance. After a few months the lessons stopped. They would have to find their own way.

At the Blue Dove

One day a man came into the Blue Dove. He returned many times. He always ordered the same thing, the specialty of the restaurant and the reason many came there, attracted by the odor of fat juices dripping on the charcoal fire in the back courtyard, the *cabrito al pastor* and the plates of *machitos,* tender pieces of goat liver roasted in lengths of intestine. These delicacies persisted on a pedestrian menu of steak, eggs and burritos.

This man sat always at the tiny corner table, a table also favored by lovers, who failed to notice the sway of the chairs, the unsteady table when the folded matchbook beneath the wall leg was disturbed. Nor did the man notice these things. He placed his folded newspaper on the empty chair and gestured for the waiter.

Standing up he was unpleasantly tall, but in a chair, and his long legs folded beneath it, he faded, distinguished only by a heavy nose and a mustache of excruciating thinness. He had a trick of looking slyly around from under lowered eyelids, never staring boldly, never letting his eyes flash. His hair was sleek and receding from his caramel-colored forehead. He came from a northern city, one could hear it in his voice. He sat quietly, his hands loosely collapsed, filling the table, as he waited for the platter of meat to come. When he was finished with the meal he placed his knife and fork on the plate in the form of a cross, lit a cigarette, holding it between forefinger and thumb of his left hand, and leaned back in the creaking chair. If he caught Abelardo's eye he would gesture with the second finger of his right hand as a sign he wished the dirty plates carried away. One evening he made this gesture and as Abelardo grasped the edge of the soiled platter the man spoke to him in a low voice, asked Abelardo to meet him across the street—he named a bar—at six-thirty. Below the cigarette smoke Abelardo could smell a pungent herb oil, a primitive and superstitious odor.

A rosary on the rearview mirror

The man sat at the end of the bar, seemed very cold and dangerous away from the lovers' table. He crooked his second finger at the barman, the familiar gesture, and a glass of whiskey came to Abelardo.

"I represent another," said the man softly. His newspaper lay folded on the bar showing a photograph of Mussolini at an accordion festival. He blew smoke from both nostrils like a bull on a cold plateau. "I offer you a certain opportunity." There was a long silence. At last Abelardo asked, what is this opportunity? He said the word "opportunity" in a light, sneering voice, no longer the busboy clearing away the man's filth.

"The opportunity is a large one. A very pleasant opportunity for the right one. I think you are that one." There was another long silence. Abelardo finished the whiskey, the finger moved and a second glass came at once. The man lit a second cigarette, let the smoke drift out of his stretched mouth in quivering rings.

"This opportunity," he said, "involves one or two simple actions. From time to time I will bring a package into the Blue Dove and place it on the empty chair, behind the tablecloth. I say to you as you are clearing away the dishes a few words, such as 'white Buick with a rosary on the rearview.' You slip the package under a dirty dish in your tub and go toward the kitchen. I have noticed the side door that goes outside to the garbage cans where the waiters smoke. It is easy to go around the corner to the parking lot." The word "smoke" sent the man's fingers to his shirt pocket.

"In the passageway you take the package from the tub and go out the side door. You say you are going out for a smoke if anyone notices you.

But this all happens very quickly; no one will even look. In the parking lot you glance at the cars and put the package on the back seat of the white Buick with the rosary. Or whatever car I have described to you. The Buick may be a Chevrolet or a De Soto. There may not be a rosary. There may be ten packages in a year or a hundred. On the first day of every month, I will leave one of these for you under my plate."

The man opened his left hand a little and in the dim light Abelardo saw a folded bill. He thought at first it was a ten, then a hundred, but finally saw clearly that it was a thousand. A thousand-dollar bill. A steaming flush rose up his right side, the side closest to the money.

The first package appeared four days later. It was, as the man had said, all very simple. It was the money that was difficult. So large a bill could not be real money. It was abstract, a thing of ferocious value, not to be showed and not to be spent. He got a can of shellac and a small brush, creased the first bill lengthwise, shellacked it lightly on one side, removed the bass end of the green accordion and glued the bill into an interior fold of the bellows. It was entirely invisible, could not be discovered except by knowing fingers, could not be seen, even if someone removed the ends and looked into the bellows. The man came into the Blue Dove with his secret packages and secret thousand-dollar bills for one year and two months. Then he stopped coming.

The exploding suit

Abelardo went to the bar across the street several times but the man was never there. He asked the bartender if he knew when the man was coming back. That one whispered it was better not to inquire. He himself knew nothing but had heard that a fine new suit had been delivered to someone, a beautiful grey sharkskin suit in a white box, but when that person put it on, the heat from his body activated volatile chemicals secreted in the seams and the suit had exploded and the man with it.

In the bellows of the green accordion were fourteen bills of the thousand denomination.

The oldest son

In 1945 they had the news of Crescencio's death and a letter from some lieutenant that began: "I only met Crisco, as everyone called him, a few days before he was killed . . ." For the first time they learned that his death was not from bullets but from a cinder-block wall which had collapsed and fallen on him when he kicked it. He had been jitterbugging

with another soldier and in a wild breakaway had spun around and
made a flying kick at the wall, which yielded. Adina put a gold star in
the window.

Smile

The two sons Chris and Baby, nearly grown and becoming insolent and
willful, played every weekend with Abelardo.

Abelardo would play the first set, then often go off to drink Bulldog
beer in the clubs and bars, listen to the Padilla sisters' voices coming out
of the *sinfonola,* leaving the rest of the night to the sons. (Adina always
had *menudo,* the fiery tripe soup, on hand for his hangovers.) From
those intervals when he left the music to them, changes began to
develop in the sons' playing; they made a shorter, staccato music, like a
knife stabbing. The older dancers complained they couldn't dance
properly to the sons' music, with its choppier, faster beat and a kind of
sprung rhythm that disturbed, but the younger ones loved them,
screaming and cheering, especially at Chris, "*¡Viva tu música!*" when he
stepped up in his red jacket, Baby in the black jacket with white piping
on the lapels. Then, to Adina's heartbreak—she blamed Abelardo and
the easy Saturday night money—both of them dropped out of school.

What was the point? All paths went nowhere. *¡Ándale!*

Acne scarred Chris's face, a hardening face as he tried for jobs and did
not get them. Weekend music wouldn't keep a chicken alive. He had a
taste for stylish shirts and wristwatches, gold chains. His ambition was
to own *un carro nuevo.* He grew a mustache as soon as he could, to draw
attention from the acne and to make himself look older. This black
mustache curved down. He wore a pair of dark glasses and began to run
with a bunch of *cholos,* especially with a rough called "*Venas,*" a black mole
on his left nostril, someone who poured money into his white Buick with
the crushed velvet upholstery, whose father, Paco Robelo, the whole
Robelo family, were rumored to be connected with *narcotraficantes.*

In a year or two Chris had his own car, a secondhand Chevrolet
repainted silver, with painted flames licking along the sides and on the
hood a portrait of himself playing the accordion in a fiery circle that
made the old women say it prefigured a trip to hell.

Baby seemed to suffer. Everything affected him—the smell of
burned food, thunder and hail, girls whispering, the shine of the stellate
scar on his forehead. The old women said he had a steel plate in his
head. Abelardo shouted, "snap out of it—we got a dance to play
tonight. You sit up there, look like your best friend just died. You see

how Chris always got a smile? The audience wanna see you having a good time."

Adina would put her hand against his forehead, worry that his heated blood might somehow be cooking his brains. But he was composing his first songs, struggling with words and music. It was all coming out in American.

Félida's helpful teacher

Mr. More's voice in the remedial mathematics class droned on and on about topological vertices, but Félida kept her head down, feeling him looking at her. He was walking up and down the rows and talking about it.

"Call the front of the room line AB, call the back of the room CD, if I walk BD, if I then cut across to A, do we have odd or even vertices where I stop? Hands?" There were no answers. Now he was walking up her row, slowing, standing beside her desk. She could smell the wool and chalk smell, see, from the corners of her eyes, the dusty brown shoes.

"Félida."

She didn't know. "Even?"

"As a matter of fact it is, but I think you guessed at it. Would you like to come up and draw the diagram on the board?"

The bell wouldn't ring! She went up to the blackboard, took the chalk. What had he said, where had he walked? Across the front of the room. She drew a horizontal line. Down the row. Then up her row.

He laughed. "What I said was, *if* I cut across to A. I didn't actually cut across to A because I can't walk through desks. Look." Beside her again, taking the chalk from her, his cold chalky fingers touching hers. He spoke very softly, not a whisper, but a low voice. "Come back here after school for a few minutes. I want to talk to you." He raised his voice, raised his hand with the eraser, rubbing out her lines and replacing them with his own. She went back to her desk feeling nothing. Nothing at all.

When she came to the room after three o'clock he was standing by the window watching the school buses pull out.

"You know how many years I've been doing this? Nineteen; fourteen of them here in Hornet. I came down here from Massachusetts. I had some dream about living in the southwest. I just thought it would be different than it is. You have to eat. Teaching, and in Texas, for Christ sake. After a few years you're in too far to get out. So here I am. And there you are. Come here." Moving to the side of the window.

And it was the same thing, the chalky cold fingers going up her neck

and into her hair, pushing it up against the grain, which she hated, and
then he pulled her up against him and the bony hands came up to her
breasts and felt them, down her ribs to her waist, her hips, then up
under her skirt and the cold chalky finger digging under the elastic of
her panties and into her as he ground against her thigh. Hopping
adroitly back when someone in the hall laughed and the clack of heels,
some woman teacher, rattled past. She thought maybe it was his wife,
Mrs. More, who taught typing and business math.

"Listen," he mumbled. "She's going to a meeting in Austin. I want
you to come to the house. Tomorrow around five o'clock. I've got this."
He pulled something from his pocket, paper, unfolding it, showing it.
A five-dollar bill. "For you. You can play your accordion for me." He
smiled faintly.

The accordion had started it. She had gone to his office the year
before because he was the school guidance counselor on Wednesday
afternoons, told him she wanted to be a musician but the problem was
her father, well known, a famous accordion player, and her brothers
who also played the accordion and were admired and demanded all
through the valley, while she was invisible even within the house. Her
father had a strong prejudice, she said, against women in music unless
they sang; it was all right if they sang. But she had been singing all her
life and he had never noticed. She had taught herself to play the accordion but had no confidence. She already knew thirty *rancheras*. What
should she do?

"A beautiful young girl like you shouldn't be worrying about a
career," Mr. More said. "But I'd like to hear you play. Maybe I can offer
you some suggestions. I once had a dream of playing the classical tuba."
He had patted her arm, two slow pats, the tips of his fingers just grazing the down on her arm and making her shudder.

The criminal daughter escapes

When he woke from his little nap in the red Saturday evening a few
weeks before Félida's *quinceañera* there was no one in the trailer.
Abelardo dashed water on his face, patted himself dry, sprinkled talcum
powder into his groin, slapped his face and neck and shoulders and
belly with Sea Breeze. Now the careful arrangement and spraying of his
hair. The pressed trousers, the new black socks of some smooth silklike
fiber, white shirt and a pale blue tie, a pale blue polyester jacket to pick
up the color. Last, the gleaming shoes. In the mirror a good-looking
man of deep health and intelligence. He went for the green accordion,

for he was playing for Bruno tonight, a man who appreciated the plaintive voice and the hoarse crying of the old instrument. It was not in the closet, not under the bed, not in the living room nor the kitchen. His heart beat with fear. He raged into his sons' room and for a moment thought he had found it, but it was only the old Italian Luna Nuova that he had given to Baby years before. One of the bastards had his green accordion and he had no time to run around the town looking for the dirty little thieves. In the end he had to take the Majestic, but the tone was wrong for this music and he played so angrily and powerfully on it that he broke a reed tongue and the buttons jammed.

Long after midnight he returned, drunk and still furious, but the green accordion stood on the shelf in the closet again. He opened the instrument, his fingers probed the creases of the bellows. The money was undisturbed. The shreds of fear solidified to fury. He strode to his sons' room, ready to denounce and tear them. The beds were empty. It was inconceivable, but Adina must have had it.

"Get up!"

"What is it?" Bolting up in fright, wide awake and trying to recognize the danger.

"Why did you take the green accordion? Where did you go?"

"I? The accordion? I took nothing. You've gone crazy." He raised his arm as if to strike her in the face with the flat of his hand, left her weeping on the pillow. *Ah, now it comes out!* she thought. *Brutal man!* While he went to the refrigerator and groped for the ice water. He thought, *Félida!* And rushed to hammer on her door. Shocked by the burst of defiance from the other side.

"YES, I TOOK IT. I was invited to play for a teacher!" It was too late for any kind of truths. For she had not even opened the case before the teacher was on top of her, grinding her into his dusty carpet where she could see forlorn strings hanging from the underside of the sagging sofa.

"Not even the most criminal son would speak to his father this way! You slap my face with insolent words!" Rage swallowed everything. He felt interior stormy chords as if madmen were pummeling the timpani of his guts. He shouted.

"A woman cannot play the accordion. It is a man's instrument. A woman cannot get other musicians to play with her, nobody will hire you, your voice is not strong enough. Your character is bad, you are disobedient, you have no future in the musical field." He was almost crying. "After all the money we intend to spend on your *quinceañera.*" And kept it up until Baby came in, calmed him, until at two in the morning it was silent. Chris was still out under the moon somewhere, driving his taxi, was often out all night taking drunken soldiers back to the base.

In the earliest morning Adina heard the door close. The outside steps creaked. In the window the margin of the moon was dark silver as though tarnished. A deep and ominous silence. Abelardo breathing thickly beside her. She touched the side of her face lightly with her fingertips. Where he might have struck her, where he almost had struck her. In a few minutes she got up and went into the kitchen, felt sand under her bare feet, no, it was sugar. Sugar and salt spilled across the floor. Heard the hissing gas before she smelled it. *Dios,* they could die! She turned off the gas burners that were pouring the noxious stuff into the house, opened the door gagging and coughing at the stink of the gas. She stood on the porch in her nightdress looking down the wet dirt street. Somewhere a rooster was crowing, a maniac of a rooster. The street was entirely empty. Betty/Félida was gone.

Trembling, she stepped back into the kitchen and saw the green accordion on the table. A knife protruded from the bellows. It was a message that the daughter wished to stab her father to the heart.

"Never mention her in this house again," Abelardo mumbled, weeping. "I have no daughter." Yet before he spoke he drew the knife out of the instrument and examined the bellows slowly, carefully, for signs of other invasive cuts and slices and he spent the afternoon behind a locked door repairing the damage by gluing a thin piece of pigskin over the tear inside the bellows and working a rich leather preservative into the outside to keep it supple and willing.

The remaining sons

After the war the minutes flew by, the hours, the weeks and years and there was no word from the daughter. Adina became very religious ("Lord, I cannot bear these burdens alone"), going out with the Leaks to knock on doors and persuade others to become Yahweh's Wonders. Chris and Baby continued to play music with Abelardo, but an animosity was growing between them, a dislike of each other's music. Nor did the weekend playing bring in enough money to live. The traditional music was not so popular now; it was all swing and big bands.

When he was twenty-three, twenty-four, around 1950, Baby got the idea to grow chiles, to do some throwback thing, associated with a regard for the agricultural laborer, passionate rhetoric that flowed from union organizers who came to the region after the war, and his thoughts of his unknown grandfather whom he wished to believe a hero. The idea was vague. He had to lease land, had to learn how to grow chiles from the agricultural experiment station agent, an Anglo who pressed him to specialize in a thick-bodied cultivar named S-394, developed at the University of Texas, and not the old local chile, *la bisagra,* the hinge, for its crooked shape. The timed application of chemical fertilizers and irrigation were the key procedures. He found this boring, lost interest as soon as the plants started to grow. The chile-growing he had imagined, had heard described by older men, was a complex thing of crossbreeding for drought resistance and special flavors, of virtuoso weather readings, of gauging the soil's temper, of prayer and fate. He thought he wanted to understand these things, be a part of that life, but only discovered he had no talent for agriculture.

While he had the land, Abelardo was drawn to it, came out as often as he could get away to see how the plants were coming along, talk a little, now increasingly about his life in the past.

His drowned father had played the guitar, *vingi, vingi, vingi.*

"So there was a little music in the family," said Abelardo, squatting on the red soil at the end of a row, smoking his cigarette and watching the irrigation water trickle into the ditch. He said it was a sour, hard music that forced the ears until he, Abelardo, came along and stunned everyone with his fabulous playing.

"I learned to play in the fields, from Narciso. Narcisco Martínez, *el Huracán del Valle,* started it, started the *conjunto* music. Look, before World War Two there wasn't truly nothing, just guys playing together, all the old Mexican bullshit stuff, mariachi . . . Then Narciso, then I came, and pretty soon, after the war, there were four or five good *conjuntos*— me, Narciso, Pedro Ayala, José Rodríguez, Santiago Jiménez, Jesús Casiano. I loved that music. At first it was just a little one-row accordion, maybe another instrument, whatever was there; then we got the two-rows and added the *bajo sexto,* and just those two instruments made a lot of good music for dances. I had a man, we called him Charro because he had this Stetson he always wore, played *bajo sexto* with me before Crescencio, poor Chencho, was born, an older man, very strict in his ways. Well, he couldn't really feel the music I was trying to play and we broke up because in those days I drank a lot. Then I got a *tololoche*—*ay Dios,* what a beautiful sound that instrument makes with the accordion."

"I rather have the electric bass. Makes them dance. Drums, too, get them moving."

"Yes, now you younger ones make fun of how we played, but you got to think back who this music was for then, where it come from. It come out of poor people, didn't have money for fancy drums and the electric instruments—even if they were invented then, you got to have electricity to play them. Who had electricity in the thirties? So we played the left hand, played the bass. Narciso said '*conjunto era pa' la gente pobre*,' and he knew what he was talking about. And he knew about being poor; he drove a truck, worked in the fields most of his life. That's where it happened, this music, in the fields. And of course you know there were plenty of them that looked down on the *conjunto*—your mother, for one."

No, he said when Baby asked, he had never cared to take up the piano accordion with its forbidding-looking row of keys like teeth—an instrument that breathed and had teeth, that had a way of showing the human hand as a small trampling animal.

Baby looked up the rows of the chile plants, the curved first small pods curling in under the leaves and the white blossoms enticing the bees. Why did the old man talk so much?

"Now it's getting popular, this music, our music, and you know why? *Tejanos* carried it through the cotton fields, all over the country, up in the beet fields, Oregon and wherever—*sí*, they danced on Saturday night, maybe just for the chance to stand up straight. I remember those dances very well. We all played the taco circuit. Most of us worked all week in the fields too. You had to tie a bandanna over your mouth and nose the dust was so bad, the dancers jumping around made plenty of dust. Narciso made a polka, '*La Polvareda*,' about this dust cloud. I got it on the old record; you heard it. The accordion was so natural, a little friend. Easy and small to carry, easy to play, and loud, and can play bass rhythm and melody. Just the accordion and nothing else and you've got a dance. It's the best instrument for dancing in the world, the best for the human voice. This music, this instrument—your mother"—he spat—"your mother wants to make you into imitation *bolillo*, an ass-licking Anglo doughball. You'll never be one of them. You can't. Learn a million American words and so what? They'll still kick you in the face with their big salty feet." He grabbed Baby's right hand, stretched his sweaty arm out, the brown skin taut over the muscles. Skin brown as though varnished with strong tea. "But don't expect to make a living with music, with playing the accordion. It cannot be done, even if you play nothing but American music. That's the tragedy of my life." He held out his own hands, fingers splayed.

The son Baby, this lagging chile grower by day, this part-time accordion player at night, drifted along. On the weekends he played for dances with Chris, mostly *rancheras* and polkas; they sang in the classic two-part harmony, *primera y segunda*, Baby's voice a raspy tenor that could soar to a quivering and incandescent falsetto, Chris's voice with a thick nasality that gave the sound substance and richness. Their big days were in October, especially *El Día de la Raza*. They split off from Abelardo because there were too many dances to waste three accordions on one place. The dances were exhausting, the strain of playing and the lights, the sweat and heat and thirst, the noise like pouring rain, and always a table of roughs waiting for Chris, youths opening in *el grito,* "*Ah-jai-JAI!*" when Chris stepped up to sing.

Though so many turned to the big-band sound and the strange hybrid fusion of jazz, rumba and swing, would rather listen to "Marijuana Boogie," the Los Angeles Latin sound, than "*La Barca de Oro,*" there was an audience that liked their music, who found value in it. These new ones, many of them veterans back from the Korean War, some of them university students, embraced *conjunto,* and this music was not for dancing but for listening. It had a meaning beyond itself.

"They listen," said Chris, "not because we're good, though we are good, but because we are theirs. They are not just jumping around in the dirt until they drop." But the zoot-suiters booed them off the stage, went crazy for the Mexican-Latin stuff, *música tropical,* a kind of hot, tripping swing.

Chris was in small troubles constantly, half hiding behind Baby while they played because someone was looking for him; he was always fooling around with somebody's woman out in the parking lot and when the break was over he didn't come in too many times and Baby had to start without him, got used to being the only accordion and started to play one or two of his own songs. "Your Old Truck and My New Car" was well known, and "I Never Knew About the Front Door."

Chris drank. Got into fights. He was arrested, three, five times. Beaten in jail or on the way there. Stories went around. He had a gun in his pocket. He was mixed up with the Robelos. Then his friend Veins was found clubbed to death in the folds of a dirty carpet.

With two sons like that, what kind of path could they find through the world? Chris had a job driving a taxi and was out all night, night after night, working or not working. Half the time he didn't show up on the night they had to play.

Conversion

The change was sudden. In 1952 Chris accepted the contorted religion of Yahweh's Wonder in order to marry Lorraine Leak, the daughter of the missionary couple who had come for many years to the Relámpagos, spooling out "and the Lord said" and "Jesus tells us." Chris was twenty-four. The missionary daughter, Lorraine, a pious washed-out blond with a thick face, spoke in tiny, inaudible words. Her parents, grizzled and unhappy, but caught in the trap of their own preaching about brotherhood (never dreamed it could boomerang like this), stood silently during the ceremony and did not come to the fiesta Abelardo and Adina arranged. It was just as well because Abelardo drank enough to make a public speech to Adina.

"You see, you joined their religion long ago, now Chris does the same thing, so you are of the same religion as Señor Leak, no? But he holds himself above you, him and his wife and their rabbit-eyed daughters. What can come of this marriage?"

Chris shaved off his mustache, ordered his hair cut short, dropped his old friends. He quit drinking and smoking, and was often seen to clasp his hands, bow his head and let his lips move silently.

The thing that did not change was his great hollow laugh. Chris and Lorraine came to visit on Sunday afternoons, Lorraine sitting dumbly on the sofa watching the Sears Roebuck television with its skinny rabbit ears and suckling the child. What a stick, thought Adina.

Chris sat on the porch railing, one leg swinging, the other foot touching the porch floor. Looked over at Baby, who still lived at home, in the sly way he had when he was getting ready to duck out of something.

Baby said, "what? Something on your mind. You got a girlfriend on the side and you want me to tell Lorraine you got to go out of town?"

Chris was fatter now, his shaven face ballooned up, and because he always felt the urge, he said, for a cigarette, he ate fast food when he could get it, burritos, tacos, hamburgers, Pepsis. Driving a cab made you hungry but you didn't get any exercise. The front seat crackled with his paper bags and candy bar wrappers.

"You don't change, still got a dirty mouth on you. No, no girlfriend. It's I can't play at the clubs and dances no more. It's against my religion, now, and it's making hard feelings with my in-laws. So, I'm like switching over to the organ, play at services, you know, hymns? Religious music. I mean, I know Jesus now, and that's where I'm aiming my music. I used to be wild, but I'm tryin to do better. Guess you and the old man got to keep it going for the Relámpagos." They could hear the baby crying inside.

"You not going to do the recording deal with me and him? That's set up for months. He won't like it. We'll prob'ly lose the contract—suppose to do the two Bernal songs with three-part."

"He'll have to accept that my life has changed."

"Well, you do what you have to do. Still driving the fucking taxi?"

Yes, Chris answered, he was still driving the taxi.

"Must be a good job, you got that new camper van." Nodding at the street where the beige van gleamed.

"What you trying to say? You saying something?" He drew his face into a turtle's expression.

"No, man, nothing. Just a fucking idle question, y'know?"

"Nothing is right. So fuck off."

So he knew Chris was lying about Jesus and that something was as crooked as the river.

A prodigal son

The chile-growing fiasco was behind Baby. He'd come out of it with no idea of what to do next except junk jobs, pick up a little money on the weekends, playing anything, mambo, cha-cha-cha, Tex-Mex, polkas, Cuban *danzones,* yeah, swing. He applied for a job as a bus driver. Sometimes it looked like a great job, that big bus, the nice uniform, fresh air when you wanted it, the chance to look over hundreds of girls. Bus drivers were famous for wolfing around. But there wasn't a chance. The company hired only Anglos. He'd never go back to school, and he hated the ones who came home from college looking around like they smelled something bad, making it a short visit because they couldn't wait to get back to the world they were trying so hard to enter, putting up with the little jokes behind their backs. He remembered private thoughts when he was a kid about being an architect, wondering how to begin, how did you become someone whose ideas turned into buildings? He didn't regret leaving school.

He painted a kind of mural on the front wall of the trailer, trying to get all the great old accordion players into it, painting from his father's photographs, with Abelardo in the central position, Narcisco Martínez smiling over his shoulder. The disconnected heads with fixed mouths and glaring eyes floated in the air, some high like gas-filled balloons, some near the ground.

He seemed immune to the lasting power of love, specialized in brief infatuations, a day or two, then he lost interest. After these little breakups he played like a demon, speeded up the music as if he was trying to out-distance the other players. At these times he was attracted to angry dissonances. The women were always after him, whispered among themselves that he had certain powers, that his body was like a heated iron drawn from the coals. "*Ay, Dios,* my mouth was burned, he left a scar down my whole front, breast and arm, belly and leg!" Smothered laughing and questions about more intimate regions. He could have anyone he wanted and he didn't want any particular one. Although he never lost his temper he was feared. It was remembered that as a child his hands were always hot, his touch feverish. It was said that if he slapped someone in anger the skin of the abused adhered to his fingers.

The right thing

Then, like a traveler who suddenly notices the sun moving down the west, the daylight condensing into an hour or two of dimming light, he decided to marry, quickly chose one of the first women to come near him, Rita Sánchez, a graduate of the university up at Austin, a teacher, busy with community actions and the new politics, already known as a strong woman who fought to get sewer lines into the *colonia* southeast of Hornet, a nightmare place where the residents were mostly poor *mojados* who had crossed the river in danger and now suffered bizarre diseases—leprosy, bubonic plague, tuberculosis—and were reputed to live on roadkills the women picked up on the highway, darting into traffic for the crushed flesh.

He made her pregnant on their wedding night, and his life slipped into the ancient human groove of procreation, work, cooking, children's sicknesses and their little talents and possibilities. For the first time he saw he was no different than anyone else. Their daughter was born with birthmarks like red arrowheads in her groin and armpit and on her neck. The next year, a boy was born the day after Stalin died (the newspapers all read in thick inky letters "*José Stalin ha muerto*"), whom they named Narcisco in honor of the friend of Abelardo's youth. Rita began to put aside her community work, resigned from the committees one by one. Her children ate her up.

For some reason, after his marriage Baby's musical abilities increased tremendously.

"Ah, that's because you don't waste your energy wondering where you're going to get it," said Abelardo. He came often to Baby's house, at all hours, enjoyed his morning cup of coffee under clouds the color of salmon eggs, walking around and criticizing Rita's basil, full of little beetles, the smell of yesterday's heat still in the dead air. In the back they had made a tiny patio. Rita planted a tree, watered it, and already it was large enough to cast a little shade. Its roots were pushing up the adobe tiles and the children fell often when they ran there.

"You could be very good, you know. Famous. You have the stuff."

"Yeah? And change my name, like Andrés Rábago to Andy Russell?

And Danny Flores to Chuck Rio? Like Richard Valenzuela to Ritchie Valens? Na, na, na."

Now Baby understood his father's greatness without jealousy or envy. Saw his inventiveness, his place in the history of the music. When they sang together now, he felt his voice embrace that of his father, a kind of sexless marrying like two streams of water coming together. Together they were in a closeness not even lovers could know, as the shadows of two birds at different altitudes cross the ground touching.

The accordion, too, he truly embraced, holding it against his breast so that its breathing commanded his own, its resonance made his flesh vibrate. He had many accordions; they seemed to come to his hand like lost dogs. In a strange city someone would come backstage, hold out an old instrument and offer it for sale, sometimes give it to him. Going back to Texas, there was always a strange accordion with them. And at home he'd take it up, play it, discover its little secrets, hold it near the sensitive skin under his chin to discover air leaks, learn its voice and individual ways, retune it to his taste. Abelardo never allowed him to play the old green accordion.

"Two eyes in one head," they called the father and son. Now came audiences smothering them in admiration, rolling them over and over, the waves of applause breaking and subsiding only when they stepped forward together, their breasts glittering with the instruments, only when they opened their mouths and sang "*Yo soy dueño de mi corazón . . .*"

Spider, bite me

Abelardo felt nothing in his sleep. The spider had bitten him and he slept on, his swollen feet enjoying the ease. But woke in the morning in the shallow silver light that precedes the coming day, with a sense of doom. Beside him, his wife breathed and her heat drew him to her as a shuddering wave swept down his spine. There was a tickling scurry in his groin and his hand went down. The spider bit again. Now he leaped up and threw down the covers, exposing his wife's body in her faded pink gown, her jackknifed legs and folded arms. He saw the brown recluse rush over the sheet, over his wife's leg and down into the darkness beneath the bed.

His heart was hammering. His neck itched, his groin. He wanted badly to be asleep, to be comfortable against his warm wife in the silver morning, tingling now with blue.

"What," murmured Adina.

"*Araña.* Spider. Spider bit me. Went under the bed."

She was up and in the doorway, her hair pressed down on one side, roached up wildly on the other.

"The brown spider?"

"I think so." He turned away, peered into his groin, his foolish long hair trailing onto his shoulders. He felt his neck.

"It got me twice, I think. I don't know how you're going to find it, but it's down there under the bed."

She went to the kitchen, down under the sink for the poison spray.

"Don't do that now," he commanded. "Get me some coffee. *¡Ai, ai!* That this should happen." Pulling on his clothes, shaking them first in case of other spiders.

Sat on the kitchen chair drinking the coffee. The nausea began, very strong.

All day he vomited, all day diarrhea poured from him in a green burning stream, a consuming fever came on mixed with the scent of insect spray, his teeth crashed together, he was freezing. He wanted badly to lie down on his bed and sleep but feared the spider. Anyway it was better to lie on the couch to be near the bathroom. Thank god there was a bathroom and not like at the old Relámpago place or in the stinking *colonias* where the ground festered. He was glad he did not have to run through the mud to the little house, with griping bowels and heaving stomach. The buses roared.

At noon his wife called for a taxi to take them to the clinic.

"They will give you something," she murmured. He was too wretched to argue. In that place they sat side by side on torn plastic chairs. Adina filled out the complicated forms. The room was crowded with people, wailing, coughing children, an old woman who kept passing her hand across her brow as though to stroke away some pain that lay near the surface, an emaciated boy. More people pressed in, leaning against the wall, squatting or sitting on the floor.

"We're lucky we got chairs," said Adina. Abelardo said nothing, leaned his head against the wall, but twice had to stagger into the toilet with the plywood door. In the waiting room they could hear him retching. When he came out his hair straggled down, and even in his sickness he tried to push it into place.

They waited two hours. Although more people came, no one seemed to leave. Finally Adina made her way to the smeared glass partition and rapped on it until the Anglo receptionist looked up, her eyes pale and furious.

"Will it be much longer? My husband is very sick."

"Yes, it could be a long time. The doctor is at the hospital for a meeting. If you people would make appointments instead of just crowding in like this, instead of just coming in without an appointment."

She went back to Abelardo. A dull-eyed woman with a limp child was sitting in her chair. Adina leaned over and whispered to him.

"The doctor isn't here yet. She says it could be a long time."

"Get me home."

He lay ill on the sofa, eyes closed against the droning television. He could swallow nothing. Adina talked with a neighbor or two, to old María bent and deeply wrinkled but still strong, who said, "I'm disgusted. You should have taken him over the river to the Mexican doctors. They are very good over there, their courteous manner makes one feel better. You don't have to sit waiting until you are a thousand years old. And the best is that they charge you only twenty dollars for a visit. At the clinic it is eighty. The drugs, the same drugs you buy on this side, the same packages, everything, over there you pay only five or six dollars for what costs a hundred here. My son's wife taught me all this. We all go across the river when we are ill, and I advise you to take him there at once."

Mara, who worked in the Community Action office, a university graduate who dressed in a long skirt, a rebozo dangling and catching in doors, her bare feet in sandals, the yellow, unvarnished nails showing, reproached her as well. "You should have had the *curandera,* Doña Ochoa—I've seen her help people who were truly sick that the doctors couldn't touch. There's something to it, you know."

She called Chris but Lorraine said he was gone, she didn't know where, maybe he would be gone for another week, she didn't know. It sounded like she had a sore throat, her voice strained. In the background Adina heard Mrs. Leak's raw voice say, who is it—is it him?

That night the convulsions started. Each attack was prefaced with an ominous sensation of something dark and heavy as a locomotive rushing toward him. He sat up, tried to withstand the hurling sensations, sat through the night alone, his wife lying on the bed in a stench of insect-killing spray.

A tightness began in the lower part of his back. His legs began to tremble, then danced up and down despite his will. His jaw clenched. Fine tremors like a tuning fork's vibration set him quivering. Stronger and stronger he vibrated, the quake radiating from the clenched back, until he felt his body sounding, a dull, low note. His lower jaw clacked faster than any castanets. He seemed to be in a red darkness and fell to the floor, legs jerking. In a minute it subsided and he got back up, panting, sat again on the couch.

Again and again the attacks came, each preceded by flutters of dread.

His chest tightened, it was difficult to breathe. He was burning up, his stomach clenched down to the size of an apple.

But on the second morning he was a little better, although his face was the filthy color of old coffee mixed with skim milk. He tottered up from the couch for the little bowl of rice Adina cooked for him. Its cloying odor repulsed him and the nausea seized him again, his body hooped in painful dry heaves.

"You get in the bed, Abelardo. I've sprayed and sprayed in there, all the slats and joints of the bed, and aired it all out. No spider could live through that. If I could sleep in the bed last night you can lie in it now. You need to rest."

Staggering, panting, he let himself be steered into the bedroom. The long hairs straggled wildly and he did not notice. She took off his stained bathrobe, sponged him with warm water and scented soap. How grateful his crusted burning body was for the wet cloth. Adina was frightened at the weight he'd lost in two days. A modest man, he held the towel over his inflamed groin, but she glimpsed the red, oozing swelling there and on his neck. She took his nightshirt from the hook behind the door, got him up, drew it over his head. She turned back the covers. He swayed forward and half fell onto the white sheet. His wife left the room.

The room seemed hot and filled with burning light, then chill and swept by strong wind. His eyes hurt. He moved his trembling legs, half rolled on his side, and the persecuted brown recluse in the sleeve of his nightshirt, squeezed by the taut cloth, bit again.

"Juan," he said clearly. "Juan Villareal! I will play '*Pícame Araña*' as no one has ever played it. You see, it is no joke. It must be played cruelly!" And struggled to get up, to get his accordion. He stood swaying beside the bed. The damaged spider dropped from his nightshirt, limped into a floor crack.

For a moment he felt very well, full of a young man's energy and joy. He sang in his mind. "*Hoy me siento vivo, me siento importante . . .*" He was not surprised to discover one did not need to have an accordion to play it. The amusing *huapango* of the dancing spider filled his mind, but he played the notes very, very fast, vicious, mordant stabs of sound. Before he reached the part where the accordion fell silent for the guitar solo, he dropped to the floor and that was more or less the end.

El Diablo

There were hundreds at the funeral. It was necessary to rent a black funeral accordion, although Baby had to go to Houston to find it, *El*

Diablo written across it in silver. He played on and on at the graveside, all the songs and tunes his father had made. The afternoon wore on, people became restless, shifting on their feet, thinking, after all, not everyone should die along with the corpse. Still he played on, *redovas*, *rancheras*, polkas, waltzes, *canciones*, displaying the treasures that his father had fashioned from his life. Yet he played with joy, for it was as if a certain heaviness had gone out of his own life.

After *El Diablo* was returned to the music store, the clerk (who later invented the slogan *The Accordion—A Music Education in a Box*) noticed that the buttons appeared scorched.

(A generation later, an Air Force jet crashed in the cemetery killing the six people aboard and the elderly maintenance man who mowed the plots. The crash demolished more than nine hundred headstones, among them the red granite of Abelardo Relámpago, *"Un gran artista,"* his hand-tinted photograph broken from its enclosing circle of glass.)

The capture of a drug criminal

It was good, Adina said, that Abelardo had died, that he had not lived to see the stories in the paper headed *"Conjunto* Musician's Son Seized in Drug Raid,"* and the photograph on the front page where Chris resembled a furious tortoise in handcuffs.

He was arrested in the stupidest way, as he came over the bridge and through the border checkpoint at Weevil at ten in the morning, driving the camper van, Lorraine beside him, the kids in the back. The checkpoint was busy, probably what he'd counted on, thought Baby, the line moving slowly past the landscaped island of bright flowers where a Latino woman watered plants with a green hose.

The U.S. Customs Service agent, a young Anglo with short red hair, pimple-spatched face and eyes like bottle glass, his white t-shirt showing at the neck of his shirt, walked around the van, looked at Lorraine, at Chris. He spoke to Lorraine.

"Your relationship to the driver?"

"My husband."

"He's your husband. Are those your children?"

"Yes."

"He's the father and you're the mother, right?"

"Yes."

A muscle jumping in Chris's jaw, but his hands casual, loose on the wheel. The agent walked around the van again, stooped, looked underneath. He rapped his knuckles on the propane tanks at the rear. Again. Turned the valve. Gas hissed as it escaped. He closed the valve again, came up to the driver's side.

"You understand English, buddy?"

"Of course." Trying not to lose it. It was going to be close.

"See that inspection bay over there? Just pull over there, I want to take a look in the back, see your luggage."

He breathed a little. Maybe it would be all right.

But agents were all around them, herding them out of the van and toward the door of the inspection station and from the way that pair was going straight for the propane tanks he knew it was finished. It was stupid but he tried to run, leaped over the flowers, his feet sinking into soft soil. The woman with the hose looped it, flung it around him, bringing him down into the plants, a faceful of dirt, lassoed by a garden hose.

A father's vengeance

It was the beginning. Seven months later on the first day of the trial, in the hallway of the courthouse, a bizarre figure rushed from the men's room and down the corridor, the emaciated and trembling Darren Leak, gripping the .38 that Chris had carried under the seat of his taxi. Bullets whined and ricocheted off marble walls, echoes pounding, multiplying into a deafening barrage.

A man in a phone booth at the end of the hall shrieked. Chris's lawyer sprawled on the filthy marble floor, one middle-aged leg moving like that of a dreaming dog, glasses rucked up into his hair, a fan of papers around his head, the edges absorbing blood. A man struggled with the courtroom door as though holding up a great weight. Chris crouched against the wall, one knee up, strained eyes looking at his father-in-law.

"You dirty Mexican nigger!" Darren Leak screamed. "We took you into our church and our family! You went unto our daughter and *Knew* her! You mixed your dirty blood with ours! You lied, you concealed your evil drug trafficking behind the name of Jesus! Your every action was a lie and a curse in the face of god!" He began to bellow wordless words like a rutting bull in spring, guttural roars that shot up into squeals, then he pointed the gun at Chris and shot, the bullet tearing jaw, tongue and spinal column, lacerating the brain with needle fragments of his shattered teeth. Leak said, "Our Father," pressed the muzzle to his breast and exploded his own heart.

The burning hand

Baby Relámpago *y su conjunto*. Better known as Baby Lightning. His voice was passionate in color, his falsetto as weightless as the ascent of a hawk in an updraft. His face smiled out of posters. He was well known in the southwest, had played in Chicago, Canada, New York. He always said New York although it had been only Albany, with an unresponsive Irish audience. "In Concert," the posters said. He had played at the Democratic National Convention, had made more than twenty records. "*Los Ilegales*" was selling strongly in San Diego. He played— what?—seventy, eighty gigs a year, always for sitting audiences (there were no more dances), endured the touring life until he was exhausted and went home to San Antonio where he lived now.

He wouldn't fly because of a dream. He had dreamed of himself hurtling naked down the sky toward a field of stones. In this field, workers who were filling baskets with tiny stones straightened up and looked toward the sky at the sound of his voice. An accordion was still in his hands, the little green accordion of his father, the buttons worn and shaped by the old man's fingers, and the wind pressing powerfully through the torn bellows made an extraordinary sound, vast ropes of discordant music which he could see, writhing through the clouds in black and purple strands like handfuls of glue-covered horsehair. The workers began to run toward the horizon and he understood that they did not wish to be dirtied by the fragments of his body when he hit.

It was 1955 and they had a date in Minneapolis, a concert for something called Mardi Gras Up North. He had a bad feeling about the venue. The small audience responded only to stupid songs like "*La Cucaracha*" and "The Mexican Hat Dance."

(Forty years later in the same theater a swaying crowd packed the auditorium, shouted and whistled for Sonora Dinamita, the boiling *cumbia* group from Colombia, Gilberto Gil, Flaco and Santiago Jiménez, Jr., Esteban Jordan, Fred Zimmerle at the Hispanic Cultural Heritage Concert in aid of Latino victims of *el SIDA*.)

After the show, in the dirty dressing room, they could hear the audience filing out, a diminishing babble as though a horde fell through a funnel, and somewhere someone whistling "Three Coins in the Fountain," getting it wrong; they could smell hair spray and moth flakes and hot lights and electrical connections. Isidro and Michael did not say much, packed the instruments. He knew they were hoping they could stay the night, not have to start the thousand-mile drive against blinding truck lights back to Texas, cramped in the car, burning eyes, yawning and stopping for coffee, Isidro saying "two hours and forty minutes, *hombre,* we'd be on the ground."

They were in the dressing room. The promoter, a heavy woman in a blue rayon dress, hadn't brought them their check. He was ready; both accordions—he used Abelardo's old green accordion for some of the traditional music—were cased; he'd changed into slacks and a knit golf shirt to be comfortable on the long drive. The *bajo sexto* drained a Coke. The blue dress was in the doorway and he looked up smiling, happy for the check, to be getting away.

"Hello, Baby," she said.

He was confused. The voice, he knew the voice, but where was the check? It wasn't the right woman.

"It's Betty. Félida. Your sister." She stretched out her long blue arms.

He remembered; it was the voice, the impatience of tone like Adina's voice. His sister. He looked at her, still very young but not beautiful, broad through the hips, the black hair elaborately braided and twisted into a crown, the glasses with plastic frames tinted flesh color, the full-skirted dress, a flashy band of gold down the front, the high heels and big clumsy patent-leather purse.

She was already fat.

"Félida?"

"You didn't get my message?"

He shook his head. Did not know whether to embrace her or not. Her arms slowly descended and she folded them across her breasts. They stood awkwardly.

"I left a message at the box office to say I'd be here. To invite you to dinner, meet my husband. He's in the music business too. We got a lot to catch up on."

He could not refuse. He told Isidro to wait for the woman with the check, get hotel rooms. He gave him some money. They had to stay now.

His sister sleeps with an Italian

Their apartment was small, the furniture covered with multicolored throws and fringed covers. There was a crucifix on the living room wall and a blown-up photograph of the Bay of Naples. The husband, Tony, at least fifteen years older than Félida, heaved himself out of a tan recliner and offered a beer. Baby wished for Scotch and water. Tony was a bandleader, on the club-date circuit; he had met Félida at a Polish wedding. He nodded his square flat head, the blue-black hair combed straight back, the heavy eyebrows cresting over deep sockets, and above the eyebrows the arsenic-white forehead. The eyes showed no glint of light, so recessed were they. He held himself stiffly. Baby thought he looked like a criminal destined for the electric chair.

"She's a good player, your sister. She can fake anything, she's very good at the ethnic stuff. We do a lot of ethnic stuff. Weddings, anniversary parties. They don't want to hear American tunes. Italian dates, heavy Greek stuff, Hasidic jobs we get, polacks, Hungarians, Swedes— they all want something ethnic. You try to give them American they won't give you the money; I even had a guy throw dinner rolls at me when we played 'My Blue Heaven.' No sir, they won't even take 'Alexander's Ragtime Band.' "

The dinner was lukewarm meat loaf, white fat congealing on the plate, a salad of grated carrots and raisins, bread sticks that cracked in their teeth like rifle shots, and a bottle of red wine that made the interior of his nose swell with the first swallow. They ate at a glass-topped table. Baby could not keep from staring through it at their thighs.

"Have some more meat loaf, Baby."

The husband poured wine, slopped it on the table.

It was disturbing to hear his sister's remembered but deepened voice coming from this woman. There was something of their mother's voice there, a sarcastic edge, the way the sentences ended with despair.

The husband, Tony, interrupted every sentence she uttered. "So you play the accordion. I know the accordion like I know my mother. I play accordion myself. I got a beautiful Stradella. You want a good accordion, it's going to be Italian. Best in the world."

Baby ate the meat loaf, wondered how soon he could get out of here. But the husband kept on. He had pushed his plate away, was smoking now and dropping the ashes on his plate. He couldn't tell Félida about Chris or their father, this loudmouth would keep on talking.

"So what you play? Jazz? I couldn't make the concert." The husband.

"*Conjunto.* Tex-Mex."

"Folk music, eh? Ethnic! I'm telling you, it's something you gotta know. But if you wanna hear beautiful accordion music, you listen to Italian. The best in the world. Jazz, classical, popular, anything you want to name. It's the best. OK, now, listen to this." He went to a cabinet in the living room, threw open the doors of the cheap entertainment center, Sears, thought Baby, and the husband turned on his components, the tuner, the turntable, adjusted the high-fidelity speakers, put on disc after disc introducing the music of Peppino, Beltrani, Marini.

When he went to the bathroom, leaving the door a little open so he wouldn't lose a note of the music, Baby looked at Félida.

"A wop. An old guy, too." He could be open with his disgust; after all, she was his sister.

"What do you know! He's a nice man. He grew up with nothing! He's proud of the record player."

"We had everything, I suppose. You were young, it was better when you were growing up. You don't remember the dirt floor . . . no, you had it better."

That started it. He was too connected to her painful childhood, that enemy of her true self. The toilet was flushing. She wanted to refute his condemnation of her husband. She wanted him to leave. She was sorry she'd gone to him. A slab of meat loaf lay on his plate, a small piece gone from the corner, the rest uneaten. Yellow liquid leached from his salad.

"You haven't said one word about the family. I suppose that's a bad sign. You might as well tell me who's dead. Is it our mother?"

"I haven't been able to say anything, your husband there telling me about the ethnic music. No. She's alive. She's sick, she's got something, they don't know what it is, we're worried about cancer, but she's alive. She's the only one, her and you and me. You should have written to her. A lot of trouble, a lot of pain for her. You know about Chencho? Yes, of course. That was before you ran away."

It took only a minute, the way he told of the deaths of the father and brother: a spider, a crazy man with a gun.

For her it hardly mattered. They had all been dead for her since she was fourteen. What was disturbing was the living brother on the sofa, his mouth moving, the yellowed fingers tapping his knees, the ostentatious wincing at the billowing Italian music. She felt a meanness, a necessity to wound him.

"You know, your music hasn't changed. You play what our father played, or at least what you and Chris played years and years ago, just that same stuff, the old *conjunto.* Don't you get bored with it? Don't you want to get into the new stuff? I mean, try something different for a change? Chuck Rio's doing *norteño* rock—you must have heard his 'Corrido Rock'? There's R and B. Latin jazz? You ever get to L.A.? That's where the real *música* is happening. You're stuck."

He was insulted and furious, but he smiled. Hadn't she always been unpleasant, an awkward blunderer? He could barely speak, he was so angry. But only shrugged. "That's my music. My music, that's what they want to hear and what I play. Tex-Mex, *tejano* with more snap, more country in it, and the traditional *conjunto* our father played, that is my music." The recording of the Italian accordion music filled the room with tremolo. "There's plenty musicians try new stuff. But they come back to the old stuff too, they come to the well with their pitchers." His coffee cup was empty. He waited for Félida to notice, refill it. His hand shook. She looked across the room at the husband coming out of the bathroom, zipping up his fly. The room seemed filled with bitterness and the quivering Italian music. Baby's glance focused on his accordion case near the door, the corners scuffed, the festival stickers peeling. He pushed out of the rump-sprung chair and got the accordion, walked deliberately to the entertainment center and turned off the Italian. They didn't know what to do. They were glaring at him, frowning.

He had a feel for silence, for leading to an unsounded note the listener yearned for and finally had to supply from his mind, the stopped phrases like a held breath, the faded ending or scantily echoed notes, the thin line of a beginning like a colorless trickle down a rock in the woods but growing to standing waves, a waterfall, a whirlpool, undertow and riptide. This hostile silence he attacked with powerful and rapid fingering from the beginning, too fast to make sense, a kind of anger bursting from the instrument. He played without stopping for about ten minutes, jumping around through twenty songs, a phrase or a line, intros and transitions, broken octaves, sliding his fingers over the buttons for the difficult but beautiful *glissandi* effect. He raised his head now and then to look across the room at his sister and her husband, and stopped abruptly.

"How about you," he sneered. "You used to play. Our father said you were the true musician in the family, the one with the real Mexican soul. But that was before he cursed you, before you left in the night like a criminal, before you broke your mother's heart and turned your back on your family and your people. Before you learned to be an Italian. Can you still play your own people's music? Or is it just the olive oil crap?" He extended his accordion, held it out in courteous fury.

"How dare you," she said. "Oh yes, I should have stayed, played the chile queen until I married some Chicano fruit picker, had fifteen kids and made tortillas three times a day by hand, keep my head down, watch for the evil eye and wear out my knees on the stone church floor. You hold out the accordion to me? I'm surprised. Surely you believe, as our father believed, that it is a man's instrument. Well, I think it is the instrument of unsuccessful men, of poor immigrants and failures. I was only a child but I saw that years ago. I saw that before I left, our father the busboy and his precious green accordion—that one right there—and the way he stood, all hot and sweaty, and that ridiculous hair, and came in drunk, a drunk Mexican, a busboy with an accordion, his moment of glory, and he would let the accordion hang down, the bellows open, just let one end go, and I saw that big moldy thing hanging down and I hated him, and that's when I knew the accordion was a man's instrument and men play it like they fuck. As you have just played it. I decided to play it as a musical instrument. And it is true, I can play anything. I am not stuck with *conjunto*. Anything! I do not bother with the button accordion, a nasty toy for amateurs and drunks. I play the piano accordion and I am a professional musician in a way you will never understand, a responsible musician."

He felt a kind of horror. "What a bitch you've turned into!" he cried.

"Don't you speak to Betty—" The husband put his hands on the arms of his chair.

"Shut up." He turned to Félida. "The piano accordion makes a stupid, domineering sound—it is a clown's instrument—yes, I can see you toddling out on Saturday nights with Mr. Baton to some Jew birthday party, you and a bunch of old hacks who can't play the scale, 'Happy Polack Birthday to You—' " he sang in a whiny sneer. "Corny band playing stale oldies. 'Happy You, Happy Me, Happy Fuckups in a Tree.' "

"You bastard! You don't know anything about it. I spent years playing with fine musicians, I worked hard, I was just a kid, learning the instrument, I played many years in four-piece bands, drums, accordion, trumpet, somebody who could double on clarinet and saxophone, and we were good enough to sound like ten instruments. I'd like to see *you* do it, cover standards and Latin and ethnic and pop, yes, and swing and hot jazz, even hillbilly and semiclassical, you see how long you'd last. You'd be tossed on your tail in five minutes with your lousy, dinky squeezebox." As she shouted she was pulling an enormous case from the hall closet, a heavy black case, and from it she took a large chromed accordion—it looked to him as though it were made from the front end of a Buick.

"You bastard," she panted. "You don't even know I can replace an entire sax section. You do not even know that although I married, I continued my music!" She passed her arms through the straps and hoisted the huge instrument. Glaring at Baby she played. He thought she might do some show-off medley, some bell-ringing patchwork full of squeals and whistles, a showstopper that dumped "Little Brown Jug" into "Tickle Tickle Hee Hee Hee" and ended with "Bill Bailey, Won't You Please Come Home" or a show tune, but she surprised him. She stared at the ceiling, said, "*por Chencho, Tomás, por Papá Abelardo,*" then sang the heart-wrenching "*Se Me Fue Mi Amor,*" which Carmen *y* Laura had recorded in the last year of the war. Her bellows control technique was extraordinary, with dramatic swells and choking, *sforzati* explosive effects. She scratched and rubbed and struck the keys, ran the back of her nails across the folds of the bellows. The accordion gave the perfect illusion that a *bajo sexto* and a bass as well as a highly original percussion player supported the accordion, and from it came the melting harmony of the missing sister's voice to twine and burn with the sweet, smoldering fire of Félida's sad voice.

"It is the most beautiful music in the world," she said and went into the bathroom where her sobs echoed off the tiles.

"You ought to hear her play 'Flight of the Bumblebee,' she's fantastic," said the husband.

Baby put Abelardo's green accordion in the case, looked at the stupid Italian and walked out, leaving the door ajar like Richard Widmark, heard it slam as he punched the elevator button.

In the street Baby walked toward the lake, shivering in the evening damp. Two men walked ahead of him under the lights, but they turned off and entered a building. There was a faraway guitar, a blues line, the *but-tut-tut* of drums, escaping from an open door. He walked toward the black lake, heard the liquid suffering of the water. He thought of ships backing slowly out from their docks. After a while he began to yawn. How tired he was. And chilled. He walked away from the water and when he saw a taxi gliding toward him, its roof light yellow and warm in the northern street, he raised his hand, ran toward it.

"Fortune Hotel." *Ay*, what a beautiful, beautiful voice she had, wasted on an Italian club-band man, trampled by that large, overbearing accordion. Tears flooded his eyes.

In the hotel lobby he realized he had left the green accordion on the floor of the cab. He rushed to the street but the taxi was gone. He made call after call, no, he did not notice the cabbie's number or name; no, he did not know what cab line it was, he remembered nothing except the yellow light on top and it could not be recovered.

A smell of burning

In the apartment the agitated husband walked back and forth.

"What a yo-yo," he said. He scratched his arms. "I smell something burning," he said finally.

"It's him. He always stank of old cigarettes and burned wood." She began to cry and when the old husband came toward her with his arms out to comfort, she pushed him away. An Italian!

Hitchhiking in a Wheelchair

A CHROMATIC ACCORDION

On the streets of Paris

Charles Gagnon, whiny and given to crying (the motive, Sophie, his deranged mother, said, for her attempt to drown him), entered working life in 1912 at age five, sucking on a harmonica and begging for *centimes* on the streets.

Sometime during the Great War, when he was nine or ten, the whore Yvette, who had saved him from drowning and in whose room he sometimes slept, pushed a little one-row *accordéon diatonique* at him, a ratty castoff pasted over with multicolored stars, a gift from one of her clients who was sick of hearing the mewling harmonica and who felt some pang for the bruised macaroni-face harvesting cigarette butts from the gutter, sorry for him because of his shitty past—imagine!— trussed up with coat hangers by his crazy mother and thrown into the river, pulled out by skinny Yvette who, as a girl, had dreamed of swimming the English Channel (a decade later when Gertrude Ederle did so, she felt betrayed); but he said to Yvette who gave the brat a place to sleep, a real heroine, he said only, doesn't he get enough of the filthy harmonica out on the street? Does he have to keep on when he comes in? Here, give the little shit-ass a real instrument. And speaking of real instruments, see this?

With the button box—the buttons were loose, the bellows leaked, it sounded like a sick dog trying to bark—Charles worked the roughest *bals musette* (the fashionable men in their mink trousers and zip jackets never came there), playing doggedly for tips in the smoke and shouts and fights, the rhythm accompaniment provided by his stamping feet, sometimes alone, sometimes in competition with other players. There were no breaks. When he stopped for a piss or a drink the dancers screamed curses and threw things at his skinny back. His pay, often enough, was *un petit vin blanc* which was the cheapest and which became his realest pleasure then and forever. So he sniveled toward taking his place in the world of men, half starved and often drunk, sleeping at Yvette's when he could, when she didn't have customers, sometimes under a pair of chairs in the corner of a bistro, a part of the dockside life with his runny nose and burst shoes and a touchy hauteur based on nothing.

By the time he was sixteen this accordion irked him greatly—it did not have enough volume, it could barely be heard so much air poured out of the cracked bellows, it had an unprepossessing appearance, yes, it resembled a stiff rag, a dead turkey. Then there was the matter of the music. He was drawn to jazz, crazy to learn, to try cranky, strange progressions, but if he experimented—he had made up something that came close to "Honeysuckle Rose"—the patrons shouted their displeasure, pecked at him, come on, come on, drop that shit and play real music, the dim couples shifting around the floor on stiff western legs, the *crêpe de Chine* tubes of the women's dresses flashing around their shins, the men's two-toned feet pivoting and pointing, surrounded by candle fires on the white tablecloth plains, the music sad and jaunty, the hands and fingers of the men touching the ribs of the women through the heated fabric. The boy played derisively, mocking the flowery patterns on female rump and thigh, the brilliantined hair and cautious hands of the men.

His hero was Jo Privat who could play what he liked, *le jazz hot* mixed in with gypsy music, who sat in with those gypsy brothers Ferré and Django, was facile with the old *bourrées* and polkas, at home with the most desperate *chansons musette*. He had connections, did Privat, he knew muscle men, gangsters, he was always the star turn, *le clou de la soirée*. He was lucky, the bastard, got the lucky breaks, and Charles Gagnon never would. He had no luck, the ace of spades turned up every time. Jazz in the waterfront dives? Never, nothing but sentimental tripe with idiot refrains, songs that went with drinking and no hope, the kind of music sung by women whose men beat them, vinous crying, torrents of pained memories and defiant songs of nobodies. He got the idea that in the cosmic scheme his ill fortune counterbalanced the success of Jo Privat; if Privat went down in the world then Gagnon could rise. For a while he dreamed of killing Privat; he would rush up to him with a smile as though to thank him for his music, then make the lightning stab and disappear into the crowd. After a few weeks he would stroll into one of Privat's haunts and begin to play. At the end of the evening Privat would be forgotten and there would be a new star. But it could not happen with this dead turkey of an accordion.

He made an arrangement with Gaétan the Necktie; an *accordéon chromatique,* a big black box with six rows of buttons and a bellows that nearly took the full stretch of his arms and that sounded like a locomotive crossing a trestle, appeared one evening; just a few francs every week until a certain sum was paid, better not forget, eh? and the Neck-tie punched him on the arm with his hard fist.

He would have been content with a two-row button accordion, but in this world you take what you can get. To learn this myriad of buttons, to cast from his mind the old simple pattern, to train his fingers to dance like those of someone at a typewriter was difficult, but he learned quickly because the sonority of the instrument and the rich possibilities of the chromatic scale rewarded him. What an incredible number of notes. He would never go back to a *diatonique*. The big chromatic was loud, it was enormously versatile and it was heavy. After a night of playing, his legs trembled. But what tricks he could make it do. Now, when a drunk bellowed for some drooling *valse musette*, Charles Gagnon would scream "*ta gueule!* Shut up!" and keep playing, drown him out. The big chromatic enjoyed musette tuning: three reeds for each note, one tuned to pitch, another a slice above true pitch, the third a cut below, so a note sounded in an aching tremble. It was silver-tongued, louder, better than any *diatonique*. And because of its weight he used it with success in one or two fights, slammed it down on some *mec*'s head, the guy went to his knees, his eyes rolled up as if he were examining the underside of his brain.

With this strong accordion he became an adult, the weepy, cringing childhood replaced by a formidable presence, heavy shoulders and arms, a thick neck, and a face with fleshy ears. His eyes were dark and suspicious, the black hair parted in the middle. He had hard nerves and his mouth was narrow and tight, pinching the ends of his cigarettes flat. He was in trouble so often it did not matter.

The café fire

Sooner or later he had to get into a real mess. He was made to stand up with Julie, forced by her brothers and Old Denis, the vicious father whose motto was "*buvez et pissez,*" a walking corpse with a liver as big as a portmanteau in him, so there had to be drinks first, drinks before a wedding or a pissing as the old man said, and as Charles took his glass in the café in an atmosphere of commingled anger and triumph, from the corner of his eye he could see the satin on the girl's tight belly gleam and darken as sunlight sifts through cloud shadow; it was the kid inside squirming. There were a few more drinks and a crowd pressed into the Café Girandole, named for its dusty chandelier with most of the crystals missing, decorated for this occasion with twisted streamers of crepe paper, and after an hour or two all of them were drunk and Julie, short and already stout, dancing like a cow with an electric prod *au cul,* when there was an uproar of Senegalese at the door.

Olive, the elegant black girl he liked, advanced on Julie, fingers crooked like a garden fork and a blowtorch of abuse pouring from the pomegranate mouth, her round, hard belly advancing into the battle ahead of the rest of her body. In the doorway were her male relatives, enormous black men with bunched muscles and sleek cropped heads bearing greased ears that could never be gripped. The eyes of these men were red-veined and focused on invisible phantoms about a meter and a half in front of them.

Julie's brothers and father leaped up, smoke and curses pouring from their mouths, throwing down their cigarettes. The two pregnant women shrieked and darted at each other; Julie gave Olive a tremendous slap that sent blood arcing from her nose, and Olive returned it with a blow on the satin belly, and then Old Denis lunged at the door, bottles and knives glittered, chairs splintered, the women rolled on the floor, a black man got Charles's unshaven cheek in his teeth and began to chew. Moisture fell on them, there was a flash of light, a narrow flame ran along the floor and burst with a soft *hus* into a ball of fire. The crepe paper roared. He tumbled through the door with the black man, his shirt on fire, rolling in the wet street, and got away, clean away, leaving a piece of flesh in the teeth of his opponent, leaving the women burning up alive and his quickening bastards in their permanent dark chambers. Old Denis, badly scorched, got away as well and swore death to Charles by melted lead poured into his eyes, his ears, his mouth, slivers of steel pressed under his nails, up his urethra, fillets of flesh cut from him with a carpenter's saw.

À Montréal

It was 1931 and Charles worked his way across the Atlantic to Québec, found a woman almost at once, and in less than a year was a father, married, and living in the east end slums of Montréal in the middle of the Depression. He had a job for a few months delivering white ashtray sand to luxury hotels and apartment buildings, but the concessionaire replaced him with a nephew and then there was no work. The big *accordéon* was in and out of the pawnshop. Besides, he disdained the drawling, mangled language and the Québécois musette style, hurried and without savor, worse than anything he'd ever heard. There was no jazz at all, and he despised the stupid reels and gigues of the carrot farmer and *bûcheron,* the gibberish mouth-music of crazy syllables and the way musicians danced their feet while playing. He stole a few records of Jo Privat although he had no Victrola, imagining the taste of Paris in his throat, the flavor of his old street life.

The wife, Delphine, went stale quickly, changed from a not-bad-looking girl, quick to bring him little comforts, to a woman nailed on an invisible cross. She came from an impoverished farm family undistinguished since an ancestor of quarrelsome temperament had landed in Québec in the late seventeenth century and within six weeks was brought before the court for calling his neighbor *"une sauterelle d'enfer,"* a grasshopper from hell, *"un bougre de chien,"* and striking him with a hen, for which mischief he was sentenced to a fine and a public *amende honorable,* a statement of repentance and apology. He quickly left the settlement and went on to become a *voyageur* and *coureur de bois,* scattering mixed-blood children across the continent before settling on a small acreage on the west bank of the *rivière* Saguenay and fathering seven more children on a half-Abenaki woman. (Delphine's father, descended from one of those seven, died in 1907 when the cantilever railway bridge in construction across the St. Lawrence collapsed and he tumbled, with seventy-three others, assorted wheelbarrows, shovels, poles, blocks and tackles, and lunch pails, into the black water.)

Delphine's elaborate upsweep of glossy hair, the pouf of curled bangs became a crooked side part, straggling hair held back with a plastic barrette in the shape of a seahorse. Oh how she talked and complained. If only there was some money, she said, if only she had not married him, if only she could be a child again.

He didn't have patience. It was easier to give her a slap and tell her to shut up, to slam out the door when she sat weeping at the table, the ragged line of flesh-toned slip dipping below the hem of her cotton dress. She had a nervous cough, and despite his reminders of her place, kept at him day and night, begging him to cross the border, saying, there's a chance there, maybe, oh I know the Depression is there, but my brother says the sawmills are still running, some of them, there's more there than here, here there's nothing! She held out her thin arm to make the point—not enough to eat, that was it. And her hand grazing her belly, all women did that, the argument of the belly that a man couldn't win. Her brother, who hovered over their talk like the ghost of an ancestor, had a job in a box mill in Maine. She wrote to him, asked if there was a chance at a job for Charles. Not much, came the answer, but maybe something part time. Maybe. If Charles wasn't choosy. He would have to take what was available, it was all a gamble, have to learn to talk American. They could stay in the brother's house for a few weeks.

Random

They crossed the winter border on a back road through the woods late at night. Her brother, Indian-looking face sour between wrenched smiles, was waiting on the other side, guided them to a nearby house to warm themselves for half an hour before the final leg of the journey—a hovel, really, a tiny fingernail of a stranger's house in the wastes of snow, the stovepipe shooting sparks into the night. They each drank a cup of bitter coffee, dirty children peeping from behind a torn blanket, and went on with the brother in a nail-sprung sled pulled by two horses.

Both Delphine and Charles found the dark cedar swamp through which they passed terrifying and immense. To Delphine the heavy scent from the trees was the smell of illness, of vapors and poultices, and the wind soughing through the needles was the sinister sound of the limitless forest. Charles recognized his brother-in-law's reluctance to have them, burned with humiliation that he had married into a half-breed family unknowingly. He whispered angrily to Delphine. She denied Indian blood, her brother was dark-complexioned, that's all. Beyond the shuddering exhalations of the horses, the squeaking thuds of hooves on the packed snow, the hissing pines, there was resentful silence.

The box mill

They tried to fit their lives into the place—the brother's crowded house, the rough commands in American and chopped-up French. As soon as they had enough money they rented a low-ceilinged shack lit by kerosene lamps. They took possession on a biting-cold day. Charles pushed open the door with his foot and stepped in, said *mais non!* and dropped his armful of stove wood. Delphine, behind him, carrying the baby, saw the decaying carcass of a dead hanged cat against the wall, the plaster clawed to the lath where it had struggled to escape.

Delphine chopped ice from the brook every morning and hauled water, slipping on the icy path, slamming into the kitchen drenched and weeping, swearing oaths that she would keep her children clean if it killed her. She was repulsed by the Irish family who lived out by the dump in a hut built of Triton Motor Oil cans, ignorant immigrants who sewed their children into their clothes in the autumn and peeled the gummed rags off in June.

A year passed, another, then two more and with the twins they had six children. They stayed in Random, afraid to make a move after Delphine's brother, whom Charles now called Chief Warbonnet, went to

Rhode Island to work in the woolen mills; some of his children were old enough to bring home a pay packet. So they were alone in the alien forest. Charles cursed the filthy, freezing, fly-infested country, was sick with longing for his old, lost life, the streets and the music, the wine. He cursed Jo Privat who had all the lucky breaks.

If hell was a great fiery-hot music hall, he thought, where untuned instruments scraped and shrieked in diabolic cacophony, all chaos and noise and maimed devils capering, then entering the box mill was like stepping into *l'inferne* through a side door. The machinery boomed and rattled, metal ground against screaming metal, moving belts roared overhead, the air filled with fine dust. One got used to it or left. The Yankee foreman watched him at his planing machine, the boards screeching through. Dollar and a half a day for fifteen hours of work and lucky to have it. Then he was too tired for anything but shoveling food into his mouth and sleep. But Saturday night he would drink and quarrel, then strike, then mount Delphine. It was, he said to her cruelly, just for relief. Only a blind man could desire her, a blind man with a clothespin on his nose and gloves on his hands, for she stank and her skin was as rough as that of a crocodile. It was necessary to show her he was someone to reckon with. On Sunday afternoon he killed his hangover with more whiskey—there was no wine in this lousy country—and at these times he got out the accordion and tried "Honeysuckle Rose" with fingers stiff from handling boards, dreaming of the clubs and the cobbles gleaming under the streetlights in the rain.

Random was proof of his black star. He had been duped and cheated all his days since his cursed mother had twisted the wire hangers tight to hold his arms at his sides and slapped him to the edge of the quay and into the greasy Seine, he had been forced to Québec where they masticated the language into a sodden porridge, tricked—yes, tricked and trapped by wily redskins—into an unsavory marriage, lured to Maine, a brutally provincial cul-de-sac, with false information. He had another proof in the spring of 1937 when the planer sheared off three fingers of his right hand, leaving the index finger partially severed and, in a few days, fat and green with infection. The doctor arrived at two in the morning and after a squinting look said the kerosene lamp was worthless and he couldn't see anything. He went out and drove his shock-sprung Buick up to the kitchen window and, in the headlight glare, examined the remaining finger.

"Got to come off."

Charles couldn't understand how it had happened; it had simply occurred in a moment indistinguishable from a million others that had passed safely.

He recovered slowly, his stubbed fingers a raw sensitive pink. They were on the dole, a box of food each week—weevily flour, a can of lard and a small sack of beans. The box mill folded suddenly and everyone was out of work, robbed of their last week's pay because the owner skipped with the money. Families slank away in the night, heading south to Woonsocket, Pawtucket, Manchester, for the mills of woolen, cotton, silk, shoes, where relatives already in place could help.

Charles cursed his life, and his morose nature, sanded to the quick by difficulties, exposed a sublayer of permanent rage. He tried once after the accident to play the accordion upside down and backward, with the left hand pressed into service, but his own clumsiness made him wild and he shoved *le maudit instrument* into the stove to punish it, crammed and hit with the poker, did it damage, but it wouldn't fit the firebox. Delphine yanked it out and threw it in the yard. Burning like that, it made too much smoke. In the morning she brought it in again, wrapped it in brown paper and put it on a shelf.

That winter Delphine walked in her sleep, walked barefoot in the snow. When she came back inside, her feet were like red wax, the hem of her nightdress clotted with frozen crystals. On a night of red snow under the aurora borealis Charles told her he was going down to Bangor the next day to look for work, that special job the one-handed man imagines. He left the shack early in the morning. By the end of the week she knew he was gone for good, back to France, with a life and a family and a half-learned language to forget. The baby, Dolor, was two years old.

(Back in France when the Second World War broke out, Charles acted as a courier for the Resistance, was seriously injured in a fall from his bicycle on a moonless night, yet crawled ten miles on hands and knees to deliver the message which was, after all, of little importance. He abruptly switched allegiance to the collaborationists, took part in anti-*zazou* raids, standing in the shadows outside swing nightclubs with his pair of clippers, eager to scalp the greasy pompadours of the callow, egotistical youths as they came out into the streets, exhausted from dancing "*J'ai un clou dans ma chaussure.*" Call that music? It wasn't jazz, that swing, nothing but noise, the dancers stupid with their popping eyes and snapping fingers, jerking their arms and leaping about like fleas on griddles. After the war he hung around nightclubs for years, running errands, sweeping out rest rooms in the predawn hours, enough for the six bottles of *vin blanc* he drank daily. In 1963 he was still working the clubs, still sweeping, and ended polishing faucets at the Golf Drouot Club, fell under a sink with a heart attack and died surrounded by the synthetic-stockinged ankles of a circle of young *yé-yé*s.)

What was she supposed to do? She wrote to her brother in Providence although she knew he had moved south not only for work but to get away from the burden of the Gagnon family. Then come on, he answered sourly. I'll send the money for the bus. But you can't bring all the children. Life is difficult for everyone. Only the two oldest. They can work. And you can take employment as well.

Birdnest

In Old Rattle Falls the finest building was Birdnest, an ornate mansion built for a nineteenth-century railroad baron, the facade crenellated and bow-windowed, topped with an octagonal widow's walk, fronted by a porte cochère and two immense Chinese urns, girdled by a twenty-foot-wide porch. In 1926 the town seized Birdnest for back taxes and turned it over to the county to be used as an orphanage. Those tall rooms papered with imported William Morris wallpaper, the ceilings worked in wedding-cake plaster, the carved linen-fold panels, stained glass, walnut banisters, the ballroom, all were converted and partitioned into orphanage appointments: dormitories furnished with metal beds, ballroom transformed into a potato-smelling cafeteria, parquet floor painted grey. Metal file cabinets crowded the breakfast room. The linen closet became a punishment cell. The gardens, designed by Calvert Vaux, turned rank and wild, with Virginia creeper smothering the ornamental trees, branches littered the marble stairs to the grotto, ash saplings crowded the flower beds, and the perennial bulbs were eaten by skunks.

He was two years old and at first he cried for the shack and the familiar smell of the wood stove and his mother's lean, hard hands, the sound of her nervous cough. Even at this time, barely out of infancy, hours of depression visited him when the only thing possible was to sleep or lie still with his eyes closed, inhaling, exhaling, breathing in, breathing out, in, out, slow, slow, slow.

His twin sisters, Lucette and Lucille, and an older brother, Lucien, were in another part of the building though he did not know it. He spent his days with the babies and toddlers, long, long hours in a wooden crib, in a row of cribs, each with its caged child, rocking, babbling, wailing, head-banging. Two women came in the early morning, changed diapers and bedding, handed out bottles of bluish milk, saying little and handling the children as though they were billets of firewood. Dolor had been weaned for a year but discovered the solace of the gummy rubber nipple. For a single hour in the morning the babies were carried into a large room—the morning room where the railroad baron's wife wrote her dull letters in post–Civil War times—and there put on a grimy square of carpet to play with wooden blocks so worn the corners were rounded and few traces of paint remained. Running was forbidden. The sound of French receded; all the new words were American. Sick children stayed in their crib prisons. Birdnest was a place of orphans and adult women. The only men who came there were the doctor, the county inspector, and once a month a Pentecostal minister who shouted Jesus, Jesus, until the youngest ones cried. The older children went to Sunday school in the church bus, a stubby green vehicle with canvas flaps on the sides, rolled up in summer, a wonderful outing. The bus creaked down the long hill and through the town past the SLOW sign changed to read VICTORY SPEED 35 MILES when the war began, and over the gravel road along the river. In the spring they gaped at the huge cakes of ice thrown up on the banks.

The population of the orphanage changed, a few children reclaimed by mothers or a mother's relatives. Fathers never came there. Some children went to the hospital, and some to the morgue. Some children were adopted, indeed Dolor himself was adopted for a few months when he was six, but the family decided to move south when the man got war work and returned him to the orphanage. They said he was a quiet child. What he remembered of the time with them was speckled chickens who ran forward when he threw handfuls of cracked corn on the ground, the smell of their hot, louse-crammed feathers and their clucking voices asking him questions in poultry language. He answered them with similar words. He also remembered the man of the house sitting at a player piano whose keys rose and fell by themselves as though an invisible musician sat in his lap, while he sang in a thick voice, "Oh bury me not . . ."

In school he was a small child on the edge of things, too timid to speak, hesitating even to stare or watch openly how others did things. He was fastened tightly into himself, sometimes made tiny smiles and nods over imagined conversations. The best thing was the *Weekly Reader,* a real little newspaper; it made him feel tremendously grown up to hold and read it. In Current Events he sat facing a cardboard sign, GIVE IT YOUR BEST. Sometimes he was allowed to fold the flag because he was quiet.

Birdnest was the first stop the school bus made, ten minutes from the school, so there was no reason to say anything to anyone, just file out of the bus with the grey bag the county gave each of them for books and lunch, and always, in front of him, walked a girl with blond braids tinted a strange green color on the ends where they had been dipped in the inkwell until the school district abandoned ink and everyone had to bring a ballpoint pen from home. Birdnest passed out pens that read *LeBlanc's Mortuary* on the side. Fat William, wheezing with asthma, often afflicted with earache, was his best friend in the fifth grade. The Birdnest children stuck together. On the bus there was an older boy whose pants were too short; the others called him Highwaters or Frenchie. He was always fighting and his nose ran.

"That guy's your brother, and he's bad," Fat William told Dolor, who began to watch for a sign of recognition, but Frenchie looked past and never said anything to him though he could speak French a mile a second and swear terrible curses, said Fat William, and then he wasn't on the bus anymore, gone, and no one knew where.

(The twin sisters, Lucette and Lucille, had been adopted their first year in Birdnest by a couple who moved to Rochester, New York. In 1947, Lucette, who sang "White Christmas" in a pure voice and suffered from a perplexing chronic skin disorder, entered the hospital where she was injected with plutonium in a secret medical experiment. In 1951 she died of leukemia. She was seventeen years old yet weighed only sixty-three pounds.)

After Fat William's worst asthma attack a lopsided woman appeared and claimed him as grandson; now the one Dolor watched was Winks, the school clown, a sore-eyed kid with curly, dirt-colored hair, two or three years ahead of him. Mugging, reeling and pretending he was drunk, making squeaking noises in class, tickling girls, rubbing his shoes on the floor and tapping nervously during tests, the pencil, his feet, fingertips all going at once, he was a one-man percussion section at the back of the class.

"Winks!" the teacher barked and he stopped for a few minutes, then started again.

Dolor stood behind him in the lunch line and as Winks turned and looked down the seething lunchroom, searching for a place to sit, Dolor saw chaos in his eyes, could see right through the thin circle of blue surrounding the distended pupil, examine a naked anxiety that repelled. He turned away, pretended interest in the cook's stainless-steel ladle and the orange gruel punctuated by minuscule cubes of turnip, but through his eyelashes watched Winks swagger down the aisle between the tables bopping kids on heads and shoulders, slopping his milk and going *pah, pah, pah, pah* with his mouth.

Standing in the back rows and holding silence did not save him. In the fourth grade the older boys fell upon his name.

"Hey, Dollar! You must be rich! Give me some money!"

"Doughnut! Hey, Doughnut, how's your hole!"

Mrs. Breath, the director of Birdnest, tapped her fountain pen on a note from the school.

"You know, I think it would be better for you if you had a regular boy's name. Which do you prefer, Frank or Donald?"

"Frank," he whispered. And so he was renamed and another fragment of self fell away like a flake of rust.

A disappointing inheritance

When he was eighteen he finished Old Rattle Falls High School but did not go to the graduation ceremony. The thought of having to climb up the wooden steps, cross the stage and shake the principal's hand, then grasp the diploma, gave him a blinding headache, made his joints ache intolerably.

The mirror reflected an oval face, dark hair parted on the left, brown eyes under black bushy brows, a long nose with a slight bulb at the tip. His ears were well proportioned and set close to his head, the horizontal mouth somewhat full and unsmiling. He made himself smile, showed the crooked teeth, the high cheekbones and skin very pale under the black hair. An arrow of black hair descended his torso. He had neither photographs nor memories with which to compare his image, and he did not expect anything from anyone. He was free to leave Birdnest.

In the office, the steam radiator hissing despite the leaves still on the trees, Mrs. Breath gave him her good wishes and a large, awkward parcel wrapped in brown paper and tied with dark red cord. It was heavy.

"Yours," she said. "Personal belongings from when you first came here. It was in the storeroom." He blushed, did not want to open the package in front of her, believing in family letters and photographs never seen. She handed him a white envelope.

"Good luck, Frank."

On the bus to Portland he got a seat to himself in the back, opened the envelope, though he knew what was in it—a twenty-dollar bill and the standard Birdnest letter of good character on a sheet of paper decorated with the image of a bird bearing a writhing worm in its beak. He put the money and the letter in his new vinyl wallet. In the front of the bus a natty man, hair touched with grey, fingering his sandy, pockmarked face, got up and moved down the aisle testing different seats. He settled across the aisle from Dolor, pulled at the sleeves of his brown jacket.

"Don't want to sit with the sun in my eyes," he said to the window and began a pleasant, modulated conversation with himself. He spoke in a rapid southern accent. "Now I'll split it," he said. "Thank you, Inspector." A gold wristwatch with an expansion bracelet showed at his wrist. "I can offer you three hundred dollars. I'm taking this trip, this important trip and I don't know how it's going to come out. Hmmm, hired—hired?"

To keep from staring, Dolor got down the brown-paper parcel from the overhead rack and worried it open, carefully undoing the hard knot, its twists dark with dust, pulling the paper away gently, embarrassed by the way it crackled, made the southern man watch him.

He didn't know what to make of it. Nothing but a wrecked accordion, the wood case charred on one corner, the bellows torn open. Rows and rows of little buttons on one side and on the other black and white keys. The name "GAGNON" on the end looked as though it had been scratched in with a jackknife blade. An odor rushed up from it, the smell of softwood smoke and damp. A lousy burned accordion. Suddenly he heard his mother's cough, though he had not known she coughed until that minute. Now he was sure of it. Maybe she'd given him up because she was sick. He examined the instrument, the paper it was wrapped in, but there was no message, no note or photograph or letter, and his past remained unknown.

"I never smoke now," said the man in the brown jacket. "Never. I no longer drink."

In Portland Dolor got off the bus, walked to the army recruiting station. The back covers of *Double Detective* and *Weird* and *Argosy* all ran the same ad—HELP YOURSELF GET THE JOB YOU WANT IN THE ARMY. He carried the instrument, rewrapped in the brown paper, under his left arm. He gave his name as Dolor Gagnon, signed up for four years. It was 1954 and the job he wanted was television repair but the closest thing was electrician and they were full up. They put him in the quartermaster corps.

In some ways the army was like Birdnest: he did what he was told and kept out of the way. When they landed on him he never complained. He got through basic training by being quick and invisible, barely looking at the bigger men, the loudmouths and smart alecks who attracted the interest of sergeants as limping hesitation attracts predators. He was assigned to Germany.

"Be fuckin glad you got the Fräuleins instead of Frozen Chosen," drawled the sergeant standing behind him. "Be goddamn glad you didn't have to go to Korea. There was nothin worse than Korea. Guys froze solid standin up."

All around him men talked of getting married when they got back home. Everyone had a photograph in a wallet, girls, girls, looking the same with their rolled-under shining hair and deep-colored lips, the pastel sweaters and the distant tender gazes. He found one of these photographs in the pages of a book from the base library and kept it in his wallet. The girl looked Swedish, with crayon-yellow hair and protruding blue eyes. He invented a name for her, "Francine," he would say, "that's Francine, we're getting married when I get back, she's a kindergarten teacher."

In Germany he took the wrecked accordion to an elderly man in a cold, dark hole of a repair shop. The man was as thin as a sheet of cardboard, beside him slouched a young girl with a ferret face and lipstick although she was not more than ten or eleven. The girl watched the old man attentively as he examined Dolor's accordion.

"*Französisch. Sehen Sie hier?*" Pointed to the metal crest. *Maugein Frères—les accordéons de France.* His nasal voice sounded as though he were close to weeping.

"How much to fix it?" muttered Dolor. "*Wie viele?*" The old man did not answer, shook his head, pointed at the burned wood, the scorched buttons, gently stretched the cracked and torn bellows. He touched the brittle folds.

"*Diese Plisseefalten . . .*" He leaned over and talked to the child in his sadness.

She looked at Dolor. "He says he cannot repair this, all the folding parts must be new, he cannot get the right kind of wood for the end, the keys are ruined, it is burned, you see, and even if it is new it is not good. French accordions are not good. You must buy a German accordion, these are the best ones. He will sell you one."

"Naw," he said, "I guess not. I don't even know how to play it, I just wanted to know if it could be fixed." It was the only thing he had. The old man didn't wrap it up again and he left the shop with the paper loose around it, trailing string and the smell of burn. Back in the barracks he separated the end piece engraved "GAGNON" from the instrument and threw the rest away. He, too, had a passion for cutting his name or initials in everything he owned.

A few weeks later in the damp German spring he caught a cold which developed into pneumonia. The illness ebbed from his lungs, seemed to shift to his legs. He was in the base hospital for two months, wobbling around half paralyzed, a cane in each hand, sucking air through his teeth with the pain.

"Frankly, it may be paralytic poliomyelitis," a doctor with a pointed mole on his right nostril said. "I see they gave you this new vaccine, this Salk vaccine, when you were inducted, but who really knows how efficacious it will prove to be?" Gradually he recovered, but the same doctor said he was unfit for active duty and after a year and a half in the army he limped out on a medical discharge in the summer of 1955.

The taxicab

He was supposed to get a plane to Boston, then catch a train to Portland where he would be processed out, but the plane landed in New York and seven hours later when they gave him his new ticket he tangled up with a parade of kids in red, white and blue costumes and moved into the second leg of the mistake, dodging a boy disguised with a paper Uncle Sam beard and a tall blue hat pasted over with stars, getting away from the acned girl with a sign on her breast, AMERICA FIRST, he somehow boarded a civilian flight heading, not for Boston, but for Minneapolis. He sat next to a woman in a polka-dot blouse that reeked of dye and underarm odor.

"You dumb shit," said a sergeant at the recruiting booth in Minneapolis when Dolor turned up, nervously showing his travel orders and asking for help. "Didn't you see at the gate it said Minneapolis? Can't you read the word Minneapolis? Is that word too big for you to read? Did you think it said Marmalade or Mystery Booth?" He made telephone calls, letting Dolor stand there, shifting from one foot to the other.

"I thought they were going by way of Boston. I thought they'd stop at Boston. The girl didn't say nothing when she took the ticket."

"You thought so. Yeah, that makes a lot of sense, don't it, go to Minneapolis by way of Boston. Like Los Angeles by way of Singapore. What a moron. OK, here's what you do. You're gonna stay in a hotel, here's a chit, the Hotel Page on Spivey, and I will personally see you get to Boston. Don't expect no cushy civvy plane, soldier. You are going on the dirt-bag train at nine ayem *mañana.* You be right here where you're standing right now at eight tomorrow morning. I'm afraid you might see the Boston sign and think it says Bingo."

He walked around for a while, taking in the city. There was a black man on Prairie Avenue playing an alto sax, "I Left My Heart in San Francisco," the instrument case open, some quarters and halves lying on the blue crushed velvet. It sounded good. He threw in two dimes and a nickel. The guy didn't even look at him.

He ate at Happy Joe's Café, lured by the sign in the window, "It's Air

Conditioned COOLER Inside," ordered the special and got some kind of strange food, little meat dumplings and steamed cabbage with white sauce and plenty of bread, the custard pie dessert, all for sixty cents. There wasn't any point in going to the hotel until he had to, so he drank two beers in a place where they spoke a foreign language, he guessed Polish, but it was a good place and the beer was cheap, then he found a movie palace, gilt and marble inside, where *Seven Samurai* was playing. He sat in the dark eating licorice. He didn't understand half the action because the subtitles were hard to read, and it was funny as hell to hear the actors spouting Japanese. He left halfway through the film and went across the street to see *The Killer Shrews,* decided it was the worst movie he'd ever seen, blamed it on Minneapolis.

When he came out of the movie into night, the neon blue and yellow of a café, a woman in a clear plastic raincoat, carrying a spray of ferns, her white shoes flashing over the sidewalk, the shine of trolley tracks and stoplights reflected in windshields dazzled him. He heard music crisscrossing in the street, slow piano like a dripping faucet, a snare drum. The hotel was twenty-seven blocks away. He was dog-tired after two days on planes and the mix-up and hauling his duffel bag around, but he started walking. The streets were swarming with people—midnight kids on junk bikes, a blind woman led by a dog, a man whose suitcase pulled his shoulder down, black people. After two blocks he saw the same saxophone player on the sidewalk ahead of him and somehow he didn't want to pass him again. His legs hurt. The guy was still playing "I Left My Heart in San Francisco." Probably the only song he knew. He held up his arm for a taxi and, although he waited for a long time, caught one as it pulled away from a hotel back up the block.

There was something on the floor of the cab, a kind of case, an overnight case. Furtively he seized the handle. When he got out of the cab at the Hotel Page, a dump of a place, he carried his duffel bag and the case, telling himself if it had the owner's name in it he would call the guy up and say, I found your overnight in the taxi, and the guy would maybe offer a reward. Or if it was a woman's suitcase, he'd call her up and she'd say, why don't you bring it to such and such an address, we'll have a drink, you're very nice to call, and she would live in a beautiful apartment with white rugs and he would miss the train. He couldn't believe what he found. Another goddamn accordion, like it was a message from God, or something. For something to do, he spent an hour with a nail file picking out the glass rubies that formed the letters *AR* and scratching "GAGNON" in the wood while he watched *The U.S. Steel Hour,* some army show about sergeants, on the hotel's dinky metal

TV, a round seven-inch screen, like looking out of a porthole in a storm. The sound was bad and he couldn't get the gist of the action, ended up watching the ads for Breast o' Chicken tuna and Winston cigarettes.

Maine

In Maine again, he spent a few days in Augusta trying to get a copy of his birth certificate, bought a used Chevrolet truck, a secondhand RCA with a twelve-inch screen, though he really wanted one of the new portables, then headed up to Random. The birth certificate did not say much. The date. Both parents from Canada. His father, Charles Gagnon, had been twenty-nine, his mother, Delphine Lachance, twenty-eight. Five living children before him. His birth weight, six pounds, one ounce. That was all.

Through the rain-streeled windshield, Maine appeared as alternating plats of spruce, slash and clear-cut, withered acres of poplar and cherry, rolled-up leaves like charred scraps of paper on the defoliated trees, dark, too, with rain, and roadside moose the shade of old butternut husks, darkness unrelieved by whatever pale strip the sky unrolled, the crippled rivers and chains of lakes bordered by tattered horizons. He drove over a maze of roads that circled, looped, crossed and recrossed.

Back on the edge of the slash he saw tar-paper shacks and churches with hand-painted signs nailed to skinned poles—Church of Christ Coming Again, Church of Redeeming Grace, Church of New Faith, Temple of Christian Beliefs and Practices, Church of the Big Woods, Sanctuary of the Last Times—set among pale sand and gravel quarries, among the shattered trees, a stipple of mauve clouds like petechiae against a flesh-colored horizon. He would have to be careful.

The stranger in his birthplace

He did not expect to recognize anything. He knew only that Random was situated between woods and potato fields and that he had been born here. The light in this place was the first light he had seen after the blindness of the womb. His eyes kept filling with tears. He felt he might be slipping back into an archaic time when clans roved the forests and he was running along behind them, belonging with them, yet an outsider. He felt the somber light, the black softwood and the sound of rivers from the earth's core rolling over rock. He passed a stumpy clearing where there were three or four old trucks with homemade plywood caps built into the back beds, a woman in a gypsy skirt placing a stick on the red fire.

Random was a small town with two general stores, a post office, a café, a garage, school. No one knew him, but he began to study their faces and learn their names. He liked the peculiar dullness of the buildings with their film of age, the evocative smell of spruce and potato dirt, the vague roads that petered out in the slash.

North of town another road branched off through the bog holes. At the junction he saw the Esso station and the Pelkys' clapboard farmhouse, the ell divided into four apartments, two up, two down, in the distance a barn against a wall of black spruce.

"Mr. Pelky raised potatoes—we had one of the biggest potato farms in Random County—but you know how it is, you get older and your kids is all somewheres else. He fell off the tractor two years ago and the tractor runned right over his head, made him lose his mind for six months, but gradual he's got it back and he's as good as anybody now, but they say he can't farm no more, so we fixed this up for apartments." Mrs. Pelky wiped the checked plastic tablecloth as she talked to him, pushed the salt and pepper shakers into the central position. Her aquamarine eyes winked behind plastic harlequin glasses. Her green housedress was printed with yellow sombreros. "Home-cooked breakfast goes with it. I hope you got adventure in your heart. Like I tell Mr. Pelky, I can't stand to cook the same old thing every day. Mr. Roddy rents a unit but he don't take the breakfast, goes into town and eats a greasy mess at the diner." The linoleum was a crazy pattern of many colors, the wallpaper a jungle of poppies and elephant ears. Mrs. Pelky sang her little song, " '. . . *des bottes noires pour le travail et des rouges pour la danse* . . .' now, if you want furniture and you don't mind used, there's secondhand in the barn up the road, that used to be our barn but we sold it to the Dentist. If you can stand the Dentist, the dirty old thing. He's like some of those old men get, you know what I mean." With a piece of cheese she coaxed her little dog to sit up and beg, told Dolor another dog, even more enchanting than this one, had been seized the year before as he stood near the fence, leg lifted, by an Arctic owl which carried him off in the moonlight.

His apartment was on the ground floor, two long rooms with sloping wooden floors, the flyspecked windows looking into a straggle of spruce. He stood in the kitchenette taking in his gas burners, the tiny refrigerator no higher than his knees, a white enamel table and mismatched chairs with chrome legs. There was a metal bed in one room and on certain evenings the sound of Liberace came through the walls.

Every morning Mrs. Pelky labored to his door on her bad ankles with a plate of curious cookery: Orange Buds, Pork Fruit Cake, Deviled Clams and Bean Mash, Lentil Loaf, or The Poor Man's Omelet—bread sopped in hot milk. Her passion was experimentation. She clipped recipes from the papers, pasted them into her "cookbook," a turn-of-the-century salesman's catalog for soda-water apparatus; the recipes obscured photographs of fabulous machines in onyx, red-veined Breccia Sanguinia and Alps Green marbles with gleaming spigots and ornate woodwork and German-silver labels for the sirops. From behind the luteous clips for "Appetizing Relish" and "Egyptian Stew" peeped the gas-lit Ambassador, the Autocrat with twelve spigots and double-stream soda-draught arms. He ate everything she brought him for it was better than his own strange combinations, a peach and kale sandwich, macaroni and vinegar, canned salmon and rat cheese.

He needed some shelves, a bookcase, an easy chair, a dish cupboard. He steered toward the secondhand furniture barn and saw hulking figures in the yard, immense naked women twelve feet high, carved of wood and with breasts like watermelons, pubic triangles the size of pennants, staring eyes and glistening hair, painted in exterior enamels. They stood among wooden cacti with nails for spines and plywood spruce trees. Inside he examined basins and two-gallon coffeepots, rusted calipers and axe heads with broken helves still filling the eyes, bucksaws and crosscuts, wedges, scratching awls, snatch blocks and snow knockers from old lumber-camp days.

The Dentist was bandy-legged and filthy-mouthed, his words drenched in brown tobacco spit. "How do you like them babes I got out front? That's my hobby, carvin women. Don't know who I am, do you?"

"The one they call the Dentist."

"Call me the Dentist? Why, they call me *everthing* from a two-handled devil to a three-legged bastard to a four-eyed fool. Some call me Squint, short for Squint-Eye. When they don't call me *Dentist,* 'cause I was the fuckin *filer,* filed the saw teeth. Ain't a fuckin son of a bitsie *left* knows the difference between a goddamn tuttle tooth and a sterling tooth, goddamn scissorbills cannot find their *eyes* in the sockets." He had worked in the woods in the old days, out to the Pacific and back, and the only people who mattered to him were dead men, men whose exploits and scars could never be equaled by the soft maggots of the contemporary woods.

Dolor bought two chairs and a small table from him, a chest of drawers with wooden thread spools for knobs. The chairs were upright, with cracked wooden seats that pinched his ass, but if he wanted comfort he could always lie down on the bed. At night he wished Francine were with him, forgetting for long moments that he had invented her; he'd thrown away the photograph in Minneapolis. He listened to the radio, it was better than the TV late at night, the distant hillbilly music and sermons and promises of cures from the wildcat border stations down in Mexico—funny their signal could reach all the way to Maine—offers for weight-loss tonics, pills to make you put on pounds, plastic broncos, moon pens, zircon rings, Yellow Boy fishing lures, apron patterns, twelve styles for just one dollar, rat-killer and polystyrene gravestones, send no money, send your name and address in care of this station, less than a penny a capsule, for each order received before December 15 you'll receive in addition, absolutely free, while this special offer lasts, insist on the genuine, prosperity, plain brown sealed wrapper, a package containing rigidly inspected pharmaceuticals, if you are nervous and wakeful at night. He never felt the voices were directed at him, but at all the silent millions out there lying in their beds unable to sleep, needing Restall and switchblade knives to end their suffering. He was not one of them, only eavesdropping, until he heard Dr. Bidlatter one night say, in his deep, comforting, fatherly voice, "trying in vain to get help for your physical or emotional problems? Are you unhappy? Are you depressed, anxious, fearful? Are you lonely? Have you been told 'it's all in your head' or 'there's nothing wrong with you, forget it, take a vacation, quit your job, move to the sunbelt, get a divorce'? If so, you may benefit from hypnosis and behavior modification. Call 462-6666 today for a consultation with Dr. Bidlatter." He wrote the number down but never called.

He'd filled out a little in the army, still not big, but wiry and well knit, supple and with a good sense of balance. He thought about trying for the forestry service through the G.I. Bill, but took a job as a limber in a small logging operation, Parfait Logging & Haulage. Through the autumn and into the winter he worked, bent over the felled trees with his chain saw, cutting limb after limb, hauling them to brush piles, monotonous, physically difficult work, his clothes covered with pitch and bark dust, but except for the chain saw exhaust, work done in the midst of resinous fragrance. He saved his money, ate at the café where gradually they recognized him, then knew his name, and finally heard that he had been born in Random but taken away as a baby, that he didn't know the whereabouts of any living member of his family.

"So you might say you're a stranger in your hometown," said Maurice, the cook, waiter, janitor, but not the owner. His wife, Jeanette, was the owner and he was just an employee, just a humble oppressed employee with a mop or a spatula, until deer season when he metamorphosed into a hunter with a lethally crooked finger. But neither Maurice nor anyone else remembered Dolor's parents. The family had lived in the township, he had been born there, they had made no mark.

In December, after a light fall of snow, the wind came out of the south, the temperature rose into the forties and suddenly the air was charged with an ineffable sweetness, a perfume as of invisible flowers. Was it some fragrance borne on the wind from the tropics, or the held breath of summer released by the untimely snowmelt? It persisted three days and then disappeared as a cold air mass seeped down from the Arctic and new snow fell, rinsing the air of all scent, covering the decaying leaves and raw earth, the single leaf of the grass-pink, sprawling woodbine like a dark violet wire among the rocks, the increasing white weight matting ebony spleenwort, pulling down the plumes of faded goldenrod.

On weekends Dolor didn't know where to go, and kept himself company reading *True Adventure* and *Detective Stories* and carving a naked girl on a pine board, sure he could do better than the Dentist's colossal women, or watching TV. The only thing to do in Random was get drunk at the bar or drive around trying to get stuck in a beaver wash.

There was a night when the old Dentist came crashing in, ricocheting between the walls, slam, scrape, hung on the doorknob making a trilling sound and calling "Mr. Gagnon, why *don't* you answer your goddamn fuckin doorbell," until Dolor opened the door and looked at him.

"Only the Dentist come in for a *little* drink," he said, in his withered arms a brown paper bag of beer bottles, in his pants pocket a new pint of cheap whiskey, in his hand another, half gone. Dolor steered him to one of the chairs.

"Think I'm kegged up, don't you? No, I'm *not* kegged up or you'd know it."

The Dentist looked at the ceiling, the shelves on the wall, the half-carved deer head, into the corners of the room, nodded at the instrument case at the foot of the bed.

"There's a 'cordeen for you, ain't it?" He took a drink.

"Remember that short staker come *through* one winter? Couple of weeks and he was *gone,* but the tunes he knew, son-of-a-bitchen bastard knew a hundred of songs, made them out of his head. Played the *squeezebox* 'cordeen and sang like a dog with his nuts in a wringer. Suppose you want to hear me do a goddamn one of 'em?"

"Go ahead," said Dolor.

The old man folded his arms across his chest, one foot beat time loudly, and he began to sing in a strong and amazingly loud voice although he barely opened his mouth.

> *"Oh loggers come and sit by me—*
> *Here's my little 'cordeen 'pon my knee.*
> *I'll sing to you of Danny's game*
> *And how he come to his end up in Maine*
> *On the bold Penobscot, the Penobscot cold."*

The steady voice grew louder and harder as he sang, the lines thrusting into the room like pike poles. Although it was singing, it was speaking as well, a kind of commanding and rhythmic recitation that pulled a listener inside the singer, straight into the old woods, the clink of log chains and snorting horses, the creak of laden sleds.

> *"His age was only twenty-two,*
> *His wife and child was almost new.*
> *He had a trick so slick and smooth*
> *When it was done there was no proof.*
> *On the bold Penobscot, the Penobscot cold."*

He stopped singing and drank whiskey, did not resume the song. When Dolor asked him to go on, he claimed he'd never sung a note in his life, what was on the TV tonight, weren't it the night for *Dragnet*? But they got Myron Floren playing "Tico Tico" on the Lawrence Welk show and the Dentist made gagging sounds.

"I wouldn't buy no Dodge," said the Dentist, "unless it was one of them Power Wagons."

You Are My Sunshine

One of the skidder operators kept looking at him, came up to him on a payday Friday. He was a tall, stoop-shouldered man with light eyes, hair cut in a duck's-ass style, gleaming with Brylcreem.

"You know somethin, pretty sure I remember you. Yeah, I remember you. Couple years behind me. I was at Birdnest when you was. I know you was there. You're Frank. I remember you, the way you'd duck out of sight when there was somethin goin on. I was put there after my fuckin folks got killed on the bridge, comin across that bridge right down the hill in town. Guess my old man was drunk. They tell me he drank a lot. The cops was chasin them and they crashed. Right through the rail into the river. Guess they're still down there. They couldn't get them up. Never found them. Current's too strong. I often thought how it would be to dive down there, look around. Maybe there's somethin of them's still down there, a watch or a wallet under a rock. I fish in there, put a big sinker on and a bare hook, see if I can get a hook into my dad's wallet. But so far no luck."

Dolor looked at him, at the bony face, ears like urn handles and a nose wedged between wide-staring dilute blue eyes and an upper lip that arched tightly, gave his mouth the shape of a croquet hoop. His coarse hair was thicker than grass. There was a scar like a sickle on his right cheek where a fragment of metal broke from the edge of his axe on a cold morning splitting wood for his kitchen stove.

"I got that last winter; my foreman seen it, he says 'two things you never wanna do, and one you *do* wanna do—never grin' down your blade fine, and never leave her out all night so she gets brittle. And the best thing you can do for a cut is let a dog lick it.' Suppose he thought I was gonna let a dog slobber all over my face."

Dolor didn't remember him. He shook his head, shrugged and smiled.

"Yeah, you remember *me*. Wilfred Ballou. Watch this." He crossed and uncrossed his legs and his arms rapidly, writhed his face through maniac expressions, his feet tapped and shot out, knees bent, a rubbery burr from his flabbering tongue, his ears went up and down.

Dolor laughed. "Winky. Winks. Jesus. Yeah, course I remember. You used to get in trouble with Mrs. Breath. We'd go past the office and see you in there like headed to the electric chair."

"Wilf, not Winks. Hated that damn name *Winks*. Hey, I met a guy once was *really* going to the electric chair. I got in some trouble after I left damn old Birdnest, they give me a choice, join the marines or go to jail, this was '52, the choice wasn't too great because if I joined up I'd probably be on my way to Korea. Anyway, they told me to think about it overnight in the county jail, and there was this guy in there that had just killed his brother over a woman. They both wanted the same woman. Later on he got it, he got the chair."

"Which did you pick?"

"Oh, I joined the marines. I went to Korea. See this?" He unbuckled his belt and pulled down his pants, presented his left buttock where Dolor saw a fist-sized depression, a mass of fibrous scar. "That's my souvenir. Man, that was my ticket home. When I got rehabbed and got so I could walk good again, went to Old Rattle Falls, got a job in construction, met Emma, my wife. She comes from up around here, comes from Honk Lake originally. She got family all around here, so we moved up. So what are you doing here?"

"Born here. My people left a long time ago. And I was in the army. In Germany." Dolor didn't know what else to say.

"They say you play the 'cordion."

"Get out! Where'd you hear that?"

"My wife's aunt and uncle. The Pelkys. You rent from them. They hear you. They say you got a long way to go. They say you're pretty bad."

He blushed furiously. "I don't know nothing about it. I just fool with it. I found it in a taxi when I got out of the army. My father used to play the accordion—not this one, another one, with like piano keys. It got burnt up in a fire when I was a baby. He saved us kids but his accordion was ruined and he lost his life. That's how come I was at Birdnest. I just, you know, fool with the accordion. I don't know how to play it."

"Bullshit! I had a dollar every time I heard that story I'd be drivin a Cadillac. Every kid in Birdnest used to say the same thing—dad got killed saving them from drowning or from a fire or a car wreck. Dad run off, that's what. Ain't that right?"

"I don't know. I was too little to know anything. Anyway, his accordion was burned up pretty bad, so there was a fire."

"Well, my old man died because he was so drunk he couldn't stay on the road and he killed my mother with him and if he was alive instead of dead I'd kill him myself for what he done. I wish you did play that 'cordion. This'll knock you on your can—I play the fiddle. You believe that? I'm not much to listen to yet, but we got no mice in our house. Emma's dad plays the fiddle. He's pretty good if you like cowboy songs, that Grand Ol' Opry stuff. Say what, you ought to practice up with that 'cordion. Anyway, come over to my place we'll drink a few beers. One thing about livin around here, they love two things—music and likker. God, how they love them things. And dancin. There's a dance every Friday at the Yvette Sparks Center."

He put it off for a month. When he did get around to driving over, it was without the accordion. The kitchen was very small and clean, with curtains at the window, a wedding photo of Emma and Wilf in a round frame, salt and pepper shakers in the form of windmills. The calendar was fixed to the wall with a green-headed thumbtack and a chromo of Jesus with his raw heart like something from a meat counter hung over the refrigerator. He leaned on Emma's table and listened to Wilfred saw the fiddle.

"Jesus, Wilf, I can't even play, but I can make a better noise than that," he said. "I never heard nothing so rotten."

The next time he went to Millinocket he got an instruction book for the button accordion at Yip-I-O Music and, after ten days of sweat and fumbling and cursing, learned to play "You Are My Sunshine" and sing it at the same time, which was like patting his head and rubbing his stomach. He put some money down for a record player that took the new long-playing records, thinner than a coin, made of some jaw-breaker plastic, polyvinyl chloride.

Wilf and Emma watched him open the accordion case. "OK," he said, "you asked for it, and here it is." By the time he got to the refrain, Wilfred sawed in, playing his rosiny fiddle by ear. They were rescued from their own ineptitude by the astonishing sound the instruments made together, a rich and wonderful sound. "Fuckin greasily bears," said Wilf. "It would sound *good* if we knew how to play the damn things. That's a nice little 'cordion you got there."

Pulp truck

That winter on Saturday nights he drove over to their place; his suffering truck broke down often enough so that half the time he hoofed it, snow or sleet in the face, or deep cold icing the hairs inside his nostrils, making his teeth ache and his hand go numb where the strap of the case bit in, and over his shoulder a feed sack with six quart bottles of beer that would be half frozen by the time he got there. The accordion had to warm up for an hour on a chair in their kitchen before he could play it. Emma was always a little dressed up, her hair curled and rouge on her cheeks, like she was going out on a date. She wore a dress with a big circle skirt; her brown and white spectator pumps and those high heels did make a kind of festive feeling for all of them. He and Wilf drank beer and talked about the days at Birdnest as if they had been good times, while Emma fixed supper, some kind of special dish, had a glass or two of beer in an old amber glass dimpled with dots that had come to her after her grandmother died. Dolor left a five-dollar bill under his plate, his kick-in for the casserole or the Pork 'n Pineapple or Curried Tuna Surprise she fixed from the *Betty Crocker Cookbook*.

"I don't cook that old French stuff my mother cooks, *ployes,* and baked beans take three days, them old *tourtières.*"

If he got too drunk he slept on their ratty couch, covered with a Frenchie quilt.

When she went to the woodbox in the entry, Dolor said, you're lucky, Wilf, got yourself a good wife, a kid.

"It ain't that hard, Dolor. First you find a girl, then you get married, you get the kids with three box tops and puttin it to the old lady regular—" and shut up when Emma came back in, kicking the door shut with her foot and stuffing the chunks into the firebox, pounding a big one with the lid-lifter until it dropped down. She'd heard what he said. "You watch your big dirty mouth," she said. "Or you might start missin it regular." Dolor didn't know whether to laugh or keep quiet. Emma sat down at the table. "You know what your name means?" she said to him.

"No, what?"

"Irregular," said Wilf.

"You won't get none now," said Emma, but to Dolor she added, "*Douleur*—pain. *J'ai une douleur dans les jambes*—my legs hurt."

"That's the truth," he said. "They do hurt."

"More like *j'ai une douleur* in the ass," said Wilfred.

Around nine o'clock they got going with the music, the kid asleep, Emma putting the last dish away, getting her tambourine out of the closet, the head blackened by striking fingers. Wilf tuned his fiddle, the familiar bending notes as the tightening strings sought E and A and D and G, the accordion took in warm breath and at last expelled such a sonorous chord that the kitchen shook with it, the beer trembled in their glasses. They warmed up with "Smiles," "My Blue Heaven," "Little Brown Jug" and Dolor's standby, "You Are My Sunshine," then tried whatever Wilfred had worked out from listening to the radio, "Get Out of Here," "Kansas City," and "Dance with Me, Henry," similar but not the same, twisted around to what he could play, and Dolor followed along, sometimes guessing wrong, but it sounded pretty good and it was getting better.

By summer, when the long evenings kept them out on the porch playing and slapping mosquitoes and drinking, they had two dozen songs, hillbilly, popular, a hymn for Sunday morning. Once in a while they didn't play but hit the dance down at the motel lounge in Random where a local band, The Saw Gang, played "Purple People Eater" five or six times, loud and fast, the dancers crowding around a tub of ice and beer between sets.

"Hell, we sound as good as them," said Wilf. "That's just crap they're playing."

"We're better." Though Dolor saw what dancers needed, a forceful steady rhythm that made them hop and kick when they were half dead.

In 1957 Wilfred quit Parfait Logging and started driving a St. Cloud pulp truck from Maine over to New York State, sometimes down to Massachusetts. When he got a chance he'd hit the music stores in different towns, pick up new records. He got a ten-inch record in a sleeve showing three men in weird masks wrestling an alligator—*Mardi Gras with Cajun Bill and His Honeybears.* They listened a couple of times. Wilf took up his bow and tried to follow the music but it was too much, and Emma, in capri pants and ballerina shoes, hands clasped before her on the oilcloth-covered table, caught French shreds of the songs and repeated them, "... *acheter du coton jaune* ... *à bal chez Joe* ... *'coute toi-même* ..." but shut up when cries and gasps of sorrow came from under the needle. When the record ended, Dolor went at what he'd heard, threw himself at the double time, but he got only a little of it. They did better with popular songs and once in a while some country-western.

Emma, short and rumpy, dark circles under her eyes, said, seems funny, you being French but can't talk it.

"Yeah." He knew all about how funny it was, his name taken from him, the language lost, his religion changed, the past unknown, the person he had been for the first two years of life erased. He saw how a family held its members' identities as a cup holds water. The person he had been as a child, a French-speaking boy with a mother and father, brothers and sisters, had been dissolved by the acid of circumstance and accident. He was still that person. He would return someday, like an insect cracking out of its winter case, he would wake speaking, thinking in French, a joyous man with many friends, his lost family would come back. And he always saw this transformation occurring in a warm room dominated by a wood-burning stove. There was a blue door and someone coughed. In French.

French music is hard to find

"Hey, you know, Wilf, the songs we're tryin to play—I don't know what it is, but that ain't what I want. There's a kind of music I want to play but I don't know what it is. What are we messing around with? Stuff off the radio, 'Michael Row the Boat Ashore,' 'Tom Dooley.' Folk music. It's like it isn't real music. It's somebody else's, you know what I mean?"

"I thought you liked the Kingston Trio. We spent two months trying to work out 'Scotch and Soda.' What do you want to do, 'Surfin'? How about a little rock 'n' roll, a little 'Blue Suede Shoes'? You like that Pelvis Presley? *'Ah-ha wah-ha-hant yew-hoo!'* Hey, did you see that movie *Blue Hawaii*? What a load of shit that was. Or how about some blues? Or them Lawrence Welk bubbles? *Bluh bluh bluh bluh.* Hope to Jesus not. I don't want to play that stuff."

"No, no, no. Look, is there such a thing as French music? I mean, is there a kind of music that's like, French? I mean, the Frenchies around here?"

"I don't know. Emma! There such a thing as Frenchie music?"

"Yeah. *Ouai*." Her voice came from the kid's room. "It's all a bunch of old-time *gigues* and reels for dancing. There's nobody around here that does it no more. You got to go up to Québec probably. If they still do it up there. Fiddle music, piano, accordion. You ought to ask my dad. That's the kind of music he used to play. He's got all them old seventy-eights, Starr records—I remember that '*Reel du pendu*,' the hanged man. He must have fifty, sixty them old things. Sometimes when he feels like it he plays a little. But not so much now."

"And there's that Cajun stuff," Wilfred said. "That's French. But Jesus, I can't sing like that, sounds like your guts are being pulled out with the pliers. You want to try workin up one of those? '*Jole Blon*,' maybe? There's a new Jimmy Newman album out, *Folksongs of the Bayou*, I heard a cut on the radio the other day, some New Hampshire station, but I couldn't play that fiddlin style if you put a blowtorch on me. It's mournful stuff, but real tricky at the same time. You know what we ought to do is get out of here, get out of the kitchen and go listen to what they're playin around here, you know, around Random, Millinocket, there's roadhouses on Route Thirty. Hit a few bars maybe, where they got live music. We need to get out of the kitchen." He was flipping through the new *Playboy*, half listening for Emma coming down the hall, Emma who would say, get out of here? You been out all week. Try staying home for a change.

"We could do that."

The bedroom door hinge groaned and he shoved the magazine in Dolor's accordion case.

Getting out

Emma's father, who was a weekend gunsmith and held his fiddle to his shoulder like a rifle, turned down the volume on *Maverick*, said he'd taken all the old Starrs to the dump four or five years before. They had hurled them into the air and shot them with the bird gun.

"Oh, it was a lot of fun. Those old things, they was wore out. But some great music. I use to know it all, how I learned. LaMadelaine, everybody had his records—boy, he could hypnotize you. He come out of the woods, learned fiddle from his father—that old-fashioned sound. Traditional, *hein*? But Soucy, he was a genius. Nobody ever played like him, not even this guy they got playing now, Jean Carignan? Why I switch to hillbilly. There's too many good ones up there. Then the accordion come in strong, so I got interested in that, learned to play a little. In the old days we use to have kitchen parties, everybody come, dance, but the new new houses, the ranch houses? The rooms are too small. So you got to hire a hall, go out to a hall or something got enough room."

Dolor tried to imagine the old music.

The next Saturday night they got dressed up, big jackets, Wilf in a pink shirt half unbuttoned, Dolor in black, and tried the bars in Bertrandville. Emma couldn't get a baby-sitter and had to stay home. At the North Star, there was a guitar player moaning over "The Tennessee Waltz." They ordered Bud.

"How about country music? Remember that night we tried to get 'Abilene' goin? It sounded pretty good."

"Yeah, maybe." The guitar player was mauling "Which One Is to Blame?"

"Christ, the guitar's a stupid fuckin thing."

They went down the street to a neon sign that first winked COCK-TAILS, then became a stemmed glass with a green and red olive. Inside they ordered whiskey sours which sounded sophisticated and went with the music, a tenor sax, an organ and a bald black man from somewhere else stroking brushes on his drumheads and shaking his head as if he couldn't believe he was in Maine. When they left, the street was empty but the signs flickered, and they kept hitting the bars. The sleeve of Dolor's new duffel coat caught on a protruding nail and the fabric tore.

Dolor overheard bits and pieces of French fly past him.

"*Je m'en crisse!*"

"*Mange de la marde!*"After a while he had the feeling he could speak French and tried French-sounding words, but it was like talking to the chickens: the tone was there but without meaning. Wilf's submerged side slowly came up under the influence of whiskey until he was in a homicidal mood. Dolor remembered the crazy-eyed Winks with his lunch tray.

"I hate drivin that goddamn truck," he screamed and started to punch faces, tore at coats on the backs of strangers and chopped at their necks with the edge of his hand, tried to gouge and bite. Dolor got him back to Random, the truck veering over the road and swaying toward trees and other headlights, wrestled him into the house. Emma gave him a cold eye and said, I hope you're satisfied.

"It wasn't much of an idea, I guess." He wanted to jump her.

Maybe the wildest time they had was on a snowy March night when the Penobnocket radio station announced it had stuffed five thousand dollars in a Coke bottle and hidden it somewhere in town. Men, women and children came from a hundred miles around, spent two days shoveling snow and searching motel rooms, tearing booths out of taverns, invading the courthouse, the post office, garages and the Extension Service office, ganging into the radio station itself, until the state police called everything off and sent them all home. Wilf heard later that the bottle had been hidden in the locked trunk of the station owner's car. Who could find that? He refused to listen to the station again even though they'd donated the money to a new playground.

Bad thoughts

At twilight in the deepening wood, the pale sawdust spurting from under the teeth of the cutting chain, he felt the pain in his legs again, blamed it on the whole day, the weeks, the cold months leaning down, holding the saw at awkward angles so his back seized up. And rolling and heaving on the trunk to get at the branches pinned underneath, breath gushing from his chapped and cracked lips, chin stubble picked with beads of frost, the smell of oil and two-cycle engine exhaust, of resin and raw wood and crushed needles, the smell of snow and his own reeking armpits and cigarette smoke, thought, was he going to do this the rest of his life? Was he crazy for Emma? He thought he wanted Wilf's life. He knew he wanted Emma, most deeply because she was French, because she had made a kid for Wilf and because of her dozens of relatives, the Comeau and the Pelky clans, the complex interconnections of blood extending up over the border and to the St. Lawrence south shore and down through New England and into the south, Louisiana, uncles, cousins, second cousins, aunts' sisters-in-law, brothers and sisters and their husbands and wives and children. The wealth of blood. He dreamed sentimental family thoughts through tunes as he cut along the bole, trying to limb with certain rhythms, though awkward branches constantly ruined the songs, thinking of those lost records, the blue and gold labels powdering over the dump, the music of dead fiddlers, something Irish-sounding but swingier, a slipping, reeling line of music, wildly ornamented but broken and lost among the wet mattresses and rinds. There was something about the green accordion that repelled him. He could feel how the buttons had been worn by the earlier owner's fingers, the strap twisted to fit another's thumb. Ancient dirt packed the joints and cracks—dust from dance hall floorboards, human grease, motes of decayed matter, lint, crumbs. A ghostly player moved into the circle of his arms whenever he took up the accordion. He wanted Emma, yes, but he wanted her to stay with Wilf as well. What did that leave? A marriage with two husbands and awful intimacies. Or maybe Wilf would die and he'd get her. This desire became a template for distorted thoughts and for no reason he began to check if he was pissing blood, worried that the urine would be pink-brown when it hit the snow, although there was no reason for this fear. Then, for weeks, he got in the habit of counting how long it took to empty his bladder. One morning he got to forty-two seconds and expected death from internal rupture in the near future.

The first gig

He was sewing a barbwire tear in the leg of a pair of work pants when he heard the hiss of air brakes, an idling motor, then footsteps as loud as a horse on the Pelkys' flagstone path. The outside door slammed and Wilf galloped down the hall and into the apartment. He jerked open the refrigerator and took out two beers, opened them, handed one to Dolor, clinked the foaming lips.

"What's it all about?" said Dolor. "You get elected Driver of the Year?"

"We got a job. A gig. A guy I know, trucker, drives a truck, is havin a surprise party, it's his wife's birthday. We supply the music. You and me. We get paid. Twenty bucks. Saturday night. Listen, we got to practice. This gotta go well. After this we'll play a lot, I know it, if it goes good. Come on, let's practice. This is the best thing ever happened to us. We're on our way now. Come look in the truck, see what I got—a amp and a couple of speaker horns at the army surplus. Come on, what the hell are you doing, sewing at a time like this? Goddamn, just like a stupid Frenchman."

He was calm when the night came. He could remember every note; the fast runs fell off his fingers, the beat was punchy, strong for dancing. But for the first hour it was no good because Wilf shook with stage fright. He shook so hard he could not tune his violin, he overtightened the bow and stripped the screw, had to use the old bow missing half its hair, and when he started to play his hand trembled ferociously, the notes skittered and squalled and he forgot tunes.

Dolor cursed himself for not noticing while they were setting up. The speaker horns were round, made of pot metal and painted khaki green. The Bogen amplifier, under its coat of dust, bristled with glass tubes. They couldn't find a place to put any of the equipment in the crowded kitchen, finally put one horn on top of the refrigerator, the other on a chair near the back door and the amp on the back burner of the electric range. It warmed up into a steady hum. Wilf was wound tight.

"Christ, that sucker's heavy."

"Why do we need this stuff?" said Dolor. "It's only the kitchen, they can hear the music good."

"They can't! Once they get dancin and scratchin their feet around and laughin and slammin the door they won't hear us. You *got* to have a amp, that's what bein a professional is all about." He kept shaking his hands as though they were wet, changed the placement of the horns five or six times until Big Bubbie, already drunk, yelled, come on, let's have some music. His wife was white with rage, had been truly and unpleasantly surprised, for her birthday had come and gone unnoticed two weeks before; now, gripped by savage menstrual cramps, both kids hacking with bronchial coughs, she had been slopping around in a torn housecoat, the place a mess of strewn socks, dirty dishes and dust kitties, when cars and trucks began to pull up and disgorge strangers who wished her happy birthday, lit cigarettes and started to drink.

Dolor and Wilf, dressed in matching red Airtex shirts and crepe-soled shoes, squeezed themselves into a tight corner of the kitchen. People going out the back door kept tripping over the speaker wire. Big Bubbie kept shouting "Awright!" The refrigerator door opened every ten seconds, jarring the horn on top. The sound from the speakers was screechy, Dolor thought, all the bass strained out, Wilf's fiddle notes straight from hell in piercing power.

"Break," yelled Dolor to Big Bubbie when Wilf's fingers skidded off the fingerboard like a hockey puck on new ice. He pulled Wilf out into the backyard, through a crowd of drinkers to the quiet of the garage, gave him a beer. His eyes were white with panic.

"Jesus, drink that and settle down. You're nervous."

"I know it. It's all them faces looking at us. There's this couple keeps trying to dance and I think, 'oh no, I'm gonna fuck up and they'll stop and give me a dirty look'—and then I do and they do and I feel like I want to get the hell out of there. Look, am I crazy? Did Bubbie's wife give us the finger? I feel like I'm gonna throw up."

"It's OK," said Dolor. "She'll get into it. It's kind of fun. Just don't look at nobody. Look at me, just pretend like we're at your place with Emma, havin a few beers and playing for the hell of it. Anyway, they like it, except her, even when it falls apart. They like the instruments there in the kitchen, it makes everybody feel good. It makes me feel good. It makes your pal there, Big Bubbie, feel real good. I heard somebody tell him it was the best party they ever been to. Everybody's happy except Mrs. Bubbie and she'll get with it when we play 'Happy Birthday.' Come on. We're not doin bad. Except for those goddamn speakers—them things sound like somethin out of a train station."

Wilf calmed himself down by looking rigidly at Dolor. Now he hit hard and clean on the notes, the double-stops true, a kind of goatish leap in his playing that had never been there before, that cooked out as a raw and slangy sound. Dolor was getting good music out of the box, rich and competent, despite the bad speakers, a yard ahead of his usual cut. The dancers were pulling the music out of them. People were dancing, bumping into the stove, the table, the kitchen floor was undulating, Mrs. Bubbie was washing dishes and slapping the clean plates into the drain rack, they were dancing through the door and into the backyard, when somebody slammed the refrigerator door and the speaker rolled off, bouncing from Mrs. Bubbie's shoulder into the dishwater where it simultaneously broke, exploded and loosed a savage current that raised the birthday girl's hair in a crest and threw her, staggering, into the crowd of dancers.

Minutes of chaos passed before Dolor yanked the speaker wires loose, jerked the amp plug out of the outlet. Mrs. Bubbie, white and shaking, sat in a chair, Big Bubbie wept on her knees and begged forgiveness, someone brought a glass of whiskey, another a can of beer, another a towel to dry her wet hands, another a blanket covered with dog hairs, and in half an hour, after three glasses of whiskey and abject apologies from her husband, she had recovered enough to command the music—without amplification—to begin again.

"I told you," said Dolor, feeling this was the right moment to play "Happy Birthday" in waltz time and then move into some good hard dancing stuff. A little later one of the kids sidled through the dancers and said, Mama, there's smoke comin out of the wall.

At two in the morning, after the fire truck had left, they pulled away, the wreckage of the sound system rattling in the back of the truck, their hot breath misting the windshield so that Dolor kept wiping it with his hand to clear the glass, Wilf passing him the pint of bourbon. They were exhilarated, groaning, laughing, still hearing the music, still seeing the way a roomful of people sprang and shuffled and swayed and pressed against each other because they had played the twenty songs they knew, still seeing the sparking voltage in the sink and feeling relief when Mrs. Bubbie, not dead, looked at her husband and said through stiff white lips, you pinhead.

"What a night," said Dolor. "Without them goddamn speakers it would have been good."

"Yeah, except at the beginning when I couldn't get it together. I don't know what happened, I just started shaking."

"If you leave that out and leave out almost electructing his wife and almost burning the house down, it was good."

"That fire was Bubbie's fault, putting foil in the fuse box."

"Somethin else. Before the trouble started, this lady come up and asked for a song, something French, *la danse du* something or other. I told her we didn't know it, she said, shame on you not to play the music of your people."

"Fuck her," said Wilf.

"Yeah. All right. But I happen to think she's right. All I want to know is where the hell is this so-called French music? It sure ain't around here."

Virtuosi

The closest he came was once or twice on the way home from the woods he tuned in *Le Réveil Rural,* on Radio Canada, heard a fiddle reel with tiddly-pom-pom piano accompaniment and the twangy buzz of *la guimbarde,* the Jew's harp, then something that sounded untamed and feral, demonic flying runs, a harsh, exultant music that imitated waterfalls, locomotives, a band saw, an accordion huffing, the strike of ice spicules on a tin pan, a screeching, rambling, shrill, mad cascade of music that made him pull over to the side of the road. "*Wah!*" said the announcer. "*Soucy l'incomparable!*" Another time he caught a program featuring *les accordéons diatoniques, musiciens du Québec;* the brilliant and vigorous playing seeped through the static, overrode the scratches and scars of old wax discs; Joseph-Marie Tremblay, Henri Bisson, Dolor Lafleur, Théodore Duguay, murmured the announcer. At least he knew what it was called now: traditional music, *la musique traditionnelle.* It must have been this that his father played on the old burned accordion. He couldn't get past the idea that his father had died saving his children from an inferno.

"What do you think we go up to Québec and get some records and learn that music? I got to have records to figure it out. Let Emma come to translate. We could go up to that town, they say there's a lot of accordion players."

"Yeah, yeah. Montmagny. I was up there once, pick up this special saw blade." But Wilfred wasn't crazy about the idea, wasn't crazy about the music, either, and kept putting the trip off. Dolor wondered if he had figured out how he felt about Emma and was jealous. Emma called from the kitchen, "they don't give green stamps up there," and that seemed to end it.

But he woke up on a rainy Saturday morning with the idea of driving to Montmagny himself even though he did not understand the language. If he brought the green accordion he wouldn't need to talk.

The logging road bucked and twisted under him as he drove through the slashed woodlots toward the border checkpoint. He had expected it to look the same on the Québec side, but the country flattened out into clustered villages with long, narrow farm fields stretching out behind them. It was all farming, cows and crops, and this surprised him. As he drove over the flat roads he sensed a demonic energy coiled inside the houses and barns. Yards bristled with whittled objects and moving parts, robots constructed from tractor parts, bizarre flowers constructed from plastic bleach bottles, windmills, flying ducks, miniature houses set among the stones and emitting clouds of resident wasps, pinwheels, donkeys made of bottle caps, a canoe balanced on a stump and manned by carved paddlers, bouquets of tin cans, lath figures in scarecrow clothing with Halloween-masked faces. The rain faded and he drove toward a clearing horizon and sunlight.

The trip became a journey, through St.-Georges, St.-Joseph-de-Beauce, St.-Odilon, St.-Luc, St.-Philémon, St.-Paul-de-Montminy, Nôtre-Dame-du-Rosaire. A heady feeling rose in him that he was returning home. Somewhere up here was his source. He wept when he saw the great river, the deep bolt of water shot into the heart of the continent.

It was late afternoon when he reached Montmagny. The sun was low. The old stone houses with graceful pavilion roofs along the river glowed yellow and the water seemed made of sheets of torn gold. He drove around until dusk. There was no traffic on the street, only a woman walking a small black dog. He felt he had come into another century. He was hungry, he was afraid, excited. He found a place to park a few blocks away from a building that looked like an inn; dozens of cars were parked on the streets nearby. The swinging sign picturing the musicians read LES JOYEUX TROUBADOURS. He carried his accordion case. Before he opened the door he heard the music.

A young woman with red lips and black hair curled under at the ends sat at a desk, the panel of a green door behind her painted with two dancing rabbits, looked up from a handful of papers, saw the accordion case and smiled.

"*Bon! Un autre accordéoniste pour la veillée.*" She consulted her papers. "*Quel est ton nom—?*" Her voice was husky and hesitant, as though she had suffered a throat injury in the past and it was still painful to speak.

"I'm sorry," he said slowly, "I cannot talk French. I come up here looking to hear some accordion music." She looked at him gravely. He smiled and lifted the case a little. "I do not speak French, I'm sorry," he said, wishing there were a language of thoughts.

She pursed her lips, raised her right forefinger and gave it a little shake as if to say wait one extremely brief minute, and disappeared behind the green door, leaving it ajar. There was an accordion on a chair near the door. He could make out the name *Ludwig Sapin* and see the image of a little spruce tree on it. Was it hers? He imagined himself married to the young woman, in love with her, combing her black hair, waking in the morning to her ragged voice. He could hear the music plainly now—a fiddle, an accordion and spoons; no, it had to be two accordions; the thump of the musicians' heels. The woman came back, followed by a red-haired man in a suit that was too tight for his robust frame, adhesive tape across the bridge of his nose.

"What can I do for you?" he said in American.

"I drove up from Maine," said Dolor. "This sounds dumb but I'm trying to find accordion players, I mean, the traditional music, you know. I'm French but I can't talk it. Name is Dolor Gagnon. I'm trying to find out about the old music. I play the accordion a little, but not the traditional. I can't find any records. I can't seem to find anybody who still plays it. Not in Maine, anyway."

The man laughed. "Buddy boy," he said, "did you hit the jackpot! In that room are some of the best. Anywhere. In the world! If I tell you Philippe Bruneau is in there and Joe Messervier's boy Marcel, and a kid named Raynald Ouellet, Marcel Lemay and one or two more—maybe it doesn't mean anything to you, but take my word for it, it's the best. Tonight is the night of the *Veillée du bon vieux temps* in honor of the late Monsieur Duguay, *accordéoniste extraordinaire.* You're welcome to sit at our table if we can find you a chair." He spoke American without the trace of an accent, moved fluidly in and out of French, introduced himself as Fintan O'Brien, an overseer at the Thetford Mines and a fiddler of Celtic airs, born in Ireland, raised in Philadelphia and Halfmoon, Idaho, now marooned in Québec, he said, a man without a country, ha-ha.

The dim golden room was packed with people at round tables illumined by candles. Along one wall he saw a long buffet covered with platters and dishes and dozens of bottles of wine. The red-haired man led him to a crowded table and found a chair for him, introduced his wife, Marie, in a scarlet dress, announced to the table that here was a lover of the old music, a traveler from Maine who could not find what he craved in the States.

To Dolor he said, "it's a special night. They're losing the traditional music in Québec too—big band, folk music, pop songs from the States, that's what people want to hear. But not here, maybe the last place where this music is alive and well."

An elderly man sang a line and every face turned to the front of the room where he stood on a dais. The accordions and the spoons glittered in the rich light, the knees of the musicians rose and fell in metronomic vigor. All over the room people were nodding their heads, prancing their fingers on the table, swaying and clicking their teeth in rhythm with the *cuillères,* the *os,* the *pieds* of the *accordéonistes,* until the tables were cleared away and dancing began.

He was in a room of French people. There were similarities in bone structure, in the fine hands, the dark hair and eyes. He told himself these were the people from whom he had come, he was genetically linked to those around him. He felt a curious thrill. It became the great night in his life, the one he later pulled up from submerged dreams, though the memory was flawed by a phantasm assumption. He believed that on that evening he had understood and spoken French.

The music was stunningly brilliant, joyous with life and vigor. The dancers sprang over the floor and now and then they would draw back and give room to a step dancer whose rigid back, erect head and straight-hanging arms accentuated the clattering, tapping, rapping, knocking, flinging feet whose steps stuttered in and out of the music. He wished Wilf could hear the fiddler, the sound like a flock of birds, a flight of arrows striking all around him, from a growling, clenched-teeth mutter on the G and D strings to harmonic shrieks and stair-tumbling runs— Jean something, a taxicab driver from Montréal. He stared, he listened so intently that what he heard was fixed forever. He remembered everything. His attention fell particularly on a brawny, square-jawed young accordionist with a pompadour of gleaming black hair. When the man played he seemed in a trance, his face fixed and expressionless, his eyes glaring into a distance beyond the room, his leg springing up and down like a piece of machinery, a fine *accord de pieds.* His music was muscular, with a full, ringing tone, very rapid and technically flawless. On and on he played, the music surging, circling, twining in and out of itself like a nest of snakes. It created a blue ozone mist around the player. No one was better than he and when he stopped, the throats of the people in the room roared. Dolor clapped until he thought his fingernails would fly off.

"Who is he?" he shouted to Fintan O'Brien in the din of applause. The man answered but Dolor could not hear him.

A hollow-voiced man with a black, twenty-past-eight mustache announced a quadrille and played a curious "Français" accordion, very small, with only seven folds in the bellows. A bicycle bell attached to it signaled the change for each new figure of the intricate dance. The sound was too small for the room. Not far into the tune, the dancers stopped and looked accusingly at the accordionist who shook his head in apology and began again from the beginning.

(The hollow-voiced man went to London the next spring to play this instrument in a program that included Malcolm Arnold's "A Grand Grand Overture" for three vacuum cleaners and solo floor polisher.)

Toward the end of the evening the black-haired young woman from the front desk stepped forward with her little spruce tree accordion. She sang a *complainte,* a deep, slow drone from the accordion, and her voice issuing from a closed throat seemed unearthly and strained to him, the voice of someone in the grip of an invisible power.

When the musicians put their instruments away at eleven o'clock he left, a scrap of paper in his pocket with Fintan O'Brien's address, a promise to stay in touch. His head rang with wine. Outside the dark village he pulled the truck over and slept cramped up on the seat, dreaming something unutterably sad that he could not recall when he woke up in violet river fog to the flapping of ravens' wings and remembered that in the bed of the truck were three bags of garbage he had forgotten to bring to the dump.

What's the use?

On the return journey he could feel the familiar depression lowering onto him like the premature darkness that foreshadows a coming storm: a chronic, tearing misery that never completely retreated. He drove, yawning, the truck swaying over the line and touching gravel from time to time. He could not have Emma, nor the black-haired young woman at the green door. He wanted to play that music, music that belonged to him by blood inheritance, but could not learn it because he didn't speak French, because he lived in a place where the music was no longer admired or played, because he could never be as good as the tranced man with the piston leg. Random had revealed nothing, meant nothing and held no meaning for him. The journey to Québec had only compounded his sense of alienation and inadequacy. He could never be those accordionists. And of himself he knew what he had known when he was two—nothing, *rien,* nothing. He threw the scrap of paper scratched with Fintan O'Brien's name out the window and went on.

Une douleur

In June, two months after Wilf's death, something went wrong with his legs. He woke in the morning, didn't realize it at first, looked out the smeary window at white fog, white shirts and socks on Mrs. Pelky's clothesline hanging limp, thinking it would burn off by ten. The black flies had been bad the day before; his scalp and neck were lumpy with their bites. He was ready to quit for good, fed up with the woods and the dirty work, and whatever he thought, his mind kept slewing around, arrowing back to Wilf.

The days were warmer but the roads were still icy in the higher elevations where Wilf steered loads of pulp through the New Hampshire mountains to the paper mill in Berlin. They worked it out later that he must have whipped the truck around the sloped hairpins, taking them a little fast, then hit a section where a spring in the cliffs had frozen down the rock face, overflowed the ditch and crawled onto the road, a fan of blue ice two inches thick, slanting toward the precipice. The truck soared off the road at speed, fell through the icy air upright and into the trees, old black spruce, dense and brittle. As the trailer broke away and tumbled into the ravine spilling four-foot logs, a long broken stub speared up through the cab, pierced Wilf's back so the bloody jag exited at the lower sternum, tearing away the xiphoid process and stabbing into the roof of the cab. Wilf, impaled, lived on. The ambulance came keening through the trees, and to his rescuers his moans were no louder than the wind in the rocks but far more memorable.

Mr. Pelky brought the news to him, his voice low, shaking his head, adding the bloody details and spinning out the telling.

"They had to cut off the stub, see, top and bottom, with a chain saw and bring him to the hospital with that stub still in him. They couldn't lie him down in the ambulance, see, with that wood in him so they had him strapped on boards along his sides, under his arms, see, and they held him up. It didn't do no good. He died on the way."

Dolor could not go near Emma, did not go to the funeral. He went to his distant slope the third morning after the funeral, the back of his truck in grimy order, the scarred Stihl, toolbox and dented gas cans, red paint chipped and marred, the tools becrusted with oil and leaf dust, sawdust, road dust. A light rain smeared the windshield, the sky dull along the east rim of mountains, the houses he passed, inmates in the deepest sleep, his headlights gouging a way through the trees. He yawned, still warm from the bed, a row of stale doughnuts sliding with the candy wrappers on the dash, a cup of coffee sloshing in the homemade wooden holder he'd lashed in place with wire, one by one eating the white sugared cakes, jelly spurting, until his mouth clogged with disgust of the sweet half-raw dough and he had had more than enough. His legs ached.

By noon he could barely keep from fainting when he straightened up because of the pain in his legs. He told the foreman he was sick, staggered to the truck.

As the day wore on, his vision blurred, he hyperventilated, he fought to keep from strangling. The next morning his legs did not hurt so badly but he could barely move them. The Pelkys did not knock on his door until the end of the week, and by then he was feeling better, he was moving around the apartment at least, thought it might have been arthritis, everybody who worked in the cold damp woods ended up with it. Mrs. Pelky came and said Emma was with the kid at her parents' house in Honk Lake, she was probably going to move back in with her mother and father, she sent her love to Dolor.

"I'll go up and see her in a few weeks," he said but didn't do it.

In the months after the accident he became preoccupied with his body. Strange sensations overtook him. Enormous sensitivities prickled: loud colors, bright light, the beeping of dump trucks in reverse, slamming doors and the conversations around him scraped his nerves raw. He developed allergies to dust, mold, apples and tomatoes. He was constipated, bought packets of laxatives at the Cut Rate drugstore in Millinocket, but nothing worked. He heard of a health food store that had just opened in Portland and made the long drive to forage through the jars of blackstrap and honey, the coarse bran and dark apricot ears. He bought packets of ginseng tea and nerve tisanes but developed abdominal pain, sore throat, shooting pains in his joints. One night pain spread through his face, a dull, severe ache that was unbearable at night. It hurt to rest his cheek on the pillow but if he turned on his back the pain flowed in waves from ear to ear. His mouth was burning up, his tongue swelled until he could barely speak. He woke at two in the morning with groin pains shooting up one leg and into his abdomen, across and down the other leg, circumscribing an endless circle of pain. It hurt to urinate, to defecate. He wrote out a list of pain and suffering in a shaking, paralyzed hand and brought it to the doctors at the V.A. Hospital. Diverticulitis, they thought, or a spastic colon, a back problem or a kidney problem. Kidney stones or nephritis—

The aches coiled and uncoiled. He was cold, yet there was internal heat as though a ferocious furnace was stoked in his depths. It was too much; one morning he tried to get out of bed, managed a few steps, then fell on the floor where he stayed until the Pelkys heard him pounding with the heel of his hand.

The Pelkys helped him into the back seat of their old sedan, Mrs. Pelky stuffing a bed pillow that still smelled of her night hair under his shoulder. Mr. Pelky, his driving confused by a sense of emergency, squealed onto the highway and sped for the hospital. The trees were in heavy bud, the wet road under the maples covered with their fallen blossom, as dark red as coagulated pools of blood. The car whirred past sloping maple, soft buff and genital-flesh blur, and below this purpled arc a line of popple flashed, then past veins of birch, then the curving line of the ridge and through the branches the puzzled sky, and they were past the roaring arms of the pines and the swamp filled with stalks, coming to the first fields and scratchy lines of red osier, bramble hoops, and all of it strung together with birdcalls and apprehension.

Nothing wrong

They didn't know what was wrong with him. He had them arguing, diagnosing unseen injuries, germ warfare, malingering, childhood polio, psychosomatic paralysis, a slipped disk, chronic fatigue, central nervous disorder, psychogenic pain, loss of pep, muscle spasms, an unknown virus, bacterial infection, a hereditary disorder, posthypnotic suggestion, infectious mononucleosis, depressive hysteria, hypochondriacal delusions, Parkinson's disease, multiple sclerosis, brucellosis, or encephalitis. But after three weeks, there was no change and they sent him back to Random in a wheelchair. If he could manage to stand up he could totter a few steps, but that was all, and the pain in his legs and back was relentless.

The social worker at the V.A. helped him get a small government disability pension, but it wasn't enough to live on because he had to pay Mrs. Pelky to cook for him and help him get to the toilet and in and out of bed. Mr. Pelky built a plywood ramp down the entry stairs.

When he had to get out of the oppressive rooms, when he needed things in town—beer and groceries, haircuts—he pushed himself out to the highway in the wheelchair and stuck his thumb out. Pickup trucks were the only ones that could give him a ride, and the driver had to get out, help him into the cab, put the heavy chair in the bed of the truck, get back in, drive to town, then the whole business had to be repeated in reverse. Not many bothered to stop and he could sit out there for hours, shivering and cursing, before someone pulled over. His strong, muscled torso fattened from lack of exercise and the fried pork, peanut butter sandwiches and beer he consumed. He became a familiar figure on the Random highway, slouched in his wheelchair, long black hair straggling down, raising his gloved hand in supplication as trucks came in sight, and when they didn't slow sometimes yelling words that could not be heard but were easily guessed, accompanied by an upflung finger.

Only once did the Dentist come on an errand of mercy, kegged and roaring lumbering songs, with a six-pack in each hand, telling lugubrious tales of mishaps in the woods of the horsepower generation.

"Here, ya little bastard," he shouted, "have one." He got the accordion out of its case, dumped it in Dolor's lap. There was nothing wrong with his arms except a minor shooting pain, but even with three or four beers he couldn't play. It was not just that Wilf was dead, but he kept hearing the formidable virtuosi of Montmagny, kept thinking of the unknown player who had possessed the green accordion before him.

"You ain't a lot of fun," said the Dentist.

A lost chord

One afternoon when the door opened it was not Mrs. Pelky with her sauerkraut ragout, but Emma.

"Mrs. Pelky said you wasn't doin that good," she said, looking around the stinking room. She'd never seen it, and he was ashamed of the dust and empty beer cans, the dirty clothes in the corner and the crusted dishes in the sink which waited sometimes for days before Mrs. Pelky could get to them. Emma went straight to the sink and the hot water gushed over the greasy plates. He was excited, suddenly happy and maneuvered the wheelchair to the sink where he could watch her lashing the suds up. She looked fine to him and all at once he guessed why she had come. He blushed, ready to cry from excitement. Emma!

"How'd you get down here?"

"Come down with my folks. There's a wedding, one of my cousins, Marie-Rose, and they asked Dad to play for the dance after. He's going to play some of that old music. I thought it was a good chance to see you, see if you want to hear it. I remember how crazy you was to hear the old music."

"Look at how I am! Can I go to a dance? I can't even get to the V.A. Hospital once a month without half an army to move me."

"Dad's comin over with Emil in his pickup truck. They'll put the chair in the back, you in the front. There's gonna be a real good accordionist there." She laughed slyly. "You got good clothes you can wear?"

"Yeah, yeah. How you doin up there? The kid OK? Who's Emil?"

"I'm doin real good. I got a job, just on the line at the toy factory. The kid's growin big—you won't hardly recognize him—and I get to bring him home free toys, that's a benefit. Emil is—it's not only my cousin, it's in the air—next month we're gettin married, me and Emil. He's a nice guy and he likes the kid. They need a father, you know kids need a father. He works at the toy factory, too, in fact he's the foreman. You'll like him. He's the one that plays the accordion. I wasn't gonna tell you, it was gonna be a surprise, but I guess I told you."

"Guess you did." It was only a few minutes since she had come in but he had soared high and plunged into the abyss since she walked through the door. He wanted to yell at her, it's only eight months he's been dead, and what about me, I been crazy about you forever. The dishes were shining in the drain rack, she was polishing the faucets and talking to him. He remembered her dress very well, the cadence of her sentences. He couldn't say a thing.

The wedding reception was at the V.F.W. hall, and a big crowd shuffled along the buffet, paper plates bending as they heaped on sliced ham and turkey, potato salad, the peppermint chip chiffon cake and orange Jell-O molded desserts. Children ran back and forth, crawled under the chrome-legged Formica tables, bawled in corners, pushed and howled. He sat at a long table covered with paper printed with a design of silver wedding bells. The napkins carried the names of the bride and groom, *Marie-Rose & Darryl.* He sat between Emma's father and Emil, didn't know many of the others. Emma's pale yellow bridesmaid dress made her look sallow and tired. At the bottom of the table sat a fat man with a black eye who kept telling Frenchie jokes in a broken dialect, who winked and said he got his black eye when he walked into a door.

Before the dancing began, Emma's father announced, "We're gonna play a little bit of the old music, mostly for the older people in the crowd, not too much though, I know you younger ones don't go for it. But you know, it's good music, you can't listen to it without tapping your toe and feeling good. Myself, I regret we don't hear it so much no more."

Dolor was disappointed in the music. He remembered vividly what he had heard in the north beside the great river. Perhaps it was because the first tune Emma's father and Emil tried after the falsely enthusiastic announcement "Here's one for the old-timers!" was one he had heard the stiff-faced man play in Montmagny, the "*Quadrille du loup-garou,*" the "Werewolf Quadrille." Even with two accordions Emma's father and Emil skimped on the runs, lost notes, played at a dragging tempo and cut the complex piece short, wheeled immediately into "Blueberry Hill," and then the wedding guests danced, the men sweating in dark suits, their oiled hair breaking loose and flapping against their foreheads, the women's skirts belling around their nylon legs.

They tried a fast *gigue* that brought an old man onto the floor, clacking and kicking with stiff legs, only an echo of the youthful dancer he must have been, keeping it up even when Emma's father forgot the tune and quit playing, though Emil plunged on, his solo and abbreviated playing far short of the intricacies of the St. Lawrence valley, but spirited enough to keep the old man dancing, an animated skeleton. At the end Emma's father leaned into the microphone and said, "well, that was some pretty fine dancing by Charley Humm, and that's it for the old stuff. You know, you get a certain age in your life and you forget some of the tunes you used to know and I apologize for that. Now here's a little haymaker music, Maine's own Hal Lone Pine's 'Cryin' Cowboy.' I heard Hal and Betty Cody do this over in Machias years ago in a thunderstorm, the lights all went out, their sound system died, but they sang and played in the dark with the lightnin flashin outside. Now that's a real performer for you. So here we go, all you country fans," and applause and cries of *yahoo* filled the room. This was Emma's father's territory. He wrung heartbreak and yodeling and wailing harmonies from his fiddle and Dolor had to admit he was good. As for Emil, he played well enough, but he was grade C, like everything else in Random.

An aunt of the bride loomed behind him suddenly, sat in Emil's empty chair, smiled, drank from a smeary glass, coughed in his face as she lit a cigarette—one of those wiry Frenchie women who'd buried two or three husbands.

"They tell me your name is Gagnon."

Emma leaned forward. "Dolor, this is Delphine Barbeau from Providence, Marie-Rose's aunt, her father's sister. Delphine and Tootie gave Marie-Rose the fold-up TV tray-tables. Delphine, you know me and Emil is next. So you better stay right here and you don't have to come up again in a couple of weeks."

The woman drew on her cigarette, coughed. "I shouldn't even be up here now. I had pneumonia. Me and Tootie was drivin along and the car broke down and we had to walk for miles and miles. Oh, I was soaked, and the wind just chilled me to the bone. So I got sick. They told me at the clinic, don't travel, no excitement, don't go to work. I was out of work three weeks. I work at Ferris Combs, they make the hairbrushes, combs that glow in the dark. You work there long enough you start to glow just like one of them combs. So here I am. Yeah, those TV trays are cute. I don't know if they eat those TV dinners. If you're gonna get married next I might get you the Toastmaster Hospitality Set, it's a toaster and these snack trays." She laughed. Her voice was flat and loud as though they were in a room full of machinery. Dolor thought she might be drunk.

She leaned closer to him, cut Emma off. "You from around here?"

"Well, I was born here, but I grew up somewhere else. Old Rattle Falls."

"Uh-huh. How come you're in a wheelchair? You always been like that?"

"They don't know. Just something wrong with my legs. It just started this year."

"Delphine! Come on, we're going! Come on, it's nine hours' driving. I ain't waitin." It was Tootie, the fat man, the front of his shirt marked with a triangle of sweat, his matted hair straggled over his brow.

"OK, here I am." To Dolor she said "glad to met you," got up and cut through the dancers to the fat man.

Then Emil was back, pulling Emma out onto the floor, and he was alone, looking at the litter of crumpled napkins and rinds of ham fat on the mustard-smeared plates around him.

"Hello, Frank. I've been looking for you." It was Emma's sister, Anne-Marie, who called herself Mitzi, with her charming little stutter, her scent of lily-of-the-valley, a silver cross lying against her bridesmaid breast, a fluffy skirt of tulle, yellow satin slippers with Cuban heels. She was not pretty, did not have Emma's robust vigor, but there was a delicacy about her, a tenderness that flattered him, a private and restrained tone in her voice when she spoke. Each time he had seen her she seemed deeply interested in how he felt, what he thought. Wilf had told her about the name Frank back at Birdnest and she always used it.

"Having fun?"

She looked at him. "Dead on my feet. These shoes are pretty but they hurt. They didn't send my size, five and a half, so I had to wear these fives." She sighed, drank a little from her glass of wine. "Frank, can I ask you a personal question?"

He knew what it was going to be. "Sure."

"What happened to your legs?"

Christ, maybe he should make up a printed pamphlet. "Nothing *happened.* Just something went wrong. They don't know what. I was OK until a couple of months after Wilf—Emma's—after it happened, then I just woke up one morning and boom! There I was. They don't have no idea of what it is."

She nodded as if he had explained cause and effect. "I brought you something," and she handed him a tiny metal figure.

"What is it?" He turned it over. It was a silver leg, less than an inch long, with a hole pierced at the hip.

"It's an ex-voto, a votive offering? You offer it to Christ or to a saint and pray that your legs will be cured. See, you can put a pin through the hole? To pin on the saint. You know something, you ought to go to the shrine over at Lake Picklecake, the shrine of St. Jude. He's the most American saint, he's the one who looks out for the impossible cases, the ones that baffle the doctors. Before that we went once to Sainte-Anne-de-Beaupré up in Québec, but there was gypsies there, hundreds of them. I got a girlfriend, she had terrible headaches, a spike being pounded into her head with a hammer, they didn't know what caused it, but she went to this shrine of St. Jude and she did the stations of the cross and prayed for deliverance from her suffering and gave St. Jude a little silver head and after that she—she never had another headache. This was two years ago. I went with her."

"Is it Catholic?" he said in a low voice.

She looked at him pityingly.

"Do you remember last year when Mother and Dad"—Emma said "*Mamam et Père*"—"were trying to sell their house and nobody even came to look at it?"

"A little," he lied.

"Well, they had it on the market for a year and nothing happened so they went up to the shrine and prayed and asked St. Jude for help and left like a little house Dad made out of a bottle cap, he flattened it out and cut it with the edge of a chisel, it's all straight lines. They drove home and walked in the house and the phone was ringing. It was a woman from New York who saw the FOR SALE sign last summer when she was driving through, wrote it down. She said she had been looking in her purse that afternoon and found the address and remembered the house and was it still for sale, and of course Dad says yes, and you know the rest. It was St. Jude that interceded for them and made it happen."

Dolor vaguely remembered Emma saying that her parents had sold their old log house on Honk Lake to someone from out of state and built a new ranch next to the high school baseball field.

St. Jude

It was two hundred miles and more to the shrine, all the way across the state, then over a bridge and onto the island. She drove him there in her little Volkswagen, a good driver, steady and not too fast so they could see everything. The land was flat and swampy, then it rose a little. All along the lakeshore were empty summer camps painted cherry, chocolate, lemon, vanilla. The wind riffed and slapped up whitecaps; he squinted at massing clouds like twisted wet sheets.

"It's going to rain."

"What difference does that make? It's to test you."

They crossed a pistachio green bridge to the island, turned onto a mud road. A sign pointing vaguely toward the water said only "St. Jude." The rain started, fine drops needling the windshield. She pulled into the gravel turnaround. There were no other cars. The rain came in gusts and the wind tore at their hair and snapped the nylon fabric of her pink jacket. She wrestled his wheelchair out of the back seat and helped him into it, began pushing it toward the lake, toward a small corrugated-metal shed. The wheels gnawed through the gravel.

The shed faced the lake and the front was open to the westward weather. On a wooden bench at the back stood a carved figure, a lumpy wooden St. Jude with a face like a beagle, black with rain. Once it had been brightly painted, but years of lake squalls and driving sleet, reflected sunlight and seasonal roasting and freezing had scoured away the pigment, and mildew mottled the figure. Mitzi pointed at the dozens of ex-votos pinned and nailed to the wall behind the saint: the miniature house her father had made from a St. Pauli Girl bottle cap, arms, legs, lungs, kidneys, trucks, a tiny chain saw painted on a scrap of plywood, an eye, part of a report card, a fishhook. A second, weatherproof plastic representation of the saint, only a foot high, stood in a hollowed-out television set. The knobs were gone and there was no maker's mark, but Dolor thought it was a Philco sixteen-inch. The mahogany veneer had buckled.

The rain slammed sidewise into the shed, and through his wet eyelashes Dolor saw the drops bouncing up from his wheelchair arms. His jacket and pants were sodden. The water was pouring from his hair, running down his neck and into his clothes, runneling St. Jude's ruined visage. He could not see Mitzi behind him but heard her voice, serious, intense, believing. The lake was hammered white by rain. The world seemed compressed in a bare sumac branch. He leaned forward, pressed the pin into the wet wood. The tiny silver leg glinted. Some unknown sensation—was it faith?—stirred in him and he thought, no, he was *sure* he heard a holy voice.

All the way to the motel, as she drove through the belting rain and the car windows steamed over from the moisture in their wet clothes and hair, he felt his legs growing strong. Their rooms were side by side and she pulled the car up in front of his door.

"Don't get the wheelchair," he said in a low voice. "Just come around to my side." As she walked around the car he opened the door, shifted over, swiveled his legs out and, grasping the top of the door, stood up. She stared at him, her face clenched. He stepped forward on trembling legs, and when he had to let go of the car door, he put his arm over her shoulder and shuffled eight steps to the motel door. Inside the room he kissed her, the salty tears in their swollen mouths, his shaking legs moving them to the stiff white bed.

"No," she said. "After we get married. I made a promise to God," she said.

The wedding guest

He recovered very quickly, such is the power of miracles. They were married a month later, the bridegroom eager for connubial bliss, but they spent the honeymoon in Providence for the funeral of the bride's aunt Delphine Barbeau, who had been a death's-head at the wedding, at the reception choking and gagging from her cancerous throat but still demanding cigarettes and still swallowing brandy and asking those around her if they watched that chimp on TV. She croaked demands to fat Tootie who carried her in and wrapped a blanket around her.

He came over to Dolor, lighting a cigarette, his oily forelock dangling.

"She wants to see you," he said, pulling at his sleeve. Dolor bent over the waxy face, trying not to shrink from the fetor issuing from the black hole of the mouth. The woman crooked her finger.

"Tell you. Now you married your cousin. You fool."

"What do you mean? I don't have any cousins."

"Wife," she said accusingly, "you married your wife," and coughed and coughed, racked with coughing until the fat man carried her out.

Ex-voto

"Frank," she whispered, rolled fast in his arms, looking at him from the distance of a few inches, the waxy curve of his eyelashes, the dark stubbled chin and jaw, his red mouth and the wet teeth disclosed when he smiled at the sound of her voice. "I dreamed we went on a boat and the boat sank and everybody drowned but us and we just floated on the water like soap and we couldn't sink because we were saying Hail Marys and that's what kept us up. Frank, I dreamed that you promised to give up playing the accordion for God and St. Jude who restored your legs, I dreamed that we moved away from here to Portland or Boston and our lives were so different, so beautiful and happy and successful."

She told him what was wrong with the place. Random was a twilight place that made people moody, tripped the switch for tears, boiled up a sense of loss and the feeling that the good things were out of reach. Men rushed into hopeless situations. Women threw themselves away on roughnecks who beat them and made them suffer, men with faces pitted and blackened like aluminum pots, who humiliated them and showed them the worst of everything. It was a place that pulled you down, that made it so you could never get ahead, just trapped in some halfway life that nobody but those ensnared recognized. It was because everybody in Random was French but nobody was French—they weren't anything; they were caught between being French and being American. Those who went away had a chance; they became true Americans, changed their names and escaped the woods. She asked him what he thought of the name Gaines to replace Gagnon.

" 'Frank Gaines,' " she said. "It sounds good. A good name for a child, easier, more American than Gagnon. What did that French name ever do for you? Kids made fun of it, right?"

"Yeah. But French kids made fun of it too, so I think it was me, not the name." He didn't care about these things the way she did. He was limp with happiness, unable to think of anything past or future, alive only in the moment.

"Frank," she said, weeks later. They lay close in the bed, from the other room the sound of the new color console Zenith her parents had given them for a wedding present. Mitzi had turned it on before she went to the bathroom, then to the kitchen to put on the kettle. He was weak with pleasure lying in the warm bed while the television voices bubbled like a porridge pot on the burner, listening to the sound of her voice for its buzzing timbre rather than its content.

"You know Emma and Emil been planning to go on their honeymoon when the weather got good. They're going to Louisiana, we got some relatives there, and Emma, she got to go down there, got to have her way, see what it's like, just for once. She said if you want him to, Emil could maybe take your accordion down, get a good price for it. Better than around here. She said Emil said he could maybe get a hundred dollars for it because it's kind of unusual. It's not like you play it anymore. I think you owe something to God, Frank, to St. Jude who healed your legs. And it's, you know, sort of a instrument they make fun of, a Frenchie thing, you know what I mean." There was a long quiet minute, with only the television voices and their breathing. He wanted her to understand what he was thinking, to know how happy he was and how little he cared about the accordion, about anything, if only he could lie there with her and drift on the buzzing of her voice.

"Frank," she burst out, "I want a chance too. I want a chance to do something, do something with you. I want our kids to have a chance at the world, not stuck in the boondocks here. Frank, I cry when somebody, when a Yankee, is nice to me in a store. The rest of them give you that attitude, that here's-another-Frenchie look, they make you feel like dirt. Frank, there's no sense in being French, in staying here. You don't talk French, you don't know who your parents were or where they come from, nobody here remembers them, they were just passing through for sure."

"Yeah," he said. "Why not. Why not sell the accordion. Somehow I lost the urge for it. I don't care. Whatever he can get. Yeah," he said. "Whatever you want, we'll do it. It's a good idea, maybe, to get out of here. I used to think about getting into TV repairs."

"Frank," she said, "you can go to college, you can be anything you want."

"I'll tell you something though. I don't change my name to Gaines. Frank, OK, but Gagnon stays. The only thing I got of my people is that name."

And she slid out from under the covers, went to the kitchen to make his coffee and a plate of milk-soaked toast with maple syrup which he ate in bed under the silver crucifix while she brushed his trousers and rubbed his work shoes with neat's-foot oil. He thought he would cry with the joy of it. But already the red idea was simmering that such intoxicating sweetness of life couldn't last. He thought of what the man in Montmagny had called it, *douceur de vivre*. Yes, his bones were marinating in that bowl of wine, but how long would it be before he was impaled on the spit again and roasting over the flames?

While she was in the bathroom he pressed a pin under his fingernails until the blood came as a reminder of the pain and loneliness from which God and St. Jude had released him. The traitorous observation that he suppressed lurched up from the pit—he could feel the pain and weakness waiting to seize him again; he was not cured.

Emil's joke

Emil looked the accordion over. He thought it needed work, one of the buttons stuck a little, though the fine leather bellows were still tight and sound and when he blew smoke into the instrument to test the bellows for leaks none escaped. It had a special tone, sad and emotional. They would like it in Louisiana.

"They'll buy it, somebody down there will. You know, I don't want to say anything against the French people, but those coonasses, they're, you know, impulsive, not too smart? You heard this joke: Thibodeaux goes to the barroom to have a drink with his friends, both ears is bandaged up. 'What's the matter with your ears?' says his friend Boudreaux. 'Oh,' says Thibodeaux, 'I'm sitting in my kitchen, next to the ironing board, Marie she's gone out to use the little house, and the telephone rings. "Allo, allo, *cher*," I say, but oh my god, I pick up the hot iron instead and burn my ear.' 'What about the other ear, Thibodeaux?' 'The other ear? That damn fool calls back.'"

He roared, blew his nose in one of Emma's paper napkins stamped with silver bells, left over from their wedding. If he couldn't get a good price, he told Dolor, he would buy it himself and keep it in the family. That way, if Dolor decided to take it up again it would be there.

"No, I'm not going to play no—anymore." Mitzi was correcting his grammar.

Going to Louisiana

"My God, this interstate road system is something," said Emil to Emma, "you can drive across the country in half the time."

"'Drive your Chev-ro-lay, through the U.S.A., America's the greatest la-la-laaaa,'" sang Emma in a mocking baby-voice. They were in the new car, a thistle grey Chevrolet V-8 sedan, though Emil had wanted a station wagon. In Kansas City they heard Polish polkas at an all-night dance, the wild Kansas City style so crazy they couldn't even dance to it, though there was a couple who did the fastest polka while working a single Hula Hoop around their mutual hips to great applause. "They could have started a campfire that way," said Emil.

They had stopped in Des Plaines for the fifteen-cent hamburger at a drive-in called McDonald's a gas station attendant told them to try, and turned south down Route 66, stopping every night to go to a drive-in movie, through Pontiac, Ocoya, Funks Grove where Emma bought a can of maple syrup, past grain elevators and truck stops and hot dog eateries, the Dixie Trucker's Home, a thousand filling stations, Texaco, Shell, Mobil, Phillips 66, and Emma picked out the tourist cabin for the night by the signs, HEATED—QUIET—CHRISTIAN ATMOSPHERE, the car wheels thumping over the tar seams in the four-lane highway. Near Sand Owl they passed a bad wreck, oil and water and gasoline all over the road and three cars in the ditch, one upside down, a man bucking in the grass, his white shirt mottled with blood and the red lights of the police cars flickering.

"I'm not lookin," said Emma and they rolled on to St. Louis and Rolla where they started noticing the increasing heat, turned south to Little Rock and a sign that spelled out

What Was
The Last Miracle
Jesus Performed
Just Before He
Was Crucified?

but the answer was missing, and on to Cuba, dodging possums, to Alton where an American flag flew in the middle of a cornfield, Searcy, Lonoke, Fordyce, Natchitoches, Bunkie, past roadhouses, a café with a giant milk bottle on it that reminded Emil of the phonograph record factory with a dog on the roof and Emma said that was nothing, they had a gift shop in Kennebunkport shaped like a whale, but all these were eclipsed by a drive-in ice cream place shaped like an enormous black bear and you drove between the bear's legs and said what you wanted into a microphone and it was ready when you drove out under his tail, and finally they were in the flat, hot country almost on the Gulf of Mexico.

The last night on the road, Emma called her mother to say they were almost there, how was the kid doing, was he still up or in bed, hello honey, it's Mama . . . pretty soon . . . next week we start back, I'll bring you a surprise . . . bye-bye . . . hello *Maman,* he sounds good and— what? What? WHAT? She came back to the car, stone-faced and twisting the strap of her purse, threw herself into the seat with force.

"What's the matter," said Emil. She wouldn't say for a long time, an hour. He drove carefully and slowly, looking over at her, patting her knee and saying tell me, tell me, is it the kid, then what, when she shook her head, your mother, your father, then what? Eh? What's wrong? Eh? Finally he pulled over. There was a gravel turnout beside a bayou under a mass of trees with festoons of Spanish moss. The air smelled rotten.

"Now tell me."

"It's Dolor. Dolor killed himself. Emil, he had everything to live for, they don't know why he did it. He left her a note. All it said was 'I am happy.' My poor sister, they got her under sedatives."

"Jesus Christ. When?"

"Saturday. The day before yesterday. We was driving along and laughing and having fun and his little green accordion in the back seat and he was—" Please, please, Emil, she thought, don't ask how.

Don't Let a Dead Man Shake You by the Hand

A PIANO ACCORDION

A new owner

There was a truck parked on the lawn, with a hand-lettered sign in the windshield: FOR SALE $400. In the driveway a sedan panted, crowded with dim people, the back seat writhing with children, and lashed to the roof a long metal cow-feed trough. The wife's posture in the front seat marked her as pregnant. The driver's door stood open admitting a torrent of small black mosquitoes while the driver, Buddy Malefoot, a muscular man in white jeans and white rubber boots, a pearlized raccoon foot he'd found in an oyster hung on a chain around his neck, leaned under the truck hood jiggling wires, hooking his finger under belts to gauge their stretch, reading the bone-dry oil dipstick, then coming out from under to kick the flaccid tires with his good foot. He had a bony, rectangular face like a box, the jaw as wide as the brow, the top of his head squared off, and two jug ears that had resisted the adhesive tape of his infancy. His greasy cap sat high on black curls. He was right-sided, from a mole on his right ear, to his dexter eye, larger than the other, five long hairs near his right nipple, fingernails that grew faster on his right hand, a longer right leg and a foot a full size beyond the left. In the house a shape hovered behind the screen door, cracked it open, but Buddy held up his hand and shook his head, got in his sedan and backed out.

"Idn't it no good?" The voice came from his father, Onesiphore, in the back seat smoking a cigarette, a man with the same square jaw as his son but stubbled with white, his yellowed hair crested, eyeglass lenses reflecting the rice fields and watery sky.

"No damn good at all. Look like hell struck with a club." He had a smudge of grease like a caste mark on his forehead.

"Yeah, well, hate to see you spend that compensation money enna-way. Seem like y'all got a TV and an accordeen. You ought a save some of it." He flipped the cigarette out the window.

"What I think, too," said the daughter-in-law up front, half turning and presenting Onesiphore with her buttery profile. She wore a striped maternity minismock, and her bare thighs were stippled with mosquito bites.

"Seem like it was me got hurt. Seem like you forget don't nobody tell me what to do. *Va brasser dans tes chaudières.*"

The sedan slouched over the road on its bad shocks, squatting on the corners.

"*I'll* tell you what to do," said the back seat. "Y'all drive straighter or I'll put a chair leg to you. You ain't so big I couldn't make you dance. I want to get home and see that accordeen good."

"That's right, *Papa,* make your poor hurt-footed son dance."

"Your foot's as good as mine. I hope it's a D chuned." Onesiphore Malefoot craned over the front seat to look at the black case resting between his daughter-in-law's feet.

"Yeah? Like to see *you* walk on it for more'n a minute. Told you, it's a C."

"Me, oh yeah, I'm gonna like to have a D. That beauty Ambrose Thibodeaux got, that old Major?"

"Dream along."

"One time a son wouldn't speak to his father like you, when I was young we lived at home, ate the good homegrown food, oh yeah, none of the supermarket food, but *sacamité,* the good okra gumbo, *boudin* like you can't get no more, yes, oh yeah, then the kids were good—trouble started, and this is true, when they made the kids go to school, talk only *améri-cain.* You, you and Belle used to talk French, perfect French, when you was little, now I don't hear a word, and the grandkids, they don't know a cheeseburger from a *tortue ventre jaune.*" He lit another cigarette.

"Yeah? See how far you get out on the rig talkin French. These oil guys come here from Texas, Oklahoma, they got the money, they hand out the jobs, everything, bidness strictly American and you got to make your reports, all that the same way. What good is French to me? It's like this secret language don't work. It's like kids doing pig Latin, *Iay ovelay ouyay.* It's OK for home, talk with the family, sing songs in." His right eye fluttered, a tic brought on by the strain of conversing with his father. One of the children was lying on the back window shelf; the other, Bissel, crouched on the floor arranging stray pieces of gravel on his grandfather's boot toe. (Sixteen years later Bissel, who was playing drums in a disco band in Baton Rouge, came back for a visit, saw ten thousand screaming people give the old man a standing ovation at the Cajun Music Tribute. "That's my fucking grandfather," he said furiously to his girlfriend as though it had been a secret kept from him all his life. When the old man died of trichinosis Bissel switched to accordion, imitated his grandfather's singing style with eerie accuracy for a year, then slid over into swamp pop.)

"Grandpa, did you see a turtle when you were little?"

"See him! We ate him! Catch him in the summer when the swamp dried up, dig him out. Sometimes we find it after the thunderstorm. Keep him in a pen until we ready to eat him. You get the woman turtle full of eggs you got something good. We use to feel, feel that turtle with our little fingers, see can we feel eggs. *Maman* fricassee the meat, and the best treat is the yolk of the egg right there on your plate, taste just like chicken. You kids never ate no turtle yet? It's good! You know, you cook them eggs all day and all night and all the next day and the white never get hard. You got to suck it out of the shell, they got a shell like leather. I don't see one of them turtles for a long time, couple of years. Smell that *café!* Always down this road a good smell of *café,* oh yeah. Me, I can use some of that. Let's hurry up and get home. *À la maison, mon fils!* That *petit noir* is already jumping in my mouth. '*Le café noir dans un paquet bleu, le plus je bois, le plus je veux,*'" he sang in his celebrated voice, vibrant and keening, the wailing style anciently linked to the music of the vanished Chitimachas and Houmas. "Me, I say we gonna get more rain. See out there?" A mass of blue-black cloud was moving in from the Gulf. Only his daughter-in-law glanced to the southwest and nodded to foster the illusion that they were conspirators, allied against Buddy and Mme Malefoot. Onesiphore patted her shoulder and sang on, smoking, as the sedan rolled through the hot, flat country.

The Malefoot family—their enemies said the name derived from *mal-frat,* or gangster—was a tangled clan of nodes and connecting rhizomes that spread over the continent like the fila of a great fungus. Anciently they came from France in the seventeenth century, crossed the north Atlantic to *Acadie* in the New World, ignored the British when France ceded the land to England who renamed it Nova Scotia and demanded oaths of allegiance. The Malefoots and thousands of others along the littoral of the *Baie Française* ignored the preposterous request, a lack of enthusiasm the British interpreted as treason. Thousands of the Acadians were shipped away to the American colonies, some made their own way to refuge. The Malefoots went first to St. Pierre, then to Miquelon, scraps of rock off the coast of Newfoundland, then were shipped back to France where they languished for months, crossed the ocean again to Halifax, and from Halifax took ship to New Orleans in French Louisiana, an ill-timed choice, for a few years after they arrived the territory was ceded to Spain. The refugees traveled north and west into the hot, dripping, watery country of the Opelousas, Attakapas, Chitimachas, Houmas, to the Acadian coasts, the bayous Têche and Courtableau, learning to pole fragile bateaux and live in the humid damp. They mixed and mingled, blended and combined their blood with that of local tribes, Haitians, West Indians, slaves,

Germans, Spanish, Free People of Color (many with the name Senegal, for their homeland river), *nègres libres* and Anglo settlers, even *américains,* shaping a *méli-mélo* culture steeped in French, and the accordion, borrowed from the Germans, livelied the kitchen music of the prairie parishes, the fiddle had its way in the watery parishes.

Along the great bayous stretched alluvial deposits of marvelously fertile loam. In the Attakapas country the Malefoots planted cane and corn and worked the plantations alongside imported Chinese laborers, driving big sugar mules, though no Malefoots lived in fine mansions; in the Opelousas, their crops were small-farm cotton and corn, sometimes worked on shares. They kept a yam patch, rows of Irish potatoes.

They built their houses on islands and back up the bayous in the Creole style, the houses standing above the ground on cypress *piliers,* the broken-pitched roofs borrowed from the West Indies that covered built-in porches and outside stairs with a *fausse galerie* roof extension to keep the slanted rain from striking in. They smoothed the inside walls with calcimined mud and moss, grew Blue Rose rice, and in the Atchafalaya Basin, the great freshwater swamp, they gathered moss, shot alligators, poling through the marsh where snowy egrets took flight before them like tablecloths shaking, threading the briny maze of quaking earth, oyster grass, wire grass to the edge of the Gulf. In the Gulf the Malefoots, once cod fishers and whale killers of the North Atlantic, dragged for shrimp, tonged oysters, fished, and, since 1953 when the government authorized offshore drilling, worked on the oil rigs, but had not forgotten the slow glide of the pirogue through black channels, the hiss of the boat as it parted the grass, the nutria in the trap, *la belle cocodrie,* snout brilliant with wet duckweed. Malefoots enveloped in whining clouds of mosquitoes, slapping at blood-mad deerflies, still poled through shimmering water, sky and marsh grass, but they complained that it was all changing, with alien water hyacinth choking the waterways and the shrimp nurseries dying since the Army Corps of Engineers had blocked the natural flow of the delta-building Mississippi with their levee system, cutting off the rich silt deposits that had traveled all the way from the heartland of the continent and that had fed the great marshes forever, now spilling the silt wastefully into the ocean. The swamps and marshes were dissolving, sinking, shrinking away. (A generation later, five hundred square miles of land had melted into water. Men closed off the saline marshes, flushed them with fresh water for a crop of rice, pumped them dry for cattle pasture and the quick money that Texas feedlot entrepreneurs would pay for scrub calves.)

There were square-jawed Malefoot relatives in New Brunswick and in

Maine, they were all over Texas, Beaumont on the Gulf, up in the Big Thicket country through Basile Malefoot who had married into the Plemon Barko rednecks with their cur dogs and whooping coon hunts on a dirt-yard frontier, Basile who on horseback could round up unmarked pigs with his dogs, rope a young porker and haul it squealing up on the saddle, clip its ears and release it. A twirl of his rope, a cry, and he had another.

Basile's older brother, Elmore Malefoot, herded cattle and raised hogs, fought Texas fever, ticks and flies on the north edge of the Calcasieu prairie near the pine flats where spits and points of woodland projected into the grassy flat plains like headlands and capes into the sea, where groves of hickories and oak and the small indentations of prairie, reminding the homesick of the irregularities of the lost coastline, were named coves and bays and islands. In the woods to the north of the prairies lived a strew of Scots Irish and Americans on their lonely square tracts, insulated from the pleasure of company and the comfort of good neighbors; the Germans down from the midwest to raise rice instead of wheat had been swallowed up, had gone French after a taste of bayou water.

The third brother, Onesiphore, had stayed in the small settlement of Goujon. Long, narrow strips of farmland ran out behind the houses as on the distant St. Lawrence centuries earlier. Onesiphore raised hogs and cane and grazed a few scrubby cattle on *gazon,* grass that grew lush and thick but failed to nourish and died and rotted when winter frost was followed by the inevitable rain. The state paved the old gumbo roads in the thirties and now, in 1959, people built along the macadam, no longer a mire of mud or choking dustland, as they had built once on the river, arranging the land in novel patterns.

Onesiphore Malefoot could remember his father, André, a man who always looked as though he were leaning back in a chair even when he was standing up, hauling their new-built house (constructed in Mermantau, near the sawmill), with teams of oxen and the help of his brothers, Elmore and Basile, over the open prairie.

"It took three days to get to Goujon. Oh yeah, they couldn't get more than ten mile a day. That poor lovely man, he has the luck of a skinny calf. He get it move and what a trouble, he forget she's jacked up and in the night—and he goes fall off the side of the house and break his leg." The house was buried in four immense cape jasmines, the drugging, drowsing perfume of home for every Malefoot who ever lived within its walls, a missing sweetness that made Buddy uneasy when he was out on the rig doing his fourteen days, making good money and dying of homesickness.

"Tell me again about this accordeen thing and how you found it and what's so good about it. Why you buy this? We got accordeens plenty, the

Napoleon Gágné, the blue one, we got the Spanish three-row, and you, you got that pretty little Soprani, and we could get fixed up the funny one—I forget all them name, but the one I wish we got is that old black and gold Monarch. Oh yeah. We got now *un mystère* accordeen, is it?"

The daughter-in-law opened her mouth for the second time.

"Pete Lucien's Marie got her niece Emma down from Maine, her husband Emil plays some music up there, the accordion—"

"Country, he plays country and western music. You know, 'Saddle my yodelin bronco and ride through the campfire at night—'" Buddy gargled an imitation yodel. "What the hell they're doin with that kind of music in Maine? You got a cigarette, Papa?"

"How about right here? Happy Fats, oh yeah, he ain't influence by country-western? The Rayne-Bo Ramblers, Hackberrys? *Diable*, they was playin it when I was a *bébé*. How about Frank Deadline, after the war? I play it myself, oh yeah, western swing, *you* play it, what you play sounds pure country sometimes. Hell, country all you hear on the radio. You told me yourself country is all you get out on the rig. So this poor Emil, he plays country-western accordeen, come down here, listen some Louisiana music, he decide, oh yeah, give up his accordeen because he can't never play so good as Cajuns?"

The daughter-in-law, wreathed in grey smoke, snickered. "Nothing like that."

Buddy said, "nothing like that. He don't like our music, too sad, not smooth. No, he keeps his own accordeen, just a big piano accordeen, white, weighs three or four tons, don't make so much sound as a little ten-button. This one here is the accordeen of some other guy, married to the niece's sister. The niece is Emma, her sister Marie, call Mitzi. The guy up in Maine, married to Marie, I forget his name, he's the one that had the accordeen"—and he gestured at the case between his wife's feet—"and he was crippled up bad, I don't know it had ennathing to do with that accident Emma's first husband died from, remember we heard about that?"

"Truckdriver-accident man the only one I heard about, oh yeah."

"That's him. Emma's husband, first husband, *before* this Emil-with-the-accordion-to-sell that belongs to the friend of Emma's truck-accident husband, the friend that marries Emma's sister Marie call Mitzi and got bad hurt legs, I don't know his name. That's the songs they supposed to play up there, French songs about chain saws and log trucks. But no, they got to get cowboy hats. So this bad-leg friend of Emma's truck-accident husband—he's a friend of Emil too—it's his accordeen, he's in a wheelchair, he makes a promise to god, if he gets his legs better he's gonna give up the accordeen. That's what happen. He gets better.

And then! He kills himself. Married two or three months and kill himself. So Emil and Emma is already on the road for down here to sell the accordeen for him, somebody down here will like to buy it. Now Marie, she's the wife calls herself Mitzi, she's Emma's sister, of the bad-leg-wheelchair-friend-of-Emil-and-the-truck-accident-husband, she need every dollar.

"Ennaway, nobody up there like the button accordeen no more. Bad as here. They say it's Frenchie stuff, so everybody going for the guitar, play rock and roll and all that. So I squeeze it a little bit, I can hear she's special, Papa, you gonna like the sound of this instrument, and she's got a big long bellows, plenty of squeeze in her, a crying voice. Oh she's a nice little girl accordeen, lonesome for the pine trees in the north, for that poor dead man, she cries on her pillow all night."

"*Vite! À la maison!* I am on flames to hear this accordeen."

"He scratch his name on the end, but I guess we sand it down right away. Leather bellows, *très bon* kidskin, pliable. He put something on it, what they used to put on the harness of the log horses, this Emil says, so it don't dry out."

"It's not stiff, it don't fight you? Leather bellows fight back, oh yeah, they do. I remember one that Iry Lejeune had before he got run over—like squeezing a corpse." He blew out a rod of smoke through pursed lips.

"No, it's easy. She's in pretty good shape, I think. You'll look at it, Papa."

Trois jours après ma mort

They were nearing the village now, past the gas station at the crossroads.

"Wait, wait, wait, wait. What is this?" Onesiphore pointed at a building going up, the Marais brothers nailing up exterior sheathing, gaping rectangles in the facade for plate-glass windows.

"Gonna be a restaurant. Somebody from Houston behind it. Call it Boudou's Cajun Café, jambalaya, crawfish boil and live music every night. For the tourists."

"Who is this Boudou?"

"Nobody. They just make up a name it sounds like Cajun, French ennaway. Building up the tourist industry, employ local people, that's the Marais brothers."

"Y'know," Onesiphore said, squinting up his eyes malevolently, "my generation we just live. We don't think who we are, or anything, we just get born, live, fish and farm, eat home cooking, dance, play some music, grow old and die, nobody come here and bother us. Your generation split up. All of you talk American, no French hardly at all. Some say 'oh, I got to learn French, I got to be Cajun, quick, show me some words and give me a *'tit fer* I can play Cajun music.' So then these *bébés* here, they coming up in a time where strangers get in, make a restaurant, nobody's gonna eat at home and go to the dance, but they go to a restaurant own by some guy from Texas, a place for tourists come to see the Cajuns, like monkeys. *CAJUNLAND!* Put up the sign."

Buddy rolled his eyes. They were past Dumont's store, abreast of the woven wire fence topped with two rows of barbwire in front of Bo Arbour's new ranch house, window trim painted sea blue, plaster ducks in the rank-growing grass and the first of the row of television aerials that marked the air with loops and curves resembling the old skillet-full-of-snakes cattle brands.

"You never could tell, you look at that nice house, old man Arbour died from leprosy. Oh I remember, they said his leg was like cheese, his big toe fell off in the bedroom, then they took him away to Carville there with the lepers. Kept it secret for a long time so he can stay home."

"Oil rig work built that house," said Buddy out of the right side of his mouth. They passed Onesiphore's cow pond and turned into his driveway. Buddy and the daughter-in-law lived on the far edge of the village near the rice field, in the modular house Buddy was still paying off. They pulled up behind Onesiphore's old truck, the paint completely gone, a dark red shell of a truck eaten out by the damp salt, dented all over from the old man's accidents and dance hall parking lot bashes with fried drivers. There was a spatter of shot holes in the cab from the night Belle was killed.

"Let's get this cow trough down first," said Onesiphore. "I wanna put him over by the fence where it's that old wood one." Cigarettes in the corners of their mouths to keep the smoke from their eyes, they carried it to the fence and pulled away the splintered, broken wooden trough that had been there forever, as long as Buddy could remember, and Onesiphore lashed the new one to the fence with wire. The galvanized metal gleamed.

"Those cows don't butt it away now, oh yeah, when he's empty," he said. "We try it out with a little hay, get them used to this good new trough," and he broke a bale into it. There was a rumble of thunder.

Belle

The daughter-in-law made the children take off their shoes in the entry; Mme Malefoot kept a bitterly clean house, and it was one reason Buddy and his family did not often go there. The white gas range against one wall balanced the gleaming refrigerator on the other. The clean blue light from the window reflected from the surface of the white enamel table and from the polished glass ashtray. The floor was white linoleum, waxed to a watery glare. Mme Malefoot had ordered the flooring after the death of Belle, dead years ago in a parking lot in Empire. Three other people had been shot or stabbed in separate fights that night, two of them blasted by an enraged and drunk troublemaker named Earl, thrown out of the bar for pissing on customers' legs (he later had a fatal coughing fit in the penitentiary). In the moiling darkness customers had rushed from wall to wall, into the parking lot and back, like ants trodden by horses. Belle, her silhouette mistaken by Earl for that of the bartender—both were slender and short, both had frizzy halos of hair—took a charge of buckshot in the chest and died at the hospital the next morning. The waiting room had smelled of guinea pigs.

Always tidy and fine, Mme Malefoot began after Belle's funeral to clean obsessively, spoke little, fell into silences. She left Onesiphore's bed and slept in the room of her dead daughter. In the flow of the rising moon it seemed sometimes the girl was only away, visiting her cousins in Texas. A slow, holy music, pure voices arcing through the broken clouds, slid into the room with the moonlight. A net of light appeared on the wall, a delicate mesh in a curving form like a drawn bow, with a deep band at the end and a fringe of filaments, long threads of moonlight given motion by the warm air above the electric heater through which the light passed. She could not find the source of this odd and beautiful dispersion and in a few minutes it was gone, the wall an ordinary dull white. She took it as proof of her daughter's ascension and presence. She secretly purchased a selection of tubes of paint and when Onesiphore was away from the house tried to re-create her dead daughter's face, first on paper plates, then on squares of canvas, unstretchered, laid flat on the table, copying from old photographs. She painted her as an infant, as a child holding a snapping turtle above her head, on her knees saying her prayers, as a young woman sitting beside her father striking the *'tit fer* that had caused her death, for had she not played music in the rowdy dens with Onesiphore and Buddy, had she not worn American blue jeans, had she had a fuller bosom— poor child, she was as flat as a wall—she would not have been mistaken for a man in that rough place and would still live. Had she not been a little slow, an innocent who was not wary of evil, all would have been different. Onesiphore himself had a great scar from eye to jaw from years before when he had played at a country dance hall ("Hit the floor and start dancin!"), a dangerous place where the musicians were not protected from flying bottles by a chicken-wire cage, all that smoke and so hot their eyes as red as Christmas the next day, and Buddy was always in a fight, partly because of his combative nature, his truculent anger, but so far had felled all attackers with right-left punches and a knee in the groin. The best painting of Belle, showing her as a child holding a calico cat, hung in that bedroom, framed in a black-enameled toilet seat with gilded margin, the lid hiding the portrait unless it was lifted.

Onesiphore examines the green accordion

White muslin curtains framed the incoming storm. A painting of three diaphanously clothed angels flying through a rainbow, also from Mme's brush, one angel with the features of Belle, hung over the insurance company calendar. White china plates leaned against the rail of the sideboard, cups the white of peeled eggs, a white sink and a white porcelain drainboard. The daughter-in-law felt as awkward as a burned moth bumping against the enameled surfaces. In all this chill paleness only Mme Malefoot, dressed in her cream polyester pants suit, the smell of fresh-roasted coffee and the chairs seemed lively and warm. The chairs were homemade, with thick legs and plain ladderbacks, the wood scraped smooth with a piece of broken glass, the seats of red and white cowhide with the hair still on. Near the window was the cat's chair, and out in the grass inspecting the new trough stood the cat himself, immense, squarish and orange, resembling a suitcase, his tail a broken strap. The storm cloud darkened the grass and he moved toward the back door.

Mme was stout and proud, her grey hair fixed in a tight double bun at the top of her head. Her large face, like a china plate itself, floated above a lace collar. She embraced her daughter-in-law without feeling, kissed the children coldly, set out pecan cookies on a foil pie tin instead of good china which the daughter-in-law perceived as an insult, began to grind the coffee beans, halted in midgrind to admit the cat who was clawing at the door. He marched to his chair, sprang up and began smoothing his fur in short, displeased licks.

Buddy opened the instrument case, lifted out the green accordion and handed it to his father. Onesiphore, on his chair, legs cocked open, examined it minutely, undid the clasps. He worked the buttons, nodding at the action, then lifted his arms, elbows down, and began to draw music from it, the vigorous double time seizing the kitchen, kicking up the rhythm with his octave jumps. He stopped after a few minutes, looked at Buddy and winked, then turned away and began to play again, lifting his voice over thunder so loud the china plates quivered against their dish rail, threw down a sobbing gulp at the end of the lines as though he had been punched.

> *"Yie, chère 'tite fille,*
> *Ah, viens me rejoindre là-bas à la maison.*
> *Trois jours, trois jours après ma mort, yie,*
> *Tu vas venir à la maison te lamenter à moi.*
> *Yie, garde-donc 'tit monde . . .*

"Oh yeah, man that made this knew one or two somethings. Buzz on the E, probly a loose reed. She's quick, got good action, but she's noisy. You hear how she clacks?" He lit a cigarette, squinted into the nearly empty pack with sorrow.

"Me, I like that sound. That's part of the music. That's Cajun, that clacking."

"Tell you what's not Cajun is that valves—you hear her make that gurgle, a kind of throat sound? Listen." He played again:

> *"Fais pas ça ou ta maman va pleurer.*
> *Viens avec moi, yie, là-bas,*
> *Non, non, ta maman fait pas rien.*
> *Yie, toi, 'tite fille,*
> *Moi je connais tu ferais mieux pas faire ça, yie, yie, yie"*

and they could hear the rough sound, could hear too the first strikes of rain as though called down by the music.

"My car's gonna get a Mexican car wash," said Buddy.

"That's your leather valves. They'll curl up over time." He had the instrument open, examining the reed plate. "It's an old one, see it how it's made, oh yeah, everything by the craftsman hand, everything good. Look here. We replace the valves. Just one big reed plate. See how he puts a little bend in the reeds at the tip? That gives you more metal at the tip, the tone is deep, more full. You know, I think we give her new reeds, retune, flatten the thirds, give her a good sharp bite. *'Anodder man's waaaaaf.'*"

"Sounds pretty good."

"OK. Then replace the gasket around the treble box—she's no good. Take the grille off. Pretty, but it smothers the tone. We get it ready for Saturday. They say some woman photographer come here, wanna see

Cajun life, oyster tong, *fais dodo, la boucherie.* How much you pay for this little box?"

There was an anxious silence in the room. Buddy leaned against the sink, crossed his feet at the ankles. A tremendous thunderclap, and a simultaneous stroke of lightning turned the room blue.

"Don't sit near the window, *cher,*" pleaded Mme Malefoot to the yellow cat.

"One hundred and fifteen dollars." He ignored the storm, his mother.

"*Mon dieu!* You Jean Sot! Too much money. It's a fortune. You throw money away. Don't you point out the problems to him? You could get him down maybe to fifty, sixty? She's worth something, oh yeah, me, I don't say she's not, a handmade, a special one, but needs work, and if you was smart you could jew him down, *non?*" and crushed the smoking stub of his cigarette into the glass ashtray.

"No. Listen, Papa, you getting tight as the skin on a dead goat. I got a good reason. That poor woman up in Maine after what happen she need every penny. She'll never, never, never get over it, Emma says."

"She find him?"

"No, thank the saints. Somebody work in the woods near him, finds him and run out like a crazy man." He lowered his voice so the children wouldn't hear, although they did. "*He cuts off his own head.* He makes a thing in the woods, tie up the chain saw between some trees and get it running, and then he—and then he walk into it so it—*zut.*" He drew his hand across his neck.

"*Non!*"

"Yeah. But you know what? He done his day's work first."

"That's the Frenchman for you!"

"Grandpa, the cows fell down and now they're sleeping in the rain," said the boy.

"Eh? Oh, oh, holy god!" He flung open the kitchen door and looked at the three cows, their bodies steaming in the downpour, looked at the tilted pole, the power line from it trailing on the fence, at the metal trough half full of wet hay and sparking. Yet they were not dead. In twenty minutes they were standing with wide-spraddled legs, and nothing ever induced any of them to eat from a trough again. Onesiphore had to pitch their hay on the ground and even then they were suspicious.

Women at the *fais dodo*

The photographer, Olga Buckle, a tall blond woman with Afro-frizzed hair and wearing red bell-bottoms, skilled at setting her foot in an advantageous spot and shoving until she got into the center of things, parked in the lumpy dirt yard outside the plank-sided dance hall faced around the bottom with corrugated metal and roofed with the same material. She drove a new De Soto with Flair-Stream fins and push-button drive. Her great shot had been on the cover of *Life* the year before, college students squeezed into a telephone booth, and a close-up of an agonized face with bulging eyes at the bottom of the pile, a twenty-year-old pole vaulter dying as the shutter clicked.

She was on assignment for the Folklore of the American Hinterlands Institute in Washington, a government-funded archive staffed by trim little men with grey goatees. She could never relax, did not drink even when someone said a drink is a Cajun handshake, wouldn't dance, couldn't see the point of *bourée,* yawned at horse races, was a stranger to hog and beef killings, had never tasted the white tailmeat of *cocodrie,* could not keep her balance in a skiff, had never slept on a pillow stuffed with dried moss, was not Catholic, had never before seen a rub-board or thimble rhythm section, rice or cane in the field, nor driven a mule, nor ridden a horse, nor caught a hog, could not understand French and did not like women. She was a chain-smoker. Almost all the pictures she took were of men, though weaver Granny Reneaux (who looked like a man) appeared in one or two, weaving, and Mme Fortier, five times a widow, tufting a quilt and shooting glances out of her rare violet eyes, got a shot.

Inside the hall the writer, Winnie Wall, sidled up to her and said, "I thought you were lost."

"I never get lost."

Winnie Wall was a youngish woman who had abandoned her brassiere, dressed in a sprigged calico Mother Hubbard and lugged a recording machine. She asked hundreds of relentless questions in a French so stiff and peculiar that people begged her to speak English. She seemed always about to faint, her underarms wet with sweat, her rough-skinned face without makeup or lipstick, streaked with perspiration, and her damp hair matted down.

"She is very sick, she has a sickness in a private place," whispered Mrs. Blush Leleur, the *traîteuse,* to the daughter-in-law's pale ear. Both women stood in the room off the main dance hall, the children's room where the big platform bed was made up for a dozen babies. In the main hall they were playing "The Unlucky Waltz." The daughter-in-law handed her plate of Marshmallow Krispy Treats to the *traîteuse* to hold while she put Debbie down. At the end of the waltz Archange, the announcer, spoke into the microphone.

"Driver of the maroon and white pickup, you lights is on."

The *traîteuse,* tall, with large, strong hands, was dressed in rose-colored slacks and a purple rayon blouse with cloth-covered buttons and a Chinese collar. She wore twelve strings of false pearls around her neck, one long and descending below her waist. Although she was sixty-five her hair was as black as soot and as curly as sucked dandelion stems. She wore gilded harlequin eyeglasses with tinted lenses. On her withered earlobes were clamped pearl disks. Her face was wrinkled, the same blunt but agreeable expression as that of a turtle, her mouth colored with black-red lipstick called Barbecue. The daughter-in-law covered her wide-awake child with a red shawl and sang, half American, half French, " 'go to sleepy, little *bébé,* when you wake you shall have some cherry cake . . .' " Her white, sleek arms looked airbrushed. The music stopped and the microphone squealed and whistled.

"Driver of that two-tone pickup, you don't shut the lights off you be hoofin it. You battery almost dead."

"I can smell this sickness. It is in her private parts and she wears no underclothing because of the pain it causes her. She can speak of it to no one. The photographer, she dislikes her and did not wish her to come. They are here to learn Cajun ways." She laughed with good-natured malice. Through the doorway they watched the young woman take a bottle of beer from an outstretched hand.

"That will make it worse," said Mrs. Blush Leleur, "beer is very bad for this one's condition. There was such a woman in a certain parish a dozen years ago, she swelled up so her private parts resembled two slices of watermelon, a terrible itching and burning of fire. Her husband—he was an albino and at first I thought it was because of something coming out of him, *you* know what I mean, that made her like this—but he could not even enter the same room. She prayed for death and wept day and night because the pain was so intense."

"What caused such a thing!"

"Beer. And other foods and spices, wholesome for others, simple good things as okra, yams, beans and peanuts, pecans and even grits. It came to me in a dream. I dreamed of her drinking beer and suffering. First I made her fast for five days and drink only rainwater to clear her body of poisons. Then I gave a little corn bread and lettuce, rice and other little things that nourished her and did not inflame the susceptible parts. She lived many happy years until she was frightened by a bone in a jar some evil one placed on her top stair and went into a cataleptic trance and wasted away. How is Mme Malefoot?"

"She's in good health except for the arthritis, but very coldhearted.

She barely touches her grandchildren. She cares nothing for the child that is coming. Onesiphore sleeps alone in their bed. She spends much time in Belle's room. What must we do? Is there a cure for this?"

The music halted again and Archange's hollow voice said, "you better call you mother, pickup owner—you ain't got no transportation."

"Do you wish to engage me?"

The daughter-in-law thought for a moment. It was not her affair or her place to interfere. Onesiphore and Buddy should speak to the *traîteuse*. Yet she thought they would not do so. She thought of her children, so coldly embraced by their grandmother whose glance fell away from them as though they were worms.

"Yes."

"Very well. This woman has frozen her grief. This woman has sealed her heart up by will. She fears nothing for herself now, not death or God, feels herself damned to hell on earth. She feels nothing for her husband for she has left his bed. She feels nothing for her grandchildren for she is cold to them and does not see them. You she does not see. But what of the other son, Buddy. Is she frozen to him as well?"

"To everything. Except her yellow cat. In the storm that knocked down their cows—she laughed as they lay in the mud—the cat sat near the window and she pleaded with him to move. She called him '*cher*.'"

"Maybe this is good. She still feels something. Not good that it is a cat who engages her affection. Still, perhaps we can pry open this little crack into her heart to pour in a warm medicine that will make her return to her family. Let me put this matter under my pillow. Come to my house if you can in a few days and I will have a plan."

In the house of the *traîteuse*

One did not enter the kitchen of Mrs. Blush Leleur but stepped into a cramped hall containing a coatrack and a chair with a cowhide seat, a hooked rug in a design of roses. She had come by her fearsome powers as a child. One day in the late autumn her father, an alcoholic cow horn salesman, leaned against the barn wall and jealously watched a stranger enter his yard, knock on his door. A gypsy. He imagined he saw his wife smile and wink at this gypsy man selling painted wooden fruit. When the gypsy left he gathered armfuls of dry leaves and grass and piled it in the yard, dragged his wife outside (the child watching through the window), threw her down in the tinder and set it on fire. The wretched woman ran shrieking and aflame for the bayou, emerged sobbing and muddy, burned on her arms and legs, the side of her face white with dead skin. The child directed a savage thought at her father, that he become small and weak. That night her father began to shrink. The process was agonizingly slow, but in ten years he was the height of a child, withered and tiny, his arms like hollow stalks, and when he finally died he was no larger than a loaf of bread. His scarred and ruined wife threw him into the yard for the hens to peck. (She remarried a blind egg farmer and enjoyed a decade of vigorous affection before their car was struck by an Amtrak train, the engineer's timing distorted by the hallucinatory by-flashes of utility poles.)

The hall opened into an intensely crowded parlor, the walls obscured by photographs of Leleurs and Prudhommes singing, graduating, marrying, paintings of Christ blessing the multitude, Christ like a girl with a mustache, crucifixes large and small, stamped metal maxims, bunches of dried flowers, silent clocks, calendars, a recipe for butter cookies on a painted breadboard; every flat surface was covered with a cloth and every cloth was of lace. On a table in the corner lay a bible, a spiral notebook in which visitors were invited to write their names, a ballpoint pen that formed the tail of a ceramic hound dog, three vases of plastic flowers, seventeen saints and Christs, eleven photographs of grandchildren, five candles, a folded newspaper, a stack of postal flyers and supermarket coupons, a Zippo lighter, a bottle of Troutman's cough syrup, a camera, a ceramic owl, a blue candy box. The television, new and blond, with splayed spindle legs, flickered in the corner. Pinned to the wall was a newspaper article featuring a photograph of Mrs. Blush Leleur dressed in her rayon blouse and strings of beads.

She invited the daughter-in-law, who had fetched a plate of green cupcakes as an offering, to take a chair near the table, brought her a demitasse of *petit noir* and said, "if this cat dies, her affection will take flight and fasten to the first one who approaches her with consoling words. You must see that it is you, her grandchildren, her husband and son who comfort her over the loss of the cat. She will love you all. And that's what we want—when people's gonna love you, when evrabody's her friend and she won't never do no wrong against you and the grandchildren again. Just gonna love them." She bit into a cupcake.

"Oh, *chère,* what good frosting."

"But the cat is healthy and well."

"Things change," said the *traîteuse.*

Death comes for the yellow cat

The yellow cat was nine years old and had not spent one of his lives. But, as sometimes is the case, he had to pay up everything in full in a few brief minutes.

Like many fortunate beings he had become self-centered, would not eat crawfish unless Mme Malefoot removed the shells, spurned skim milk, preferred *sauce roulée* to butter but had been known to lick the butter down to the pattern on the dish, and had only to scratch idly at the back door and Mme would come flying and coax him in with promises of cheese, for he liked squares of good strong cheese above all else excepting fresh-caught young mice, so young they had not yet grown throat-catching fur to spoil the treat, could be swallowed alive, bones and all, their wriggles providing a pleasant *frisson.*

He rarely left the Malefoot farm for he was too heavy for adventure, knew the boundaries and fences very well, had timed to a nicety the distance he could travel in the adjoining goat pasture before the old billy would charge and helplessly clang his horns on the fence while the cat licked his paw in safety. He crossed the road sometimes to the neighbor's where he ate the dish of scraps the child set out for a thin dog, but looked both ways first and never let himself be approached by pedestrians, especially those with guns, sticks, ropes, whips, branches, stones or other harmful objects in their hands. No one could touch him but Mme Malefoot, and sometimes he pulled away from her or clawed her caressing hand. Before he became too heavy, he was a great cat for climbing the chinaberry tree and capturing birds. In his prime he had torn swallows from the air, and he was still a first-rate rat and mouse catcher, crouching silently near the long grass for interminable lengths of time until he detected the faint stirring in the grass, then, with hindquarters setting and resetting, tail twitching and eyes ablaze, he sprang, and an hour of amusement was guaranteed as he let it go, sprang again, released it, batted it up in the air, caught it in his hind feet like a ball of yarn, rolled on it, pretended to lose it utterly while watching the grass quake and tremble as the wounded mouse staggered off, then flew upon it once again until the mouse was worn out and dead, and even then he smacked it about hoping to revive it with a little roughing up.

Two weeks after the *fais dodo* the photographer was still hanging around, though Winnie with the tape recorder had gone back up north. The photographer had exhausted the tamer aspects of Cajun life and had turned now to illegal cockfights, flashlight alligator hunts, horses being

fixed with charms and potions to win or lose races, miscegenation, arm-
wrestling matches where the winner snaps the loser's ulna, staring
matches, bad-blood ambushes, shooting victims, raped and disheveled
girls telling their stories, raids on stills, swamp hideouts with escaped con-
victs in residence, or, what was now promised for Saturday night, dog-
fights to the death. She felt no personal danger when thrusting into these
dark affairs; she held her camera as a shield, felt her position to be one
of privilege and safety, for she had an important reputation, came from
the north, and *she knew better.*

The yellow cat was taken in surprise ambush. As he helped himself
to orts in the neighbor dog's dish, a croker sack came down over him
with violence and such speed that the dog's dish and the fatback rind
and cold grits in it were swept up as well. At first he tried to claw his way
out, razory talons protruding from the sack mesh, but the abductor tied
a double knot in the sack neck and threw it and the cat into the back of
an idling pickup truck which squealed onto the highway and sped into
the golden evening light. Inside the sack the cat wrestled and clawed,
slumped, despaired, howled and swore vengeance, bit the dish with
such fury it cracked, shat with rage but was still in the croker sack when
the truck arrived at a waterfront warehouse where men, dogs and the
photographer waited.

The dogs were streamlined for fighting, their ears cropped away,
their tails bobbed. They had no rest. Tonight's winner had to fight again
the next day and every fight was to the death. How long a dog lived
depended on how long he kept winning. Big money exchanged hands.
A good dog man could live on his ring earnings without working. The
yellow cat was the opening entertainment, an appetizer to get the dogs'
blood up, in the mood for killing.

The yellow cat was dumped into a sandy ring about twenty feet
across, surrounded by a chicken-wire fence with a rail top. Men, smoking, chewing, rolling cigarettes, gnawing on buffalo chicken wings or
biting their nails, sucking at their fingers, picking shreds of meat from
between their teeth with horny nails, hung over the rail, rested their
arms on it. They shouted when the yellow cat tumbled out. Grits were
matted in his fur. He was huge, bristling with insult, fright and rage. He
streaked for the chicken-wire fence, searching for the way out. Three
dogs were released into the ring and they went for him at once, growling, snapping, skidding to a stop and turning on a nickel as the cat spun
and wove and dashed between them. There was no respite. Every
frontal feint was answered from behind. He clawed a dog's nose,
another dog seized him by the back and shook, his hindquarters were

paralyzed, yet his eyes continued to blaze and he lashed out. It was over in a few minutes when his head was taken in the jaws of a stubby black dog and crushed. The yellow cat was dead.

But when the dogs were called off, the cat's body, instead of being shoveled out the back door into the bayou, was dumped in the croker sack again and the same pickup spun out to the east. Someone heaved the corpse over the Malefoots' fence and it landed not far from the back door. A few minutes later the truck cruised past the house of Buddy and the daughter-in-law and the horn sounded four times. Buddy was out on the rig, the daughter-in-law did not wake up, sunk in a dreamless moon-under sleep.

A strange encounter

The photographer struggled to drive a straight line in the rose dawn, her eyes smarting with smoke, her legs like rubber from standing up all night and her breath fetid with cigarettes and soft drinks. She yawned a horrible cavernous yawn, her eyes filling with tears, jaw cracking and a roar bursting from her stringy bowel as she steered through the puddles (rain in the night) and came abreast of the Malefoot yard to see a middle-aged woman limping around the corner in nightgown and mud-caked slippers, face swollen with weeping, trailing a pointed shovel in her hands. She leaned the shovel against the steps, sat on the damp bottom tread, put her face in her hands and sobbed.

The photographer slowed, stopped, aimed her camera through the greasy window, thought better of it, got out, leaned on the hood, sighted through the clear air at the bereft woman lighted by a great swath of green sunlight and began snapping pictures. The woman did not lift her head. The photographer advanced, leaned over the fence and shot. The woman looked up. Through her tear-filmed eyes the female figure at the gate, heroically large against the rising sun, holy in its streaming rays, seemed to her to be the angel of Belle come to console her mother.

"Oh *chère,*" she sobbed, "thank God you come to me." She got up and staggered toward her with her arms outstretched. The photographer, using her camera as a shield, clicked again and again at the advancing woman and still she came on. She could smell her grief, a bitter, briny odor.

"Belle," the woman groaned. "*Bébé. Ma chère, ma fille.*" She embraced her, felt the camera, saw her face, so changed, but understood why she was wearing this ugly carnival mask—no one must know she had come back from the dead. She seized her hand and dragged her toward the door.

Inside the kitchen the photographer sat at the table, ill at ease. In habit she raised her camera and began to take interior shots of the chair by the window, the glass jar of rice. Mme Malefoot understood this perfectly. If her daughter was called back to Paradise, at least she would have photographs of home to ease her loneliness. She led her daughter upstairs to her old room, showed her the portrait waiting in darkness behind the toilet seat lid, smoothed the pillow. She took her into every room, to the parlor, the pantry and the kitchen, tried to give her a plate of red beans and rice, coaxed her to the porch and up the outside stairs to the room where her father lay sleeping, grey hair in a pointed muss, guided her outside to the tree where she had played as a child, and around the barn to see the yellow cat's fresh grave. A siege of herons flew up from the bayou across the road.

"Got to go now," the photographer said when the woman came pressing close again with a yearning expression. It was awful. What was wrong with the old broad? It was as though she had fallen in love with her, this big flat-faced, middle-aged woman with her damp caresses and tear-streaked voice.

Mme Malefoot understood. The angels were calling her child back to them. She had the photographs of home and they would be developed in heaven. She seized the girl in her damp arms, kissed her shoulder (she had grown tall up there), wept and clung as she pulled away.

"Will you come back?" she called. "Will I see you again soon? Come at night. I'm sleeping in your room!" She couldn't hear the answer, but the photographer lifted her right hand and saluted to her. A girl does not forget her mother! And she drove away like an ordinary person, but of course that was part of the disguise.

(Two decades later the photographer was blinded in the left eye by a nine-millimeter semiautomatic pistol in the hands of a nine-year-old boy firing from his family's apartment window at cars stopped for the red light. There was a good side to the injury; she became a celebrity victim and within months her work was displayed and awarded, she appeared on television talk shows and in radio interviews.)

Out on the rig

"Your oil rig is a fuckin crazy place," said Coodermonce, who'd given up the invisible-vinyl-repair business for the steady rig paychecks. He was part of the confusion, for on this rig worked Cuddermash, Cuttermarsh,

Coudemoche, Cordeminch and Gartermatch, all variations on the original name, Courtemanche. Buddy liked the work for the pay and the wrongo heads on the rig, hated it for the Yankee bosses and the lonely feeling of being out in the Gulf with no way home, shut up for two-week stretches hearing the same goddamn record on somebody's turntable, something bad like Gypsy Sandor or the Voices of Walter Schumann, having to hear the endlessly repeated stories of the old guys, high-tempered toolpushers, riggers, derrickmen and chuffy roughnecks who remembered the pipeline walkers, oil witchers, shooters and doodlebug men, who had seen everything twice, jamming around through Oklahoma and Texas drinking pop-skull whiskey and sleeping it off in bowl-and-pitcher hotels and now telling their salted stories to the Louisiana French boys, these babes who had never worked the oil fields. Carver Stringbellow, sunburned red, a single blond eyebrow and sandy-gold hair in deep crenellations, never without his pair of white gloves, told about the wildflower man who drilled where wildflowers caught his fancy and always struck oil, had seen drill pipes blown out of the hole, shooters disintegrate into bloody pieces the size of dimes in the old liquid nitro days when it exploded prematurely, had experienced a tornado that tore the rig apart and threw the toolpusher's new sedan into a swamp, a Texas windstorm that pasted a metal Nehi sign across his back and then ran him over the ground as fast as he could go, running on his toes and praying not to lift off into the dirt-filled air. He was a big old boy from Odessa, six foot five, top-heavy and dedicated to fight and drink. He always arrived at the rig lamed up, bruises fading into chartreuse and yellow, married and divorced seven times and claimed to have fathered more than fifty kids, from Corsicana, Texas, to Cairo, Missouri. He ran a comb that he carried in his back pocket through his hair twenty times a day, said he had been out to the Middle East, worked for Socal in Bahrain in the thirties where he learned to relish sheep's eyes, during the war when Socal and Texaco merged as Aramco he worked in Saudi Arabia, knew crazy Everette Lee DeGolyer with his passion for oil, chile peppers, and the *Saturday Review of Literature,* ate lunch once with management in the Hotel Aviz in Lisbon at an hour when Calouste Gulbenkian was seated at his private table on a platform of some altitude, had seen the half-mad Getty, richest man in America, with his surgically tautened face, chewing oysters thirty-three times per mouthful and smiled when Jack Zone, who'd asked him to the lunch, speculated whether or not that old crocodile was wearing the famous underwear he washed himself by hand each night in a little gold basin. He could tell the weather three days in advance and drank thirty cups of black coffee a day, lived boom or bust, pockets stuffed with money or jobless and on the grass, read about bullfighting and said it was his idea to go to Spain and see Ordóñez someday, to see Hemingway in the bar and talk with him afterward.

"Listen, last year you know what he did, Heminway? He shot the ash off the end of a cigarette that Ordóñez was smokin at a party. They do that to test each other's nerve—and smoke it down to a short butt, like this"—he drew on his inch-long Camel—"and then they shoot the ash off. With a twenty-two. This one guy, he says, 'Ernesto, we can go no farther. I felt it brush my lips.' Somethin like that." For years he had saved money to go to Spain, but whenever he had nearly enough something happened—a woman, a poker game, one winter a long stay in the hospital with broken knees.

"You want money you ought to help me find this painting," said Screw-Loose, from Beaumont in the coastal part of Texas known as Louisiana Lapland. "You know that whiskey, Sunny Crow whiskey, gonna give a reward to the one finds this painting. Twenty-five grand'll buy a lot of bullfight tickets. I got a good idea where that lost painting is, oil painting by Frederick Remington of a calvary charge. About fifty guys coming right at you, hell-bent for leather. Now, see, I know I seen this painting somewhere one time, I know it like I know the feel of my old lady's ass. I seen it. Then I seen the picture in a magazine couple of years ago—Sunny Crow run a photograph of the painting in a magazine—when Remington died they found this photograph in his stuff, but the picture, the painting? Nowhere to be saw. They know he painted it, the photograph proves it, but they can't find it. And I actually *seen* it somewhere. Every night I go to sleep I tell myself 'tonight you're gonna dream where you saw that painting and when you wake up you are a rich man.' It'll work one of these days because I remember seeing it. I just can't remember where."

At least this time there was some new music and maybe he wouldn't get sick of it before his tour was up. He'd brought the accordion out once, but it went over like a lead balloon.

"Don't play that fuckin coonass chanky-chank, boy," Carver said, combing his hair. "That fuckin music is worse than killin pigs."

"Yeah? Don't call me 'boy' like I was a nigger unless you want your face changed."

"Yeah? I was you I'd watch my mouth. Accidents happen pretty easy to guys with big mouths, 'specially a fuckin coonass." He smiled like a skull.

"Yeah? I was you I'd get a pair of eyes in the back of my head. It's better than that fuckin castanet shit you play."

"Yeah? You know what they say, 'look all around a coonass's bed, nothin but bedbugs, shit and crawfish heads.'"

"OK, fella," said Buddy, "I'll see you ashore." Fighting on the rig meant instant dismissal, with the company launch out to pick you up within the hour and your name guaranteed on the blacklist.

(By the time his hair was starting to grey up and the Louisiana oil boom was over, Buddy was the toolpusher on an offshore rig in the North Sea, working with burr-voiced Scots.)

The third day into this tour somebody saw the boat breasting toward them, bouncing through the white crests and giving the occupants a hell of a ride.

"Fish man ahoy!"

Buddy recognized the fishing boat of Octave, black and wiry, a good boy on the *'tit fer* when you could pry him away from that nigger zydeco shit, did odd jobs and sold fish on the side, came out to the rig twice a week if the weather let him, Tuesday and Saturday, with catfish and a couple of sacks of mudbugs for a boil, once in a rare while a slab of gator tail. He got double the going price from the rigs. This wasn't his regular day.

"Somebody with him!" Everybody tensed up and the men on deck shaded their eyes and strained to see the second person. A second person meant news of trouble.

It was the daughter-in-law. She crouched in the bow, staring at the rig, trying to pick Buddy out. Her eyes were not good. He recognized her before they were in hailing distance. Octave was bailing with a flattened coffee can, his eyes hidden behind blue-tinted glasses, his old cowboy hat hiding his dark face in darker shadows. The sky above was packed with clouds like wadded gauze.

"Now what," he muttered. She'd done the same thing the year before when they'd taken his mother to the hospital after she'd painted her face and hands and dress a mess of thick colors, the lampblack and gamboge and viridian streaked everywhere in the white kitchen. He could see it was a new disaster.

"What is it?" he shouted.

"Your father, Papa Onesiphore—he's gone."

"What! He's dead? Papa's dead?"

"No, no. Gone to Texas. He stopped by, his truck all loaded up, said he was sorry but he had to go. He left your mother. He says he can't take it anymore, living with a crazy woman." Everyone on deck was listening now.

"Did you see *Maman?*"

"Yeah. She don't know but she thinks he's going up to stay with his brother Basile in Texas. She thinks your sister came back from the dead and she's up there too. In Texas. There was them cousins she liked so much."

"*Non.* The cousins she liked was Elmore's kids—Gene and Clara and Grace. He can't be going up to see Uncle Basile. He hasn't seen him since he was twenty years old."

"What shall I do? Can you come home?"

"Can't you take the kids over and stay with her a few days? I'll be home in ten more days, goddammit."

His wife began to cry. She was wearing a pale blue cotton dress and black rubber boots. She cried silently, letting the tears roll down her face. She looked at him. Octave's boat rose and fell.

"Go home! Stay with her. He'll come back in a day or two." He glared at Octave in the stern who smiled enigmatically. "You, Octave, you shouldn't of brought her out here. Take her back." He turned away, smarting with rage, heard his wife say "last time I tell you anything," then the stutter of Octave's motor drowned her out.

After a while Adam Coultermuch said, "my father run out on us when I was four years old. I don't even remember what he looked like. Never saw the bastard again."

Quart Cuttermarsh said, "hey, you was lucky. I would of give anything if my old man run off. He'd get drunk up, beat the shit out of us. You wanta see something? Look at this." He pulled off his shirt, revealed round scars up and down his arms. "Cigarette. He'd burn us to watch us cry. I hope he's roasting in hell. I heard he got knifed in a bar in Mobile."

"My dad was OK when we were kids, I mean, he didn't do nothin to us, always workin or sleepin, but when we come up a little, about fifteen, sixteen years old, god, he turned mean," added T. K. Coudemoche. "I was in a car, car belonged to the father of a friend of mine and my friend was supposed to drive it down to the railroad station and meet his dad, we was both sixteen or seventeen, going along the road there nice and steady when this car come up behind us. It was my dad and he was trying to pass. Well, my friend, he didn't know any better, thought he'd have a little fun, so he pulls out in the middle of the road and don't let the old man pass. I tell him, that's my old man and you better let him by. He's got a temper. But my friend says it's just a little fun and he don't let him pass. Well, the old man tries five or six times, puts on his lights and toots the horn and I'm sittin there shakin because I know he's gonna follow us to the station. I got this plan when we get there to get out and run so he don't know I'm in the car. But we never got there. My friend got kind of careless and the old man gets abreast and then edges us off the road into a ditch, just locks fenders and butts us off. My friend stops in the ditch and gets out and here comes the old man swingin a tire iron and cussin everything in the world, and he lets my friend have it right across the nose with the tire iron, you could hear it go crunch, he gives me a terrific crack on the arm, breaks my arm, then he set to work on my friend's father's car. He smashed that thing, glass everywhere, he pounded on the fenders, sprung the hood, tore up the doors, and for a finale, pulled out his whacker and pissed on the front seat. Didn't say a word. Just got back in his car and drove off. I didn't even bother to go home. I lit out for the oil fields and been there ever since."

Iry Gartermatch cleared his throat. "My father was normal until he was seventy-five, then he married a girl of eighteen, simpleminded, she had three kids and he died when he was eighty and didn't leave none of us nothin but trouble."

They were trying to make him feel better. Where the hell could a seventy-five-year-old man run off to? And he was right.

The green accordion brings a good price

When he drove down the road ten days later the old man was sitting on the porch with the green accordion on his knee playing "*Chère Alice,*" cigarette in his mouth, and out in the yard Mme Malefoot gathered shirts and tablecloths in the calm sunlight as though life had rolled sevens and elevens all the way.

He pulled into the driveway, stared at his father. "I heard you gone on a trip."

"*Oui,* yes, *mon fils,* just a little trip, me, '*go put on your little dress with stripes . . . ,*' just want to see how they are doing in the world. Just a little change for my eyes. Yes, I am very happy to be home again on the bayou. We play tomorrow night for a dance, the barbecue dance at Gayneauxs, '*she didn't know I was marrrrrried.*' That *Saturday Even Post* comes with a photographer. Every week we got one, click the flashers in your eye. You come here tonight with your accordion, play a little in the kitchen. That black guy Octave comes by. You know he say he love this green accordion very much. He say he give two hundred fifty for it."

"Where the hell would that nigger get two fifty? Eh?"

"Sell Gene Autry seed packs, rob a bank, fix TVs. Sell fish to the rig."

"You serious?"

"Oh yeah."

"If he got it we'll take it. I can get Mr. Pelsier to build one just as good, better, for a hundred. Take the money and run."

"I think so. Even when I got her painted nice." He had commanded his wife to paint a row of red waves below the buttons, with a devil's head at each end and the words *"flammes d'enfer"* to set them off.

Here's looking at you

Octave did not like playing with the old man and Buddy—the old man, dirty Cajun, cheated him on the money every time—but he clanged the *'tit fer,* blew into a sonorous bottle, a teakettle, rapped horseshoes, rattled boxes and tapped a mule-hide hand drum, got into the *Saturday Evening Post* photographs as much as he could and nobody knew his private thoughts, that he regarded the music they made as a lugubrious whine.

He wanted the accordion. He played the accordion better than any Malefoot that ever lived, but no way they'd let him sit up there with them and outplay them, so he did washboards and triangle and acted the fool singing their praises. He wanted the green accordion because it sounded good and loud and could sound better, but most of all because it had looked him in the eye. He'd been sitting to the left of old Malefoot a few weeks before, the old man swinging the accordion around and squeezing it, warping in his slurs and slides, singing a little and then playing a little, moving constantly in that old-man twitchy way, and somehow or other the mirrors on the accordion had lined up just right and when Octave glanced over, the damn thing was looking right at him. Of course he knew it was his own eyes reflected but figured the odds were a million to one they could line up with the mirrors that way. It made the instrument powerfully alive, looking at him, watching him, saying "what you gonna do? You gonna git me? Better git me, nigger, or I git you." It was a scary thing.

Sold in America

"One hunerd, one ten, one twenny, one thirty, one forty, one fifty, one sixty, one seveny, one eighty, one eighty five, one ninety, one ninety five, two, two ten, two twenny, two thirty, two thirty five, two forty, forty five, forty sic, forty seven, eight, forty nine, two hunerd fifty." But the old man had to count it all over again and he kept making mistakes and finally Buddy took the money and counted silently, lips moving, said it's all there and threw the green accordion up in the air so Octave had to backpedal to catch it. He knew he was paying too much and that what he really needed was a triple-row. He'd even thought about a piano accordion but doubted he could learn the chord-bass buttons or get used to an instrument that didn't depend on push and pull to make a tune. He liked to see that too, the notes according to the draw of the bellows. It was like a natural law.

"Where's the case, Mr. Malefoot?" he said.

"Aw, don't have no case."

"Mr. Malefoot, I seen you bring it in a case many a time, you see what I'm sayin? I under the impression a case go with this 'cordion." Buddy thought about it a minute, the money felt good, it was warm and dry and there was a hundred percent profit. He could give Octave a hard time, stiff him the case, but then he might stand back on them when they needed a washboard, or stop bringing fish out to the rig. Octave was capable of meanness.

"Back over there back a my daddy's foot."

(Thirty years later, in Scotland, coming late and drunk out of a pub, warp-sided face atwitch, Buddy glanced into a parked van in the glare of a streetlight. He saw an accordion on the seat, stealthily tried the van door. It opened, and he seized the instrument, carried it under his arm to his hotel. In his room he opened the case. It was a beautiful instrument, leopardwood with chrome-plated buttons. The maker's name was unknown to him, but it was a Cajun beauty and it came from his home country. He played and sang and wept for vanished times and places until the pallid Scots light of morning tinged the window, then he wondered what in the hell he was going to do with a stolen accordion. He left it in the hotel room.)

Don't let a dead man shake you by the hand

Octave, good-looking except for a drooping eyelid like an eternal slow wink, brown-skinned, had his getaway money saved up, folded in an empty tobacco can hidden under a certain tree root. He had his suit and his white shirt in a cleaner's bag on a red plastic hanger suspended from a nail in the wall of his mother's house. In a month he'd be gone, Kansas City or Chicago or Detroit, hadn't made up his mind yet, but there were a few fool things he had to do first and one of them was get new steel reeds in this thing and make it jump. He would bring it to Mr. Lime, get some of those good reeds made out of clock-spring steel. He was skipping his regular weekend gig on the crawfish circuit so he could play over in Houston on the edge of Frenchtown alternating sets with Clifton, a nice balance because Clifton had the big piano accordion, was into rhythm and blues; he had his own style, might be closer to Boozoo, but pushier and revved up. It was well known people danced hotter to the button than to the piano, not a jook, either, but the Blue Moon Dance Heaven that had been a grocery store back in the forties with an icehouse next to the store. Thinking about the icehouse, he remembered—memories came to him sharply, let him fly backward into childhood—the big cake of ice swathed in burlap bags on the porch of the store in Féroce where some-times Uncle Pha would chip off a big crystal dagger for nothing if some-body was buying ice and you were standing around, the delight of watching the pick drive a line of stars and then the piece would break off clear and shot through with frozen bubbles. You could stab somebody with it and kill them, it happened once when Winnie Zac stabbed her boyfriend in the neck and the weapon melted in his hot blood. That was how Amédée Ardoin played, that *'tit nègre,* stabbing the buttons with ice-dagger fingers. Nobody had cakes of ice anymore. And in Houston the Blue Moon icehouse was long gone, you couldn't tell it had ever been there looking at the dance floor not much bigger than two bedsheets and the tiny bandstand, but an acre of tables and a fifty-foot bar, and nobody would know what hit them when he came out there in his black pants and shirt and red satin vest and his white lizard boots and this green accor-dion with its roving eyes. He would make this thing burn pure zydeco, ring bells. He was going to touch home base.

Wilma came with him, dressed in a red and white striped rayon tube, red wedgies. She looked good, a peppermint woman, sat at a little table next to the bandstand smoking Spuds and squinting at the dancers. The place was already packed to the walls and more people coming in, greet-ing and hollering at each other, the women throwing down their purses on the white oilcloth tables, reflections of cigarette lighter flames bouncing off the upright studs wrapped in aluminum foil that sup-ported the tin ceiling, swags of dusty red crepe paper overhead and on every table a plastic rose in a cut-off beer bottle—somebody got a bot-tle cutter for Christmas—the windows covered with black cloth for that nighttime feeling. The floor in front of the big zinc bar gave a little under the feet where it was rotten from the years of dripping ice. A big poster in red and black was nailed to the peeling clapboards under the sign NO MINORS ALLOWED:

CLIFTON & OCTAVE
ZYDECO KINGS
ALL NITE $1

Next to it another poster flapped in the air:

Friday!
Zordico King Sampy
and the Bad Habits

They were lined up outside and the sun was still over the horizon, tinting the heavy thunderheads coming up from the Gulf blood red, Cato Comb taking the money at the door and inside the phone ringing off the hook and Etherine, six foot ten and red-colored hair processed to ruler straightness—"fried, dyed and laid to one side"—answering it and saying, yes, yes, well, so many people worryin me at home, and telling the caller it was Clifton and Octave, yes, two 'cordion, *frottoir* and drums, and laughing at something the caller said, huh huh *huh* huh huh. She handed a cold beer to Octave, shook her head when he asked, Clifton here yet? The tables were filling up, people three deep at the bar, rayon dresses with vines and hibiscus, pink pleats and cayenne red.

It was warm, the heat of bodies sweating up the room, the glasses and bottles clinking and in the corner a raw voice climbing over the roar of talk. The phone rang and rang. "Yas, yas, huh huh *huh* huh huh, no, no. Yeah, he here. Well, what happen? What you want me to tell 'em? Hello, hello, OK, goodbye." Etherine hung up and looked at Octave. She could hear distant thunder, a long, irritable mutter; that tightened her up, thinking about the tornado last May that tore off the back end of the dance hall and killed a man. Octave leaning on the bar, looking at her with a questioning expression, she looked back, seeing his easy cocoa-brown face and strong neck, the mustache above the rich mouth, spider fingers, the charm of that chipped front tooth.

"You ought to take them blue-ass shades off, let the women see your *beaux yeux*. That there's Clifton. Look like he can't get here. They in a car wreck over Louisiana, up at Dimple. Nobody hurt but the car. He say it's all yours, you better make 'em hot. He get here if he can but don't count on it." She watched him walk over to Wilma, coming down hard on the heels of the white boots, the pointed toes like arrows showing which way to go, bend down to her and talk, then sip a little of her drink before he got up on the bandstand. That was his trouble. He come down too hard on his heels.

He stood at the mike, to the side Bo-Jack with his drums, Studder with his fork and gleaming metal breast, the faces turning toward them, a few voices hollering "where's Clifton, where's Mr. C.?" Studder clowned with the *frottoir;* he was wearing the funny one made with a pair of silver breasts so it looked like a blackface robot woman was scratching away under her titties with that stubby fork.

"All right, folks, Clifton just call up and say he got a breakdown and a wreck over in Dimple, Louisiana, not hurt none, say he want to hear you all jumpin and hollerin all the way to where he is at. We gon' play zydeco, we gonna stomp and be happy and get hot and if you dead when he get here he bring you back to life, let's GO!"

He started hot and hard, held the accordion over his head for a triplet bellows shake, rotating the corners of the bellows in a semicircular twist, rolled out like a plane flying acrobatics into diatonic clusters using every inch of the long bellows and shifting its action skillfully, swooping and diving into a rocking palm section that had the dance floor jammed tight in three minutes. He knew what to do. He screamed, "ah, ha, ha! You gonna burn! You burnin yet?" Then it was "*J'ai trois femmes*" slap-staccato bundles of notes hitting the dancers, the drum knocking their hearts, the rub board hissing and rattling like a snake, *hincha ketch a ketch a hinch*. Bright drops of sweat flew. Etherine shouted, "you sweat and stomp, you hot, you *will* be back!" The half-open door showed blue-white and with the concussion of thunder the lights flickered and he could hear the scream of wind outside. Etherine knocked back a shot of pure gin and prayed. She didn't want to look out there and signaled Cato to shut the door.

Octave was bending at the knees now to drive the intense nervous energy up into his hands. His fingers raced and hit, trills and violent tremolo, the notes vibrating with the force of his upward lunges, a left-hand trill going on and on and the heel of his right hand knocking hard and quick against a mass of buttons, a jam of close notes, discord that pulled yells from the dancers and then a sudden stop leaving everybody panting and laughing, and then—it's a trick, folks—right back into it again, wringing and twisting out modal harmonies, the dancers shaking snake hips and pop-locking, off to the side a couple jerking their pelvises in the Boody Green. But under the hard dancing he could feel their reserve; they were holding back from him, longing for Clifton and his big glittering piano instrument.

"I don't put you too cold, do I," he bellowed. "Come on, here we are, like they say, too French to be black, too black to be French," and made an accordion joke with an old Cajun two-step reheated on high and time doubled and syncopated, notes blued and broken and the whole tune moving in a fast sad tangle that was mockery and sympathy. "Go on, go on, go on, go on," he called and one couple, old and muscular, smooth as wet silk, cut a wedge in the music. The other dancers moved out of the way to watch them execute the old zydeco jump and wheel, swift and beautiful. Cato Comb stepped in from the rain, wet clothes plastered to his long body. The wind was roaring outside and a bristle of hail ran across the roof. Octave leaned into the mike, his lips grazing it, his breath filling the room.

"You all remember what this come out of, know what I'm sayin? You remember it all come from what we go back to, LaLa, remember that old LaLa, we all done that. Make you feel at home. Don't nobody cross they feet, now." They were hot but he felt their coolness.

Plates of food were being passed down the tables, gumbo and chicken, and over the room hung a heavy pall of smoke, the glowing ends of cigarettes shining in the darkness of the room. The heat was tremendous and the dancers' clothes were soaked with sweat, their slippery hands unable to grasp, and dancers slipped from each other, ricocheted against others but kept dancing, rubbing their wet palms down their thighs. Overhead the big fan turned the smoke. The storm was passing. Somebody yelled for Clifton's "*Eh, 'tite fille*" and he gave it to them, jamming in the blue notes and running the triplets like the strong man, setting the dancers' backs quivering with tremolo.

"God darn it, sound better here than anywhere!" screamed a white dancer moving in a flat-footed, spraddle-legged way, one of five or six who came slumming down to Frenchtown. A black woman answered him. "That's right. It's pure Louisiana." But women called from the floor in discontented voices. "When Mr. C. get here? Bring me Clifton, y'hear? He play pianna AND button, what he want. You good, boy, but you ain' no Mr. C."

An old man danced with a young woman. He wore yellow patent-leather cowboy boots with chrome toes, an orange leather jacket with a pinch waist and flared skirt like an old-time gunfighter, a blue shirt and a bolo tie held by a gold death's-head with ruby eyes. Nobody on the floor could dance like this man, the smooth glide, the trapezoid back that rippled like a snake shedding skin, the twisting hands scratching air, the yellow boots winking and tapping across the waxy boards, the long muscled legs bending and dipping, swiveling hip sockets, fragments of a hundred dance steps echoing, the buzzard lope, Texas tommy, the grind, funky butt, the fishtail, the twist, the Georgia hutch, the Charleston, the shimmy, the shout, the crazed turkey.

"Give him a glass a water," somebody shouted, for he was a known balancer and an end-man dancer who could spin and leap, balancing a glass of water on his head steady.

"Thamon! You a baaad man on the floor." He was seventy-three, his body as pliant as a child's.

Octave's eyes were red with smoke and his throat was like a furnace duct at the end of the hour and he shouted "Rest time" and sat with Wilma, mopping his neck and face, signaled Etherine for beer and cigarettes, for a whiskey and another beer and another, and then into the second hour with "Don't Let a Dead Man Shake Your Hand," buttons clicking, the bellows sucking in breath and jetting it out in puffs, distorting the tones by swinging the accordion over his head, slamming into swells and then choking it down, scratching and rubbing and rattling the backs of his fingernails along the ridges of the bellows. Cato Comb opened the door wide and let the sweet rain-washed air cool them off, the night sky fluttering with lightning to the north of them now, but Etherine frowned—it was her experience that people liked to be good and hot, wringing with sweat, hearts pounding, lungs demanding air.

Octave wasn't satisfied. He was in it now but couldn't win their hearts, couldn't make them forget Clifton. He was giving the green accordion all he could, it was breaking out breathy sobbing roars as though from a strongman's heaving chest, it was an instrument of sweat and that big crying voice talking to them, but even with the grille off, even with the new reeds, it wasn't right. It didn't have the range. He didn't like that devil's head and the flames painted on it. He'd paid too much for it, beguiled by the reflection of his own eyes. His mind was made up. He'd bring it to Chicago and sell it to some homesick squeezer and he'd get himself a big-key strong-back like the one Clifton played, more notes than he'd know what to do with, the one the beautiful women threw their underwear at, wriggling out of damp scanties on the dance floor and hurling them at the big accordion which caught them in its folds and squeezed and kneaded the flimsy scraps of nylon, like Boozoo Chavis who at intermission sold extra-large panties printed TAKE EM OFF! THROW EM IN THE CORNER! That accordion fool, drunk and wild, fell off a barstool onto the floor and kept right on playing. Nobody'd ever thrown underpinnings at him, but in Chicago he was going to fly, he would smoke. It was 1960, and yes, that old Illinois Central train was waiting, don't play no blues, we here for zydeco.

(Thiry-five years later Rockin' Dopsie sat on a straight chair on somebody's porch in Opelousas and remembered the night Octave tore off the roof with that green two-row, making huge sound. "He never played that good again." But how did he know that? He recognized the single burning night that comes at the top of a life, and it's all downhill from there, no matter what happens.)

Joe Chilly City

It was a hard, hard time in the winter misery, a wind off the lake loaded with raw sleet, low on money, sleeping in a dirty room, gigs hard to find, they didn't want no zydeco up here, they wanted weird progressive shit, nobody danced, it was all blues, blues, blues, not the old delta blues neither, not rock, not anything but electrified guitar urban blues, loud and fast and gritty and he understood why. It wasn't like times he'd heard about after World War II when they come up from the south, thousands and thousands, trains packed full, and everyone find a job an hour after getting off the train. That hungry city, Chicago, starved for good strong-arm, start-at-the-bottom cheap labor like there used to be in the old immigrant days, what made Chicago rich, not hogs and wheat but cheap labor to butcher the hogs and move the wheat. They were still shambling up the long route by the thousands but the work wasn't there anymore, there was some deep kind of economic shift going down so it was sit around and wail out some black-heart music and drink, smoke, fight, fuck, listen to somebody singing J. Brim's "Tough Times," anything to get your mind off the problem. Some of the guitars was making it, getting recorded by those polack brothers, but nobody was rushing to get any zydeco on wax. They didn't want to hear it up here. It was getting so he didn't want to hear it himself, not after he telephoned Wilma long distance and wrote her a song afterward she was never going to hear.

"It rainin at your house babe, same like it rain here?" he'd said, voice bending down the wire, voice dropping low and sad. Heard a live silence, the wire breathing and crackling with the depth of miles. The silence, the hammered silence. Too much to say.

"If I could be with you," he breathed, "to talk and love you, get *in* you. Miss you babe, so bad, so bad." Everything he said jerked through the wire in broken fractions. Missing. Missing you. Doin it for you, babe.

And when she hung up it seemed to him she was still there, still on the line, still connected to him and still trying to say something but couldn't, and didn't have to because he got the message. He was gone.

He still had the green button accordion, though he'd lost the grille and thrown away the case, couldn't sell the motherfucker. It sat on the top of the cardboard wardrobe looking at the opposite wall, the eyes always catching some blank light that made it look blind. The strap on the case had broken a few minutes after he struggled off the train at Central Station; it had happened inside the station when he was trying not to seem awed by the arched windows and the oval echoing hall, the restless mass of people with bundles, suitcases, strings of children, and when it hit the marble floor the accordion fell out and went down some steps with a bad sound. Somebody yelled, "hey, man, you drop somethin," and he fumbled for the instrument, cramming it into the case, furious with embarrassment, everyone gawking at the rube from the south, and he rushed out onto Twelfth Street without knowing where he was, only that he had to find Indiana Avenue. The treble end was cracked. He'd kicked the case away at the station, cursed bitterly, and carried the naked instrument through the streets. He thought Buddy Malefoot might have done something to the handle.

On the street, instinctively he turned south, lugging the instrument and his suitcases, making his way through a cluster of Salvation Army musicians, trumpet, drum, English concertina and a tambourine for the incompetent on the end. He smelled Chicago, the distant animal stink of the stockyards to the southwest, the sharp acidic flavor of exhaust and wafts of hot, greasy frying meat. He passed movie theaters and shoe stores, palmists' upstairs signs with pointing fingers, a dreadlocked Rastafarian bumping along, storefront churches, ". . . *talkin 'bout the Christ of the bible, am I right? 'bout Solomon's temple, 'bout the wheel in the middle of the wheel, am I right 'bout it? I know that's right, 'bout the bridegroom looking forward to the bright mornin, people, you prayin with me? That's right, I know that's right, you can't give off light 'less you on fire . . . ,*" heard a thread of blues locked inside a room, the blatting of horns, the rolling hiss of tires, the throat hawk of a doubled-up bum leaning against a wall and from every direction the brittle rap of women's high heels, the clicking skeins of biped rhythm crossing and recrossing. It was a kind of music. He tried not to walk on the pictures a legless man on a mechanic's trolley was drawing on the sidewalk with colored chalks, making pictures of Jesus and his adventures in panels like a comic book, the words in yellow chalk, the shapes of the letters curved like bananas.

The best he could do was a basement kitchenette, a dark hole with a hot plate and saturated with a strange, sweetish smell, but cheap. (The building was one of hundreds, green Zs of fire escapes zagging down the stained walls, a glimpse of the lace bridge, factories with glassless windows tipped open, the swollen monograms of graffiti, letters obscuring letters, layered, jumbled, meaningless except the words FORGET IT on a viaduct.) On a shelf in the closet he found a dirty white comb, a yellowed newspaper ad, "get with the rave sound so popular with teenagers . . . ," and a letter addressed to someone named Euday Brank that said "Flyto nede a sax man, call 721-8881." The envelope was postmarked Kansas City, 1949. He wondered who Flyto was, had been, dead now maybe, threw the letter in the cardboard box that was his wastebasket, got remembering the cardboard box that was his earliest memory, lying in a dim room and looking at the edge of a box flap, the pale brown color, the row of little dark tunnels that went off into someplace he knew was frightening and strange, saw a tiny red insect appear at the mouth of one of the tunnels, gaze at him with its shining eyes and go back inside.

"You can't remember that," his mother told him. "It's true you in a box, but you a baby. Nobody remember when they a little baby. You grow so fast I put you out of there in a month. It a soapsud box, Rinso White. People come in and see you there and joke about it—I tryin to lighten you up?" Even now the smell of that detergent gave him the ineffably sad feeling he associated with tiny cardboard tunnels.

He could see the dust on the green accordion and he knew dust was bad but he just couldn't get to wiping it off, couldn't get to much, he could still play it but he didn't much want to. He'd played it all the time at first, cracked or not, but it made such a pumping, breathing body sound, like running or hard work, like screwing, and he missing somebody so bad, yeah, made a sound like what a human being would make if it got turned into an instrument, that after a while he couldn't stand it. Sound like somebody choking. He couldn't find work. It looked like he going to end up bringing it to the pawnshop and go back home.

"I can't be satisfy!" he said angrily, blaming himself for the lack of jobs, knowing there was something dead wrong with him, that he wasn't no good, he didn't have it, whatever it was.

Guess I'll hang out

The day came a year or two later when he decided to bring the accordion to the pawnshop, not for a ticket south but because he had a little habit and his paycheck was lagging behind and when you gotta have it you gotta have it. He was staying. He had a job in construction, apprentice carpenter, going to try for his union ticket, no hurry, plenty of work on the new projects filling up with black people as soon as the last windows went in, the whole huge area divided from the city by the Dan Ryan Expressway. All that goddamn talk about integration in the south—they ought to look up here, rock-solid segregation with a moat around it. Could be somebody planned it that way?

He was crazy about two women, feeling good about it, Bo-Jack and Studder come up from down home and got straight into the music scene, they looked up to him, show them where it was at, only half a joke when they called him B.N.I.C., and he took them on a tour of the black-and-tan clubs, down among the cluckheads, down where the pimps coasted by driving their white hogs, slumped in a gangster lean, and when they got out showing their knife-creased pants and gator shoes, walking the pimp limp. Bo-Jack told him Wilma got married, moved away to Atlanta. They wanted to hear something different, some strange sounds. He steered them to the Diamond Dot Club to hear a Nigerian Juju band with a diatonic accordion, *sekere,* talking drum, cymbals and gongs. Bobby went crazy, *boom!* became a disciple, and any idea Octave might have had about starting up their old thing again was dead. He didn't want to anyway. Now he had a little money, enjoying nightlife, buying a big piano accordion on time (two dollars a week) and owning a black silk tunic, a paisley scarf knotted around his head and an ankle-length Afghan coat of some yellow fur, and if not living large, at least larger—certain things a man had to have. A taste for urban blues growing in him, but he still played zydeco, ashamed because it was southern nigger music. He understood one night listening to some cross-eyed fool from down the bayou playing away in a club, nobody paying no attention to his little trembly voice that kept catching and leaving rough patches of silence in every phrase, just caught and held on the nail of a sung word. Even when that fool's accordion knocked around the beat like a push-button machine he heard it was wrong. What was right was that Louisiana swamp-pop shit, that whitey two-chord E-flat B-flat shit, that was going down. He wouldn't play it.

He didn't know why it was, but he had raised a temper, flared into anger at little things that never bothered him in Louisiana, maybe because of the TV, come at you all the time with cars and shoes. He had to keep himself up with plenty of good times, upstairs in the building and down the block, rent parties, card parties, party parties, Saturday night and every night if you had a taste for them and weed and coke and good likker, if you liked that kind of thing. He did. Chicago was jumping. He liked to hear the saxophone and the electric guitar, it was cool, beautiful. He had an unsatisfiable appetite for good times, a scarce commodity in his early life, wouldn't mind some gold rings and chains. He had a bookshelf and six books on it: *The Condensed World Encyclopedia, High School Subjects Self-Taught, Great Men of Color, Female Sexual Anatomy, Riplow's Universal Rhyming Dictionary, Introduction to Musical Scales.*

Things were happening, or so it seemed, and then he got laid off and blacklisted and the jobs began to melt away, they just weren't there any-

more. The economy had coiled back on itself. Well, he'd just stick tight
and wait for it to come around again. It had to; so many people needed
the work.

You got no idea where you come from

His great-great-grandfather had been captured and chained in a coffle
of slaves, a bitter irony for he was spiritually intimate with metal, from
an ancient line of smiths who beat glowing rods on their anvils (and this
made him a prize), transported on a Nantes slaver to New Orleans, then
sold to a planter who brought him to the Mississippi delta where he
died in early middle age after shaping iron window guards and gates,
andirons and trivets, shackles and tools, sometimes working decorative
shapes and designs that carried secret harming powers unsuspected by
the whites who used the objects and later fell sick.

The metalsmith's son, Cordozar (great-grandfather to Octave, Ida
and Marie-Pearl), born a slave and trained by his father to forge work,
made off for Canada at age twenty-seven, hiding out in the swamps
with the Indians and traveling by night. He had promised his woman
that if he made it he would work it so she could escape and follow with
the baby, Zephyr, join him in the north. But he had been in Toronto
only a few months when the Civil War erupted and, on fire, he went
down to Boston and enlisted, burning to shoot, fought from Pennsylvania to Virginia, wounded twice, drove an ambulance wagon and
seemed to forget the woman and child. Two years after Appomattox he
went west with the Tenth Cavalry, one of two black mounted regi-
ments, and died on Prairie Dog Creek when his horse, gut-shot by a
twelve-year-old Sioux, reared and fell on him.

The girl he left behind him

The child Zephyr grew up sharecropping cotton and picking banjo in
Vanilla, Mississippi, living the poor, hard delta life from furnish to settle, on one of the richest alluvial soil deposits in the world, cheated
annually of the money he earned, deprived of arithmetic and literacy,
healing his sicknesses and injuries with bean blossoms and prayer. He
got out of it for a few years playing banjo with a carnival show touring
the territories, doubling as the African Dodger, his head through a hole
in a sheet, winking and grinning at the crowd of white men and boys
who one by one, arms cocked, hurled a ball at him, while a Victrola
cranked out "Dancin' Nigger." The carnival broke up in some hard

Nevada sheep town and he was stranded, forced to sell his banjo for two dollars which bought him a train ticket halfway to Vanilla. He walked the last half, coming home footsore, back in the sharecropping cycle for good, taking his small allotment of pleasure in sex, drink and music. A white man from the Farm Security Administration took his photograph in the 1930s, standing there in his work clothes, a strange suit of rags sewed on rags sewed on rags, hundreds of fluttering threads and frayed ends, a hat of moth-laced felt. He got children on four women and let them shift for themselves. He owned a no-breed blind dog, Cotton Eye, who cured wounds by licking them, a service for which Zephyr charged a nickel. During one mean, yellow year a pigweed of inordinate size grew in his garden. He gave it extra water, suffered no other plant in its territory, admired its hugeness, its stalk as thick as two thumbs. It reached a great height of ten feet, then toppled of its own weight, the mightiest pigweed ever seen, remembered by all who saw it.

He spoke little, except through the banjo, never talked from the secret side of his mouth, never said what he thought, only what he wanted, and he wanted only what he could have until, after he saw a demonstration of the new International Harvester cotton-picking machine, after Mr. Pelf told him at settle time he'd made only three dollars on a year's work, he made a final monthly funeral payment, lay down on his ragged bed and called for roast beef and champagne (two dietary articles he had elevated to iconic status having tasted them once fifty years earlier on the Fourth of July when the carnival boss had a feast sent out by jitney from a fine restaurant in Des Moines, paying with counterfeit bills). His daughter Lamb, the only surviving one of his children who still lived in Vanilla, brought him a saucer of fried fatback and a glass of cloudy water. He was eighty-three, worn out and so wrinkled he looked quilted.

"No," he said, and he rolled up in the grey blanket and faced the wall, closed his eyes and did not move or speak, dead in two days, worn out by the grand tradition of struggle.

Bayou Féroce

Lamb stopped the alarm clock on the windowsill, covered the clouded mirror with a sweater, took the photographs of her children off the dresser and folded them in paper. After the old man's funeral, in May 1955, Lamb and her three children, Octave, Ida and Marie-Pearl, moved to Bayou Féroce, Louisiana, with her boyfriend, Warfield Dunks (pale brown eyes circled with a rim of purest blue), where they bought a radio

and began to listen to Professor Bob, king of the turntable, out of
Shreveport. The first hour in the rented shack, Marie-Pearl got into a
yellow-jacket nest and came tearing through the weeds in her old flowered dress, jumping great wild jumps, leaping high, her thin stung girl's
legs shining in the sunlight.

Poor Warfield died a highway death after they had been there a year
when he stopped to watch a six-hundred-pound wild boar running
down the midline of the highway and a Chevrolet driven by an elderly
white woman struck him from behind. Lamb was working in the kitchen
of a white college president's house (permission to take home skin, fat,
feet and heads of pot chickens, potato peelings and the heels of stale
loaves) at five dollars and fifty cents a week. She hoped someday she'd get
a chance at the upstairs, snap out the cream linen sheets, dust the pale
windowsills, arrange the pairs of Mrs. Astraddle's shoes on slanted shelves.
Her children were growing up. Octave, almost a man, was fishing in the
Gulf. He needed a better boat, one that didn't require bailing every ten
minutes, one with a good motor. She prayed that Marie-Pearl would keep
out of trouble, though it didn't seem likely, she was so good-looking and
so boy-crazy. The real trouble was Ida, six foot two and almost three hundred pounds at eighteen, homely and dark black, with a big potato nose
and gap teeth, always the one to turn the rope when the girls played double Dutch jump rope. She should have been a boy. She had a disposition
to fight, a stentorian voice. She might get happy after she had her first
babies, might not, swearing the way she did that she hated men and
wouldn't have no babies, said no man was ever gonna get on top of her,
knock her around or up, and the space under her bed was piled with old
books and yellowy magazines, the dustiest mess Lamb had ever seen. Old
ladies knocked on the door day and night bringing her more junk.

"Way you look, don't worry," said Lamb. "No man gonna worry
you."

"I know how I look. You been tellin me since I could stand up and
walk."

Hair pulling

In the eighth grade Ida got her friend Tamonette to go downtown with
her and pull white people's hair. They walked the dusty road holding
hands and singing "Jesus on the Phone Line." They shared a dangerous
humor, the sort where laughter must be stifled to avoid implication of
guilt. Tamonette was thin and short, felt an obligation to be daring
because of her grandmother's sister, Maraline Brull, who had gone to

Paris in the 1920s as a white family's maid and there learned to fly an airplane, returned to the south as a crop duster until a white farmer shot
her out of the sky in 1931; even then she went fiercely, aiming the diving
fiery plane at the man in the field with the rifle, and got him, too.

"What kind of jeans you wearin," said Tamonette critically.

"Ask me no questions, I'll tell you the answers. Whatever," said Ida,
twisting to look at the label.

"You fool, that's the kind got the KKK behind it, making money off
us. They behind that fried chicken you like, too. You better get rid them
ugly old jeans."

"Tamonette. How you know?"

"Everybody *know*, fool."

It was four miles to Féroce and the town frightened them with its
cars and sidewalks and traffic lights. Every white person seemed to be
looking their way, reading their minds.

"Now listen," she said. "Only one hair—you don't be grabbin a
whole bunch, just one hair—then if you get called on it you say 'sorry,
ma'am, musta got caught in my watch strap.'"

"You don't got no watch and me neither."

"That's right, but you *say* it. Remember, just one hair. It hurt more."

Crane's Department Store with its crowds was the place, but not the
main floor near the escalator. They needed to ease away and get lost as
soon as they did it. Tamonette pointed with her eyes at the Returns &
Check Approval counter, white people crowded five deep waiting to
return defective junk they'd wasted money on, all of them jostled
together talking and straining to see if the ones at the counter were
almost done or not.

Ida picked out two fat women, Number One, with white hair and a
man's face, in a big pink dress, talking to Number Two, potbellied, with
violet clustered curls. She edged close enough, heard their talk.

"Doesn't Elsie belong to the Daughters?"

"Sugar, she did but gave it up."

"Her family lived in Mississippi for the longest old time."

"Will you look at the short skirt on that one?"

"Those skirts, I think they'd be cold."

"Oh, the styles are just awful."

"I'd like a new dress, but I can't . . . well . . ."

"You know Elsie's car? I always bump my head when I get in her car."

"I always do that! I'm glad to hear somebody else besides—*OW!*" Both
hands flew up to the back of her head, she looked right and left, up at
the ceiling, wondering about a canary loose from the pet department.

"Well, honey, a hairpin must of hit a nerve—"

"Somebody pulled my hair."

"Well, don't look at *me*," said Violet-Curl, affronted, and Tamonette and Ida were two aisles away examining notebooks with mottled black and white covers, not even smiling. (Ida bought one of the twenty-nine-cent notebooks: she had already started scribbling down certain things she heard.) Later they got a girl with long red hair parted in the middle, then changed to another store and Tamonette got a youth with long straggles, and still neither one of them even smiled, not even on the long walk back, though it was pent up in them until they were safe in Ida's house when they roared and screamed and reenacted sidling up to this one and that one, selecting a single hair, the sharp yank, the drift away with poker faces.

Lamb was home, sewing some old rag of Mrs. Astraddle's into something Ida or Marie-Pearl would end up wearing and hating. The radio was blasting Reverend Ike, pouring out words like handfuls of BBs: "*I am the greatest, I am stupendous, I am beyond all little kinds of measuring sticks and ordinary classifications, I am somebody, I am something coming to you like a BULLDOZER and I am looking good and smelling twice as good and I am telling you, get out of the ghet-to and get into the get-mo. Get some money, honey. You and me, we not interested in a harp tomorrow, we interested in a dollar today. We want it NOW. We want it in a big sack or a box or a railroad car but we WANT it. Stick with me. Nothing for free. Want to shake that money tree. There is something missing from that old proverb, you all know it, money is the root of all evil. I say LACK OF money is the root of all evil. The best thing you can do for poor folks is not be one of them. No way, don't stay. Don't stay poor, it's pure manure, and that's for sure. I want you to know—*"

Lamb believed in Reverend Ike, sucked up the stories of the blind beggar woman who bought one of his prayer cloths and minutes later the phone rang and she had won a Cadillac in a sweepstakes, and a man rewarded with a South Seas cruise or the one who found, on a bus seat, a wallet of crisp bills with no identification. She ordered her own prayer cloth, kept it hidden in the toe of her patent-leather Sunday shoe and waited for it to start working, said every morning "I feel and pray that God will make me rich sometime."

Ida gets in it

In 1960 Ida was eighteen and Tamonette, who had dropped out of school in the ninth grade, was as big as a house with her second baby.

Ida graduated and came up against the dead end she had always known was there. There were no jobs for black women except housework and field work. What was the point of social studies and algebra if the best thing out there was scrubbing some white woman's rancid toilet? Lamb said something to Mrs. Astraddle, maybe Ida could help in the kitchen, maybe part time, but Mrs. Astraddle glanced at Ida, standing there scowling and swinging her big arms, said, I don't think so, Lamb.

Her notebooks and papers were all over the house, pages curled, loose papers gliding to the floor when anyone came in off the porch.

"Can't you get rid of this shit?" said Lamb.

"Shit? You don't know what I got here, do you?"

"No, and don't give a care. All I see is one great big papery mess. All I see is you gettin bunches a writin paper from some old woman. What you doin with those old woman papers? Scratchin away instead of lookin for work."

"It's stuff they tells me."

"Better get a job," her mother said bitterly.

Joe McNeil, Franklin McCain, David Richmond and Ezell Blair, Jr., sat at the Woolworth's lunch counter up in North Carolina on the first day in February and in a few months sit-ins were happening everywhere. Ida dumped all the notebooks and papers in a box, pushed it under the bed.

"I *got* to get in it, *got* to get in it. I'm going up to North Car'lina," said Ida.

"You fool," said her mother. "You be killed. Those white men kill you. You are not *going*. It's *college* kids, college students doin these things, black ones and *white* ones, they got it all organized, you just don't go runnin up and say 'here I am, little Miss Ida from Bayou Féroce.' These people got charm bracelets, wearing pink shirts. You don't know nobody. You don't be part of no organization. I'm tellin you, it is dangerous, girl, like you don't even understand—I'm talkin mortal unto death dangerous. You be picked off like a drumstick on a platter."

"I can march. Can sit in."

"March? You can't even walk to the store without complainin. Look at you, solid blubber, you melt before you walk a mile. You haven't got the sense of a potato bug. I swear, I rather see you scribble on them old woman papers. Go all the way to North Car'lina to get killed."

"I won't get killed."

"Happen every day to quicker, smarter, better-lookin ones than you. I bet that's what poor Mr. Willie Edwards thought over there in Alabama the first day on his truck route when the Ku Kluxes made him fall off a high bridge and die, hammered his fingers with guns to make him let go. For nothin. I could tell you things all day and into the night but I might as well save my breath."

(A few years later Redneck Bub, on his way to record his only hit, "Kajun King of the Ku Klux Klan," "for segregationists only," broke down in front of Lamb's house. He came up to the door. "You got a phone?" he said. "Lemme use it." She knew who he was, let him use it. He drove home the same way two days later, and as he passed Lamb's house again the worst headache of his life came down and stayed for a week, caused him to throw up in his car.)

Reverend Veazie's grease bath

Tamonette snorted, choked on smoke. "You don't need to go to no Montgomery Alabama or no North Car'lina for a sit-in. They having a bad sit-in over in Stifle Mississip' Saturday afternoon. At the Woolworth's lunch counter."

"How you know that?"

"Because me and my mother and the Baptist Young People gonna be in it. Reverend Veazie takin us down there in the church bus and we gonna sit in."

"You? Girl, since when you interested in sit-ins?" That mealy-mouthed old chicken-eater Reverend Veazie at a sit-in, driving a bus full of people to it, was too much to imagine, and Tamonette's mother was not the sit-in type. Tamonette herself, a watermelon balanced on a pair of toothpicks, had never said a thing about civil rights in her life.

"I'm coming, then."

"Don't say nothin to nobody about it."

The sit-in

She didn't dress up; they didn't make dress-up clothes big enough to fit her. It was the same old men's blue jeans and men's work boots unless Lamb sewed up a tent-sized skirt for her, roughly ironed with cat's-face wrinkles all over. Tamonette couldn't fit into anything but her old orange maternity dress, but the boys wore their go-to-church jackets and pressed pants, the other girls and women were henned-up in good rayon prints, belted and nyloned, and some wearing hats and even gloves in spite of the heat. Up front she saw Tamonette's ex-boyfriend, Relton, the father of the unborn baby, sitting beside Moira Root, his long narrow feet in tan boots.

"That why you so interested in the sit-in," she hissed to Tamonette.

"You hush your mouth. It is NOT." But it was. Ida's hard eye saw Tamonette's coming life, letting men walk all over her, and she'd have one baby after another, wearing the old orange maternity dress until it fell off her, things never working out.

On the church bus Tamonette's mother and Reverend Veazie, sad-looking and bumpy-cheeked, a white handkerchief sticking up from his pocket like the peak of Everest, sat in front, and Tamonette's mother started singing as soon as the bus rolled, a woman who could not resist harmonizing with engine hum.

"Now, they don't know we coming," called Reverend Veazie. "Remember, just take a seat and sit quiet and if the waitress ask what you want, order a Co'-Cola. Everybody got fifteen cents to pay for it if she serve it? But she won't. No matter what they do to you, remember, you can keep ordering your Co'-Cola in a quiet, cool voice. Stay cool. Do not destroy or touch anybody or anything except your Co'-Cola—if she serve it. But she won't. When the police come and try to force you away, hang on to that counter. Don't say nothing, just hang on, Jesus Christ with you, make them drag you away, don't offer no resistance beyond hanging on to the counter. Passive resistance, coolness, think of Reverend King and remember you are doing an important and brave thing for all the brothers and sisters, for your people, for everybody, for the legions of justice, so stay cool."

It was an ordinary little town, hot, a few big trees, half the main street stores with FOR RENT signs in the windows. They went right through, and on the far side of town, past a tire dump, pulled into the Dixie Belle Mall. They were nervous, went in through the Woolworth's doors in a bunch, the girls gripping their purse handles, the boys stretching their necks in the starched collars and ties, stomach muscles clenched stiff. They walked to the lunch counter in single file. A middle-aged white farmer, dirt-stiff hair and crusty overalls, was swallowing the last of a milk shake, tuna sandwich crusts and blobs of grey fish on his plate. They sat on the empty stools. The man looked up, startled, put some money on the counter and went. The only visible waitress, cleaning the stainless-steel spigots and machine parts, took her time in glancing up in the mirror to see who needed a menu. She froze, did not turn to confront the row of dark faces but scuttled into the kitchen. They could hear her shrill voice asking, where's Mr. Seaplane, we got a problem out front, and the cook, old and white-haired, coming to the porthole in the swinging door and looking out, one arm up in the air so the wet grey in his armpit showed, then his face disappeared, replaced by that of the dishwasher and the other waitress.

She could feel the round little seat under her behind, wanted to try its spin capability, but could also feel the crowd gathering in back of them and looked up in the mirror to see them, mostly mean-looking white men, saying, what the hell's goin on here, what is this, what are them niggers doin, looks like we got us a problem here, hey nig, what you tryin to pull off here. A tall white man in a brown suit came out from the kitchen—the manager or the boss, nobody was sure.

"All right, you niggers, you clear out of here right now or I'll call the sheriff. I'm gon' count to three and if you ain't hightailin it for the door by the count of three I can *guarantee* you some trouble. *One! Two! Three!*" When no one moved except Tamonette's boyfriend who raised his hand as if he were in school and said, I'll have a Co'-Cola, please, Brown Suit paid no attention and counted again, said, that does it, I'm calling the sheriff and the cops, and went back into the kitchen. The police were there before the door stopped swinging so they knew he'd called before counting. A voice from the crowd said, you want a Co'-Cola? to Tamonette's faithless boyfriend. A sandy-headed short man, pack of cigarettes rolled up in his t-shirt sleeve, got behind him, held a bottle of Coca-Cola high, poured it, spattering, on his head.

"Taste pretty good, boy? Must be runnin down the crack of your ass where you got all your taste." Suddenly hands and arms were thrusting between them, seizing the ketchup bottles, the salt and pepper. She felt something like sand strike the back of her neck and started sneezing— someone had unscrewed the cap from a pepper shaker and tossed the contents. The men were behind the counter, grabbing cream and milk, butter, pie, mayonnaise, mustard, eggs, a tiny white man seized the rancid cold cooking oil, a three-gallon stainless-steel vat, poured the entire contents over Reverend Veazie. (Later Reverend Veazie said in a sermon, "God was watchin over me because that oil MIGHT a been HOT.")

Ida felt wet substances cascade down her neck and face, sneezed convulsively as pepper flew and mustard dripped, someone mashed an egg in her hair, another poured icy milk down her shoulder and breast, they were hurling handfuls of Wheaties, drizzling Karo syrup, throwing Jell-O bombs. "Food fight," said the tiny man, hurling a banana at Tamonette's mother who flinched as it struck and then began to sing "We shall NOT BE MOO-OO-OOVED," and they sang with her, sneezing and crying, but singing and still sitting at the counter when the two cops and then some of the men in the crowd began to drag them off the stools with hard little strikes from their batons, and arm-twists and quick knee-thrusts and savage guttural promises of what they were going to do. She felt hard fingers squeezing at her breast, then wiping the mustard onto her back, saying, disgusting nigger cunt, you big fat giant ugly nigger whore, move it or I'll shove this up your twat, jabbing with a sawed-off pool cue at her groin, hitting the pubic bone hard and painfully so that she cried out and half sank to her knees, hearing the reverend shout, be cool be cool be cool, and he was so slippery with oil they couldn't get a grip on him but kept falling down in his slick.

She got up. The man with the cue was in the crowd, back to her, trying to get a good lick in on Reverend Veazie. With all her force she kicked him in the behind and he went down under the boots of the others, shouting, aaah, aaah, hold it, goddammit, git off'n me, my back is broke, goddammit, git me up.

What next?

"Oh baby girl," moaned Lamb when she came home three days later, both eyes swollen shut, skinned up and barefoot, stinking of condiments, vomit and jail. "What I tell you? Look at you, you half dead, they half kill you. I follow my first mind, would of kept you from goin. I gonna lose my job with Mrs. Astraddle she hear about this. What you doin?"

Ida stripped and washed in the cold shower Octave had rigged before he went up north, came out and pulled on old blue jeans, her run-over black sneakers, got a plastic shopping bag from under the sink and began folding her clothes and packing them in it.

"Think you doin?"

"Gettin out a here. I'm in it. They ain't gonna stop me, neither. I'm goin with Tamonette's boyfriend. And don't you touch my papers and books. I be back to get 'em. We gonna look for some more sit-ins."

"You a living example, cast your bread upon the waters, it come back moldy."

"I'm in it."

A year later she was out of it. She turned every sit-in into a riot, fought and kicked and shouted, jumped up slugging. Her idea of passive resistance was to lean on mean little white deputies pretending she was fainting, then claw their flesh in a hard grip while saying "where am I?"

"You don't understand passive resistance," a group leader told her. "You hurtin the cause. You got too much top anger, sister. We got to channel rage, else it eat us up, destroy us too. You go home, figure out a different kind a way to help your brothers and sisters."

She went back to Bayou Féroce, packed the books and papers under the beds into eighteen boxes and moved to Philadelphia, got a job with Foodaire, a company specializing in the preparation and packaging of airline snacks, and there she stayed for three decades, driving her little car into the south on weekends, traveling around, getting into conversations with grey-headed women and asking those questions.

(Years later in a Los Angeles hospital bed recovering from a gallbladder operation and digesting the news that she had tested positive for tuberculosis, she read the paper: in Jackson, Mississippi, a black man stopped for speeding was taken to jail and beaten dead, the coroner ruled a heart attack; on another page, forty black men had hanged themselves in Mississippi jails in six years; Mr. Bill Simpson, forced out of Vidor, Texas, back to Beaumont, was shot dead within the week. So forth and so forth and so forth. The paper slid to the floor. It never stopped. Hadn't they done something fine back in the sixties? Hadn't people died getting the voting and civil rights laws? And since then, what? Seemed like some had got money and power, but they'd left the others behind, curling like shrimps in the smoking fry pans of cities where bodies of children were discovered in trash compactors, blood dripped through ceilings onto somebody's plate of dinner, babies got shot in cross fire, and the names of cities meant something deep bad, unfixable and wrong. Money was rolling in big waves but not even the foam touched the black shore. All those notebooks wouldn't save a single one from the hot pan, all those histories of black women, those invisible suffering ones at the bottom of the bag. Her apartment was filled with notebooks, yellow snapshots, studio photographs, diaries written on paper bags, ill-spelled pages of herbal cures illustrated with leaves and flowers and colored with dyes squeezed from stems and petals, a sharecrop account written on a shingle with a burnt stick, a letter printed on a piece of apron by a woman homesteader in Kansas describing the death of her husband, a thick manuscript in beautiful cursive script on pages fashioned from cut-up circus posters, *My Socalled Life with the O.K. Minstrel Circus,* recipes written on scrap wood with a nail dipped in soot ink, the midnight thoughts of a charwoman who cleaned federal offices during the Second World War, scrawled on pages gleaned from wastebaskets, the lines of anonymous poets, scraps of lives of thousands of black women. She'd done it on her lousy salary: used-book shops, church bazaars, yard sales, dim, dusty boxes in thrift stores, trash cans and Dumpsters, asking everyone she met, you got any books or letters or whatnot about black women, any black women, everywoman? She thought of Octave and his green accordion in Chicago: was he still alive? She'd sent a letter years ago, sent it by way of Lamb, *sure would like to hear you play a little zydeco on that old green accordion.* Never heard. Wasn't that the old evil thing, brothers and sisters losing each other? Wasn't it the old, old thing, families torn up like scrap paper, the home place left and lost forever?)

Old Green

Octave, drowsing through a bad spell that hinged on a long layoff—he'd never gotten his union ticket and there were too damn many people wanting work out there; he'd tried it all, worked fifty short jobs as a plasterer, carpenter, carpet installer, trashman, furniture mover, taxi driver, hearse driver, grocery delivery boy, short-order cook, maintenance man, awning installer, TV deliveryman, fired or quit after a week or ten or eleven days until it got to the point where he couldn't kill nothin and wouldn't nothin die; everything was turning ugly and anyway he was in no shape for construction work anymore—couldn't make out what the letter said. He discovered it again some weeks later under a chair and this time read it through. Old Green, shit, Old Green gone to the pawnshop long ago. "Yes," he said, "too bad, baby sister, but Old Green is doin time in the pawnshop for anyway three years, know what I'm sayin?"

(He did time himself for a few years and in the clink managed to get through junior college, thought about becoming a Black Muslim and changing his name to something new, start a fresh life, start over again. He thought about money and how to get it. At first it didn't seem there was anything but music and crime, those were his job categories, what the circumstances pegged him for. Well, he wasn't going back fishing and couldn't make it with zydeco or jazz or rock or any other fuckin music thing.

He started reading like a crazed bastard, read his eyes crossed, not mysteries and crap like the rest of them did, but the *Wall Street Journal* and financial magazines, small-business start-up analysis, and after a year or two of studying what the world needed, he settled on sludge. On his release in 1978, after he was turned down for loans by sixteen banks, he held up a supermarket and with this investment money went back to Louisiana, bought eighty acres and invited several metropolises to bring him their solid waste for a fee. By 1990 he owned a five-hundred-acre model landfill and was a major conduit for New York City sludge which went from him to fields in Iowa, the Dakotas, Nebraska, Colorado, Texas and California. He tracked down Wilma, twice divorced, gave her some play, got her heated up and dropped her. He never picked up an accordion again, didn't even like to hear it. "Only way out for me if I'd stayed up there was be a street musician, play in the cold, the subway, have a little tuna can settin on the sidewalk for dimes and quarters. Fuck that." But he was very careful and didn't drive at night.)

Hit Hard and Gone Down

A BANDONEON

Back of the yards

Old Mrs. Józef Przybysz had worked until she was sixty-six—"No work, no pork, no money, no baloney"—but in 1950, the same year she caught her grandson Joey smoking a cigarette from a shoplifted pack and broke his nose with her ivory darning egg from the old country, she retired, concentrated her time on church, cooking, social meetings and telling stories of the hard times they had survived.

"Tragic. We are a tragic, tragic family. All dead now but me. Yes, nothing lasts forever, my dear child. Let me change the cold cloth—ah, you will not steal coffin nails again and smoke them, will you?"

Two decades later, at eighty-six, she had outlived her oldest son, Hieronim. She was a massive woman, her furrowed and liver-spotted skin like a slipcover over a rump-sprung sofa, yet her muscled forearms and strong fingers suggested she could climb a sheer rock face without chalk. Her face was heavy, indented eyes and mouth like fingernail marks in dough, her yellow-white hair pulled up in a soufflé crown bun. Her rimless bifocals were extraordinarily reflective, flashing with the blue flame of the gas burner.

Over her rayon dresses, printed in diagonal checks, flowers, polka dots, feathers and flying birds on dark backgrounds, she wore aprons trimmed with bands of blue or Mamie Eisenhower pink, but she was so lame and bent that she could no longer search for mushrooms.

For years her son, Hieronim, and daughter-in-law, Dorothy (a real cholera of a woman), and their two sons, Rajmund and Joey, had lived with her in the tiny house on the South Side's Karlov Avenue, a solid Polish neighborhood; the house she had purchased herself with her wages as a cigar maker after her husband ran away, for, she said several times a day, "the person without land is like a man without legs: he crawls around but gets nowhere." The Chez family from Pinsk lived across the street; later they changed their name to Chess, the two boys grew up to work in businesses, a junkyard, bars and nightclubs, finally making phonograph records featuring black singers moaning the blues, and by 1960 the good Polish neighborhood had also turned black on all sides. She couldn't blame the Chess brothers, but somehow it made a connection in her thoughts—the black ones, the blues, the Chess brothers, the changing neighborhood. The Poles moved out fast when the black ones started coming in after the war and efforts to defend the neighborhood with fire and stone failed.

At first Hieronim had been a great stone thrower and urged Rajmund and Joey to throw as well.

He shouted at the black ones, "go on, get out of here, this is good hardworking Polish people here, get the hell out, nigger, you spoil our homes, go on you dog's blood, cunts will grow on pineapple trees before you live here," as boys had once thrown stones at him, calling him a dirty polack, a dumb hunky, get the hell back where you come from. The Irish, the Germans, the Americans.

Hieronim, with his small oval face and tiny blue eyes buried deep in their socket caves, a pinched mouth like his father but long-armed and with ropy shoulders made for hurling, went with other men to protest at the huge housing projects when they tried to open them up, Fernwood Park Homes, a few years later, the sly government putting black ones in a white neighborhood. There was a huge crowd, thousands. Hieronim kept his eyes open later, watching where they built others, and he'd go at night with men to get building materials, not to steal but to sabotage, to slow down the work. (On one of his expeditions he fell into an empty stairwell and hurt his back. After that he limped and complained of an aching liver.) He filled Coke bottles with gasoline for Park Manor. He started an improvement association for their block, although it did no good. He saw to it that the Polish Club had a buzzer on the door, and he went back night after night to Trumbull Park Homes in 1953 when they tried to sneak in the light-skinned nigger family, until they gave up and moved out, back to the dirty slums.

A few years later the real estate man came to her door saying, "you guys better move out while you can, get a price for your house. It ain't gonna be worth nothing pretty soon. I can get you something for it right now." But she did not sell though the daughter-in-law complained constantly because it wasn't safe, Hieronim not so much. He'd given up by that time, watched *The $64,000 Question* on television, shouting out wrong answers and finding fault with the ballroom accordion players in their sequined suits.

Next door in those days was the house of Zbigniew and Janina Jaworski; she remembered the day they moved in, 1941, both of them working, ". . . him in the steel mill, her in the ammunition factory. Oh, us women loved the war; the only time a Polish woman could get a job

was when they had that World War Two." Before the war there were thirty
women for every job and the foremen wouldn't hire them, blustered that
women were demanding and troublesome. How clean were the Jaworskis'
kids, and the yard spotless, nice flowers, she went to mass, good friends,
yes, he liked to drink but what man doesn't, and many happy hours she
spent with Janina, sipping coffee and swallowing that tender ginger
cake. Look at the house now, inhabited by a washboard black woman in
a pilled sweater and grimy slacks, shoe soles flapping and half a dozen
ragged children darting mischievously around, kicking garbage cans,
prying at mailboxes, punching each other, a detritus of bottle caps, paper
scraps, broken sticks, dented hubcaps, flattened tin cans spreading out
in their wake, the house itself shabby and peeling, the broken window-
panes blocked with warped cardboard, anything at all. And at night the
men who slouched through the loose door, shouting and singing and
fighting inside, the din filling the street. Who knew what would happen
next? But often, when her daughter-in-law was at work, she brought the
woman cabbage rolls covered with foil, gave her ragged children cookies and the tiny tin globe from old Józef's chest.

A few years before she grew so lame, on good days she had knotted
her babushka under her chins, taken up her collecting basket and set
out for Glowacka Park to search for fungi. "So many!" she whispered to
herself, her basket crammed with heavy flesh, its weight pulling her left
shoulder down. She routed the return journey so she would pass the
Stretch-Yor-Bucks grocery, past the sidewalk displays of McIntosh and
Delicious apples, baskets fitted with commercial mushrooms from the
chemical cellars of Pennsylvania. She despised these smooth beige
heads, the flavor of nothing, all poison sprays. Let the stupid Americans
eat them! What terrible grocery stores, she muttered, thinking of the
old Quality Pork & Provisions store, long ago torn down, thinking of
the huge sausages in striped bags, flitches of bacon with the square
brown rind like a notebook cover, a stiff, pale leg suspended by a wire
loop around the hoof, the ribs slanting down the rectangular rack looking like a ravine in a landscape photographed from the air, and the terrible heads of the pigs, brows furrowed with the anguish of the last
realization, the clouded burst eyes starting or sunken, the ears tattered,
the stiff snouts tilted as if releasing the last exhalation. At home she
spilled her basket of mushrooms onto the white tablecloth, these
delicious mushrooms that she stroked as though they were kittens: fifteen pounds of pheasantbacks, the speckled tawny fans an inch thick
giving off a smell of watermelon; sacks of morels, their mazed surfaces
leading the eye around and around, the hollow insides studded with

glistening bumps like the plaster ceiling in church; creamy waves of
oyster pleurotus with a fragrance of leaves and nutmeats, to dry, to stuff,
to pickle in vinegar. And all this for nothing but the effort of the exciting search. How her heart beat the summer she discovered twenty-seven
great parasol mushrooms in a clearing. But now the park was so beaten
and trampled it resembled the earthy dust of an African village.

    In her day she had cooked with passion and experience, a craftworker
who needed no measuring cup or recipe, who held everything in her
mind. She kept a garden in the handkerchief yard, tomatoes tied to old
crutches she took from the Dumpster at the hospital, she made her own
good sausage and sauerkraut, extra for her married son, Hieronim,
when he was still alive, even after he changed his surname to Newcomer—the Americans called him Harry Newcomer—a little snack of
pieroźki and the filling soup *żurek* with mushrooms and potatoes and
fermented oatmeal and good sour bread, kneading bread dough until
her hands fainted, and once when someone Hieronim knew went hunting in Michigan and brought back a deer shared out among friends she
had made again *bigos* (venison but not boar ham or the sweet dark meat
of the Lithuanian bison which few ever tasted), crying into the pot with
joy it had been so many years, and for Sunday dinner *gołąbki,* the little
cabbage rolls in a sweet-sour sauce, and always a fresh-baked round
babka or two. Józef had always recited when she made *bigos* of American beef, smoked sausages, sauerkraut and vegetables and, of course, her
wild mushrooms, he had put his hand on his breast and declaimed, "all
the air is fragrant with the smell." No wonder when her children came
home they ate ravenously, said no one can cook like you. It was true.
And did she bring good things to the Nuns' Day Luncheon? Yes. She
despised the American supermarkets full of bright-colored square packages and heavy cans, the terrible cookbooks Dorothy bought by made-
up women with American names, Betty Crocker, Mary Lee Taylor,
Virginia Roberts, Anne Marshall, Mary Lynn Woods, Martha Logan,
Jane Ashley, all of them thin-lipped Protestants who served up gassy
baking-mix biscuits, tasteless canned vegetables and salty canned
Spam without shame, the worst food in the world. Look at her stupid
daughter-in-law, Hieronim's wife, Dorothy, that cholera, who hardly
knew how to cross herself, see her open a can of soup, fry some hot
dogs, buy a stale cake slicked over with evil green icing, potatoes in a
cardboard box, powdered drinks and trays of nasty crackers and dips
and spreads and dunks, Dorothy, who made borscht with jars of baby
food, beets and carrots, had once served her mother-in-law a glass of
milk with an enormous spider struggling in it. Yet the deluded woman

thought she was a notable cook because she had taken part in something called The Grand American National Bake-Off, had won a set of aluminum pots with her imitation of a T-bone steak made out of hamburger and Wheaties, a carved carrot for the bone. *Smacznego.*

But all that was ended. The old woman sat in the back room now, her husband long disappeared, her son dead, her daughter-in-law lording it over the kitchen and her grandsons Rajmund and Joey grown men, Joey married to Sonia, parents themselves of her two great-grandchildren, Florry and Artie. Dorothy often knotted up her hard face and complained that Joey and Sonia never visited. She said they wouldn't come because of the dirty blacks all around them; she couldn't guess it was her terrible cooking.

Yes, Dorothy, her flame-shaped blue eyes winking, asked them every week, said come over Sunday, come over Saturday, come over Friday, any day, I make a nice dinner (she made also, besides the baby-food borscht and the false steak, a fish shape from cottage cheese, canned tuna and Jell-O, with a black olive eye), bring the kids over, come over and watch the television, but they never did, and now they had their own television, a portable Philco, and paying more than three dollars on it every week, Dorothy's invitations making no more impression than if she'd been throwing peas at the wall, except on Christmas Eve they came for the *Opłatek Wigilijny* and the dinner which the old woman commanded though she could do very little of the work herself now, but last year they refused to go to midnight mass, and the old woman knew they had not fasted because the little girl left so much food on her plate and whined for pizza, bunching the hay under the tablecloth and demanding to open presents, and not Sonia, not Joey, never said nothing to her. The child had the same ash-blond hair and broad cheekbones and little ski-jump nose as Dorothy. The boy she couldn't blame, he was only a baby and anyway a boy, but the girl needed correction. She was not too young to be enrolled in the dance class and learn the old dances. She was not too young for a little dustpan and broom.

Buried alive

When Joey was a boy old Mrs. Józef Przybysz had told him horrific tales of the old days. The other boy, Rajmund, would not listen, clapped his hands over his ears and rushed out to play in the streets. Oh yes, she said, she had been there—a young girl at the time—during that terrible mass when, in the middle of the service, Maria Reks, who worked for the Irish priest, came staggering through the door crusted with dirt and blood and great red scrapes, clods of soil dropping from her torn clothes onto the wine-colored carpet. Father Delahanty shook, his mouth hung open, then he turned and fled out the back of the church. Maria staggered toward the altar, then swayed and collapsed, but as Ludwik Simac and Emil Pliska held her up and the women moaned, she told them a tale of horror in a last-act voice, the congregation standing on the pew seats to get a better view. She said that for three years she had been forced into the bed of Father Delahanty, the miserable Irisher the church had rammed down their throats, and that when, last night, she told him she was pregnant with his bastard, he tried to kill her with a kitchen knife, thought he had succeeded and buried her in a shallow grave behind his kitchen garden, behind the Egyptian onions with their heavy garlic-looking heads, but she had come to, half smothered, and clawed her way out and was here now to accuse. What an uproar! The men shouted for blood and the castration of the lying Irish priest. And within a week the hair of the entire congregation present had turned white, so that when they came together the following Sunday it was like an old folks' home. The poor girl, though bathed and cleaned and cosseted, had delivered a malformed baby with a head shaped like a carrot and then had died of influenza when the baby was a month old. At the wake the accordion was played, though some said this was wrong, for it was through the accordion she had been seduced, as Father Delahanty was an adept player of jigs and reels.

Father Delahanty—let thunder strike him—was never found, and lucky for him, too. Slipped away like water. Perhaps had become a cook or a librarian in a distant place, for he'd had a taste for both the kitchen and the book. More likely a corset salesman, hands reaching to squeeze and feel women's breasts. This was in the time when the Polish Americans rebelled against the Irish priests and separated off into their own Polish Catholicism. If the girls were going to be damaged by priests, let it at least be Polish priests. That's to look on the bright side, she said. Nowadays, and on the dark side, it wasn't only the girls.

"And what have they got for a president now, only an Irish. And a painter artist who thinks soup cans a fine subject." She looked in the boy's eyes and told him the true subject for a painter was the horse.

Hieronim Przybysz a.k.a. Harry Newcomer

Before old Józef Przybysz ran off he had taken his son, Hieronim, to a ball game once. The day was sweltering and men in paper hats dragged buckets filled with ice and clinking beer bottles, climbed up and down the tiers crying "coldie-cold, cold beer, get it here, coldie-cold." He was allowed to drink the foaming bitter beer from his father's bottle, could not understand the passion of men for this stuff, and soon he had to pee.

"Dad," he said, but his father was talking about cigars with a florid-faced man. He waited, sniveling a little, whispering "Dad" now and then, his bladder aching, the contents of his head sliding around like soapsuds in a bowl. At last his father turned to him, a huge yellow cigar, freshly lit, clenched in his teeth, and said "what!"

"I have to go."

"Jumping Jesus Christ. I'm going to drag you half a mile? Here, use this"—and handed him the bottle which still had an inch of beer in it. "You'll have to pee in this, go ahead, it's all men here, nobody cares about this."

In an agony of embarrassment he tried, but his frozen bladder would not unclench and he gave up, buttoned his blue jeans. As soon as his naked flesh was hidden in the dark warmth of the jeans, the treacherous bladder relaxed and the day was ruined. The cuff on the ear, the sopping jeans, the crack of the bat on the ball and the great shout from the crowd, all around them men jumping to their feet and leaning tensely forward, shouting awright, awright, atta baby, the smell of the yellow cigar, all combined in a deadly way that made him choose fishing over watching baseball as a suitable pleasure. He grew to manhood, married Dorothy, worked and died without ever seeing another ball game, yet smoked cigars with moderate pleasure.

After the Second World War, Hieronim thought of Sunday as a day created for him, the day he could enjoy himself after the week in the steel mill. There were two parts to his pleasure, and sometimes three.

In the early morning, before it was full light, he went into the yard with his electric worm probe, the extension cord trailing from the toaster outlet and over the windowsill. He drove the night crawlers from the ground with jolts of electrical current, "AMAZING RESULTS!" He tossed the night crawlers into a rusted coffee can with a little dirt, took his Zirco rod and drove to one of three neighborhood bridges over the sluggish river. He let the line dangle in the water for hours, the rod propped against the railing, the worm down below among the silt-covered tires. He smoked cigarettes and talked to other men along the rail, men who called him Harry—he knew most of them from grade school, they were the same men he saw at work and at the Polish Club—watched the young girls ride past on bicycles, the *podlotki,* the little wild ducks, the hiss of passing cars and trucks a relaxing background music.

Once in a rare while someone caught a small grey fish with black nodules on its decaying fins. The one who caught it would hold it up for the others to see, accept their jeers and wisecracks, then drop it back in the water where it floated away under the bridge, twitching a little, or he'd drop it on the roadway where the next car along crushed it.

"What a way," he said to Vic Lemaski next to him, "what a way for a fish to go, eh? Run over by a car! Something to tell the other fish. If he could! 'Watch out when you cross the street!'"

Vic, who was a dullard, a dog's bone of an elephant, answered, "get among goats, you jump like them."

"How can that apply to a fish being run over?"

Vic shrugged, dipped into his tackle box for his pint.

Around three o'clock, half drunk, he would wind up his line, dump the remaining worms into the river, watch their ribbony forms disappear among the ghostly plastic bags and broken sticks drifting in the current.

Now came his second pleasure, the Polish Club, where he drank and ate and smoked and read and talked and watched television until ten, then wobbled home to sleep until the four A.M. alarm.

The Polish Club was for men only—his miserable father, old Józef Przybysz (what an insane name, from the old country), had been one of the founders—and in it was a smoking lounge with newspapers, *Naród Polski, Dziennik Chicagoski, Dziennik Związkowy, Dziennik Zjednoczenia,* the *Zagoda,* others in five or six languages, hanging on the rack, the *biblioteka* with paneled walls and Polish books (nothing published since 1922), a woodcut by Adam Bunsch, a 1920 oil painting of a ruined Polish village, Russian soldiers on horses drinking from bottles and smoking cigarettes, geese running frantically, dead Poles strewn like stones over the ground; in the basement of the club the café had its veined-marble tables and bentwood chairs (though now the beer was served, not in proper glasses, but in the new aluminum cans which crackled so loudly and irresistibly when squeezed), the walls covered with yellowed posters of past Polish events, singers, art exhibits, recitals, amusements and awards ceremonies celebrating dead Polish heroes, a mysterious coconut head with staring shell eyes and a fierce expression, and in the entryway an immense bulletin board with contemporary notices of a hundred little things—imported sausage casings for sale, a notice about the Cuban cigar embargo, for sale two tickets for the upcoming Sonny Liston–Floyd Patterson match.

The men who started the club back in the 1930s, many of them socialists, had been men of some education in the old country, forced

in America to work as butchers and heavy-industry laborers, painters
and garbagemen. A wry comment on human ambition. Hieronim had
heard the story again and again from his mother of how his father had
landed at Castle Garden and a month later was in Chicago working in
the Armour meat-packing plant, living as a boarder with a Polish family in Armour's Patch, this trained pharmacist, but he could neither read
English nor speak American and the immigration inspectors marked
him down as illiterate. In this way Hieronim learned that to be foreign,
to be Polish, not to be American, was a terrible thing and all that could
be done about it was to change one's name and talk about baseball.

The old days

Hieronim's youngest son, Joey, begged his grandmother for the shuddering stories of the grandfather, Józef, for whom he was named.

"Him, eh? His family was well-off in Poland but he quarreled with
his parents, his father, over something—I don't know what as he never
spoke of it. Something very bad, I'm sure. So he left in anger and with
empty pockets for America where he would make a big success. He was
a pharmacist, a drugstore man who fixed medicine for sick people,
although he wanted to be a photographer. He drank to quench this
unattainable ambition. He told me once that his mother's family was
related to that of Kasimierz Pułaski, one of the greatest warriors
mankind has ever produced, who fought powerfully in the American
Revolution. And Tadeusz Kościuszko also fought for American liberty.
And the Revolution, it was paid for by a Pole, yes, a rich Polish Jew. You
don't hear this in school, but without the Poles there would be no
America. But to Americans all Poles are peasants, peasants who dance."
Also, she said, someone in that family had crossed the Vistula on a leop-
ard-spotted horse in the army of General Czarniecki in the dead of winter, had frozen his feet up to the knees. "And now they make everything,
so aren't they the muscles of this place? Yes."

"What else?" said the child. "Tell about eating the roast dogs."

"They called your grandfather illiterate! He who had read a thousand
books, could recite from memory for one hour from *Pan Tadeusz,* who
played three instruments, a pharmacist who wrote poetry, a man who
thanked God for the day every morning he rose except after a night of
drink, yet there was no way he could make them understand that he
was not a peasant. It is not easy to remain yourself, to keep your dignity
and place, in a foreign country. He could not talk American and later
he was too proud to learn it. So it was that he found himself in the

Chicago stockyards for his first job, seventeen cents an hour, what they called a 'hunky job.' How he hated it! How he hated the other Poles, peasants and fools he called them, Galacians and Lithuanians, the ones from Russia, stupid as boot heels, but he felt sorry for them too, so ignorant and naive they were always in trouble, timid people blamed for the crimes of others because they could not understand American ways and language. They could not even speak Polish well, nothing, not Russian or German. The poor things had no place, no language, of their own. The Americans called everybody a hunky—Lithuanians, Magyars, Slovaks, Ruthenians, Russians, Poles, Slovenes, Croatians, Herzegovinians, Bosnians, Dalmatians, Montenegrins, Serbians, Bulgarians, Moravians, Bohemians—it didn't matter, all were hunkies. The Americans said hunkies roasted dogs and ate them, the women had ten husbands, that the children were lousy, the men were drunks and all were dirty, too stupid to learn ABC, too dull to feel pain or tiredness, too animal to be sick.

"You can't believe the hardship of those days for Poles—to work all week sometimes and then be robbed on the way home. The Germans would spit on us, 'Polish scum.' I didn't know your grandfather then but he spoke bitterly of those years, and especially of the dirty landlady who slept with the boarders for extra money. I'll tell you, the Poles lived like rats when they came to America, to Chicago. And everywhere *was* rats, eating the rotten meat scraps. In the meat warehouses at night these rats would eat and eat until they almost burst. In the early morning, your father, walking to work, would see them so gorged their bellies dragged the ground going to their lairs of rags and torn paper. Someone found such a nest and in it were tiny shreds of paper money. And the worst jobs. A young man, a boy, just off the boat, healthy and strong, eager to be a success in America, was sent to shovel powdered lead for his first job and got sick and sicker, wasted away and died coughing blood.

"In that boardinghouse the windows were nailed shut, another terrible house was close beside. There was a big room, the landlord divided it in half, put up a second floor with a trapdoor and a ladder so it was a room like a cake with two layers, each only four feet high. The boarders had to crawl to their beds, they couldn't stand up. Even those beds served three men, for at each shift one went out and another came in to fall on the same mattress, still warm.

"Finally it got so he couldn't stand the blood and the stink no more. He quit Armour and he went to the cigar shop. You know, it was not all terrible. Sometimes funny things happened. A cow got loose and ran around in the streets, everybody chasing and screaming. And one poor man, he came home from work so tired and went to the outhouse— that's all they had in them days—and he fell asleep while he was in there—they tipped up to get emptied—they had a hinge in the front— and the outhouse cleaners came around and pushed it over with him inside.

"My family he disliked, he disliked them. Because of where they came from. They came here from the Polish mountains, the Tatra Mountains. Górale, he called them, in American he said jumping Jesus hillbillies. He despised them. If my sister or my mother entered our house and he was there, he left, left without saying a word, just a look on his face of tasting something unpleasant.

"Why did he quit the meat plant job? Because he hated it. It was beneath him. It was filthy work. From the first day he worked there he became a vegetarian, he lived on cabbage and potatoes and onions. To him meat had a brutal appearance, as if it had been flayed from some wretched, kneeling animal. Borscht he loved, and I made it the real way, not like the stuff your mother makes, that's no good. Cucumbers he loved. He hated the stink of the yards. He was a very clean man. His luxuries were two, the bathhouse and the Polish Club he helped to start after Paderewski came to Chicago and played Chopin in 1932 in the opera house—oh, the Poles then loved classical music very much—one of the greatest musicians mankind has ever produced, and you know, he came out on the stage, your grandfather said (he went to the concert with his friends from the Polish Club), strode out very manfully, and the entire audience stood up in homage and stayed standing up for three hours of concert and two more hours of encores. Their legs ached ferociously but they were in fifth heaven. Think of it. There were thousands who tried to buy tickets but could not. On that trip to America Paderewski earned $248,000.

"Your grandfather said the Americans were dirty, he couldn't live like them, so every day on his way home he stopped at the baths. It cost five cents. 'That's my pleasure,' he said. But really it was not. His pleasure was drinking. From Friday night to Sunday night he was drunk. At first he became very lighthearted and laughing and that was when he played his accordion—Spanish airs, then ragtime American, then polkas and *obereks*. Later he became depressed and moody and then he played the violin. And when he was very drunk he was terrible, a dark, silent anger filling him up like boiling water in a kettle. Then everybody had to get out of his way, he was merciless. Still, he carved little wooden toys for his children, for your father a tiny wooden accordion—yes, your daddy was my little boy.

You could put this little instrument on a coin, and Hieronim pretended to play it by the hour, pinching it between his fingers and humming *zim zim*. I don't know what happened to it, dear child.

"Oh, poor little Zofia? That sad story again? Well, the first years were cruel. I had two little children, your father and your Aunt Wanda, and was expecting a third, poor little Zofia, poor little girl. When she was just learning to walk she fell into Bubbly Creek they called it, oh, a terrible stream, not of water but of evil that was like little puffs of cream on the poison stream. They pulled her from it, but it had gone into her lungs and she died of pneumonia.

"After your grandfather left Armour, he started out rolling seed cigars and he was slow and made very little money, then he began to get good and fast and really make some money. He had a Cuban friend, an old man in that shop, like a skeleton, his legs were all twisted—a lot of cripples worked in the cigar shops—who showed him how to use the Cuban blade instead of a knife or cutter. Well, you take a binder leaf and smooth it out on the board like this, and then you take some filler leaves, could be two or three kinds of tobacco, sweet, bitter, and you build them up in your hand until it feels right, not too thick, not too loose, and if you was doing open head work, all the tips of the filler leaves had to be at the tuck end, the end the customers lights up. The tips are very sweet. This is the most difficult part, you can't twist a leaf or make it too tight or loose. Then it can't draw good. Then you break the filler leaves—*chh!*—to the right length of the cigar and put this bunch on a corner of the binder leaf and roll it up. Then comes the hard part, the wrapper leaf, very, very thin and fine, you have to start rolling it at the tuck, roll it a spiral way with a little overlap, and at the head you put a little bit of gum stuff on a flag and smooth it over the head, it has to be perfect. No, the flag is not that kind; it is a little piece of leaf. Then you make another one. Some of the *claro* makers were artists, real artists, but I only learned this when I began to roll cigars myself. Those *claros* had to fit through a ring gauge. But at first, when your grandfather started this occupation, it was hard. We could not live on what he made. And he had to dress well too; cigar makers wore fine suits, you know. And so we too had boarders, two boarders, bed, food and laundry, and I charged them three dollars a week. *No,* I did not sleep with them. What an idea! They never stayed long. He would find fault with them on their first evening, then pick at those faults and magnify them—garlic breath, big feet, this one lacks the fifth stave, a stupid face—he always knew how to find fault, to criticize. And they would go, many times owing us rent and always hating us. In those days he played his accordion at the Polish Club on Wednesday evenings, they had something like a concert—there was a string quartet, a pianist, and your grandfather knew some very fine Spanish airs—it was all for culture, you see, but then he stopped and began to play, not polkas at first, but American music, just 'Alexander's Ragtime Band,' in saloons for money. And you should have heard him go on about it. 'Oh, that I ever could have dreamed that what I once did for careless amusement I would do in grim earnest for money—how could I have imagined it?'

"But he enjoyed playing the instrument, not so much for the sound it made, not for his devotion to music, not like you, my dear child, but because when he played he was the master of the situation, he was the boss. He said, 'I work all week, the foreman tells me "do this, do that, hurry it up," he calls me dumb hunky, he calls me stupid polack, I take it because I have six mouths to feed. I want to pull his intestines out of him with an iron hook but I do the work. In silence, because if I don't like it there's a hundred more waiting to take my job. But I pick up the accordion and if the foreman is there in the place, maybe with his disgusting fellow bosses and repulsive wife, he gets up and dances to my tunes and I make them hot to watch him sweat and twirl.' So he said, the devil. He always played for money and command, never for pleasure in the kitchen or the neighbors' enjoyment on the stoop. That's what they did, you know, in the old days, people just made music with each other for a good time, not for money, but always there was a family that was good, they all played the instruments. On Sundays we'd have a picnic in Glowacka Park, start at noon, and you could buy a hot dog or good Polish things; I sold *pieroẓki* at these picnics and made a nice bit of money. There'd always be somebody's polka band—two violins, you know, the bass fiddle and the clarinet, no accordion at all, they'd just play all afternoon and we'd dance. No music pages, they play from their heads, they were geniuses. You know, the dancers used to sing out a line of a song, or not even sing it, just shout it like, and the musicians they had to catch it, know it and play it back in the same key. Oh, they were so good. Well, your grandfather, he sees after a while there is some money starting to come to the polka band players and there was all kinds of places that wanted polka bands—Polish Homes, the Polish Club, not the culture evening but the Saturday night dance, little dance halls all over the place, the union halls, bars and Polka Dot restaurant, the Polish League of War Veterans, a lot of restaurants, Polonia Hall—oh, there was plenty of polka dancing, and a lot of fun, and weddings, weddings, weddings, everybody was getting married and you got to have polkas. So your grandfather decides, this is in

1926, he decides he's going to have a polka band. So he gets a couple of fellows together, a fiddle, they don't need the second one because they got the accordion, a clarinet, drums, and he's very good. They picked an American name, the Polkalookas. The drum was good, pick up their feet, yes? He was a shrewdie, your grandfather. He'd take two engagements for the same night, hire some extra fellows and get both bands set up at different places, then he'd run back and forth between them and collect the money for both. It was not so old-fashioned, this music, as the polka bands in the park. No, a little faster and louder because of the accordion and the drums. And he got the idea for the Baby Polka Band, he got your father, Hieronim, only six years old, and five or six other little kids and got them all going with instruments, playing little baby polkas. A comb and paper, a triangle, they had a little girl singer, so cute. People loved this very much. But he was not happy and he drank all the money from the band playing. After a while he quit, just like that, but your father, Hieronim, he kept on, played with other bands, whoever would ask him, even though he was young, and he brought every cent he earned back to me."

Grandfather's nightmares

"Grandfather's nightmares! Holy Mary, your grandfather's nightmares were terrible—his screams woke everyone. And the last time I told you about them, what happened, you woke up yelling in the night. So I better not tell them. Well, then. Remember, you asked for it. He said, 'I dreamed of a severed head garlanded with decayed weeds and roots. The mouth was torn, the eyelids ripped away and yet the eyes rolled and looked. The face was that of my mother.' Or he would tell of a head with the top sawed off so he could look inside, and in there he saw his father's old pharmacy in Poland and behind the counter was a young man and just as the young man started to look up at your grandfather—as if he felt someone watching him—he would wake up. Or he would tell of eating in his dream a horrible soup of living toads and white snakes, of crushing each with the back of his spoon but feeling it revive and struggle in his mouth. He told of a dream in which he received a wooden box from Poland, of prying off the cover to find inside his young sister covered with a thick growth of red fur, arms and legs broken to fit her into the too small box, but living and staring at him. In his dreams were horses with pigs' faces, pieces of paper that became bloody knives, accordions that disintegrated as he played them, the buttons leaping into the air, the bellows rending and hissing, the hinges melting. Then he became interested in these nightmares and no longer feared them but awaited them eagerly, and entered his own nightmares with a dream camera, photographing these strange events.

"He entered yet another world of strong odors with the cigar shop. The smell of tobacco was so strong that it made him run out and vomit in the street the first day. There's tobacco dust in the air. The windows were nailed shut. It's humid inside because the tobacco cannot be allowed to get dry. If someone who didn't know came in and opened a window, all the workers would walk out and threaten to quit. But anyway, the windows were all nailed shut so that couldn't happen. He was good at his work, his fingers were agile from playing the accordion and he had a good eye, he had the feeling in the fingertips. In a few years he was making more money than anyone in the neighborhood rolling those Havana *claros*. We found this house and began to make payments. But he was not satisfied. He swaggered about, finely dressed, worked when he pleased and smoked his three free cigars and continued to drink. He shunned our little house. A worm gnawed his brain.

"He quit working at the American Cigar Company and went to United Tobacco. He began to do what many of the best cigar rollers did: travel about the country, going to different towns, and when he found one he liked that had a cigar shop —in those days every town in America had one or two—he would show the boss what he could do, stay for six or seven months or weeks and then move on. By the hundreds, these cigar makers, Italians, Germans, Poles, on every train, back and forth and up and down, looking for the golden America they had imagined, a place they believed existed somewhere.

"He would send money home, regularly at first, but then nothing came. For months. I was crazy. I thought to myself, this dog's blood of a man, this *psiakrew*, let him die alone among strangers. I had a little money put aside and it all went for food and the house payments. I had five children. I had to take in a boarder or two. The best was Uncle Juljusz. How kind that man was! You know, he was named after his ancestor Juljusz Olszewicz, who became French under the name Jules Verne. He helped me write a plea to your grandfather—I think he must have inherited some of the gift for writing—an advertisement that I mailed to the paper; they had a paper every cigar maker read. I'll never forget it. It would make an angel cry. It said: 'The children of cigar maker Józef Przybysz need to know the whereabouts of their father as they are in need.' They ran this advertisement for one year but we never had an answer. I never heard from him again. And what did he leave his children, what did we find when we opened his precious trunk he brought all the way from Kraków and never let anyone peep into? A metal tool no one understood, a model of an iceboat, a tiny little tin globe with a drop of red paint on the place where Chicago might be, two wax records, '*Zielony Mosteczek*' and '*Pod Krakowem Czarna Rola.*' What did these things mean? Nothing! Oh, the songs? Oh, in American you say 'The Green Bridge' and 'The Black Soil near Kraków.' Old-country songs, sad old songs, I don't know why he had them. Not his kind of music. He preferred classical music or humorous smut; you know: '*Żyd się śmiał, w portki srał, żyd się śmiał, w portki srał*'—'the Jew was laughing, he shit in his pants'—that nasty stuff he liked.

"It was good Uncle Juljusz who persuaded me I could take up cigar work myself. He told me they were hiring many women in the cigar trade. At first I only did dirty work, stripping. You know you got to get the midrib out of the leaf. Then a woman showed me how to roll cigars. The work was mostly the five-centers—the good-paying Havana *claro* work was then and always only for men—but I could earn enough, like Uncle Juljusz said, to support my children. My oldest girl, Bubya, your Auntie Bubya, was twelve, old enough to look after the others.

"And so it happened. *I* worked for American Cigar. They started me off stripping, but I pestered one of the other women who had been there a long time to show me how to do it—I knew something about it, of course, from listening to *him,* the critical affair of gauging the bunch, and I progressed very rapidly. We used cigar mold presses for the five-centers. Your grandfather never touched a mold, he was an aristocrat of the cigar. You got this two-piece wood mold with hollows in it, little beds for the cigars, and you put the filler leaves, the bunch, in these little beds and put on the top of the mold and it goes in the press for twenty minutes. It shapes the filler. I enjoyed it—you can't imagine. We were all very friendly, we had little names for each other. I was Zippy Zosia because I was very fast; Eagle Eyes was a woman who saw everything. The rest of them I don't remember. We could talk anything, conversation, jokes, somebody always playing jokes, somebody put a snake in my filler leaf box once. What a scream I made! We had a reader in the afternoon, somebody would read the paper out loud or a book—we heard *Black Beauty,* I never forgot it, we all cried and it was very bad for cigar making. We would sing—one cigar place had a piano. We would bring in cakes. All my friends were these cigar-making women. My happiest years.

"I say now those were the happiest years of my life. I was making money enough to pay the mortgage, set aside a little to gain certain advantages for my children. Bubya married Uncle Juljusz, as you know.

True, she was only thirteen, but it worked out well enough. Uncle Juljusz bought her a beautiful doll for a wedding present, something she always wanted but there was never the money.

"Joey, I paid a suit for your father so he could play the accordion looking nice, I paid shorthand school for Marta, I paid chiropractor school for your father, I paid nurse school for Rosie, for my children I paid a good education, all my children went to the Tatra dance classes, they should do well and remember they are of Polish heritage and not have to roll cigars. But Hieronim disappointed me, he stopped chiropractor school and went to work for the Polonia Sewing Machine Company and got married. Of course he played the accordion too, 'The National Defense Polka,' 'Dive Bomber Polka,' 'Hilly-Billy Polka'—ask him, I can't remember. After I started the cigar job I got very active in the church, I joined pleasant societies, very good discussion and happy occasions, I became reunited with my family and my people from the mountains, and Uncle Tic-Tac who tried to teach your father the old mountain songs, urged him to write them down in a book, to gather these songs from the old generation, what they remembered from their villages, from their youths. But your father was more interested in the new kind of polka, 'The Killer Diller Polka,' and one I did not like very much but I've forgotten the name, something about 'the little man in the corner,' especially when he came back from the war and so much was lost. Perhaps you, little grandson, with your love for music, will find a way to save the old Polish music."

What Hieronim (a.k.a. Harry) said to Joey

"My old man? Hey, I don't want to talk about the bastard. The old lady fills you with lies. He was a lousy musician, interested only in the dollar. His music was coarse—'the cow shit, the bull farted, everything went into the same hole, I came along and looked and we all shit some more.' That was what he liked. Crude stuff. The lowest common denominator. Then he'd blubber all over the place when he heard the Angelus or something. He claimed to be a pharmacist in the old country, but I did some checking up and he wasn't nothing but a peasant. Tried to make out he was better over here. Once he left, it was good. I played a lot of weddings the week he left—three or four a week. I was happy. It was good times, not just because people was getting married but because he was gone.

"Hey, when I came back to Chicago after the war it was all changed. Everything! Before the war we used to have a lot of fun at dances—

there's one thing you gotta say for polacks, we really know how to have fun—there was this guy, big heavy guy with a red nose like a cherry tomato, worked at the steel mill, you'd see him at every dance the sweat just pouring off him, and he'd shout '*ale się bawicie?*' Are you having fun? and the whole dance floor would roar 'yah, yah, yah.' Weddings? They used to go on for three days. But then after the war everybody is serious, no time for fun, the wedding dance is three hours instead of three days, all the Polish halls and societies are closed down and there's niggers everywhere, entire streets, whole Polish neighborhoods wiped out. And the people are different too, I mean white people, Polish people. They don't have such exuberant fun, even though the music, and I mean the polka music, was terrific, better than in the old days, punchy and fast and loud. Hey, I think of the music—Li'l Wally Jagiello, he's the one started the business about singing the Polish lyrics, he's got a good voice, before him hardly ever anything but instrumental polkas. But hey, are we having fun? Are people warm and friendly like they used to be, a big arm around your shoulder, buy you a drink, have some more food? No, no, everybody's cool, everybody's casual, stand back a little, don't make a big thing, don't act so Polish. This cool stuff, I say they got that from the niggers who will stand there like statues, very still, never move but watch everything going on and not move a muscle, act unconcerned, *cool,* where a old-fashioned polack would be tearing his hair out and praying to the saints. See, polacks are more like wops in the emotions. And that's when the Polish dance halls and community dances started to close down, so now the only time you hear polka music is at somebody's wedding and at special Polish days, festivals and like that. Records too, records spoiled it—hey, everybody can have a polka band in their living room on the phonograph, they don't need to go out to a place where live musicians are playing. So we're losing it. I heard my first rock number with a polka beat last week, some jerk band of kids, call themselves the Warsaw Pack. Ha-ha. I predict that in ten years the polka will be dead. And don't ask me anything again about my father. He was a lousy shit."

The third pleasure

The occasional third pleasure of Hieronim came when someone—always someone else, never him—got some whore in the back room to do for all of them, whoever was drunk enough.

In winter, there was no fishing and he spent all day at the Polish Club.

But there was another reason he liked to come there. The bartender, Feliks, because of a birthmark, had an uncanny resemblance to a man who boarded in their house when he was eleven, twelve, Mr. Brudnicki.

The house seemed full of boarders after the old man left, some working at the mill, some traveling through with things to sell, sometimes musicians and actors. Mr. Brudnicki was youngish, with swollen hands and tight pursed lips, a birthmark from the inner corner of his left eye to his ear like half a mask, a series of dots and dashes, purple writing in some strange alphabet. He was part of something the men knew about, a show or some event that happened elsewhere. Sometimes he would come into the kitchen and, if no one was around, crook his finger at Hieronim, a good-looking big kid then with snow-blond hair and wolf-green eyes, already thinking of himself as "Harry," to come up to his room where his bed was curtained off from the others, and if the house was empty he would lean against the bed and Hieronim would stand in front of him. Mr. Brudnicki would open first his pants, letting the "Red Devil" (as he called it) leap out, then Hieronim's, to release the "Little Devil" which he stroked, pushing back the foreskin and pressing the head against that of the circumcised Red Devil, and then it was time for the two devils to spar, rubbing, bumping, shoving at each other until Mr. Brudnicki turned him around and pushed him onto the bed and then Hieronim would feel the Red Devil, dressed in a cold layer of lard from the can under Mr. Brudnicki's bed, enter the "secret cave" with snorting and writhing. Afterward Mr. Brudnicki would swear him to silence and give him a quarter, a magnificent sum, worth any amount of devil sparring, though the secret-cave entry gave him pain and diarrhea.

Once, restless for that odd excitement, he took his cousin Casimir up to Mr. Brudnicki's room to teach him the trick, but when he knelt to get the lard can under the bed he saw a small red trunk. It was locked. He looked then in the scabby green cupboard where Mr. Brudnicki kept his clothes and saw an extraordinary garment suspended from a wire hanger, a glittering thing, a dress of ice. He lifted the hem, heavy and cold with tiny glass beads.

"Casimir, see this." His cousin came up beside him and touched the dress. The gloom of the cupboard, a musky, spicy smell, enveloped them. He heard his cousin breathing, could feel his warm breath on his neck. They pressed into the cupboard, the beady fringe of the ice dress clicking as they rubbed each other's swelling pricks.

"I do this all the time," gasped Casimir.

"So do I," lied Hieronim, the clotty sperm hitting the ice dress, deciding not to tell Casimir about Mr. Brudnicki and the quarters, which was different from this, sinister yet thrilling and enriching. When Casimir had finished too they started to laugh, and forevermore Casimir had only to say "the beaded dress . . ." and they would both smirk and blow their lips out in half-laughter at the memory.

After a few months Mr. Brudnicki started a series of brief absences, often falling behind in his rent, and then a long absence of weeks although his trunk and his can of lard were still under the bed, the mysterious dress in the cupboard. Sixteen days passed.

"That's it!" cried his mother to Uncle Juljusz. "He's more than two weeks behind. I got good men, working men, want this room. If he don't come by Saturday it all goes out. I rent to somebody else."

Saturday passed. On Sunday afternoon his mother went into the room, pulled the blanket divider aside and began throwing out trousers and shoes, the ice dress, the can of lard and the red trunk which crashed down the stairs, unlocking itself on the way, tumbling out wigs, cosmetics, unguents, glittering masks, and a curious elastic-backed garment with a rubber front sporting a pair of large breasts with maroon nipples.

"Jesus, Mary and Joseph," shouted his mother and Uncle Juljusz came out of the kitchen and looked, picked it up. He took it to the mirror over the sink, held it up in front of himself, but it looked laughable until he took off his shirt and pulled on the breast garment over his bare skin. The effect was extraordinary. It was Uncle Juljusz, the seamed, flattened face and the straggling mustache, and the red arms with tufts of stinking hair, but then he became—not a woman, but part of a woman. Uncle Juljusz minced around the kitchen shouting "oh, you bad man" in falsetto and slapping at the air.

"Now you know how he could pay the rent!"

At that moment when they were all screaming with outraged laughter, Mr. Brudnicki opened the door. He was thin and white, a soiled bandage like a helmet wrapped around his head. He stared at them with tragic eyes, saw his glittering dress on the floor in a heap like melting ice, turned and ran down the steps, back into the street. "What was I supposed to do, wait until doomsday?" shouted his mother after the flying man.

Hieronim's worm probe

In 1967, the week before Joey and Sonia—a beauty with a flat, still face, the full, rich mouth seeming to pull the cheeks toward it, great-lidded eyes of china blue provocatively slanted—married, it rained steadily, every morning beginning with fog that thickened and turned to drizzle that turned to steady rain that turned to downpour as night fell, so that under the drumming roof they slept well. Sometime between four and five the rain stopped and for a few hours there was the hope of dry weather, but then it started again.

On that Sunday morning Hieronim believed it was going to clear. The mist was blowing off, the ragged clouds showed sky. There was a lovely freshness to the day, the smell of the country. He passed the extension cord out the window, went outside and connected the worm probe. Barefooted, pale feet with knobby bunions, a cup of coffee in one hand, the probe in the other, he walked across the spongy lawn looking for a good spot. A slight depression in front of his wife's rain-beaded ornamental cabbages, pearly violet and mauve-frilled leaves, what beauties. He plunged in the probe and turned on the current. For a moment, as he leaped into the air, he had the galvanizing sensation that he was being turned inside out as a skin is stripped off a rabbit in one sharp jerk, but by the time he landed facedown in the sopping grass he was almost dead, and he was thoroughly dead, surrounded by a halo of electrocuted worms and robins, when his wife noticed him from the kitchen window four hours later.

She had given him the worm probe for a name day gift two years before.

A dog's voice does not reach heaven

Hieronim's wake was something, the last of its kind in the neighborhood, in the old, old Polish style, and nobody would have known how to do it except Old Man Bulas from the Polish Club, who carried a blind man's watch, a curious horologe knobbed with chimes and rings that sounded the hour and minute when buttons were pressed. The two of them had drunk and talked away the years together, both of them filled with a deep and mystical regard for Mikołaj Kopernik, the father of astronomy. Nobody would know how to conduct such a funeral in future, as Old Man Bulas himself died two weeks after the funeral-wedding weekend, and was buried with a scanty American ceremony. There's irony for you, said Mrs. Józef Przybysz, slamming her cane on the floor and weeping.

In his youth Bulas had studied literature, but when he emigrated to America the only work he could find was in the steel mills where, after six years of work, he was burned and discharged with a small settlement. His right arm was puckered its length like the skin on hot milk, his shoulder was withered and shining with scar tissue, but he was the leader of singing and knew the hymns, scores of them all written down in his *śpiewnik*, a thick, handmade book wrapped in black cloth.

"Important!" he said. "Important because now they are saying the mass in English. A tragedy." He, at least, knew the poetry of incantatory words and the power of secrecy.

He came to the funeral home at dusk with men from the Polish Club, the good singers. Hieronim, soaped and shaved and dressed in a shark-skin suit, lay in his walnut case like a polished knife in a silver chest. The singers filed in and stood along the wall. To their left was a small table covered with a white cloth and on it a dish of peppermints and a saucer of cloves. The hymns and the prayers began, Hail Marys, hymns to the Mother of God, to the saints, then, after an hour, the men went out to the parking lot and drank beer and whiskey to intensify their grief, while the women said the rosary, voices elongating, drawing out the ancient words. The men filed in again with flushed faces, belching and hiking at their belts, stood once more along the wall. Darker and more morbid became the hymns, groaning pleas to God to remove the singers from the misery of the body—*I am lost, I am damned, I have sinned.* They sang of the damp grave, the final hour, and of sinful humans' vain pleas for mercy: "The clock strikes one, the thread of life slips from my grasp, the clock strikes two . . ." There was a midnight supper of black coffee, bananas and cold pork. All through the night the singing went on, Old Man Bulas's voice cracking and shrill under the strain, and at dawn they said the last prayers for the dead and Old Man Bulas started the Angelus, *I now bid you farewell.* At seven the undertaker's men loaded Hieronim into the hearse and the singers followed in cars with the windows rolled down even though it was a raw morning, the men still singing, seeing the cold sweat of the grass, their heads aching and vocal cords so strained they sang with a kind of breathless roar.

The next day the two sons had a ferocious battle for Hieronim's accordion, Rajmund crying out and dramatically striking his chest like Tarzan, and screaming that Joey was tearing the bonds of family apart, that their father had promised it to him, that their father would twist in his grave like a worm. It was an unfortunate simile; Dorothy shrieked and Joey cursed. It was all show, for in his heart Rajmund was indiffer-ent to the accordion.

Haste to the wedding

With such a funeral, thought Sonia, no wedding, not even a Polish wedding, could compete.

She was wrong. Old Man Bulas, galvanized by an atavistic need for ceremony, slept for eighteen hours after the wake, rose, made a list and sent his grandson as messenger to the parents of the bride and the widowed mother of the groom and to many others. He told his wife it was necessary to balance the solemn death rites of Hieronim with as much of the old *wesele* style as possible, although the bride and groom had sent invitations by mail instead of calling on the hoped-for guests to invite them personally or sending a *drużba*. Since the freshly buried father of the groom had been a part-time musician, and the groom himself played semiprofessionally, there had to be a good showing of musicians, beginning with a fiddler to play "Be Seated in the Wagon, O Loved One," as Sonia left her parents' house. "Ah," said Old Man Bulas. "I remember as a boy all the men shooting off their pistols and the bride-to-be getting on the wagon all covered with ribbons. It was too bad. By accident someone shot her in the heart—an accident. So the wedding became a funeral."

Three polka bands pledged their services for the reception, planned for a small room in the Wenceslas Hotel, shifted to the Polish Club's modest ballroom. Bulas announced that he and Mrs. Bulas would act as the *starosta* and *starościna,* guiding everyone through the unfamiliar old ceremony. It went well enough at first, the bread and salt, but the musicians were impatient with the Grand March which had to be started over and over when new guests came in, then, during the interminable dinner, Old Bulas jumped up every second to make speeches and propose toasts, tongue-tangled and lost in the memory of another ill-fated wedding in Poland he remembered, a wedding ruined by a harried baker who rush-rush, mixed the batter, had to do something, rushed back and forth, poured the batter into the pan, shoved the pan in the oven, later frosted and decorated the fine cake, and when the moment came for the bride to cut it, her knife felt a resistance, he said, and as she fumbled out a slice, there was disclosed a rat, a rat in the cake, dead of course, but the tail flopped out when she cut the slice and they could see the feet sticking out and my god, she vomited and the wedding guests saw this and *they* vomited, oh it was terrible, they were all full of wine and rich food and vomiting everywhere. He sang, "*Czarne buty do roboty, czerwone do tańca.*"

When the moment came for the changing of the veils, Sonia and her bridesmaids lined up, but one of the bridesmaids, perhaps thinking over Old Bulas's story, shrieked and fell in a fit. Half an hour later, the revived woman sitting on the sidelines, they tried again. Sonia's mother, hands unsteady, lifted the orange-blossom wreath and veil from her daughter's pale hair, damp with sweat, and put it on the maid of honor, and the rich, sad voices lifted and filled the ballroom, *today you cease to be a maiden and become a woman,* when the fire alarm went off. A few minutes later Joey led his bride onto the dance floor, spun on a carelessly applied blob of wax and lurched to one knee. He flushed, cursed loudly and went straight to the bar, leaving Sonia to follow or not. Slowly, after an announcement to send Polish polka tapes to GIs in Vietnam to cheer them up, the real dancing began, sedate at first, but picking up until a manic dance fever infected them all, not just the old polka one-two-three-four, but the chicken hop, the *Siwy Koń,* the Silver Slipper and other furious new steps, and it went on until the next morning, the musicians crying for mercy, collapsed dancers rolled against the wall, sleeping in their finery. Among them was Old Man Bulas, not sleeping but in the coma from which he never roused until the day of his death a week later when he opened his eyes and said, "let those I have sung for sing now for me," and his family wailed, for surely he was calling up a chorus of the dead.

Joey and Sonia

"I sure as hell guess we got married," said Joey in the motel, yawning until his jaw cracked. Sonia smiled.

"Here's to a long and happy life together," he said, clicking his glass of sour champagne against hers. "How much money did you get?"

"I don't know." She went into the bathroom with her case.

He plunged his hand into the satin bag and pulled out a wad of bills, started to count, but she was standing on the bed and wearing a short nylon nightie, flimsy, pale blue and edged with lace, and he looked up from the money. He could see the dark circles of her nipples, the triangle, her swelling calves and white ankles. She began to jump a little, the bed quivering, her feet lost in the thick duvet. He let the money fall, rushed at her the way a diver on the high board hurtles toward the blue. All she could think of as he rammed into her was the first time she had seen his penis, years earlier; she was thirteen, swimming with her girlfriends Nancy and Mildred at the municipal pool, dark heads in the water like floating bread, hundreds of people standing, walking on the wet concrete around the pool, the girls pulling at their bathing suits. She knew Joey by sight, a big boy, two classes ahead of her in school. He stood on the verge of the pool, his toes hooked over the edge, looking down at them floating on their backs, their legs yellow and wavery under the water, seeming broken and flat in the refraction. He reached up into his baggy trunks, letting them see him getting at whatever was up there. He moved to stand directly in front of them.

"He's lookin to see if he lost somethin." Nancy tittered.

"If he ever *had* something."

"Maybe it came loose."

"Oh jeez, ugly!"

He had the head of it out, poking it at them, and then he began to piss, the stream splattering inches in front of them. They screamed and backstroked, still watching him, but he dove in under the water, coming up between Sonia and Nancy, thrusting his hand into the crotch of Sonia's bathing suit, and she went under water and came up choking and crying.

Pie

It could have happened when they stopped to get the coffee.

He was groggy and his hands were numb. He'd be better off getting a Coke, she said in her hoarse voice, it had more caffeine, and while he got it she'd clean up the kids in the rest room. Artie had diarrhea and the car stank from his dirty diapers which she changed by kneeling on the front seat and bending over into the back. Whatever it was, it was catching and Florry had it too, felt feverish. It would have to happen now. The good thing about that was it made both kids listless and they slept which was better than having them jump all over the car, yelling and bawling. And he'd gone in to get his coffee and she'd followed with the kids, cleaned up Artie in the grimy sink, stuffed the stinking diapers in the tiny rest room's wastebasket, the smell filling the closet-sized room, looked in the mirror at her grey cheeks, wet a paper towel that went slimy the instant water touched it, but at least the water was hot and it felt wonderful after the cold car, the heater on the blink again, why couldn't he ever fix anything so it stayed fixed, the kids on the dirty rest room floor, but not crying, thank god. She'd get them some ginger ale. She had four dollars, and she could at least get the damn kids some ginger ale.

She came out and he was hunched at the counter drinking coffee instead of getting a takeout, and he had a wedge of cherry pie in front of him, wolfing it down, hoping to finish it before she came out and saw it, after yelling the whole way how they barely had enough money for gas and would have to hold on until after the contest. After they won, after they had the prize money he'd buy each one of them a steak as thick as his leg, even Artie who had only four teeth. She looked at him hulked over the pie; her stomach rumbled as she imagined the tart sweetness, the warm sugary crust. And they had a little fight right there when she walked up behind him and said in a low voice, will we have enough money for gas?

"Look, I got to have the energy to drive, don't I?"

"What about me? I don't count. Supposed to take care of the kids, get your clothes nice, take care of all that stuff, get up there and perform on an empty stomach. It's OK for me, huh?"

"OK," he said, very exaggerated, letting her know she was pushing him too far. "Miss, we need another piece of pie here. And make it a big one."

"I don't want it, I don't want your goddamn pie, see?" She was so angry she started to weep. "It's the way you treat me, not the pie. I don't want it," she said to the waitress who shrugged and shoved the precut slice— they were all the same size—back into the case. The other customers stared at them. A guy who looked like a truckdriver, cowboy boots and trucker's cap, had a big plate of toast and scrambled eggs and a slice of ham, the works, in front of him. The smell of the food got to her.

"OK," she said. "I changed my mind. I'll have the pie." Ashamed but hungry. The waitress yanked the pie out of the case and put it in front of her, slapped down a fork and a napkin, poured a glass of water.

She sat on the stool next to Joey, both the kids in her lap, holding one in each arm. There was no way she could pick up the fork. Joey stared straight ahead. She wedged Artie between her stomach and the counter, held Florry with her left arm. Gave Florry the first bite though she'd probably throw up later. She ate fast, drank the water and was done, heading for the door, before Joey finished his coffee. He was spinning it out, smoking a cigarette now, probably enjoying the warmth after the cold car. (By then it probably had already happened.)

She stepped out into the grainy wind—it was cold enough to snow and that would be the icing on the cake—lugged the kids toward the car, god what a beat-up wreck. The parking lot was empty. The car still smelled bad, but it was so cold she didn't want to hold the door open. She got the kids laid down on the back seat and put the blankets over them, then remembered the ginger ale. She could see into the diner, Joey still at the counter. There was a vending machine next to the pay phone.

"I'll be right back," she said to Florry and ran back to the diner. There wasn't any ginger ale, so she got 7UP and hoped it didn't have caffeine in it. Joey was paying for the pie and coffee, counting out a handful of pennies, the waitress watching his fingers pick the linty coins out of the wad of gas receipts and folded wire, knobs of string, with exaggerated patience. She wasn't getting any tip from this bozo. Dumped the pennies in the cash register without looking at him.

"Aren't you going to say 'come again'?" he asked in his mean voice. She gave the trucker a look that said, this is what we get in here now, and kept to herself what she knew—that the guy was paying her out because the wife had had the pie.

He started the car, said, it stinks in here, what'd the little bastard do, die in the back seat?

She was getting interested in the scenery, if that's what you called the thickening city, the road widening into multiple lanes, four, then six, the traffic thickening and low-slung bars and tire warehouses, railroad switchyards piling up and the buildings piling up too, higher and tight together, buses and trucks, the trucks mobbed the roads. It was like Chicago, yet unlike. They were going through the ragged part where there were a lot of black people. She was nervous when he stopped at the lights and dirty black guys with huge mouths and rolling walks came insolently up to the windshield and started to rub with wadded newspaper, but then they saw Joey's face, his heavy-lidded eyes and his big head and his slab of face set in the I'd-love-to-kill-you-give-me-an-excuse expression, and veered off to another sucker's tinted glass.

"How do you know where to go?" She tried to make her voice light, show that as far as she was concerned the fight was over, they should get in a decent mood before the contest. He didn't say anything.

"It'll be nice to get in a motel, take a shower."

He'd set that up, made reservations at a motel about two blocks away from the hall, he said, and paid in advance. The motel was a cheap place, nothing much, he said, but it was a room, it would be warm, with a TV and a bed and a crib for Artie. He knew about it from last year when he'd been driving the truck and had laid over there sometimes. Florry could sleep with them, it was just for one night, but she'd put her on the outside, remembering where Joey's hand had been the last time they'd put the kid in bed with them. He was asleep so she couldn't blame him for it. How men were. See an empty bottle he'd stick his finger in it.

"At least we're getting here plenty early," he said. "It's what, almost three-thirty, it don't start until eight. Plenty of time to clean up. I'm gonna get a little sleep, have a couple of beers, then we can run through the numbers, practice the routine." She relaxed. The fight was over. They had a good routine, though it was a little risky. First he came out onstage alone, but kind of reluctant, looking back offstage, dressed in his sky blue satin suit, carrying the purple glitter accordion, then he'd turn a little and the line of blue sequins she'd sewed up the pants seams flashed. He'd frown and look worried, look offstage, shake his head.

Nothing obvious, just really look worried. Wait. Then, just when the judges started whispering to each other, gonna have to move on to the next one, she'd come running out in her purple satin suit with the sky blue accordion and the audience would give them a big hand even before they played a note, just glad she hadn't loused it up for him. On their side. If he was feeling frisky he might knock out a breaker and pick up a laugh. Then they'd play and knock their fuckin socks off.

"That's it," he said.

"Where?" She didn't see any motel. Crumbling sidewalks, a white Pabst truck unloading, bar signs, a bakery, P.R.C.U. Club, a butcher shop, sausage strings hanging down, an old man shuffling along, arms bent outward, hands like potato forks, two men eating hoagies in a torn-up section of street, wiping their mouths on the backs of their hands.

"Right here, dammit, you blind? Want me to get you a pair of glasses?" He pulled into an alley, forced the car around to the back of a grimy brick building, nudged a garbage can which scraped against the car. HOTEL POLONIA MOTEL. There were seven or eight orange doors with numbers, a hand-lettered sign in a window spelling "Office." A couple came out of number five, the woman young, wearing black slacks and a fake fur coat, some kind of orange fur, supposed to be fox, she guessed, the man middle-aged and heavy, smoothing at his hair. He didn't look at the woman, but walked past her, heading for a parked delivery van, "Lakeshore Officeland Everything for Your Office." The woman spat on the ground, got a cigarette out of her purse and lit up, headed for the street.

"It's a hot-bed motel."

"So what? It's cheap." He went into the office for a key, left the car running. She watched through the windshield, saw a few hard flakes of snow come down, saw him inside laughing and nodding at someone invisible, a gesture with his head, nodding again. He came out and pulled the car up in front of number one, next to the office.

"Margie's gonna keep an eye on the kids tonight. She's the manager. She'll be right there in the office, and if one of them starts to cry or anything, she'll come in and fix them up."

"Is there a crib? Did they provide the crib?" She knew there wouldn't be a crib, they'd all have to sleep in the same bed, Artie shitting his way across the world.

"Yes, there's a crib. Jesus, take a look first before you start in on me, will you?" He got out and unlocked the door, threw it open and extended his hand elegantly toward her. She hoped at least there was a shower. Florry called from the car.

"Mama. My stomach hurts."

There was a sink, an unscreened toilet in the corner of the tiny room, an alcove like a niche in the wall with a dripping showerhead and an orange-flowered mildewed plastic curtain, a three-quarter bed, and jammed into the space between the side of the bed and the wall, a grocery shopping cart. She couldn't figure out what it was doing there until she saw it was made up like a bed, with a folded blanket for a mattress. No television. She knew better than to say anything. She went out and got Florry and Artie. Put them both on the bed. Joey threw himself down on the swaybacked mattress, next to the children; the bed squeaked like a lunatic.

"Howsa wittle baby, howsa wittle girl," he said, tickling Florry. She sat up, squirming, he pushed her over, tickling, and as she got to her hands and knees she suddenly vomited and started to bawl.

(Twenty years later, the Isuzu commercial wrapped, Florry snapped the lid on her electronic hybrid MIDI-retrofitted Petosa with sixteen channels, Hall-effect magnetic switches, after-touch, dynamic bellows control, key velocity for bass and treble, tempo control, transposition capability and movable keyboard splits, nodded at Bunny Baller the engineer—a bad case of razor bumps, goateed, hair-netted—out of his booth and swigging a bottle of Evian, the drops sparkling down his mesh shirt, and pulled on her patent-leather coat, heard Tommy the producer say, that was some well-played shit, and she said, yeah, but Miss Platinum's got a salivating problem, you gotta get that spit out of there, and he said, don't worry, but she was out the door looking at her watch, looking for what came next with a terrific headache and that swimmy, fevery feeling again, the flu? Walked to her silver Camry, got in and leaned forward to turn the ignition key when something fell from the cloudless sky with force, hit the hood hard enough to rock the car and broke into three large fragments. She got out and picked up one of the pieces. Pizza—frozen pizza—what, somebody threw it out of an airplane? A message from God?)

"For chrissake," he said. "We're in the room two minutes and the pukin' brat wrecks the place. CLEAN YOUR KID UP!" he shouted at her, heaving himself off the bed. He went out to the car.

It had probably already happened back at the diner, maybe even before, but it could have happened in those minutes in the motel room.

"You couldn't hold it, could you?" she whispered furiously at the child, bending her roughly over the toilet while she retched. She heard him slamming the car doors, heard the lid of the trunk go up with a loud squeak. The motel walls were like paper. He'd bought the car from a dealer in revitalized wrecks; the frame was a little bent, the doors and trunk squealed, the tires wore on one side, but he'd got it cheap. He was back in the room before she got the bed cleaned up.

"Did you bring in the accordions? DID YOU BRING IN THE ACCORDIONS?"

She shook her head. He was frightened, she heard it.

"They're not in the trunk. They're not in the FUCKIN TRUNK." He looked under the bed, ran out and began throwing everything in the car on the ground—the kids' blankets, maps, crumpled bags, her suit-case, the box of diapers. He went back to the trunk and opened it again, as if the accordions might have reappeared, perhaps back from a stroll around the block. He got in the driver's seat, the place he always sat, the only place where he was in control of things. He tried to think. Went back into the room.

"I put them in, I put them both in, it was the last thing I did, I remember checking the catch on yours right there in the trunk—it comes undone."

"Yeah."

"Look. If I find out you did something with those accordions I'm going to kill you."

"How could I do anything with them? I been right where you are since we left."

"Yeah? How about in the diner? When I was finishin my coffee you went out. You were out there. You could of taken them out and shoved them under the car. I'd take off and never notice. Did you do that? DID YOU DO THAT?" He clamped her chin in his heavy hand, twisted her head toward him. She couldn't help it, tears spilled down her face. He made her look at him. She couldn't talk because her mouth was distorted.

"Mo. 'idn't touch 'em."

"Tell you what you did do. You couldn't wait in the car while I was getting the coffee, could you? You knew the fuckin trunk didn't lock, you knew those valuable accordions were in there, worth a couple grand each. But you left 'em unattended, just came on in, couldn't let me out of your sight. What'd you think I was gonna do, bang that waitress with the face like a baboon behind the counter? You left the car unattended so any son-of-a-bitch could come along and open the trunk and see what was in there. The guy must have shit his pants when he saw those accordions, he must have said, 'oh Lorda Mussy, dis be mah lucky day!' Some fuckin nigger took them accordions, one under each arm, and run down the street. Bet he watched us drive away, bet he laughed until he pissed his pants, laughin how he put one over on us." His voice was taut. He was crimped with rage. He went out, leaving the door open. She heard his voice through the wall, talking to the motel manager. He came back into the room.

"What was the name of that diner? You better remember what town it was in. I'm gonna call the cops there and tell them some coon swamphopper ripped off my accordions. Then I'm goin out and find two goddamn accordions we can play tonight." He looked at his watch.

"It's quarter of four. You be ready at seven-thirty and have my clothes out." He dropped the suitcase on the bed. "I'm comin back with two accordions if I have to steal 'em myself."

"Can't we borrow from the guys that'll be playin?"

He was out the door, didn't hear her. Bulling through the problems like always, even when there was a simple way. "Those are good guys. Wally'd let us use his, he always brings two. Eddie and Bonnie be glad to."

She studied the veiny map, the thruway a main blood vessel pulsing down the state, and the vein roads leading away east and west and then branching out into fine capillaries that ended in small towns. She thought about the morning, packing and getting ready to leave, tried to remember seeing him bring the accordions out. She'd gone over to the apartment window where Florry was watching the street, looked down. Their car was there, the trunk closed, Joey walking back to the apartment building with that heel-banging stride. Across the street, in front of the Stretch-Yor-Bucks, a bread truck, behind it an old Cadillac idling, a spew of oily smoke gushing from the tailpipe and the swarthy driver drawing on his cigarette. Two women in long print skirts came out of the grocery store. "Look, Florry, there's gypsies."

"Where? Where are they? Do they bite?"

"They're people, silly, they don't bite—what do you think?"

But the door banged and Joey had yelled, "come on, let's go, we're ready to roll."

She thought about asking the manager, Margie, to keep an eye on the kids while she went over to the performance hall, explained the problem, see if anybody could help them out. But didn't dare.

Pawnshops

It was getting colder. The digital temperature readout on a bank facade, "8° F." Filmy snow came down like mist, he could see advancing waves. The light was fading, streetlights came on, neon signs. He put on his headlights. His breath froze on the inside of the windshield and he had to keep scraping it with the kitchen spatula, little curls of frost showering down. He'd ripped two pages out of the phone directory and kept squinting at them when he pulled up at a red light. The traffic was stop and go. He saw an empty place, nosed the car into a taxi stand, left it running to show he'd be only a minute, then came back and turned it off, put the key in his pocket. Somebody steal that, he was up shit creek with a balloon in one hand and a stick of dynamite in the other.

The door was locked, there was steel mesh over it and a sign that said "Go to Window and Buzz."

"Buzz, buzz," he said aloud, but at the security window pressed the buzzer.

"Yes?" said a voice. "State your business, please."

"I'm looking to rent two accordions. Somebody ripped off my accordions and I got to play a contest tonight so I'm in a spot. I'm looking for two accordions."

"Read the sign, mister. Gold and silver, coins. I don't deal in accordions. Try up two blocks, at American Investment. He's got accordions. He's got trumpets. Guitars."

"OK." He was back in the car, nosing out into the traffic again, the headlights catching in the damn frost his breath made so he could barely see out the windshield. He went past the hall where the contest was going to be. The lights were blazing, a big red and white misspelled banner strung across the front, *NAZDROWIE!* 1970 POLISH POLKA PLAYOFFS TONITE. There was a list of players, headliners in big red letters with a white star for a dot over the letter *i*: Walt Solek, Mrozinski Bros., The Connecticut Twins—shit, they didn't count for shit in Chicago—Tubby Kupski, Big Marky, Happy Gals, and got a glimpse of his own name in pretty good-size letters, Joey & Sonia Newcomer. They had everybody but Frankie Yankovic, probably thought he was too big for this. Slovene anyway, not Polish, a buttonbox guy with a taste for the banjo. He wasn't worried. Most of the ones in the duet class were a bunch of pretzel benders, they didn't have his sound. Except for the Bartosik Brothers who were extremely good and extremely dangerous. They'd taken a big one from them in Gary with a novelty arrangement of "Blue Eyes Crying in the Rain" in the styles of Elvis Presley, the Beach Boys. They were bastards.

American Investment & Pawn was big, and the gold and silver guy was right, he could see accordions from the car, Christ, looking at a wall of them. This time he was lucky, caught a parking place as a truck pulled away. There was a crooked poster in the window: ENJOYING LIFE? YOU'LL *REALLY* ENJOY IT WITH AN ACCORDION!

The woman behind the counter was built like a football tackle, hard face made of suet. He gave her the song and dance about the accordions being ripped off. She didn't say a word; the look on her face said it all: I don't believe a fuckin word. But he read her like a newspaper. She had the genes, the look, of his grandmother.

"Look," he said as if talking to a dummy, but keeping his voice patient, "my wife and me, we're Polish, we got a act, a real good act, and we play in the contests. Duet polkas and she sings. We got three tapes out. There's the big contest here tonight, down at the armory, a polka playoff, and we got a very, very good chance of taking the first prize for mixed couple duet, a thousand bucks. I'm not shittin you. Some diner up the road, a couple a jigaboos broke in the car while we was takin our sick kids to the toilet and stole our accordions, we didn't even know it until we got to the motel." He let a little emotion get in there, let his voice break a little bit.

She said something to him in Polish. He smiled, hiding his quick rage.

"I don't talk Polish, just picked up a couple words from my grand-mother. *Na zdrowie.* You know." He sighed. "It's a shame, ain't it, how the generation lost the language. I'd love to know it but—" He spread his hands in despair.

The woman shrugged, pointed at the accordions with her thumb. He wanted to look at accordions why go through the song and dance? He was going to try something funny, she knew it.

"Let me see that green one. Up there." It had to be on the top shelf. She slid the rail ladder over, climbed up, watching him under her arm in case he tried anything funny. His eyes were moving over the accordions, not the cash register. Maybe he was on the level, maybe not. Came down with the accordion and set it on the counter. Dusty.

He didn't know why he'd asked her to get this one; it was a button accordion, not a piano accordion. Neither one of them could play the damn thing except Sonia, a little. Her old man was a crazy man on the buttonbox, had started her out that way. He examined it, an old instru-ment, too old and too small. Leather bellows and still supple despite the dust. He picked it up and made a couple of chords, set it back on the counter, looked at the shelves of melodeons, Cajun open-valved diaton-ics, big square Chemnitzers, English and Anglo concertinas, a small sin-gle-voice bandoneon, electric piano accordions, Yugoslavian *melodijas,* plastic accordions, a Chinese *mudan,* a *bayan* from Russia, two Pakistani harmoniums, and row after row of Bastaris, Castigliones, Sopranis, Hohner Black Dots—god, look at them all, every immigrant in Amer-ica must have pawned an accordion here, chrome Italian names curling along the cracked lacquer and celluloid and wood, Colombo, an Italo-tone, the Sonda, the Renelli, a Duralumin shaped like a harp, who'd play that?, big chromatics with their five-tier stacks of keys a nightmare to learn, over there a lone Bassetti like the jazz guy Leon Sash played, and Bach, he played Bach too, you could do that with an accordion.

"Let me see that Colombo polka model, the black one there, that's actually what we play, piano accordions. Put this buttonbox back—I must of thought this was a piano accordion up there in the shadows." The woman brought him the big Colombo. He could see there were five or six on the shelf. He tried them, one after another, most of them messed up in some way, stuck keys or the reeds bad, bellows leaky or the action stiff. There was a Guerrini polka box with Slovenian tuning; he didn't want that.

At last he got it down to three. They could play these, and he pushed back the thought that it could be hard to win with them. He rattled out a fast minute of "Money Money Polka," showing off their style, that wild honkying minor, a barbarian tension, the feeling of being on the edge of losing control that made their sound, which nobody else had, that made dancers go crazy. Looked at the woman to gauge her reaction; she looked surprised in a sour way. He grinned at her, pouring on the charm.

"Guess you can play, all right," she said.

Now beef up the sob story, and make a deal with the old bitch.

Getting ready

The kids were asleep, Florry in the bed, Artie in the shopping cart, when he came in, and Sonia was leaning at the mirror, dabbing on her makeup, bare legs showing beneath her bathrobe. Their clothes were hanging on the back of the door, not a wrinkle in them.

"Got 'em," he said, slapped her on the rump. "It's only six o'clock." He cracked open a beer, took a pint of V.O. from his jacket pocket. "Wanna shot?"

"Yeah. They any good?" Looking at the instruments. Big old black things, they wouldn't go with their costumes. She picked up one of the Colombos and played a little, ran through the opening chords of their old novelty ethnic number that they didn't use anymore, "Dyngus Day Drinkin'," where the music got progressively sillier and looser and he mimed putting down the shots with beer chasers, then he switched at her legs with imaginary pussy willows and she jumped, still playing the accordion, did a big bellows shake. The tone wasn't lively and she could hardly jump, the instrument was so heavy. Anyway, they'd dropped that number for a complicated medley of tricky rhythms and familiar tunes. Joey knew that winning duets stayed away from weird stuff, gave the audience something familiar and comfortable yet played fast with a lot of tricks: "Love Ya," "Happy Us," "Wonderful Times," "My Happy Baby." She thought of their lost instruments, Norwegian spruce soundboards, handmade reeds, the grilles cut out in their names.

"It's heavy," she said. "It sounds muddy." She tried the other instrument. It was a little better, maybe, but one of the keys was loose and made a clack every time she hit it. She wanted her blue accordion. Actually it was his; he'd gone to court against his brother over it when old Hieronim/Harry died. The old man left only one accordion and both of them wanted it, but Rajmund could hardly play and Joey got a cheap lawyer to make the case that the one who could play should have it. Rajmund just wanted to sell it and have the money. He'd do anything for money, but things went against him. Those long arms like an ape. He'd grabbed a package of bills, three tall stacks packed close and bound with a brown paper wrapper, from the woman behind the check approval counter at the Kmart, did it on impulse, all that money and her just standing there with it, trying to hold open a canvas bag with the other hand. He ran out. But in the parking lot the package blew apart, sending out a big cloud of red dye that got all over him, up his nose and all over his face and neck. He dropped the money and ran to his old maroon van, but there was a cloud of red floating behind him and red all over the van where he touched it, and the engine wouldn't turn over.

Now in the hot-bed motel Joey started the salty comic piece "What's That Thing Between Us?" and their voices fitted together, hers husky and full, his reedy tenor surprisingly pure and high from that heavy chest, so that she carried the melody and he took the harmony. It was OK and she relaxed. Maybe they'd pull it off. The voices counted for a lot. She started to practice the runs, hating the loose key, sipping at his boilermaker. He played better when he was a little drunk. So did she. And it made it easier to drink the liniment mixture.

"You rent them?" she said.

"I made a deal. Don't worry, it's OK. You think of the name of that diner? And the town it was at? I'm getting those accordions back, don't care what I do."

"I looked on the map. It must of been Morley, because I remember it was after that long road with nothin on it, then we come to this town. But I didn't see the name on the diner."

He gave her a disgusted look. "What the hell good are you? Tell you one thing, we're gonna pull out of here tomorrow morning and spend the day in fuckin Morley until I find the guy that took 'em, then I'm gonna run over the black bastard until he turns into strawberry jam." He took a hard belt of the whiskey and smacked the glass down.

"OK, get it over with. Get the stuff." She got the bottle of Dr. Jopes Red Rock Healing Liniment, with the silhouettes of horses galloping across the label. Joey measured a capful into her glass and topped it up with beer.

"Drink it slow so it can take effect."

"Don't worry!" The bitter, corrosive sensation began with the second swallow and her vocal cords tightened. When the glass was empty her mouth and throat were dry.

"Enough? Or do you need more?" He was hard about the liniment bottle.

"I'm ready, I'm ready, it's good," her voice harsh and high, the sound he loved, the sound of ecstasy and raw pain.

Polish honor

They took a cab to the Polonia Ballroom so the accordions wouldn't be chilled in the sharp cold. The street was jammed with traffic, horns hooting, a mounted cop beckoning cars forward.

"Big crowd," said Joey as they passed the ballroom, swung around the corner to the back entrance. He felt his mood lift. A good crowd was what they needed. Now he was solicitous of her well-being.

"You all right?" She didn't answer. They walked through the big room, already packed with people shuffling along in front of the con-cession booths and tables displaying giddily painted eggs, embroidered vests with triangular lapels, carved wooden cups, loops of kielbasa, cakes, intricate paper cuts of the Tree of Life, roosters and hens, ban-ners, subscriptions to the *Amer-Pol Reporter,* a kiosk raising money to help the family of the Reverend Józef Jurczyk in western Poland—killed while he said mass by a madman swinging an axe—travel information for vacation transatlantic crossings on the M.S. *Batory,* pride of the Gdynia-America Line, and at one booth a red banner reading HELP DEFEND POLISH HONOR!

"You go ahead," he said to Sonia. "I want to see what this is." It was the Polish-American Guardian Society collecting signatures and money to sue the Motion Picture Association of America for producing movies defaming and degrading the Polish people and naming *Taras Bulba,* with Tony Curtis and Yul Brynner, along with *Let No Man Write My Epitaph* and a string of other movies he'd never heard of, and a separate petition urging Hollywood producers to make films portraying Poles in a sympathetic and favorable light, films based on the military careers of Pułaski and Kościuszko, for example.

There were a lot of hippies around the Polish Honor booth. He was half disgusted; Polish hippies, some weirdly dressed in high-collared old-country shirts and short pants, but most of them wearing embroidered vests, their long hair catching in the crusted shoulder stitches. There was also a Vietnam veteran contingent, muscled guys in t-shirts and cropped haircuts, each of them looking capable of swinging an axe, punching each other's arms and eyeing the coolers along the back wall that would only be opened after the contest when the dancing began. The babble of voices rose above the clack of unfolding wooden chairs in the back as the crowd pressed in, looking for seats.

The dressing room was community style, partitions separating the sinks and the mirror space. Sonia had the rented accordions out of their cases and under the dressing table near the heater. She was drawing arched eyebrows on her orange face, the lipstick next, protruding redly, like a dog's prick, she thought, from its gold case on the table in front of her. His costume hung on the hook. She looked at him, threw him a wink, nodding her head at the partition to her left. He opened his eyes at her and she pointed, nodded her head again, he should go take a look. He walked casually to the bathroom at the end of the room, glancing to see who was next to them—the Bartosik Brothers. Only Henry was there. On the way back he stopped, said, "hey, Henry, how y'doin? Where's Cass? You guys all set?" There was only one accordion in sight, one makeup kit.

"Tied up in traffic; it's a mess out there." Shot Joey a look of hate from his ice-blue eyes, turned away and fiddled with a strap.

In his own cubicle Joey grinned at Sonia and began to slather on the ruddy makeup that made them look healthy and vigorous. If Cass was drinking somewhere and didn't make it or if Cass was drunk and did make it, they had the contest sewed up, rented instruments and all.

Out front the contest had begun with the Kiddy Polka King and Queen contestants and they could hear the too fast riffle of "The Skater's Polka" and the surge of applause and whistles. It dragged on before the Best Accordion Comix started. By then he had something to worry about. They were in the next-to-last spot, but the coveted last act for the duets went to the Bartosiks. Well, there was nothing they could do about it. He sidled into the wings to watch the comics a few minutes. The crowd was roaring, laughing at anything, even the joke about the woman skiing down a mountainside while playing the accordion.

The Polish Polka Bums, Staś and Stanky, had a rough but funny act. Staś wore a hula skirt made of rubber chickens, a gigantic pink bra with Christmas-light nipples that lit up cherry red when he pressed the button taped to his palm. His hairy legs ended in steelworker's boots with big round toes. Those goofy breasts and their red lights were always getting squeezed in the accordion bellows and Staś would roar AH! AH! in mock pain as he sang "They're Always in the Way." Stanky, dressed in a small tight black suit, played bent backward, his arms thrust through his legs, his groin arched and the accordion swelling and barking between his black silk ankles. Then he shouted at the audience, "you heard this one? Why does it take four polacks to make popcorn? One to hold the pan and three to shake the stove! Hey, who was Alexander Graham Kowalski? The first telephone Pole! Hey, how can you tell a Polish airplane? It's got hair under the wings! Hey . . ."

Górka then, tall, tall and thin, dressed in a jumble of women's clothes, a red wig, a false nose, a chrome whistle around his neck—and he blew the whistle, pouring water into his ear that spurted out of his elbow and his shoe, lighting up a giant fake cigar that blew up in an explosion of green dust. He had a trick accordion mounted on a Stumpf fiddle, honking the taxi horn, ringing the bells and clacking the pie pans as he played "Yes Sir, That's My Baby." And Skippo danced out, his onyx cuff links dragging his shirtsleeves out of the jacket, an orange silk background woven with gold and green lozenges, set off by a brown velvet collar and a tie pleated up like a tiny accordion under his dark jowl.

The comics were followed by a couple of transitional acts, first the mother of Arkady Krim leading her son, the blind boy from Durango, Colorado, who at age ten had lost his sight and three fingers on his right hand fooling with a dynamite cap. Arkady was dressed in a blue suit with sequins on the lapels. He held the accordion upside down and played a religious number after announcing that music was the gift of God and that he regularly turned down lucrative offers to play in roadhouses, pledging his talent to a higher power. After two encores he was replaced by a middle-aged woman in a strapless gown who began "The Ballad of the Green Berets," worked "Winchester Cathedral" and "The Tennessee Waltz" and ended with that good old Polish tune "Zorba the Greek."

Back in the dressing room

Before they married, Joey was already doing the Polish festivals and contests, a living to be made that way, just driving around from state to state, wherever they had the ethnic festivals, dances, parish get-togethers, Polka Days in a dozen states, busloads of tourists pouring in, the California Golden Accordion Fest, the East Texas Czech Fiesta, Hub City Polka Days, Polkamotion Nites, the Houston Livestock and St. Patrick's Polka Gala, up to Fairbanks for the Polkalaska, the Polkabration Weekend at the Holiday Inn at O'Hare International, jets roaring overhead. It took a year of work before she got out there on the stage with him, before she got over being frightened of the sweating crowd and the snaky cords running every whichaway over the dirty stage, the squealing feedback and the sensation that she was going to pass out in front of everybody. And her throat feeling from the liniment like it had been scraped with a broken branch. She could hardly talk, but all the strength in her leaped into the singing. Then it got good, especially when they won a contest, exciting when they screamed out Joey's name—and hers!—and shouted and whistled.

This was the time when fancy accordions were popular, the beautiful instruments from Karpeks, every color, pearls and paste diamonds, rhinestones and script glitter letters, grilles in silver plate and even real gold, the black and white key colors reversed.

The organizers were always a heavyset couple whose lives were subsumed in polka and Polishness. They knew how to make things work, rented the halls a year in advance, planned the publicity, wrote the ads and announcements that appeared in *Accordion World, Texas Polka News, Polish-American Polka Aficionados.*

When the first festivals started up in the sixties—let the blacks see that Polish was beautiful—the more Polish the music, the better the organizers liked it, wanted performers to sing in the language or some regional dialect, preferred unusual music and difficult dances that took a long time to get going, music from some isolated Little Poland. It was all Polish people who came then. But the festivals boomed and swelled, turned into everybody-come, beer-drinking weekend good times; the organizers knew what the crowd wanted and it wasn't cultural esoterica. Mrs. Grab got Joey on the phone, explaining.

"We don't want nothing weird or extreme, you know? There's rules now, the association's made rules." She was booking them for the August Missouri Hog Farmers Polka Kick-Down. "We got the Civic Center auditorium again." Joey groaned. The acoustics were hellish, the P.A. system was a clapped-out old wreck that amplified music into a metallic din.

"What's the matter, couldn't you rent a jumbo-size culvert? Effect'd be the same."

"Now Joey. Craft booths on the east, food booths on the west, also the tables for records and tapes, then at the back we put the sign-up table for the door prize. This year it's gonna be a metallic metal-flake Aztec-blue Ford. Also at the back door the ticket takers. Now, musical performers for the contest—that's you—get six minutes apiece, and for the dance the bands change every fifteen minutes. Give plenty of variety. Line dances only, puts the dancers face-to-face with the performers, get that crowd electricity going, see, it's more satisfying, people have more fun than just watching some old-style fanatics dressed up in wreaths do a two-hour wedding dance. Line dances makes a nice display. Only one song in Polish. Most people don't understand it, but one song gives a nice ethnic flavor. That's what we want to stress, ethnic *flavor*. Let me tell you something, Joey. Ethnic music is not that old-time stuff any more. These days *everybody* is ethnic, might as well make money on it. They come for the music and to have a good time. And the beer and kielbasa. They don't want that mournful folk music sound no more or those complicated couple dances going into circles and weaving around and slapping their asses and crossing into the next lane. No more of that *Kozacy na Stepie,* Cossacks on the Steppe, stuff. Everything gets mixed up unless you got a Ph.D. in Polish clogging. It's no fun. You know, I'm not Polish, I'm Czech. What's Czech these days? It's boiled down to *kolác* pastries and polka. So get out there and play loud, fill the place up with good fast happy polka. Fast and happy. Show them what it means to be ethnic. You're guaranteed three hundred anyway, and if you win—audience response on the applause meter determines the winners—it's what, fifteen hundred and the Missouri Hog Farm Polka King crown."

That particular gig was sour. She was expecting Florry and she'd lost about ten pounds and felt lousy all the time. (Both Florry and Artie had been born on September fifteenth, though two years apart.) Joey had worked up a showy version of "*Zły Chłopiec*" which they called "Bad Bad Boy." It didn't go over too well but was better than Jerzy Wald's numbers where only three couples came out on the dance floor, and the spare applause had hardly died down when a big guy jumped up, his thin long hair pasted to his sweating forehead, and began to shout at them.

"This is not Polish polka, not Polish music. I am a Pole from Poland and in Poland they would laugh at you as I do now—*Ha! Ha!*—for saying this garbage you play is Polish! That is not Polish food"—he gestured toward the lawn covered with ethnic food booths, each a ten-by-fifteen canvas tent with a steam table and a cooler and some folding card tables in back and a counter manned by ladies' auxiliary types—"that is NOT Polish food, that crap you call kielbasa and kishka. I wouldn't feed them to a starving man. And that American mess, potato salad with little two-tone olives and pieces of pineapple and sugar-flavored mayonnaise. *Ha!* Language? I laugh in your faces! *Ha! Ha!* Ruined words forced into hilarious phrases, broken grammar to make a real Pole hysterical, you think this is your ancestral language? Never! Pig Polish!" And so on. Later she saw him sitting alone under a tree eating the American potato salad with a spoon in each hand.

Winners

It was all right once they got out there. The rented Colombos worked, the timing was flawless and Sonia's voice was like a blooded dagger—*this* was what it meant to be Polish: misery suppressed, injustices borne, strength in adversity, endurance—how that poignant, rusty voice could hold a note until the audience gasped and breathed for her. And then a terrific polka that got the hippies in the audience clapping in rhythm, and the rest of the audience took it up—a good sign; they were with them. They got the most applause of anyone so far, announcer Jan Reha pointing at the applause meter and shaking his head in mock amazement.

They ran into the dressing room, sweaty and high with elation that it was over and had gone well.

Henry Bartosik, ready to go on, trembling with rage, stood outside his cubicle looking at the stage back door and at Cass Bartosik who came through it tearing off his overcoat and fumbling with the hasps of the accordion case he carried.

"Where the fuck you *been?* We're on right now. I been going crazy!"

"You can't get through, the traffic's a mess, I had to walk eight blocks to get here—Christ, I'm frozen, my fingers are numb. Stall 'em a minute." He ran hot water in the sink. "Hold the accordion over the register, it's ice cold—quick, quick, come on."

"You tell *me* come on? Goddammit, I can smell the whiskey from here."

"Fuck that, I was getting something to eat. I don't feel so great, see? I had a drink, one drink, to settle my stomach. Now get off my back." One of them worked the bellows trying to get warm air into it, pressing the cold keys. "Ah, Christ!" Cass let out a series of small belches. From the stage, as the applause for Joey and Sonia died away, the announcer called out, "weren't they great? A terrific duo, husband-and-wife team Joey and Sonia Newcomer. And now, what all you young people have been waiting for, a duo covered with fresh notoriety from their Milwaukee triumph at the Polish Street Festival, those outstanding interpreters of Polish tunes in popular styles, the Bartosik Brothers, Henry and Cass BARTOSIK." The two brothers clattered off toward the stage stairs, Henry cursing and Cass belching, hiccuping, stuttering "you can't get blood out of a dead dog."

"Tonight the Bartosik Brothers—by the way, folks, Cass Bartosik is the fastest typist in the U.S. of A.—are going to change things around a little bit, popular tunes in *polka* style, and will play a memorial-tribute medley of Jimi Hendrix and Janis Joplin tunes—but they're not gonna smash their accordions and set them on fire!—so get ready to rock! The Bartosik Brothers!"

They heard the applause, the expectant silence and then the two accordions pumping out "Me and Bobby McGee Polka."

Joey laughed. "Listen, the instrument's too cold—the bellows is slow. They're in trouble." He poured half an inch of whiskey in her paper cup and she threw it down for the quick heat and the loosening sensation, the sense of relief. Suddenly from the stage they heard the slower accordion stop, a pause, and an enormous howl of laughter from the audience that went on and on though above it now were the sounds of scuffling and muffled shouting coming closer. The contestants waiting in the dressing room to go on pressed around the door, saw Cass and Henry fighting at the top of the stairs to the stage. In the auditorium the voice of Jan Reha beat against the laughter, soothing, making jokes against the tide of shrieks and howls.

"What the hell happened?" said Joey, for it was apparent that Henry was pounding Cass furiously, while Cass bent over to escape his brother's blows. Cass leaned forward abruptly from the waist and vomited on the steps.

Joey crowed. "Jesus, he threw up onstage. He must of. Oh dear blessed Jesus, oh Holy Mother, saints and martyrs, suppose we'd had to follow that? What is it today, they're throwing up all around me." But someone rang down the curtain and two women with mops and buckets rushed onstage. Henry lurched into the dressing room, leaving Cass retching in the corridor, a security man guiding him toward the men's room. Henry was beyond rage, filled with a great Polish froth of madness, about to do something irrevocable and frightful, Sonia thought, seeing his blazing cheeks and white eyes, but he only thrust his accordion into its case, put on his overcoat and went out into the night. The snow-speckled wind swept into the corridor. Onstage the voice of Jan Reha was calling their names, the winners, the *winners,* that husband-and-wife lovebird duo Joey and Sonia Newcomer! And the middle-aged lady who played between intermissions was pumping out "Climb Every Mountain" as they came up to take the check and shake Jan Reha's scaly hand.

The present

"Honey, OK, what do you want to do, go out for dinner or get something, get a bottle and some fried chicken, take it back to the motel? Listen, honey, I know the place is a dump but suppose we hadn't won— it was all we could afford if we didn't win. Look at this sweet check, fifteen hundred smackers—we got beautiful, beautiful money again. You beautiful little doll, you want to change to a different motel, something ritzier? We'll do anything you want, just say the word."

She wondered what he would do if she said yes. "I don't know. I don't want to go out it's so cold, I kind of thought we might stay for the rest of the program, eat here, some good Polish food, it smells great. They've got potato cakes with roast beef. And there's dancing." Joey liked to dance at the outdoor festivals, where it wasn't so crowded.

"Yeah, OK. Jesus, did you see the look on Henry's face? They're washed up now, they're through. He'll have to play the chordovox at the Washington Senators games. This'll travel like wildfire all over the circuit. Can you imagine him calling up Jerry and saying they want a spot on the Doylestown? And Jerry says in that sarcastic voice, 'no, thanks, we don't think throwing up onstage is a real great act.' Tell you what, sweetheart, I got to get these accordions back to whence they came from before eleven. Why don't I go back to the motel, check the kids, get the car, turn in the accordions and then I'll come back here and we'll have some fun. Go to mass in the morning, it's a polka mass, right across the street, have the Polish breakfast and start back. Stop in that town, Morley, talk to the cops about our instruments. We'll have a couple hours then tomorrow afternoon to sit down with the checkbook and get some bills paid. Like that, wouldn't you?" She nodded.

"OK, then, I'm gonna run. See you in about an hour."

At midnight she was still waiting, sitting on a folding chair and talking to people about the music and the Bartosik Brothers, looking constantly toward the door until she was too tired and walked back to the motel through the snow, eight inches deep now and drifting. Cars and trucks slid and stalled on the greasy streets and she was shaking with cold by the time the sign HOTEL POLONIA MOTEL came in sight. Under the streetlight, a few hundred feet from the Polonia, something small stuck out of the snow. She picked it up, a pack of cards with a rubber band around it and a folded paper. She pulled the paper loose, it unfolded into two ten-dollar bills. The pack of cards showed whores in bizarre display postures.

It was after two when he sidled in, hot breath stinking all the way from the door. She'd just got Artie quieted down and her throat ached from the liniment and the singing and the vinaigrette salad dressing on the sliced beets. She was bone-tired. He plunged around, swearing, found the bed and sat heavily on the edge. She moved Florry closer to the wall.

"Sweetheart," he said. "I'm late. Went to the auditorium and nobody there. Gone home."

He struggled with his shoes, the snow-wet knots difficult to loosen.

"I went to the bar where they were all hanging out. What a scene. Cass was there, drunk, had a fight. This old guy played the bandoneon, ever hear one? Tangos. A couple got up and danced. Jesus, like a couple of kangaroos with glue on their feet. They do this little kick, it's like a dog scratching. Here. Brought you a present." She could feel something square and hard, then her fingers felt the buttons. She sat up and put on the light, dimmed with a towel wound around the shade. He was a mess, hair wet with melting snow, face flushed, red-eyed, shirt half unbuttoned. He thrust a small green accordion at her.

"Here. You know how to play this. Pretty little accordion for my pretty little wife. Or give it to little Florry, if you want." His face rippled and he moaned. "Oh, sweetheart." She stretched her arms out and seized him; maybe she loved him after all. The accordion, caught between them, groaned.

"Your white powdered face . . ."

After he got rid of the accordions he wasn't in any mood to go back to the lousy motel and listen to kids whining and coughing and throwing up. He was chilled, he was excited, the check felt hot inside his breast pocket. He filled up the car with gas at an all-night station, dumped in a can of antifreeze so frost wouldn't form in the line. He thought suddenly of the dead heater, wondered if it was the heater fan fuse; why hadn't he thought of that before? It was the fuse. Should have been the first thing he checked.

Cruising down the icy street, the present on the seat beside him, the beautiful hot air blowing on his feet, he saw the red neon, *Hi-Low Club,* and the red banner flapping over the door, NA ZDROWIE POLKA FANS. He pulled into the parking lot, jammed full—Christ, it was cold—and made his way into the noisy bar, hit by a blast of hot accordion music— Cass Bartosik at the mike, drunk and brilliant—got a whiskey and beer chaser and made his way to the long, narrow counter along the far wall, the only place he saw an empty barstool. Half the people in the place had accordions; there was music or at least noise coming from all over, "Autumn Leaves" mixed up with "What's New, Pussycat?" and polkas.

He sat next to a guy in a grey sweater, an aging man with a big nose and a black hat listening to Bartosik play his rock version of "Okie from Muskogee."

"I despise this music," said Grey Sweater.

"I despise it too. Bartosik's a pain in the ass. He should go back to his typewriter."

"You know this man?" The sweater guy had an accent he couldn't place, some kind of Latino thing. An odor of tuna can lids and cat's breath came from him.

"Yeah. I just come from the Polka Playoffs—this guy threw up onstage. They laughed him out of the place."

"So, you are a player of the accordion?"

"Yeah. You?"

"No." He gestured at the square case under his feet. "Bandoneon. The finest of the free-reed instruments. Sonorous, tragic, furious and always—*always*—sensual. I do not play this pop music, these polkas—only I play tango, music of a tragic character, associated with the torture of love, the assassination of the heart, with suffering."

"Yeah?" said Joey. "Where you from?"

"Buenos Aires. Argentina. But I left a few years ago because I thought there were some opportunities for me here. There are certain aspects to life in Buenos Aires that are uncomfortable."

"Yeah?" said Joey. "How about a drink?"

"Thank you, sir. You are a man of sensibilities. I played here in many bands, almost never tango, only once or twice. Americans do not understand tango. They do not know the bandoneon. I tell you, I despise America—the food, the women, the music. My mistake is, I let this show in my face. I do certain things. I am arrogant, I admit it, because I am a superior person and come from a superior culture. But here, at first I try, then I become contemptuous and angry—it is my nature—then, because I am hungry for everything, I turn to crime. I steal a steak from a supermarket, I am drunk in public, I piss on the sidewalk, I rant crazily to all who will listen, I shout filthy words in the cinema, I make a disturbance in restaurants. I am vengeful. A man says something to me that I do not like so I plot to ruin him." The man's cement-colored face was rigid with disgust.

"You sound like a tough customer," said Joey.

"I'll tell you something," said the man, shaking a partially smoked cigarette from a crumpled pack and lighting it. "A man insulted me recently, a bartender. I waited outside until he went home. I followed him, saw the door where he entered. The next afternoon when he was at the bar, I went to his apartment for my revenge."

"What'd you do?"

"I destroyed him. I removed all the labels from the cans on his shelf." He laughed. "He will not know if he opens soup or pears."

"That's it?"

"Also I remove the bolts from his toilet seat."

"I guess I won't tangle with you. Have another drink."

"I'll tell you something. I am going to Japan. In Japan they are mad for the tango. In Japan and Finland. There they understand. In Buenos Aires I was known as the Tiger of the Tango, the Brute of the Bandoneon."

"No shit. So you're pretty good?"

"Probably the best bandoneon player in the world, better than Astor Piazzolla, and I tell you my tangos are not so dissonant, not so *new wave,* as his. Piazzolla, with his little zips like the plastic zipper of a cheap jacket, his plotted silences, the squealing like rubbing two balloons together. That is a serious, unsmiling, hard music; the faces of the dancers frown furiously; and his tempo, the beat is like climbing cement stairs in a skyscraper with fire behind the doors. And there is that quality of a paper comb that sets the sutures of the skull trembling. Those passionate swellings are musical hives. I think of short men in leather-soled shoes, the languid violin drooling, the huffings and puffings, the stertorous gasps, the runs like beads of sour candy on a strip of paper, the illusions of snow and spiderweb and falling trees. The parts like trains backing up. The business of hens. The officiousness of roosters. The dying moans of slaughtered cows. But in *my* music there is a wildness; ferocity is in my music, in my tangos. There is an animal in me—it is like a frog with sharp claws, jumping about and tearing at me." He stretched out his hands and showed the deformed thumb.

Joey had had enough of Bartosik's noise. He stood up and bellowed:

"Attention! Ladies and gentlemen. Attention! We have tonight— what's your name?"

"Carlos Ortiz."

"We have with us tonight the famed Argentinian free-reed artist, the Tiger of the Tango, Mr. Bandoneon himself, Carlo Or Tease!" Everyone clapped; they were fed up with Bartosik. Joey pushed the man in the sweater toward the mike, helping him unsnap his instrument case, urging him along, go on, go on, let's hear the tango, alternately shouting, sit down, Bartosik, go throw up somewhere.

The man stood in front of the mike, the grey and silver octagonal instrument with its glistening pattern of buttons, one hundred forty-four of them, in his hands. He sat on the chair, flexed his hands.

"Thank you. This is a surprise, of course. I play for you a few tangos, a kind of music, a dance sensual and cruel, that is far from its city of origin, Buenos Aires. I begin with something sad and a little bitter, '*Lágrimas,*' or, as you say here, 'Teardrops.' "

They stamped and bought him drinks, recognizing the difficulty of his instrument and the virtuosity of his musicianship. Intoxicated, he played on: "Evil Thoughts," "Secret Dreaming," "The Crazy Ones,"

"My Fiery Past," "Rough and Tough," Osvaldo Pugliesi's "*La yumba*," and even Carlos de Sarli's extraordinary "To the Great Female Puppet."

A middle-aged couple got up and began to dance. They knew how to do the tango—the brilliant footwork, the close bodies, the static poses and slow, drawn strokes, the deep bend, the flashing head-turn. They seemed to Ortiz exquisite in their knowledge of the somber, irascible music and he played furiously. (Later that evening, in his hotel room and after the requisite exercises that often follow an evening of tango, the male dancer suffered a heart attack and cursed the tango in his last thought.)

But the audience began to tire of the dramatic, ripped-seam music. Cass Bartosik made a funnel of his clumsy hands and shouted, "lighten *up*, man. Man, that sound is too heavy." He advanced on the Tiger and the evening ended with a tussle in front of the mike, the pantings and gruntings of the combatants amplified. The Tiger hissed, "fucking fool, do not damage this bandoneon. They do not make them anymore. Have courtesy for this finest instrument. Polka swine! I'm killing you now."

Joey left without seeing how it came out.

(In 1972, when Perón returned from exile, the Tiger returned to Argentina. After Perón died he shrugged and stayed, in love with a botanical illustrator and enjoying success with his new tangos. One day he aroused the interest of minor dogsbodies of the military junta with "*Mala, Mala Junta,*" a tango that slyly referred to bad companions, the downward spiral, the dangers of association with criminal types. He was taken in the night, imprisoned and tortured, his fingers disjointed. He did not play the bandoneon again.)

A present

Florry woke her up before daylight.

"Mama. Mama, I want french fries."

"Umm?"

"Mama, I want some chocolate milk."

"Are you hungry then?"

"Yeah." She felt the child's brow, damp and warm, but not feverish.

"You must feel a little better?" Tried to think what there was to eat in this stuffy room at four-thirty in the morning. She thought of the vending machines in the corridor, soft drinks and candy, maybe some crackers. She whispered, I'll be right back with something, climbed over Joey, snoring now with the open-mouth rasp of a sleeping drunk, went to the door with her purse and slipped the chain. She left it ajar. The hallway was a mess of melted snow, wadded paper, street handouts for slow-dance partners showing a photo of a bosomy girl with her mouth forming a suggestive O, ticket stubs, an empty pint bottle, crushed Coca-Cola cans, a sodden blue mitten. The machines hummed and throbbed at the end of the hall. Orange soda and a packet of cheese crackers was the best she could do.

Florry ate ravenously and drank like a machine. She was wide awake, ready for the day, her eyes roaming around the squalid room that they seemed to have been in for so long, her father's clothes hunched over the back of the chair, the chink of light from the hard white window, the gleam of chrome from Artie's shopping cart bars, the reflection of a quarter on the side table, and a square green object with a red ribbon bow.

"What's that?" she asked coyly, pointing.

"What do you think it is? What does it look like?"

"A present." She put her face down in the blankets, blushing at her temerity in saying the word.

"It is a present. Here, see?" She reached over Joey and picked up the green accordion, put it in Florry's hands, undid the latches and guided the child's hands in opening the bellows, pressing the buttons.

"It's a 'cordion. It's little. Mama, where are the keys?"

"It doesn't have keys. This kind has buttons. This is the kind Mama learned on. Here." She pressed the small fingers through *Baa, baa, black sheep, have you any wool?*

"Is it for me, Mama? Is it a present for me?"

"Yes. For you."

The sheriff

The sky was overcast, dark with more snow, and Joey drove hard to get as far as he could before it started. The plows had been through but the surface was icy and treacherous. The heater grudged anything and she had to keep scraping curls of ice from the inside of the windshield and the windows with the kitchen spatula Joey kept on the dash.

"Is that it? Is that the town, 'Morley, six miles'?"

"Where the diner is. Where we had the pie."

"Where the accordions was stolen. I'll bet you a hundred bucks the police know exactly where to look for these guys."

"Joey, you didn't see any guys."

"I didn't have to. I know it was niggers with their goddamn greasy dreadlocks, needing drug money. Who the hell else would steal a couple of accordions?"

They were coming into the margin of the town now, ridges of ice on the blacktop, passing an occasional convenience store, small houses fronted by squares of snow bisected by cement walks, sedans parked in front of one-car garages, unused basketball hoops nailed over the open door, then they were stuck behind a travel trailer pasted with decals of the states visited, Joey driving close enough to make out *Florida the Home of Sunshine* in red and yellow, with a smiling sun face counterbalancing the scrotum-shaped silhouette of the state pasted in the center of the rear door where plastic curtains swayed in the louvered window.

"What the hell are they doing up here in the middle of winter?" marveled Joey. But when they passed they saw it was an old torn-up trailer without plates, towed by a wrecker.

They passed the diner, half obscured by a moving van, and Joey pulled into a Shell station where a middle-aged black man dressed in midnight blue shirt and pants and cap came toward them wiping his hands on a rag, brown turtle-face glassed over with bifocals the size of saltine crackers, the lower lenses catching light in twin hammocks.

"Fill it up, sir?"

"Yeah. Where's the police station at?"

"No police in Morley. State police barracks about twenty miles north."

"What do citizens do then if somebody commits a crime, steals your accordions out of the trunk of your car, for instance, when you're eating some cold slop at the goddamn diner down the road? Then what do you do?"

"Contact the county sheriff. Five seventy, sir, check your oil?"

"No. Where's *he* at?"

"Likely at the sheriff's office in the town hall. Go past the drive-in, past the McDonald's, past the school, and you can't miss it, big white building on the right with a cannon and a tank on the lawn. That what happened to you? Somebody take your accordion at the diner? They say music cures crime." He was mopping at the smeared windshield with a swab.

"Goddamn right," cupping the change in his hot palm, passing it to Sonia.

He parked ten feet out from a sign that warned DANGER FALLING ICE, ran up the granite steps two at a time, crusted with ice and blue salt pellets. Sonia leaned over the seat to wrap the blanket from the motel around Artie again and to give Florry a stick of chewing gum, but before she turned around, there was Joey again, jumping into the driver's seat and starting up with a roar.

"Wasn't he there?"

"He was there."

"You didn't take long."

"No, I didn't take long. I took one look at Sheriff Jivemonkey and decided not to tell him my problem. The son-of-a-bitch is as black as the ace of spades. At least he didn't throw up—just give me a look. A nigger sheriff. Fuck the whole thing. We'll get new ones."

He drove awhile in bitter silence. Florry sang in the back seat, pressing random buttons on the green accordion and piping "oh the nigger sheriff, the nigger sheriff is coming to town."

"Hey!" said Joey, enraged, and she started to cry. When Sonia turned around she saw Florry had got chewing gum in the accordion bellows and she took the instrument from her.

(A year or two later Joey was mugged by three Chinese youths outside the Polish Club.

"We're getting out of here," he said. "We're moving to Texas. Goodbye, fuckin snow, chinks and niggers." In the MOVING TO TEXAS yard sale, the green accordion went on the sawhorse table with a Charlie Tuna camera, polystyrene dump trucks and guns, a Bakelite yo-yo with a frayed string, a one-legged Barbie doll, tiny useless hands raised in supplication, a desk lamp in the form of a translucent goose, acrylic rulers, a partial set of pale yellow discolored melamine plates, an atom bomb saltshaker, a waffle iron, a candy box half-filled with thread-jammed buttons, a loop of pop-it beads, three empty flashlights, a sagging box of Polonia Clarions and a stack of old 78s.

They moved first to Koskiusco, Texas, then to Panna Maria, where Joey started a catfish farm, branched out into raising ladybugs for the organic garden market, and in a decade made a modest fortune but showed he wasn't proud by still shopping at the Snoga store. Over the years, he learned to ride, wore cowboy boots and hat and a tooled leather belt with a silver buckle engraved TEXAS POLKA. Sonia's hair turned silver white, then fell out completely from the chemo treatments in the final months of her illness with throat cancer in 1985. When Pope John Paul II arrived in San Antonio in 1987, Joey and his second wife were part of the special audience for Panna Marians, and Artie chose that time to run away to Los Angeles. He found a temporary job as houseboy for three klezmer band musicians playing supporting roles in the zany hit movie *The Cheapskate,* then emigrated to Australia and worked for a while on an outback cattle station.)

The Colors of Horses

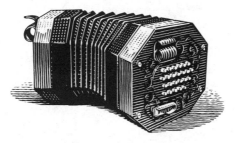

A CONCERTINA

Old Egypt

Well, the horse had been buried, and then it had come back up, heaved out of the earth by some sort of antigravity, lying on its side, the teeth in a loose dirt-crusted smile, the freckled flesh of the lips and nose slack under the snowflake hair, the lunette of the upper nostril an entrance to the mysteries of the body. One bloody ear, stiff as though listening, unraveled mane ropes, the eyes out of sight. It was Old Egypt and she wished to god Fay McGettigan hadn't shown him to her, never.

The thing on the roof

She came back to the ranch around that time in the summer of 1980 but not alone; with her she had Vergil Wheelwright who had been in Vietnam; she had written to them, this one was for keeps, the real one. He was coming across the country with her, she was bringing him to her mother and father whom she had not seen for five years, not since Simon Ults, her first husband, shot the horse and her father shot Simon. She didn't tell them that Vergil had been married before to a nurse he met in Vietnam, a bad marriage of crazy drinking, drugs, fighting and punch-ups, which broke apart when Lily, the wife, put a restraining order on him, divorced him, and moved away to parts unknown. He seemed to be over it.

She talked sporadically, told Vergil wait until he met old Fay, must be seventy years old anyway, the ranch hand who had pretty much brought her up, described the glass milk bottles of coins he had in his trailer, his skill with horses, his knowledge of equine disease. There was a picture of him, a photograph stuck to the wall with a pin, she said, taken when he was a kid—God knows who or why anybody pointed a camera his way—and he's sitting on a wooden keg, barefoot, maybe twelve years old, pants just rags, wearing a man's jacket and there aren't any buttons on it, just these short pieces of stick sewed on, probably with a grain-sack needle threaded with twine, they're curved, those needles, and inch-long pieces of stick where the buttons should have been, he poked them through the buttonholes and they worked. She talked more of Fay than of Kenneth and Bette, her parents. She told him of the times Fay had seized her ankles and lifted her high in the air upside down, the giddy swung feeling, her arms outstretched and fingers wide, whirling through the air, the yellow horizon spun hollow, the horses streaked and warped by unfocusing eyes, and Fay singing "and our funds was running low . . . ," some song he knew. He knew hundreds of old songs that no one else remembered, a lot of them dirty cowboy songs, but Irish songs too which he sang in a sad but beautiful tenor while accompanying himself on a little squeezebox.

She described the whirling as though it were an extraordinary event in her childhood, but, thought Vergil, it was as common as grass, every kid got whirled; about the shooting, details he greedily wanted to know, she said very little. She was slick at veering away from the subject. He kept glancing at her, taking in the familiar dry-wheat hair that rose from her broad forehead, the colorless eyebrows and eyelashes that she sometimes darkened with a brown pencil, a long nose that reddened in cold weather, a nose with such narrow nostrils it seemed she might have difficulty breathing; indeed, indeed, she suffered sinus infections. Her mouth was thin and uncolored. He thought of it as a Nordic face, though she said not. He didn't know what she was and what did it matter anyway? He liked pale women.

They were still two states away but it was the west, all right, and they were driving down a red dirt road. In a curving railway cut, the road crossed the tracks between cliffs so stuffed with fossils they seemed to be pouring down, eroding before their eyes into the crushed stone beside and under the ties. A tie was on fire, burning, sending up a thick rope of white smoke that coiled into the still air. The curve of the rails reflected light and their own smoothness, nothing more.

They stopped, could see where someone had built a fire of sticks and dry weeds on the tie and left it smoldering. He kicked dirt on it, she poured their jug of spring water and it steamed as though the devil were underneath, his horns just below the tie. Vergil crouched beside her, watching her serious, frowning face, the milky, untanned legs smooth and flexed, nacreous polish on her toenails, bare in earth-folk sandals, and he thought that he was doing this for her, this trip to people he guessed would be trying and awful. The parents of his first wife, Lily, had guided their lives by astrological signs and spontaneous hunches, fed him frozen tacos and canned pears, made him sit smiling while they took instant photographs, telling him not to look so serious. He had married Lily three weeks after he came back from Vietnam. In thirty-six hours he had traveled from Da Nang to Travis Air Force Base to the New Hampshire mill town where he'd grown up. He hung around the house for two hours while his father talked about how he should start looking for a good job and his mother pushed a bowl of popcorn saturated with margarine at him. He went to Boston and holed up in a hotel, spent the week on the phone talking feverishly to Lily, telling her to get a plane to Boston, they had to get married. He flushed the toilet thirty times a day just to see the water cascade.

"Why would somebody set a tie on fire?"

"It was Jesse James. Stop the fucking Express Limited and rob the passengers."

A few miles later he braked hard for a Brangus cow standing on the center line, a calf beyond the fence.

"Fuck! Fucking cow."

They went along, the junk in the back seat shifting and sliding. Josephine, puffing up the idea of adventure, had tried to find a yard sale in every state; in upstate New York they'd bought a painted plywood sign, BLESS THIS MESS, in Pennsylvania a faceless Infant of Prague and a copy of Zane Grey's *Stairs of Sand*, in Ohio a twenty-pound cane encrusted with glassies and a leather pillow with the burned-in image of a running ostrich, in Indiana the bullfighter ashtray. Illinois? Nothing but heavy truck traffic, innumerable tollbooths for ten cents, twenty cents, forty-five cents, until Vergil made a wrong exit on the edge of Chicago and she saw the yard sale first, the sawhorse table in front of a dumpy grime-stained house, the cardboard sign—MOVING TO TEXAS.

Josephine touched the doll, the goose lamp, picked up a button and let it fall, held up the bomb-shaped saltshaker lettered FAT BOY.

She said, "the winnah!" and paid a dollar. Vergil said, "fucking Lawrence Welk special," picked up the old accordion, made it wheeze a sick chord or two. Three bucks.

He mumbled, "what the fuck are we going to do with this shit?" He put the saltshaker in the glove compartment, the accordion in the back seat with the rest of the stuff. "OK," he said, "that's Chicago. What's next, fucking Iowa?"

"Fucking Iowa. Let's get out of here." The streets were getting bad, trashy, decayed buildings, the sidewalks filled with black people.

"Fucking try this," he said, shooting up a ramp, but it was blocked off halfway up and he had to back down, twisting in the seat and looking out the rear window. They could hear the roar of the highway above them.

"Christ, why not fucking block it at the bottom? OK, there's gotta be another one. Gotta hit it if we just go west under the highway, whyn't you roll us a joint?" It seemed a long time, a dangerous long time driving through the teeming streets, people drifting slantwise against traffic and lights, drunks lurching out, swirls of paper and gaudy plastic trash ankle-deep, every other shop a liquor store or a fortune-teller, and dark faces turning toward them, looking at the car, looking at them, clusters of young big men in athletic shoes and shirts slouching along, kicking, tossing, restlessly looking around.

"Jesus," said Josephine. "How'd we get down here?" But Vergil wasn't talking.

A man with a scissoring walk glared at them, mimed throwing something, and as though the gesture was a command, one of the kids bent down and picked up a pint bottle leaning against a graffitied wall, heaved it lazily in their direction. It broke in front of the car, flecks of glass pattering on the hood.

"Motherfucker asshole," said Vergil.

"Thank God he missed," said Josephine, gripping the edge of the seat, wishing the car had tinted windows.

"The fucking dickhead missed on purpose. Just a symbolic throw— these fucking guys play basketball sixteen hours a day and he could probably hit a fruit fly with a fucking grain of rice from two hundred feet."

"That's comforting." In the side-view mirror she could see them all pretending to hurl things, maybe pitching more glass bottles they couldn't see, shining missiles tumbling through the air at fifty or sixty miles an hour to take out the rear window.

"There it is." A car ahead of them swerved up a ramp and they followed, in seconds bursting into the stream of elevated highway traffic pouring west, the beginning of the rush hour. The traffic began to slow, then creep, and far ahead, by leaning out the window, she saw flashing red and blue bubble lights.

"Accident." On they crawled looking down at a brick and chain-link-fence wasteland, hearing a tremendous pounding and pulsing from a factory, seeing a grimy bar with a photograph of Pope John Paul II under a beer sign, BUD, a desolate slum of brick buildings with bad windows, the exteriors marred with wires, drainpipes, fire escapes, cables, a few small ugly shops on ground level, BARBER, RESTAURANT SUPPLIES, a prostitute leaning on a railing, glossy black wig rising from her peeled-egg forehead, carcasses hanging in a doorway under a faded sign, BANJO MEATS, SMALL BABY LAMBS, and the open backs of trucks. They crept past pylons and Vergil said, "no, it's road construction," as they came abreast of an orange sign, DETOUR, and a wattled cop who waved them back into the warren of streets below and a gauntlet of traffic lights.

"Christ! Will we ever get out of this?"

They waited at a light, the traffic choked and trembling all around them, the ruddy flare of brake lights giving the scene heat and feeling, cars and trucks packed in as tightly as shells in an oyster bed. The light changed again and again and a few cars tried to escape the jam, locking the metal knot tighter, when they heard something land on the roof, a thud and then a scrabbling sound. A mask of fur and red eyes hung over the windshield for a few seconds and disappeared.

"Ah!" cried Josephine, and Vergil said, what the fuck was that. There was a scampering overhead and it was gone, whatever it was. In another lane someone was patting a horn, *bluh bluh bluh bluh.*

"There it is." Josephine pointed at a creature bounding over the cars ahead of them, saw it leap onto the roof of a white delivery van, the rear door lettered SPEEDY. The jam began to open up, traffic crawling away from the trouble, a lockup of more flashing bubbles and street glass, and they jerked away in their lane, but the next ramp was also closed and the traffic diverted into a long underpass.

"What the hell was it, a fucking monkey?" The white van was eight or ten vehicles ahead of them. Near the end of the underpass, the grey hole opening into new streets, they felt the jolt of the wheels going over something.

"There's a ramp." Josephine looked back in the side mirror. There was nothing to see. It could have been anything.

As Vergil plunged once more into the westward stream of cars and trucks, she slumped in the seat, calm again and even loving, watched the sky, itself a tinted windshield, clear near the horizon and dense blue halfway up the dome. An isolated cloud, a strip of torn tulle, then another and another, erasures of scumbled strokes, dirty and pink. A black dot appeared, moving swiftly toward the highway from the south and crossing almost directly above them—a child's Mylar balloon, she could see now, and watched it until it disappeared, a fleck of darkness. The road surface dimmed, the blazing headlights of oncoming vehicles filled their eyes despite the lucent sky, amber and rose and filling now with unknown clouds shot with patchy glimmers.

"Let's find a place and stop," she said. She longed for a bath and a drink and an hour trying to read Umberto Eco's *The Name of the Rose,* the fat book sliding back and forth all day on the nylon carpet by her foot. She was only on page fifty-three. He didn't answer but she knew he was thinking of lying naked on the bed, the ice in his drink clicking, the hay-scented smoke muddling the television glare, watching the news, too tired to go out for dinner, why didn't she call room service and get whatever, get it and get on the bed with him and get down over his stiffening prick, do some of that good stuff, why the fuck not. What the hell was wrong with her anyway, frigid? And she would say no and do what he wanted. She switched on the radio, NPR, a drawn-out story of a man who manufactured bungalows of recycled plastic for tropical climates. They passed an overturned chemical fertilizer truck, the wheels still spinning, a drift of white across the highway.

"It had to be a fucking monkey," said Vergil. "Fucking escaped. I ever tell you about the time I ate fucking monkey brains in Nam?"

Roads

Coming out of Coaldust the next day, he asked her, how many fucking custard stands do you think are built on sacred rocks? She couldn't answer that. Well, how many fucking roads transecting the fucking medicine ravines? Didn't know the answer. I bet you think this fucking country is real, he said.

"Real what?"

By this time there was red-edged cloud over every black building and from some buildings issued vapors colored by the time of day. The exhaust from the power plant thick and beautiful like violet cloud, the moiré waste ponds azure and cobalt, magenta, the bulldozed earth heaped in vast demilunes that jet passengers peering through face-sized glass might see as overlapping fruit slices of a topographic *tarte aux pommes*. The black coal cone of a railroad tipple rising Egyptian in the thin dust, a hut with a green roof and an oil tank, window frames painted red. To the side lay the raddled ground once high plains prairie, once hissing grass stirred by wind.

Vergil drove the interstate hard, past the trailer towns with two steps in front of every door, antennaed roofs, torn curtains and open windows close to the superhighway with its blur and roar, and beyond these trailers a hundred, a thousand other trailers, a yellow sign outside a trailer café, JUMP INN. Above, the clouds in holy knots and saturated colors that transcended neon hues. Stinging hot air from trucks, the smell of diesel and hot rubber; they were coming up on night and rain.

He pointed at a darkening bluff, said up there might be stenciled hands, marks of life, remembrance. Signs and mazes on the blackest rocks, a trail of bird feces adding a curve where nothing else was curved. Over there was baked white rock that should never have been touched, yet used as a military range, turned into a crusted landscape the texture of burned scrambled eggs but pierced with the deep holes of bomb craters, still strewn with wrecked trucks, some collapsed mowing machines and reapers, a bulldozer flaking into the pocked soil. Everything over there deliberately ruined, he said, to prove it could be ruined.

The next day they crossed the river. Plenty fucking deep, he said. The greasy khaki water gnawed a quarter of a mile down into the brown rock, pulling down slopes and cliffs, licking out caves, long horizons of limestone and fossil beds, thickened shells in white reeds like bird bones, sheets of stone. And the great dull bridge itself, a ruler road atop its red arches footed in concrete, the monotonous railings more of an idea than safety catchers.

Then it was the end of the day again, at a rest area above a sulfurous pool, a scummed shallow oval of alkali water studded with beer cans, baby seats, wadded plastic, rocks. Slopes of hills around them, thirty-seven-degree slopes navy blue against a faint sky, the horizon unsettled a little. The lights on, every door open, the radio blaring, she got out and crouched on the dirt, feet wide but not wide enough to escape spatters on the ankles, and she stared at the car's white fenders. In the looming darkness the car was as nostalgic as a lighted window in a northern village.

Fay McGettigan

Bette Switch, in tight designer jeans and a man's sweatshirt, opened the door, embraced Josephine, gave Vergil her hand. Her scent mingled bourbon and perfume and tuna fish. She led them into the living room, decorated in the western style with log furniture and a bearskin rug, parchment lampshades, the edges laced with plastic simulated rawhide.

"Is this your first time in the west, Vergil?" She didn't look at him.

"No. I've been out here a dozen times. Worked on a fucking ranch a couple of summers when I was in college, the Briggins Triple-Y, about fifty miles west of here, over in the fucking Gaunt River country. Thirty-two thousand acres. Ocean of grass. And so forth."

"Well, I think you'll like the wide open spaces. It's a very healthy rural life. Kenneth and I usually get away in the winter, leave it all in Fay's hands, he's our ranch hand, I'm sure Jo told you about him, they were great pals when she was a little girl. We were on Montserrat last winter, in the Caribbean—I could live there forever, that blue-green water and white sand. And this year we're going to Samoa. Have you been in the South Seas, Vergil?"

"Yeah, I was in Western Samoa, on Upolu, two years ago."

"If you get a chance you ought to go—it's exquisite. The resort we're going to has a black sand beach. Anyway, here we are in Montana, so let's make the best of it. Cocktails at five after you two freshen up."

"I don't drink," lied Vergil, crazy for a drink and with the same feeling a fireman gets when the burning stairs behind him collapse.

"That's fine then, you can have fruit juice or mineral water, whatever. Just make yourself at home," and she went upstairs.

In less than thirty seconds Kenneth came down, shook Vergil's hand, kissed Josephine. She said, "Dad, this is Vergil. He was in Vietnam. In the marines."

Kenneth said, "fine. I'll let you show your friend around, babes. Your mother and I are having a little discussion," and he was back up the stairs, two at a time, and in a minute they heard strident voices from above.

"It doesn't sound so good," said Josephine, flat-voiced. "Some things never change. Come on, let's go see Fay. He's the one who really counts."

The first thing Fay told her was that Old Egypt had come back up the day before, her childhood horse, her good-hearted gelding.

"It was lightning, Jo, done it. Two weeks ago, big old thunderheads come up, just acrack with lightning. I'm nailing up some loose shingles on the barn—them damn things flake off bad as dandruff—and I seen Egypt grazing over by the wagon (you know Kenneth bought a old Conestoga wagon from a guy in Oregon State and hauled it home a few years back). The wind come up blowing dust and I seen him turn around and get his ass to the wind. He could of gone into the barn, the door was open, but you know he liked rain—he was a horse that sure liked rain. I'm trying to finish up before the storm hit full, but as it was, hail was bouncing off my hat and there was a god-awful crash and a big stroke, I thought I was blind, this blue glary light and a thing like a big blue rat run across the ground sizzling and hissing and setting the grass afire and I seen Old Egypt is down and his legs going like he's running away. He must of thought he was running away pretty good. And here come another one, split Kenneth's pear tree in half, so I duck into the barn and wait until the lightning gets to a more comfortable distance and I go over to Old Egypt. He wasn't moving but he wasn't dead, not yet. You could smell burned hair and there was a burn from his right ear down his nose, and all down his neck, his mane frizzled up. He was cold to touch and his eyes rolled up. I tried to get him up but he was past getting, and he give one big shudder and quit. The Conestoga wagon was smoking. What I don't understand is why he come back up now.

We dug one hell of a hole with the backhoe and it don't make sense. I think he wanted to see you one more time."

He drove his little finger into his left ear, gouging for wax, added, "anyway, what they say, 'death to the horse, life to the crow.'"

"It's too sad to think about," said Josephine, "we brought you something."

"You're a sweetheart, Jo, a darlin sweetheart."

Josephine was embarrassed at his gratitude—what was he expecting, a leather jacket, a set of imported steak knives? "It's actually junk, more like a joke than a present. We stopped at all these yard sales on the way out. I got Kenneth and Bette a saltshaker in the shape of the atom bomb. So Vergil got you this old accordion. I remembered you used to play a little accordion kind of thing. And I remember all those raunchy songs."

"Concertina," he said. "I still play it. It come to me by way of an old bronc buster and another one had it before him. They'll last your life if you treat them fair. But I always wanted a accordion, you know. Been hoping to find a good little B/C two-row one of these days; that's your man for the good Irish tunes. Let's take a look."

Vergil got the bedraggled instrument from the back seat, the bellows smeared with crayon scribbles, the lacquer chipped and scarred, leather straps hanging loose. Fay took it gently, looked at its sad rows of buttons and worked the bellows, loosing a C chord rotund and authoritative, a gibbering flash of sound, a stumble of stuck buttons and sour wheeze that set Vergil's teeth on edge.

"Well, it's a two-row," Fay said and began to sing against a scribble of notes. "*She's a dancing young beauty, she's a rose in full bloom, and she fucks for five dollars in the Buckskin Saloon* . . . There's some life in it. I can get it shaped up again, maybe. It's got a kind of chesty sound."

He threw his arm around Josephine, said thanks, but Vergil saw he was disappointed, recollected himself as a child expecting a fucking kaleidoscope—the hints had pointed in that direction—and receiving his grandfather's milky-lensed telescope covered in torn and rotting leather, through which nothing could be seen but swarming blurs.

He thought Fay resembled the seedy man at the end of the bar in any Dublin pub, straggled hair unsuccessfully combed, the flat ear, wax yellow, the bony, high-colored face, muscular strength concentrated in the lips which could extend powerfully toward a glass of bitter, wet blue eyes, though instead of the boozer's stained jacket and tie askew around a thin neck, Fay was decked in frayed shirt and drooping jeans held up by a gimcrack belt studded with glass jewels, most of them missing from the metal settings, scuffed boots and a hat so torn and blackened it could be worn only aggressively. When Vergil put out his hand Fay crushed it in a cruel grip and looked expressionlessly into his eyes, a direct stare of the sort a dog gives before it bites.

"What do you think of Fay?" Josephine asked later. "Isn't he the real thing?" She implied that Kenneth and Bette were not, that they were impostors and the Appaloosa ranch a fraud and that everything would collapse as it had twice before if it were not for Fay who held it all together through the strength of his hat.

"*Yeah,* he is," said Vergil. "I think he's a fucking nutcracker."

"Nut Cracker? That was the name of a crooked sunfisher, a bucking bronco as mean as they get, and it was a woman, an Indian woman, Red Bird, up in Oregon, who rode him to a standstill back in 1916," came Kenneth's voice from the next room.

The ranch

Kenneth and Bette Switch had come out to Montana from Boston in 1953 with a little money that Bette thought Kenneth had inherited (he had embezzled it from the credit union where he worked after the board refused him a raise), bought an old run-down ranch near the Crow Reservation. The ranch adjoined the reservation bison-project land. Kenneth liked to say years later that when they started their little cow and calf operation, they were "too ignorant to breathe without getting a lungful of dirt." They thrilled, driving down the red road, to rise up the crest and see the country furled out sixty miles and butting up against the Big Horns, and there in the foreground beasts from the west's indecent past, immense heads down and the small glittering eyes rolling; then, a mile farther on, their own black baldies absurd as painted plywood.

It took only a few years before they were in trouble, with brucellosis in their herd; the county agent told them it might be the bison carried it; they would have to destroy their animals, then after a few years they could start again, maybe.

"Anyways," the agent said, "if you don't get it bad once in a while, how do you know when you get it good? You got to learn things the hard way sometimes." It was clear he had them pegged as fool eastern-ers with more money than sense who could afford to start over every few years in the college of experiential ranching.

While they waited for the infected land to cure itself, Bette got a gal Friday job at the county courthouse and Kenneth found something with a local horse auctioneer, Gibby Amacker, at first just tallying, bookkeeping and paperwork, but he began to learn something about horses, every kind and color, duns and buckskins, grullos, bayo coyotes and bayo blancos, moros and flea-bitten greys, medicine hats and war bonnets, claybanks, bays and greys, blacks, chestnuts, browns, paints and palominos, blue corns, pintos, sorrels, paint overos, tobianos and toveros, calicoes, esabellas, skewbalds, piebalds and calicoes, roans and strawberry roans; Appaloosas with white and spotted blankets, leopard and tiger coats, snowflaked, frosted and marbled, marked with handprints or two-tone peacock spots, mottled and varnished; horses with blazes, strips, snips, raindrops, dollar spots, splashes and stars, apron-faced, bonnet-faced and bald-faced horses; saw every breed led in and out of the sale ring week after week, Paints, Morgans, Arabians, Half-Arabians, Anglo-Arabians, Appaloosas, Quarter Horses.

He found himself watching the Appaloosas with something like impatience and longing. He began to notice how their prices were moving up, had been moving up since he started working for Gibby, from thirty or so rock-bottom dollars a head to where sometimes they were bringing a hundred if they came from one of the ranchers, like Peewee Loveless, interested in restoring the breed, as Peewee said, to its old glory as the great hunting and war horse of the plains, ruined by immigrant clodhoppers and know-nothing easterners who bought up those survivors of the famous Nez Percé "palousies" of the northwest, with their striped hooves and white-rimmed eyes, the herd confiscated by the U.S. government and sold at a dispersal sale after Chief Joseph and his band took them on an eleven-hundred-mile journey across the flooding Snake River, through brutal Lolo Pass of the Bitterroots, through thirteen battles and skirmishes with ten different commands of U.S. troops, every time defeating or fighting the federal enemy to a standstill because of their superior mounts, only to arrive at the last place, the Lapwai Reservation in Idaho, where their horses were taken from them and replaced with bibles. The lucky but fool purchasers of these extraordinary horses bred them to anything that walked on four legs and had a mane, and in twenty or thirty years the spotted horses of the plains, descendants of the ice-age horses painted on the cave walls of France, of the fabled horses of Ferghana, between the Syrdarya and the Amudarya rivers on the steppes of Central Asia in Uzbekistan, of Rakush, the spotted horse of the warrior hero Rustam, celebrated in Persian miniatures and in Firdousi's epic poem the *Shah Namah,* of the Chinese Celestial Horses from the Extreme West, the Blood-Sweating horses, of the galloping mounts of the Mongol Horde and Attila the Hun, of the

Andalusian horses of Spain shipped to Mexico for the conquistadors' savage forays, of a shipload of spotted horses from the Trieste Lippizan herd landed on Vera Cruz around 1620, of the horses abandoned by the terrified Spaniards after the Pueblo revolt of sixty years later and traded north by an agricultural people more interested in sheep, to the Shoshone, Cayuse, Nez Percé, Blackfeet, Blood, Arikara, Sioux, Cree, Crow of the North American steppes known as the Great Plains, had been bred down to dog meat.

After a few months of listening to Peewee's Appaloosa tales, he asked him right out, "Peewee, you think a man could make a go of it breeding Appaloosas? You think the market is there?"

"A good question. You know, my youngest boy's home from the university just now, talking about what he's gonna do, and he breaks it to me, he's not gonna stay on the ranch. Well, I says, you don't have to to, I'll set you up good. And if I was a young feller starting out I'd think about Appaloosas, there's more people starting to look at the Appaloosa with a favorable eye. And you know what he said to me? Said, no way, I'm not getting in no horse-breeding business, because I want to get into TV camera work, I told you that a thousand times. Well, he always tooken pictures since he was a kid, but they're so damn strange nobody's gonna pay money for them things, but he says this is different, there's this new videotape stuff, whatever it is, and that's what he means. Probly get mixed up with a bunch of damn Commonists. Anyhow, he'll find out the hard way. Answer to your question, if you know something about breeding horses and you got the interest and somewhat of a bankroll or a tight belt, to my way of thinking the Appaloosa might be a good bet."

"Suppose you don't know much and your bankroll's nonexistent?"

"Why then, you'll learn or go broke, won't you? There's a couple of people around working on bringing back the good Appaloosas. It's practical because they make a damn good stock horse, yes, a fine riding horse with that natural flat-footed gait, the old Indian shuffle that lets him keep going. A couple of fellas started in the thirties but the war set 'em back. You talk to anybody yet?"

"Just you."

"I don't count! Might want to talk with somebody at Coke Roberd's place down in Coloraydo. He's been specializing in Appaloosa and Quarter Horse for long years, bred in high-quality Thoroughbred stock, some say he bred in from a Austrian or Polish spotted horse that was in a circus come through, oh, years and years ago, maybe what they call a Lippizaner, you heard of them, or they say maybe he got it off a gypsy when one of them bands come through. Then there's Claude Thompson up in Oregon, he's breeding in Arabian blood. A war vet from up around there, George Somebody, has throwed in with him and he has something to do with the Appaloosa Horse Club. I heard his great-great-uncle or grandmother or somebody bought a couple of the original Nez Percé horses at the government sale way back, so they got some of that good blood. And there's a few more been working on it. You'd have to say they are restoring what was a lost breed. It's only a couple of years since the breed was approved by the National Association. But you got your work cut out for you. If I was you I'd start myself a serious linebreeding program. Concentrate on quality, castrate anything that ain't first mark, send the duds and cripples and poor ones to the canner. You got to be hard about that. And keep real good records."

Half an hour later Kenneth saw Peewee over by the fence talking to Gibby Amacker, both of them laughing, and he knew they were enjoying the joke of Kenneth Switch breeding Appaloosas, made up his mind to make them laugh on the other sides of their mouths. (He never got the chance. Peewee drowned in midwinter when a green colt he was riding through a shallow spillway took fright at the sensation of breaking ice around his ankles and plunged into the deep water. And on St. Patrick's Day Gibby Amacker choked to death on a mouthful of rare sirloin while laughing at a string of jokes about Basque sheepherders— not the raw ones about sheep and rubber boots and crusty underwear, nor the one about shoe polish on the satin comforter, nor the one about the pressure cooker, but a childish play on words told by his brother-in-law Richard through his heavy blond mustache.

"Hey, Gibby, a family of Basques gets caught in a revolving door. Know what the moral is? Don't put all your Basques in one exit . . . Jesus, it's not that funny. Hey, Gibby, are you all right? Somebody? Hey, somebody GET SOME HELP.")

Umbrella Point

The second morning of their visit Vergil awoke to the infernal shrieking of a rooster. The electric clock buzzed and hummed, showed 5:47.

Downstairs, Kenneth poured him a mug of lukewarm coffee, Josephine and Bette still asleep. He stood nervously near the kitchen table. There was a poster taped to the kitchen door, showing a bull rider in a ball of dust over the sentence "Lord, help me hang in there." The sky was blood orange in the east. Kenneth's deep voice crowded him into a Spanish-style chair with a plastic seat and octagonal-headed tacks that cut into the backs of his thighs. The creases from Kenneth's nose to the corners of his mouth precisely mirrored the line of his chin, stamping his face with a diamond shape horizontally bisected by wide, chapped lips. His eyes were enormous, huge grey irises partially obscured by the curtains of loose flesh under the eyebrows which rested on his eyelids. These eyes were further magnified by glasses set with half-moon bifocals. His eyebrows and thin hair were the color of his skin, a reddish tan.

"How much do you know about horse breeding, Vergil?"

"Not a fucking thing." He wanted to ask Kenneth why he had never swung his daughter by her ankles, leaving it to the ranch hand.

"Well, I think that by the time you leave the Switch ranch you'll know a little bit. Give you some idea of background, I didn't know a goddamn thing either when we came out here twenty-seven years ago. What I knew about horses you could put on your thumbnail. I was smart enough to know I didn't know anything and I hired Fay McGettigan who was working for Peewee Loveless, after Peewee drowned, and Fay knew horses—knows horses—like not many men do. We had a hard time the first few years out here, especially Bette who had a lot of trouble adapting, but all it took to turn things around was one horse, *one horse,* Umbrella Point, one of the most beautiful Appaloosa stallions that ever set hoof on the soil. Those pictures in the hall and the living room? Umbrella Point." (There were dozens of photographs showing a muscular and athletic dun horse with a brilliant blanket of white over his rump and back, enlivened with peacock spots; white spotted forefeet; a white face; and on his throat a white shield. Besides the photographs there were a few bad paint-by-the-number acrylics featuring horses. Vergil guessed Kenneth had painted them. In his photographs Umbrella Point was depicted in a variety of positions and activities— galloping, calf roping, standing pensively, romping, rolling, in a sit-down halt, running for the blue in a stump race, dashing into an area keyhole, nuzzling, sleeping, and standing on a high trail under a pine branch blurred by the wind—compact but perfectly formed and with a jaunty, good-humored eye, plump cheeks which gave him a roguish air, and a wispy rat tail that Vergil thought hideous.)

Kenneth swilled his coffee through his teeth, spoke in his acquired western drawl. "The way I came by this horse is mighty peculiar, so much so that I wouldn't believe it myself if it didn't happen to me. I was in Idaho at a rodeo, still working part time for Gibby Amacker—this was just a few weeks before he killed himself laughing at the Bascos— and I was supposed to pick up a string of ponies that some Texas bronc buster had to sell and had got hold of Gibby's name some way and called him up and the old man said, you bet, I'll send Kenneth over to pick 'em up, that was typical of Gibby, it wasn't my job to pick up horses but he rode roughshod over everybody. Fay had just started working for me, so I said we'll go over there together, so Fay and me went down there and the guy's Quarter Horses looked pretty good, and he was sick about selling them but he was having some kind of money trouble. Well, that's what makes the horse world go around and around. So we load them up and I give him a receipt and one of the horses gives this nicker and the guy starts to bawl, oh that's Pearl, I can't sell Pearl, and he's shoving the receipt at me and trying to get the door unlatched to get Pearl out. Look here, I says, you told me three horses, I got the damn receipt all made out and the horses loaded up. No, he says, I'm gonna get Pearl out and give you another horse to take in her place. I got a Appaloosa stallion, been using him for roping, he's smart and quick, but I'll swap him for Pearl. He don't mean as much to me as she does. Fay gives me a look when he hears the word 'Appaloosa.' So we go over to the other side of the fairground where he's got this other horse, Bum Spots, and Fay jams his elbow in my ribs so hard I almost yelled. At the time I didn't see anything special, but for Fay it was love at first sight. Bum Spots was six years old and he hadn't been gelded and Fay knew he was perfect. Well I'm casual. Fay says, you know anything about him? I was ready to bet he was probably just some unregistered outcross breed. Oh yeah, the guy said. He's a rodeo accident. This rodeo in Coloraydo a stallion got loose and served two mares; sure enough, one of 'em was Pearl. Don't suppose you knew the name of the stallion, Fay says, offhand. Yeah, one of Coke Robert's horses, I believe it was Gee Whiskers or Gee Whizz. I paid that boy two hundred dollars for Bum Spots right then and there; no way was that horse going into Amacker's ring. And Fay says on the way home, 'that was when my heart started to go pit-a-pat, because Gee Whizz sired X-Ray Baby who just become the world champion running mare Quarter Horse, so Bum Spots is a half-brother to a world champion.' Which, of course, this gravel-headed blubbering cowboy didn't know or he wouldn't never of sold Bum Spots, a.k.a. Umbrella Point, to us."

"How the fuck'd you come to name him Umbrella Point?" The coffee was cold and the sun, streaming in hot and glittering, left him nowhere to look but at Kenneth, eating raw sausage from the package. The red light on the stove reflected in the double glass door behind Kenneth in a peculiar way that made it seem as if two intensely red berries were hanging in the disheveled forsythia shrub outside, poised somehow right above Kenneth's hair. Vergil could make them shift by moving his head.

"You know, I was looking for a different kind of name, every god-damn name you pick for a registered horse, somebody's used it already, it's hard to find a original name, but Fay and me was sitting here in the kitchen trying to think up one and I looked over at Bette's umbrella hanging on the hook over there and said, Umbrella, there's a unique name, but you know, it wasn't, somebody already named a horse that, so I says, Umbrella Handle, and son-of-a-bitch, *that* was already in use, so Fay come up with Umbrella Point and that was acceptable to the powers that be. And we never looked back. We had him until 1973, fif-teen years, and he made our living, he built this ranch. National Grand Champion Stallion, Grand Champion Performance Horse. He sired Umbrella Point's Boy, the grand champion at the Montana State Fair; Gunsight Babe who holds the world record for the four forty and three hundred yards; Chief Hardshell, grand champion at halter and racing, national champion rope race horse; Jot 'Em Down, over a hundred rib-bons and awards, every kind of cutting, reining, stump race, pleasure riding award they give; Old Egypt, that was Josephine's horse, but he won over one hundred and fifty trophies in the show ring; Pegasus, Poetry, Raisin Pudding, Target—I could go on all day." He swallowed the rest of his coffee and poured more. Vergil tilted his head this way and that, forcing the berries to hop to different branches. The hectoring voice began again.

"And then it was over, in the most *senseless* act of violence. Josephine came out for a visit with her then *husband,* this silent, sulky bastard, Ults, she got tangled up with him at one of those goddamn communes down there in New Mexico, men growing their hair down to their ass and dressed up in them psychedelic rags, jewelry and junk all over him—Christ, it *hurt* to shake hands with the son-of-a-bitch he had so many rings on. He had braids and a rag around his head like he was expecting to sweat. We tried to bring her up decent, got her a horse when she was six, give her everything we could, and what does she do, goes off to one of them weed camps and wears a pioneer dress and gets tangled up with this Ults, his father's a pipeline supplier, I think he was ashamed of his kid. Well, the son-of-a-bitch cracked, went crazy, got up one morning and took my thirty-thirty from over the door and went to the barn, led Umbrella out and shot him right outside the barn, started back in. Of course the shot woke me up and I looked out the window and saw Umbrella Point quivering on the ground and Ults walking away and carrying the rifle, this little smile on his face, you could tell he was all drugged up, not too hard to figure out what happened and what was going to happen, and I was down those stairs three at a time, I got to the back door just as he comes up on the porch, still holding the rifle, and he starts to bring it up—oh there's no doubt in my mind he intended to shoot me, to shoot us all, kill Josephine, Bette, myself, the cat maybe—but my god, I don't know how I did it to this day, surprise element, I think, but I grabbed that rifle out of his hands and shot him in the shoulder before he knew what was happening. He went right down the steps and laid there in the dirt hollering. I come back in and poured a glass of whiskey, drank it neat, ran outside to Umbrella Point—had to step right over Ults and I give him a good kick as I did—but my fine champion stallion was killed, and I called the sheriff's office and said what happened and that if he didn't come get Ults I might finish the job. Bette and Josephine was going nuts, they couldn't understand it any more than I could. Josephine blamed me, said, you didn't have to shoot him, did you? and we parted on bad terms, she drove off with him to the hospital or the dump, but you know, it wasn't too long after that they got divorced. I never knew the details, don't know them to this day, but they were divorced inside a year, that is if they was ever married. Could of been some damn hippie ceremony with dope and sitar music and tofu. I don't know. Ask her about it."

"She don't want to talk about it."

"Can't blame her, can you? I hate to talk about it myself. Fay was in town drunked up that weekend and when he heard what had happened he cried like a baby. The horse was buried by then, I did it myself." He ate another raw sausage.

"About Fay? I was going to tell you about the cook we had then. Odella Hooky, some kind of vegetarian subsect of the Holy Rollers. She wouldn't touch meat or nothing from a animal. No bacon, no steaks, no eggs, no lard biscuits, no butter. We tried to get her to cook with corn oil but she wouldn't believe oil come from corn. She was OK on beans but they didn't have much savor. Finally Fay comes into her kitchen and he's carrying about a five-pound sirloin in one hand and a hot frying pan in the other, you can see the heat waves coming off that thing, and he says, 'you cook this, by god, or I'll cook you,' and he holds her hand over that hot frying pan, about half an inch off the metal, and she's trying to pull her hand up and he's holding it down and she just hits it with the tips of her fingers and you could hear the sizzle across the room. Well, she cooked the steak, crying to beat the band, but the next morning she was gone and Fay had to do the cooking for six months which is how long it took us to find somebody else."

Vergil and Fay

Josephine was out riding. No, he told her, I'll polish your shoes and buy you Cadillacs but you don't get me on a horse, I had the fucking horse radish years ago, fucking unpredictable insane animals. Fay came up to where he leaned on the fence, squinting through his cigarette smoke, the sunlight hitting the ironed-in crease of his jeans.

"I'm headin out for town. Wanna ride along?"

"Fucking right," Vergil said, surprised. He didn't want to go any-where with old Fay but he'd go just for the somewhere of it, nothing to do but sit here in the living room with its skulls and antlers and Indian blankets and spurs, look at back issues of *Western Horseman* and *Montana Wildlife*. "Sure, I'll go with you. Give you a hand if you're picking up feed," for he had heard Bette tell the old man not to forget the chicken feed again, they were more or less out.

"Never say no to a helping hand." That flat nutcracker stare.

The floor of the truck was littered with rubbish—unopened mail trodden muddy, supermarket tabloids, 500-POUND MAN WINS RODEO PRIZE, a bottle of Hawbaker's Red Fox Urine, beer bottles, snow chains, rope, old bridles, a crushed hat, a pair of galoshes with pointed toes to accommodate cowboy boots, candy wrappers and wadded-up empty cigarette packs. He was uncomfortable, the left foot higher than the right, up on the mound of chains. The stuffing hung out of the seat. The ashtray spilled butts and Fay was lighting another. The windshield displayed two smeared arcs in a field of streaked mud. It was forty-three miles to town and Fay only hummed and sang, "*The clap-ridden slats in their ten-gallon hats ain't worth a damn that I know,*" grunting when Vergil set him a question or guessed at the depth of the snow on the dis-tant mountains or wondered whose place that was with an old railroad boxcar for a house and seventy or eighty junk cars strewn around it like fragments from an explosion.

About halfway down the trip, he thought the hell with it and rolled a joint, the last of the weed. By the time they pulled up in front of Bus-ree's Hardware in town and Fay grabbed the list from the seat, finally opening his mouth to say, meet you here at four, Vergil was calm and pleased. He wandered around town, went into the drugstore and bought shaving cream and aspirin, in the café ordered coffee and a piece of gluey red pie the waitress said was strawberry-rhubarb, looked at western-cut shirts in the Kowboy Korner, tried on a pair of Larry Mahan boots, "handmade, hand lasted and pegged, extra-wide steel shank and a good thick sole, last you a *few* years," said the clerk, grey stiff schnauzer hair, a red spot between his eyes, leaning against the wall next to a framed paper like a diploma, the Patriotic Citizens Award Given in Grateful Appreciation for Unsolicited Inspirational Patriotic Service to the Community through the Daily Display of Our National Flag, and Vergil caught on that the cloth flapping outside the show window was the corner of an immense flag secured at windows on the upper level of the building; but the boots felt strange, he didn't like that pushing arch under his foot, and the high heel embarrassed him.

"I'll think about it," he said to the disappointed clerk, glanced at the hats—god, he'd love to buy a big fucking cowboy hat, he wished he'd had one in Nam, but went outside again, looked up at the flag which was dirty and ragged. The sign in the window read BUY AMERICAN. By four o'clock he'd been in and out of every store, the tiny grocery store with the hand-lettered placard THE WORLD'S NOT WORTH A FIG. WE HAVE GOOD RAISINS FOR SAYING SO, the town clerk's office, the clinic, the post office. An old guy wearing a filthy hat, nose like a chicken's snuffbox, walked past, a placard around his neck: WOLVES. Let's Don't Breed Them. We Don't Need Them.

Fay wasn't in the truck and there weren't any sacks or boxes in it either, and he sat on the lumpy front seat for half an hour waiting and looking up aslant, seeing the whole sky driving north, long ribs of cloud curving over the land, studying a movie poster for *The Adventures of Buckaroo Banzai.*

He tried the clerk at the feedstore, one cheek larger than the other and hard to tell where his mouth left off and his face began, who said, nope, Fay ain't been in, try across the street.

He didn't see him at first, then he did. He was there, straight-backed at the end of the bar, his beer glass weighting down the shopping list, bending the ear of a nut-brown geezer who stank of sheep. Everybody in the place was wearing a message, words and images on belt buckles, t-shirts, leather labels on their jeaned rumps, names woven into hatbands, billed caps stamped KING ROPES. Vergil signaled for a beer, sat down beside Fay who swung around at once and said, "you get it all done?"

"I didn't have very much to get. Toothpaste. Some fucking stamps."

"'You remember the chicken feed?'" His voice, in uncanny imitation of Bette.

"I thought you were going to get it."

"Well Jee*zus,* 'I thought you was going to get it,'" he mimicked. "No! YOU was going to get it while I caught up on a few things."

"I didn't fucking know you wanted me to get the stuff, Fay. How much does she want? I'll get it now."

"It's on the goddamn list, heads up the whole goddamn list, every week chicken feed, chicken feed—them chickens the size of mules the feed they eat."

"You got the fucking list, Fay. Give me the list and I'll pick up the chicken feed."

"There's more than chicken feed on that list. There's booger-pickers and Tampax-pullers and a cure for Texas itch."

He took the sopping list from the bar. Half of it was unreadable, the ink blurred with beer. "Get what I can."

"You do that, you do that." And Fay started to sing in his slippery tenor, "*each range breeds its own brand of bastard, boozefighter, bugger or bum . . .*"

Out in the street Vergil headed for the fucking truck hoping the fucking keys were in it. Quarter of fucking five. If everything closed at five he was fucked. First the damn fucking chicken feed. Goddamn fucking Fay.

The feedstore clerk was glad enough to see him again, swung at a fly with a plastic bag of dried beans.

"Chicken feed."

"Layin mash? Cracked corn?"

"What the fuck does Fay usually get?"

"He don't usually get none." A crackling laugh like static.

"Use your phone? I'll call the fucking ranch."

There wasn't any answer and he half remembered them talking about going up to the big wash in the north section. They fucking all said "warsh," even Josephine. They must be up there, maybe they had ridden out on the fucking horses. He looked at the list again, what he could make out. *Chicken feed. Matches. Powdered Milk. T-post braces. Supplement. Hog ring. Keys. Popcorn.* And six or fucking seven other items he could not grasp— *raisins* or *razors, vaccine* or *vaseline, slicker* or *sugar, rump steak* or *rope clamp.*

"I'll take a bag of each."

"Fifty pound?"

"Yeah. You got any fucking T-post braces?"

"What size and how many?"

"Ten of each size. Charge it to the Switch ranch. How about supplement?"

"Ken Switch?" He sniggered. "How's his love life these days? He want horse, cow, sheep, goat, cat, dog or human supplement? Ten each kind?"

"How the fuck do I know?" At least he had the chicken feed.

Fay wasn't in a mood to leave the bar, laughing and smoking and drinking boilermakers with the sheepherder, talking about a third person, a man called High Nuts, "a bastard's bastard" and "so dumb he couldn't pull the plug and let the piss out of the sink," a man with "a head full of boiled gravel."

Well, thought Vergil, he fucking doesn't work for me and I'm not his fucking relative. He asked for and got a shot of Shark Snot and another or two. At least he had the chicken feed. He listened to what they had to say around him.

"The only good he ever done was with that rattlesnake. You know that one? He always had a plug a tobacca in his cheek. This rattler's down by the gate, he comes riding up, don't think twict, lets loose a stream a juice, it goes straight in ol' rattler's mouth, dead shot, that snake like to twistated itself inside out and finally died."

On the other side sat a pair of ranch hands, one with his head on the bar.

"I told him, I said no problem."

" 'At's the trouble. Try to talk, says I can't, but no problem, but he says stop. I says you *told* me to stop."

"I never used it. I got my own way of doing it. Short, sweet and never sober."

The bartender leaned over the counter and spoke to Vergil in a slow voice, saying, "why does a Basco carry shit in his wallet?"

"I don't know, does he?"

"For identification."

Drunk driving

It was some unknown black hour when they steered out of the bar and climbed in the truck.

"What time is it," said Vergil.

"How the hell do I know? Don't wear no watch nor rings nor golden chains. I tell you the time my daddy got a watch? Got a watch and a bathtub and a toilet and a warshing machine with a gas engine on the same day. High point of his life, fuckin miserable Irishman. Sold his cows, heavy and solid, at the right time, price up, the only time in his life. Next year the government tore the heart of him out and he lost the ranch. Well, this day I'm talking about, he's gonna use the bathtub first. Put the bathtub and the toilet—'can't say we hasn't got a pot to piss in now'—in a corner of the kitchen and hung a blanket cattercorner acrost. Blanket stops short of the floor about eighteen inches. All us kids sitting there like you see kids watching TV nowadays. Old lady heats up water on the stove, every pot and pan in the house, pours it in, he's got a big perfume bar of soap, and we hear him behind the blanket singing 'Rose of Tralee' and getting undressed, see his boots come off, then he pisses in the toilet. We can see his feet. He spreads a towel on the floor beside the bathtub. Takes his watch off—Jesus and Joseph, he's proud of that watch; never had one before—and we hear him put it on the shelf, there's a little shelf on the wall. He gets in the tub, wallows, lolls, sings, we can smell the perfume soap and hear the water, he calls for a saucepan, dips up the water and pours it over his head, he slides down and goes under, makes a noise like a coyote in the well. After an hour he gets out. We see his feet on the towel, two big old boiled ham hocks. He's got the other towel to dry hisself, and he gives it a playful little snap, all clean and pure as he is from the first bath of his life in a bathtub, and the end of the towel snakes out and she catches the watch on the shelf, flips it straight into the toilet. Which he hadn't flushed. Christ, the language that tore out of his mouth, a howl like a banshee. He reaches down in the pissy toilet to get the watch but it's no good, it's ruint. They didn't have no pissproof watches then. He keeps that goddamn thing in a cigar box for a couple of years until Donnell, my kid brother that was, takes it apart and a spring in it uncoils like a rattlesnake and gets him in the right eye and he's blind in one eye the rest of his days, which wasn't very long. So I never wanted no watch seeing how much trouble they caused. *Oh I'm a jolly baker and I bake my bread brown, I got the biggest rolling pin of any man in town . . .*"

Vergil said he fucking wouldn't mind driving but Fay was worked up and said, "The only way you drive is if I drop dead. You're drunk and you don't know how to drive drunk out here. It's a art. Now watch and you'll learn something. *She woke me up one morning, aknocking at my door, shoes and stockings in her hand, her chemise up . . .*" He backed up slowly, shifted into first and growled along the street with the lights off until not the horn blare and headlight flashing of passing cars but the darkness at the edge of town when the streetlights ran out made him think of turning them on. As they plunged into the darkness at a steady thirty-five, the right front wheel hooked on the white line, Fay talked on.

"Now, you appreciate this little pleasure, the slow drunked-up night drive with a big belly moon in the windshield. It's a empty place. You got it all to yourself. You never want to get home. *They use their pricks for walking sticks, those hardy sonsabitches.*"

"I fucking want to get home," said Vergil. "You asshole. I drove fucking places in Nam you'd be dead in five minutes. I had a string of ears. The stuff I saw and did would make you blind, old man."

"Look, I know I'm drunk and gone, but what the hell, so what, everybody's on the way out, ain't they? I'm just one of the first ones. *He ain't been rode and he's twenty year old.* Ever seen me move? Ever seen me run or dance, Mr. Wheelwright? Oh I knew how to move. Not now, of course, but I did it once, they couldn't never match me, they couldn't never deny me, the women, I could do the blood dance, dance until your shoes got blood in 'em. Big skinny old boy there, hundred twenty-eight wet in a polyester suit, big-rimmed hat about six and three-quarters inside and a face like the drag of a chalked thumb. *He ain't been rode and he's twenty year old, the worst fuckin outlaw that ever been foaled.* Mouth drawstringed and him wearing boots and never been off a sidewalk. But he plays good. Don't he. Should say played. And they put him to bed with a shovel. He's dead. *Lay off of that red-eye, get rid of that whore.* But one of the best ones I ever knewed was a woman. Dressed up the same way, white pants and jacket, cowboy hat, the boots, wax-paper face. But she did something you didn't expect would be done. She pulled out those notes like taffy until they bent and almost dissolved, and then she just untied it all like a little silk scarf and shook it in your face. Never smiled. Oh that old gal could braid you up. Never knew her name. Guess she's probably on the other side of the river now, humming through a paper comb unless they let you bring your concertina to heaven. That's the fine instrument. *The corral was all muddy and slicker than glass, I lands on a rock and I busted my ass . . . he's mean, yessiree.*"

Vergil put the window down to let the smoke out. The ashtray was smoldering with a poisonous fume.

"You're quite the shit, ain't you, a bit of a bastard's bastard, you'd pick out ticks if they fell in your food, wouldn't you, you'd forget your name if it wasn't tattooed on your dick, ah? you'd be lost without me here to guide you home through the dark of the night, yes, you need someone to turn the pages for you. Josephine's the only one in that bunch worth anything. *You been tamped full of shit about cowboys, they are known as a romantic band.* Me, I been self-sufficient since I was eleven year old. Grew up poor, old socks for mittens in the winter, picked out my clothes at the town dump, and I quit going to school in the fourth grade. Sick of the mean little bastards' name-calling and anyway my daddy put me to work. The lousiest job he ever give me to do was to kill a bunch of kittens. The old cat had a litter there, she sprang one seemed like every couple of months, and the old man hands me a pitchfork and says, get rid of 'em. *All he knows of romance is the crotch of his pants, what the hell do you think—* I hear a ringing sound, you hear that? You hear a bell in your right ear it's good news coming, you hear it in the left it's bad news. I hear it in both ears. You hear it?"

"Yeah." He did, and in both ears. Not a ringing but a long, endless bellowing moan coming from out in the countryside.

"What the fuck is it?"

"I don't know. It don't seem to have to draw breath."

And close at hand a sudden glaring light and the clacking rush of a freight train, the oxblood-red coal cars shooting past only a few yards away, Fay hitting the foot brake, Vergil wrenching the emergency, saying *fuckfuckfuck,* so close to the train they could see sparks spraying from the wheels and smell its metal.

The last twelve miles they were euphoric, death cheated, the hand of fate stayed, the grisly accident averted. Fay put the window down, thrust his face into the sedately moving air and screamed, they whooped and sang, Fay half shouting as they bumped into the yard: *"I've harvested wool in Wyoming and rawhide in New Mexico, I've weared a bandanna in Sheepshit, Montana, and got laid in old Idaho."*

And when the engine was off they stood guilty and laughing in the stunned silence, in the shelter of the opened doors, pissing on the hard ground, and their noise and the faint grey horizon in the east roused the rooster.

You sleazy cocksucker, thought Vergil, after I got your damn chicken feed. He looked in the back of the truck in the slow light but couldn't see the two sacks of feed.

"Where's the fucking chicken feed?"

Fay stepped up light and quick as though the night's peril had flushed age out of his joints, felt in the dark corners of the bed, fumbled in the cab until he found the flashlight and shone its feeble rays on a broad double track the length of the bed.

"Looks like they went the other way," Fay said and sat in the back, swinging his legs with pleasure and humming.

Vergil and Josephine

He crawled into a bed clammy from night chill, lay shivering and wanting Josephine. After ten minutes or so he got up and crossed the hall, opened her door gingerly. She was sleeping on her stomach. He lifted the blankets gingerly, was maneuvering his buttocks into position to slide in beside her when she said, did Fay remember the chicken feed?

Oooo, he whined in mock agony, wrapping his cold arms around her, pressing his icy knees into her heat, snuffing her perfumed neck and hair like a dog on a rabbit track. He was lifting her nightgown with his dead man's hands, pressing chilled mouth to her blood-rich neck with a complete understanding of vampires.

"You stink of liquor and cigarettes."

"I was in a fucking bar, I was riding with Fay. We almost hit a fucking train, we lost the fucking chicken feed on the road."

"Lost the chicken feed? Mother is going to kill Fay. How could you lose it?"

"I think when we fucking almost hit the goddamn train. We stopped goddamn fucking hard. The fucking sacks must have shot right out the fucking back. At least it looks that way. Unless they fell fucking out when we were going up some hill. I fucking don't remember any fucking steep hill."

"There isn't any hill. Stop that. *Stop that.*"

"Josephine, Jo-Jo, come on. Jo-Jo, fucking come on now," pressing hard against her, feeling the swell of blood in his prick and diving one frozen hand to her groin, pinching her nipple with the other.

"I'm serious, you can just quit right now. I'll go get the chicken feed and you get into your own bed and sleep it off. My mother hasn't had anything for those hens for two weeks because every time Fay goes to town he gets drunk and forgets it. She's been feeding them Quaker Oats and Rice Krispics. She's got a lot of problems right now and she doesn't need this. Did you get the matches?"

"Yeah."

"Dad's new slicker?"

"How about five fucking pounds of fucking sugar. It looked like sugar on the list."

"*Yeah,* it did. I'm not even going to ask about the rest of it. Come on, let's go get the chicken feed." She was up on one elbow and looking at him, a pillow crease on her right cheek.

"You're a fucking cunt tonight, you know? It's fucking miles back there. You ever think somebody else's got the fucking stuff by now anyway?"

"That isn't how it works out here." She got up, dressed furiously, jamming herself into clothes.

He wanted to hit her. Wanted to kill her. Didn't she get it? He'd gotten the fucking chicken feed while fucking Fay was drunk and swaying on a barstool, yes, he'd gotten it even though it was fucking out there somewhere in the road now. He sat up. The fucking rooster was going crazy. The hangover edged up a little. From the kitchen downstairs he could hear Kenneth coughing and clearing his throat. Fucking Christ. He thought of another fucking hour imprisoned in the Spanish chair sipping fucking lukewarm coffee and listening to the old fart boom on about fucking Umbrella Point. No wonder fucking Ults had killed the fucking horse, probably to shut fucking Kenneth up.

"Yeah. We'll get it." His voice was cold and mean now.

He was back across the hall, pulling on his rancid clothes, sopping a hot washcloth on his face, and down the stairs, not waiting for her, straight into the kitchen. The coffeepot was half full, still dripping. He poured a cup of the steaming slop and tried to drink it, turning away from Kenneth's swimmy eyes.

"You're an early riser and an ardent coffee drinker, I see, Vergil. I've been standing here looking out the window and thinking about war, about war and soldiers. Listening to the reports on the hostages. What a mess. In ancient times the Chinese had the right idea. They formed their armies from men in prison with archer's skills, killing skills, and drafted young men with bad reputations—they made a fearsome army, kept the neighborhoods peaceful and crime-free. We Americans make armies of nice kids who fight against their wills. What we ought to do is drop a nuclear bomb on Teheran, get rid of the Ayatollah and end that problem. Now, you were in the marines, you were in Vietnam—don't you agree with that?"

"The fucking hostages are in Teheran. You fucking want to kill them too?" Without waiting for an answer he was out the door, heading for the rakishly parked truck.

Back to town

The sky was clear rose, frost in patches of cut lawn grass like crusted salt, and near the ditch a fallen line of scythed weeds. Josephine sat in the driver's seat, tense and hunched forward, the ashtray empty and the windows down, and through them the damp morning air flowed, bitter with the scent of sage, death camas, lupine and crazyweed. She drove and neither of them said anything although the cab of the truck vibrated with suppressed shouting.

The sacks of chicken feed lay in the middle of the road on the town side of the tracks, faintly silvered with dew. He heaved them into the back of the truck and suddenly felt good, even happy, the coffee clicking in or the hangover departing or the glow of a fucking good deed done. He was back in and slamming the truck door when a freight train came around the curve heading out of town, empties rattling, maybe the same fucking train from last night. Josephine didn't turn back to the ranch but kept on toward town. The journey of the night was playing backward.

She parked in front of the same café where he'd drunk the fucking bad coffee the afternoon before and now drank it again, just as bad, sitting with her in a booth with red plastic upholstery, plastic-encased menus, and before them plastic mugs of weak fucking coffee, and he swallowed it gratefully and with relish ate his order of ham and fried eggs looking-at-him, mopping the fucking yolks with toasted home-made bread. There was a sign on the wall: FREE CHEWING GUM UNDER SEATS.

"All right," she said. "I'm sorry. Yesterday was a bitch. While you were in town with Fay I had a talk—she talked, I listened—with my mother. You wouldn't believe what she dumped on me. They're getting divorced. Dad's been seeing this woman about half his age, in fact I know her, she was in school with me; he got involved somehow and she had a kid about two weeks ago, a little girl—so I have a baby sister thirty-one years younger than I am. The messy part came the day after the baby was born when she got out of the hospital—they send them home the next day now. She made a beeline for the V.F.W. club with the baby, sat there for hours smoking and drinking with her greasy pals and managed to knock the baby off the bar and onto the floor. Some of them say she threw it. So the baby is in the hospital with serious head injuries—my mother wants her to die—the slut is charged with endangerment of the child's life and cruelty to a child, and my father's name and part in all this was plastered across the evening news and every paper in the state. Me—I was the only one who didn't know."

He started to speak but she held up her hand.

"Now. You're just dying to know why Simon shot Umbrella Point. All right. I'm gonna tell you. It was stupid. It was a misunderstanding. He was trying to help Dad. You know how Dad talks—he goes on and on, he never gives you a chance to say anything and after a while you get tired of listening."

"Yeah," he said.

"Dad was talking about Umbrella Point—well, that's what he always talked about—but he was hung up on what might happen when Umbrella Point got old and sick, some day in the future. He'd had a little bit to drink. He didn't feel it was right to let a sick, feeble animal hang on, getting more miserable and pain-racked. He thought old animals should be put down, but he said he knew *he* couldn't do it when the time came, that he wouldn't have the heart to put down old Umbrella Point who someday might be blind, too lame to walk, starving from tooth loss, cancerous and afflicted with skin sores that would not heal. Oh, he listed everything that could happen to a horse, and after a while, thinking about having to put Umbrella Point down, he started to cry. He said he couldn't do it; it would take just one shot to the head but he couldn't do it."

"Yeah?"

"It affected Simon. The trouble, the misunderstanding, was that he hadn't been listening very well to the first part, and by the time he paid attention, Dad was making it seem like Umbrella already had all those things wrong with him and had to be put down and he couldn't do it.

"Simon tossed and turned all night and finally he decided he would get up in the morning and help Dad out, put poor old Umbrella down and spare Dad. He *liked* Dad and he thought he should help him out. It never occurred to him that it was Fay's place to put Umbrella down if it ever came to that, but at the time Umbrella was twenty-one years old and in good health. He could have lived another five or maybe ten years, profitable years. Dad got a thousand-dollar stud fee for that horse's services. He figured Simon did him out of more than fifty thousand dollars by shooting Umbrella. And that's all there was to it, just one of those family misunderstanding situations."

"And?"

"And nothing. Simon and I went back to New York, but he was so upset about being shot and guilty about shooting Umbrella that he started to have an affair with his boss's girlfriend who was, incidentally, my gynecologist, who broke the news to him that I was pregnant. So we got divorced, he married the bitch and they moved back to Minneapolis and I never heard from him again. For years I blamed my father. He didn't have to shoot poor Simon. Just like he didn't have to fuck that slut, my old playmate."

"I think he fucking did the right thing. He said he thought Simon was coming to blow everybody away. He looked freaked out. As for the woman, who the fuck knows why this stuff happens? It happens all the time. And it's their fucking problem, not yours."

She looked at him. "You're wrong, you asshole. Totally. You don't have any moral balance. Let's get out of here and drive into the mountains. Let's get some wine and some steaks and a blanket."

"Josephine. Let me remind you that your mother is waiting for that fucking chicken feed back at the ranch."

She looked at him, at his handsome American face, both halves in symmetry; behind the prissy little wire-rimmed glasses his clear light eyes reflected a hostile spark; she saw the patchy cheek stubble and the mole beside his nose and his too hairless arms. He stared as well, and it was already, in a few seconds, as though he'd known her last year or sometime the year before. Their affection had curdled. They were moving rapidly toward antipathies.

"You don't like her, do you? My mother."

"No," he said, knowing he shouldn't say it. "And I feel the same way about your fucking father. Ults had the right idea—waste 'em."

"That was NOT what he intended. I just told you."

Still, they bought the wine and drove into the mountains and there, in a meadow blazing with Indian paintbrush, she ran from him half clothed and laughing like an advertisement for sanitary napkins; he played the game for a few minutes, then got angry with this crap, slammed her to the ground and tore her clothes, gave her a ringing, double-handed slap when she said stop, wrenched her legs apart and shoved in, bucking and rutting. The sun had heated her hair and she gave off a scent like walnut oil and hot leaves. They sweated under the purple sky, biting each other's lips, she raked his back, he pounded her with his full weight, rammed and thrust, the grasses sawed their skins with stinging shallow cuts, the wine bottle tipped over and spilled onto the earth, they rolled in it, growling and moaning, hurled their wine-stained, scratched, grass-and-pollen-smeared bodies into curious positions, shouted and wept, she cried oh god oh god, she broke a blood-rimmed nail, he damaged his knee on sharp quartz and mosquitoes sucked at his smarting back and her white legs, and when he had to piss, kneeling, she tenderly held his penis, and when she, squatting, repeated the function, he held his curved palm against the hot fountain, then came more cries to deities, more crawling and rolling in the matted wet flowers, and from each, extravagant declarations of profound love for the other, beyond life itself, all of this watched from a distant slope by a Basque sheepherder with his Sears binoculars in his left hand and his prick in the right.

"That was rape," she said.

"Yeah. And you fucking loved it."

"Your mistake," she said. "You'll be sorry."

The deerflies came. The wine was gone. They dressed in silence, turning away from each other a little. They limped from the meadow, avoiding the sight of the crushed flowers. It was finished.

The visit ended the next morning, with Vergil, before he drove away, looking straight into her eyes with sincerity and an expression that said he was a little confused and hurt about the way things had turned out (his pose of decent uprightness was a false impression for he went to prison a few years later after bilking the credulous residents of a blue-chip retirement home through his fraudulent investment company promising large returns on stocks in selected "environmentally sound corporations"), and Josephine saddled Oatmeal, a blue-marbled mare with varnish marks on her face, gaskins, stifle region and elbow, looked away from him and said, you bet, you bet. She told her parents she was going to stay on at the ranch to help Kenneth keep the stud books, and put up jam with Bette. Maybe she'd stay always, she told them, a daughterly reward for their decision to stay together after the slut's baby died and Kenneth signed up for fidelity counseling.

(But that fall she married Matthew Handsaw, a six-foot-two rancher, another Vietnam veteran, originally from Amherst, Massachusetts, who suffered a grand mal epileptic seizure on their wedding night. She sat in a hospital waiting room reading *Rabbit Is Rich,* but fell asleep at page fifty-three. They became reclusive, and in a few years, when Handsaw was convinced the federal government was red-eyed out of control and a dark-skinned, bandy-legged United Nations takeover imminent, that a lack of school prayer had destroyed the American people's moral sense, he sealed off the ranch with steel gates. Working together, they dug a series of bunkers and tunnels that grew into a ten-acre underground city with secret mole doors.)

"Bizitza hau iluna eta garratza da"

One June, on the last Saturday in the month, Fay, in knife-creased jeans, a pearl-buttoned shirt, silk neckerchief, lizardskin dress boots and a new gem belt, ground up Elk Leg Mountain in the late afternoon, the green accordion bouncing on the seat beside him, and his own concertina, cased and wrapped in a horse blanket, foursquare on the floor along with half a dozen bottles of fine Irish whiskey. He'd had the concertina a long time. The name "C. Jeffries" straggled along the wooden end. He had always thought this was the name of some waddy owner long sodded over, and he liked the instrument's hard loud voice, the gold dolphins stamped around the frame, much worn but still leaping. He'd done his best with the old green accordion but didn't know what to do about the stuck button and the ones that wouldn't sound. He wasn't handy in that finicking kind of way.

The Basques had been going all day, although the big dance platform laid out in the flowery meadow was empty, a few costumed dancers off to the side kicking their way through the incomprehensible figures of the *jota,* three or four musicians dressed up in smocks and berets and squashy shoes with crisscrossed lacings climbing their legs. They played old instruments, one piping on a *txistu* and rapping a *tambouri* at the same time, a stout man with a face as pocked as a waffle pumping the *trikitixa*, with its specially tuned reeds squeezing out "*Zolloko San Martinak*," and behind a wagon, two men with sticks held upright in their hands, pummeling a resonant wooden plank with the butts of the sticks. He didn't think the musicians were local people; maybe imported from Los Angeles.

Near the trees he saw trucks and jeeps parked randomly, people climbing in and out, a rope corral of horses. There was a delicious, smoky, greasy haze from the barbecue pits, men sat under awnings and open tents playing cards, women talked in a wash of music and nickering horses and human cries. The accumulated heat of the day loosened stiff faces, the aspens blurred in the heated air, the dust and the slanting mountain shadow.

He walked around for ten minutes, the accordion in his right hand, looking for Michel, the cousin of Javier, saw him finally half asleep, his wedge-shaped face down, sitting on an overturned box near the horses, one thigh roofed over the other, and smoking a roll-yer-own.

"Michel," said Fay, coming up. The man looked up, got up, skinned his lips back from yellow teeth and twitched his head at Fay who followed him to a mud-crusted jeep. They set off on a steep track, the celebration falling away behind them. Michel said nothing, frowned steadily ahead, the coal of the cigarette burning near his lips. Fay lit his own cigarette, offered another to Michel who took it, stubbing the butt of the first on the dashboard. The track jerked up through lodgepole pines, descended into a saddle, climbed the flank of another slope and moved slowly toward a roadless inner range, the pitching crests and the great swell of earth and rock empty of human sign, the cries of swooping kestrels and the whistle of wind the sounds of the place. The whine of the jeep engine hit an alien subtone. The track disappeared and they were grinding over rocks, skirting boulders and scree, sagebrush and mountain mahogany scraping the sides of the jeep. Michel pointed away to the right and Fay strained his eyes, staring until he picked out the scattered boulders, which might be sheep.

Michel said nothing. Fay tried a bit of song, *she wrang her hands and cried,* but the track was too rough to sing, the words jolted out of his mouth, the tune shaken from under them. "Kind of place you want a horse, not a jeep."

Michel nodded once, stopped. The sheep were still distant. Michel pointed straight up and to the right, his face tilted at the sky. There was a path. He avoided looking directly at Fay, settled back and closed his eyes.

"I'm waiting here," he said. Already a small cloud of mosquitoes had formed around him.

"Not gonna be long," said Fay, stepping into a weedy patch that gave out a scent of licorice, taking a piss before he started up. He slung the accordion over his shoulder with a rope loop and climbed, cursing and slipping in his boots. But it wasn't far, a few hundred yards, a tight twist under a pair of boulders shaped like buttocks, and on a flange of flat-cropped meadow he saw Javier's sheep wagon, the round top like a white can, the door open and Javier sitting on the sill cleaning his rifle. Up here the wind streamed, the grasses and purple lupine undulating, Javier's shirt first billowing out and then plastering close to his body.

As Fay came up, Javier turned his face to the left, morose and shy from too many years alone in the mountains with the herds, his long oily nose gleaming. The dog under the wagon growled.

"Michel's down in the jeep. Don't you guys get along?"

"Get along good. Sometimes. He's a-scared. He's the reason I need that box. He left my old one on the front seat of the truck in the sun for five hours while he was gettin drunk. You should a seen it. Nothing to do but throw it out, all warped and the wax melted all over the inside. Anyway, he's a sorehead. He's the kind of guy thinks about how tough life is. He's the sour type—nothing goes for him. That it?" He took the accordion, looked it over, grimacing at the painted devil and his worn flames.

"Nice place you got here. Lawn mowed pretty good. Garbage collection don't seem so good though," Fay looking at the cairn of tin cans and bottles.

"Camp tender pick 'em up next time. He can drive up here, go around the back of that rock, down the east side. Michel brought you on the south." He tossed a can of warm beer to Fay.

"You're missing the big party, Javier. They tell me you're the only Basque around still goes out with the sheep, everybody else hires Messicans and Peruvians. They tell me all the other sheep wagons are in museums or rich ranchers' yards for decoration."

"Yeah. I'm too old for it, too. Get antsy when I'm down there. Good enough for me up on the mountain, come down and get drunk with you sometimes. The old dog can't change his tricks. Used to it. Don't want to break no pattern. Got no ambition. Anyways, let's look at this thing." He kicked out his left leg as a brace, turned the green accordion in his hands. "Shit, it's a mess."

"I fixed the thumb strap, not much else."

Javier looked at the big wood screw pinning down a loop of leather.

"You don't want to go into cabinetmaking, your next career. Anyways, I can fool around with it. It'll be all right for up here; you don't want something good banging around the wagon. Yeah, I'm too old to be up here, but that's why I'm up here. Too old to get into something else. Sheep's all I know. I'll go out with it. There won't be no wool left in the world, all synthetics anyways."

He scowled over the accordion, turning half away. He ran his finger over the scratched lacquer, cracked buttons, the metal eyes blind with rust, the ratty bellows with Fay's duct tape over a hole, the grille gone, the finish worn away and in one end the faint letters of a French name though the wood had been sanded. He placed his stained, muscular hands in position, drew the bellows open slowly, slowly closed them. Again. He began to play, some of the notes silent or wheezing, another button sounding two notes at once. He sang in a husky mournful voice, a melody loose and wandering, sliding from note to note and slowly rising in pitch until it had left the beginning key far behind. *"Ah, what a fine friend I have who brings me music, who comes up the mountain smoking his cigarette, eager to drink a Budweiser, leaving behind in the boulders a slippery fellow who owes me plenty, who is too weak to climb up to the song of this old angel—"* and from below came Michel's cry, a shrill warbling neigh that ended with a shriek too high for human ears to hear although the dog felt its pierce and yapped.

"Wait," said Javier, disappearing into his wagon. He came out wearing a long strange necklace of small bones that hung almost to his knees.

"What is it, Ind'an?" said Fay.

"Nah, Basque, old-style Basque. I made it. My grandfather had one, but I'll tell you the bastard ain't satisfactory." He hooked the forefinger of his left hand in the end of the necklace and pulled it taut in front of him. In his right hand he held a polished stick. He began to strike the small bones with the stick and a brittle, chill music, rapid and fragile, fell into the clear air. He sang softly, a plaintive tune in his tobacco-hoarsened voice: *"Ah, bizitza hau iluna eta garratza da, this life is sad and bitter . . ."*

"What is it made out of, bones?"

"Eagle. Meadowlark. Goose. Hawk. Sage grouse. Bird bones. Ten feet away you can't even hear it."

"You better keep it hid under your bunk. They'll put you away for ten years for that eagle bone music."

But Javier was looking at the tongue of cloud moving in from the west, curved veils of rain and hail falling on some distant place, sick of company and longing to be alone in the pearl hour of twilight, the time between dogs and wolves.

Fay shrugged and started down the track. He had a five-hour drive ahead of him before he got to Padraic's place, old Padraic, who was all his family now. The Bascos weren't the only ones who could have a party.

In the army

On a night of full moon in January 1863, sixteen-year-old Riley McGettigan, tightly made, with doll's feet, had left the family croft, teeming with his half-wild sibs, and made his way to Galway where, in five nights, he was able to rob enough drunks to buy steerage passage to New York. The last sight for his sore, peat-smoked eyes was of a penitent leaning on a short stick and inching along the cobbled shore on bloody knees.

In the fabled city, penniless and famished, he tried the same robber's work with some success for a month or two, then was caught and beaten but, through his captor's gin-soaked inattention, escaped back into the streets where he joined in with a gang calling themselves Lads of Ireland, playing hot and heavy in the draft riots, joyously beating any blacks they caught, busy at three hangings and in the mob that set fire to the Colored Orphan Asylum on Fifth Avenue. In late summer he accepted a sum of money to serve in the army in place of a Yankee hardware merchant's son (how the Americans loved the cannon-fodder Irish during that war) and found himself with three dozen other paddies in Sherman's army slogging through the south, a few of the half million who had come to get rich, not to die, and who ended their lives marching behind a drummer whose sticks might have been thighbones, following a banner that should have showed a death's-head.

He marched from the defeat at Kennesaw Mountain down Georgia to the sea, singing a catchy rebel song, "The Rock Island Line," and laughing at Sherman's witty dispatch to President Lincoln, "*I beg to present you as a Christmas gift the city of Savannah,*" learned to play a pennywhistle and liked the rough life well enough to reenlist after the war to fight Indians.

He married Mary Blunky, a poverty-hardened girl with red ears, drifting along in the wake of the Union Army, dreaming of husband and home, no matter how lousy. The husband she got, but, pregnant and terrified of red Indians, she stayed east of the Missouri when Riley marched to Fort Phil Kearny on the Bozeman Trail in the autumn of 1866.

In December he was in the column that rode out under the bragging command of Captain Willy Fetterman to protect a wagon train of lumber coming from the pine groves eight miles away. Fetterman, steeped in the myth of white invincibility, rode willfully into a trap. A thin Indian boy fled just ahead of them, seemed scared to death, dodging and evading, but never opening the gap. This clumsy youth, this easy kill, led the galloping column off the trail and onto a ridge where the grass and boulders and gullies and brush suddenly vomited arrows, and a horde of ululating warriors, the decoy Crazy Horse now with them, dashed chopping forward with razory axes and hardwood cudgels, loosing hissing swarms of darts, and annihilated the column in twenty minutes. Riley McGettigan, nineteen, wondering at the brevity of life, swooned with an arrow in his neck.

(He was not dead. Hauled back to the fort by the nervous collectors of bodies, he was sent down the line to recover but, satiated with the Indian experience, escaped from the field hospital one moony night and made his way to Texas where he scrounged a poor living stealing cattle and in 1870 was caught red-handed by a rancher with a sense of humor. The rancher's hands killed and skinned the cow, shot out Riley's elbows and knees and sewed him up inside the animal's skin, his head and feet protruding from each end of the stitchery, and left the arrangement in the sun, promising to come back in a month and buy him a drink. The hide shrank and dried in the heat of the day, tighter and tighter, while the nearby deliquescing carcass stank and attracted coyotes, their slavering and gnawing his night music, while in the beating day buzzards peppered the sky.)

Mary McGettigan did not marry again for four years though she bore three sons with the handy surname McGettigan in the period— Riley junior, then one who in the toddling age fell against the hot stove and died of the burns, and the youngest, who succumbed to cholera. Finally she moved to Dynamite, Montana, where she married Francis Dermot, a railway laborer who broke her heart singing "Beautiful Dreamer" in his delirious Irish tenor. On her in the next decades he begot four more sons and three daughters, all of whom survived and scattered across the continent, becoming wives and mothers, an assayer, a cardsharp who expired in a punitive barbwire corset, a muleteer, a railway laborer who wrote exquisite poetry on Sundays.

Fay's old man

Riley junior, Fay McGettigan's old man, was a hard-luck feller, the natural luck of a McGettigan, he said. He worked as a ranch hand and stayed single until he was forty when he had saved up enough to buy a dry, scabby ranch and lure a mail-order bride to him from Ireland, the seventeen-year-old orphan Margie, silent, hardworking, quick-tempered and a singer, especially of "The Snowy-Breasted Pearl," accompanying herself on a tiny fingering diatonic she called a come-to-me-go-from-me. The gift she gave to her children was a taste for song, the human voice pitched against waving grass, four walls, a sky lowering on invisible chains. Whatever befell her or them the woman had a song coiled in her lung for it, knew hundreds of verses and hundreds of tunes, remembered every sung fragment she ever had heard, and had a quick knack for imitating birdcall. She could tell the name of an unseen horse by nicker, whinny or neigh, heard a windstorm approaching the day before it struck, harbored true pitch somewhere inside her like a lodestone, and wept in the street the first time she heard a phonograph, in 1921, playing a recording of tenor Tom Burke's "If You'll Remember Me."

Her husband, Riley junior, was hard-willed, sought relief in drink, burned impatient with men, women, children and animals; barely literate, he got seven children on Margie and one day in 1919 walked out of the house, mounted his good horse and rode into the sunset, leaving her with the foreclosure, a sucking baby, and a hundred twelve gaunt mortgaged cattle.

(He got as far as San Francisco where he was struck down by a touring Cadillac with an electric self-starter.)

Fay was eleven when the old man pulled out; the next child down the ladder was ten-year-old Padraic—the desperate boy, their mother called him. (He got the name when he was five years old and they took him to town for the first time. He was with his mother in the general store, he goggling at the objects hanging, standing, leaning, shelved, at the glassed myriad candies, when someone opened the door a little and a dog entered. Margie was examining a paper of needles, looking for one large-eyed enough to carry wool yarn, and a few feet away Padraic studied the candy jars in agonies of choice, a nickel heavy in his hand. The dog, unnoticed at first, staggered down the brown aisle, rolling its dry hard eyes, an edging of foam on its black lip. It slammed into a display, jostling oil-lamp chimneys, and at the glassy rattle the clerk looked up. "Oh godamighty, mad dog," he cried and climbed onto the counter, his shoes slipping on some piled-up paper fans, hauling up the lady customer at hand. Padraic saw the dog as it marched past him but his mother did not turn until the dog, growling, seized her skirt in its champing jaws. She shrieked and stretched her hands to Padraic to lift him to safety. He thought she cried for his help and there was nothing for it, he wrestled the heavy octagonal jar of cinnamon red hots into his arms, came forward and crashed the candy jar onto the mad dog's head. The dog fell to its side, dazed, its legs scrabbling until the clerk leaped down and bludgeoned it dead with a cane. The desperate boy was celebrated the length of the street and puked sugar all the way home, a pair of bloody dog's ears in his pocket.)

"You're the men of the house now," their mother said. "You'll have to work. We've got to work to live." She believed she had no choice but the classic occupation—taking in laundry. Fay's memories of his mother were of pulpy hands and the slosh of water, sweet-sung lines of "The Snowy-Breasted Pearl."

Love denied

As a child Fay recognized himself to be a poor, graceless, homely and uneducated mick, out of the running for family life. This painful condition was compounded by his helpless private crashing headlong fall into love with every fine-looking woman and girl he saw—photographs as well. He blushed and burned, looked at the charmers only from under his lashes or by way of window reflections.

In the midst of the Depression, when he was twenty-four, there had been a woman ranch hand at the R Bar, Eunice Brown, skin and bone and a mad preacher's face—two intense, glaring eyes and a mouth misshapen by the scar of a burn put on her by a slit-eyed cousin with a branding iron. She took a liking to Fay and embarrassed him by casting sheep's eyes whenever he had business at the R Bar. Old man Rubble said she was as strong as a man, worked cheaper, and was a better cowboy because she didn't drink, but Fay thought he must be blind and deaf in the nose, because she kept a pint in her bosom and he'd had a swallow or two of that. But he only loved the beauties and that was the way of it.

Like his old man he did ranch work, moving from one ranch to another in the basin, taking offense and quitting over imagined slights, getting tired of the food or bunkhouse company, only to shift a few miles to another marginal operation with a desperate rancher and quixotic weather, for a few months bunked with a man named Ballagh who played a concertina with buttons fashioned from a mermaid's finger bones, or so he said, and taught him how to play the instrument.

It was the Drowsy Ranch but they called it the All Checked Out because Old Man Drowsy always said that—"I want it *all checked out.*" There was a deep canyon on the ranch and, at the bottom, a well. To catch the wind, the windmill sat at the top of a one-hundred-ten-foot tower. The most hated, god-awful job on the place was the weekly climb up the tower to grease the bearings, the whole rickety thing groaning and swaying. The first public music Fay played on the unknown cowpoke's concertina was at a celebration of the canyon fire that burned down the windmill.

He came to work for Kenneth in 1957 when he was forty-nine years old because he fell in love with Bette at the first sight of her and the Irish face on her, the lovely auburn hair like twisted copper thread, her belly swollen with child and dressed in an old-fashioned cream linen smock with coffee-dyed lace at the neck and cuffs, a maternity dress designed to make the wearer resemble a little girl, and before that fire burned out in favor of the black-haired mail carrier with eyes the blue of a Steller's jay wing, he'd been working there too long to stop. Ever since, he'd had a partiality for the pregnant ones. But for himself asked only the saddest whores, the ones with drug habits and scabs, gnawed red fingernails and no interest in anything.

Dancing on cold linoleum

The long weekend with the desperate boy once a year was a rite for both of them, two ugly, drunken, aging brothers with no gifts or grace beyond whiskey and music, for Padraic, with his quiff of white hair, his crooked eyes, his slanted mouth, played the uilleann pipes, and when Fay put a bottle of whiskey on the table in front of each of them and took up his concertina and Padraic drew the first breath to squeeze into the plaid lung under his arm, they had a precious hour.

Their music was the songs they'd learned from their mother, songs built in rhythm and interval from an old language neither of them had ever spoken and rarely heard. Padraic wrote down the names of these songs on a list and each year one or the other would have recollected a fragment of "The Barefoot Bachelor," or "The Coulin," or "Jenny's Chickens." The desperate boy knew all the songs of love for he had been married during World War II for four days, but Fay didn't know what had happened, no one did beyond Padraic and the female, wherever she was.

Now the two brothers stood in the desperate boy's hallway and gripped each other by the elbows, each laid his head upon his brother's shoulder, taking in the familiar smell of the other, despite tobacco and whiskey overtones, connected with the warmth and safety of the brown blanket they had shared seventy years gone.

" 'Tis the Irish Hour," said one, tossing off the first glass from the bottle the other had brought, in a mimicking brogue that was their own joke. "Never think of getting yourself an accordion in a nice flat key, say E flat?"

"Yeah, but I thought about a B/C sooner. You can do it all on them. Yeah, if I had the money and the time to learn, maybe. Anyway, I'm OK with this. Good enough for old waddy Jeffries singing to the longhorns, good enough for me." The fingers of his right hand twisted and sprang into "The Dogs Among the Bushes," and from the concertina issued rolls of triplets, a bouquet of ornamentation so floral and richly colored that Padraic could smell the music's perfume, sweet and a little oily.

He had a stack of Irish papers for Fay to take home, and for him Fay had a story or two and some tapes for the player in his truck. And he thought of the poor Basco up on his lonely slope with the sheep and the pathetic instrument of bird bones, never a brother to keep him company and sing the childhood songs.

"Here's what I think," said Fay. "Mesas and buttes and rough country is the breaks, ain't it? Broken land? Well, ain't it the same thing with music—you make a sound, it breaks the air up? It's the breaks again, invisible but there."

Late at night, the two of them drunk back to limber youth, the desperate boy got up and to the tickle and bounce of "The Broken Plate" did a step dance that took the breath out of Fay watching, and he, not to be outdone, laid his instrument aside and danced out the silent tune on the dirty linoleum of the kitchen floor.

The Little Boy Blue Pawnshop

For a long time after Fay left the mountain Javier played, he played and sang into the thickening dark, drinking and singing, his voice and the green accordion's warped and ruined chords and lunatic notes—he didn't care—echoing off the boulders, while he imagined tracers of notes making trapezoidal and triangular figures as they bounced from boulder to stone, and it was beautiful, beautiful to hear it, alone.

But the next day he opened it up to see what could be repaired. The reeds were rusty, that was sure, and the axle, the pivot point for the keys, was probably corroded, grabbing and making the buttons stick. He could think of better places to draw out an axle than in a sheep wagon rocked by wind, something of a delicate operation, but he couldn't make the instrument any worse. He wasn't worried about replacing the valves—there was a roll of leather and skin and whang under the bunk.

He scrambled through the tools looking for a pliers to grip the end

of the axle, but for some reason there wasn't one. At the back of the
drawer he turned up two pairs of rusty old sheep shears and an ancient
pair of castrating forceps.

"Them'll work," he said to the accordion, "maybe," but used the
fencing tool instead to get a grip on the end of the axle and pull it out
straight. It was bad enough.

The silent reed suffered from a grain of rust jammed between the
reed tongue and its vent, and this he eased out with a silk thread from
his fly-tying box. The steel reeds were coated with islands of rust and he
scraped at them with the blade of his knife but was afraid of lodging
more fragments under the reed tongues. He cleaned the reeds with his
toothbrush, blowing out the dust until he was dizzy.

He could see it needed everything—new bellows, new reed, new
springs, reed plates reset, grille replaced, and more. But it had a wonderful
voice, sonorous, plangent, shouting in grief to the mountain slope.

Late that summer, at another camp farther west, he laid the accordion on the earth and went with the dog to discover the source of a far-
off sheep's nervous blat, nothing to be seen but some disturbed earth
that made him wonder if there was a cat around, but there were no clear
tracks, no dead sheep or signs of a killing. The dog took little interest in
the roughened place.

He was gone for two hours, three, and when he came back he leaned
down to pick up the accordion, still thinking about the cat he now
believed was up on the slope with him, scraping the bellows over the
rattlesnake resting beneath the instrument and receiving the fangs in
the great vein in the crook of the elbow.

The camp tender found him ten days later, his skin blackened by the
high-altitude sun. He thought, heart attack, poor old bastard, loaded
him into the back of the pickup with his belongings. Javier was buried
at the back of the cemetery without a stone, and his goods stored in the
Basque hotel where he had spent the winters and the morose times
between work.

Two summers later the owner sold the hotel to a young Vietnamese
couple and returned to his ancestral fishing village, Elanchove, where he
had been born sixty-seven years earlier, hoping for a bride and a few
years of home comfort. The new owners cleared out the back room
packed with boxes of old clothing, bibles and catechisms, spurs and
boots and worn saddles, yellowed calendars with day after day crossed
out in crooked slashes and Xs, shepherds' crooks, rifles, ancient trunks,
and a green accordion. All that seemed salable went to the Little Boy
Blue pawnshop on commission.

Back Home
with Reattached Arms

A CHEMNITZER

Harmless

Ivar Gasmann, the youngest son of Nils and Elise Gasmann, grandson of immigrants Gunnar and Margaret Gasmann, was a familiar figure in Old Glory, Minnesota, in the late 1970s, pushing his grocery cart with the groaning wheel along the streets, picking up cans, bottles, a pair of muddy, tread-printed underpants, nor did he ignore odd-colored rocks, slouching along, his hands on the handlebar, blond hair lying in dusty ropes over his shoulders, hair that he would knot and tie under his bony chin when the wind blew at his back, blinking eyes the color of sky-reflecting glass, a fine-faced man but slow in mind and dirty in person. People saw him as soft, yet potentially violent, some said he ate lost dogs, and anyone could see he lived like a swine.

Yet he was useful in the community. For him women set out things they no longer wanted: three-legged side tables, leopardskin print cushions, a soap-flake-premium cookie jar in the shape of a bulldog head, sections of toy train track, wall plaques of three flying geese *moderne,* dusty eucalyptus leaves, papier-mâché bananas and artichokes, a pink crib whose occupant had died in the night. These objects he hauled to his shack in the lilac trees, near something that had been a livery stable at the turn of the century, a gaunt building slumped at one end like a rising camel, the roof patched with flattened baking powder cans.

He had never had sexual intercourse with a woman. His feeling for men, after a peculiar encounter with a short-order cook at Chippewa Willy's Grill, was ambivalent.

Nils and Elise

When Ivar was born, a year before World War II ended, his parents farmed north of town on land once black with the dense shadow of giant pines. (The forests went down long before old Gasmann bought the farm, cut by axemen and sawyers from Prince Edward Island, Maine, Québec, New Brunswick, Finland, Norway, Sweden; as the loggers moved west, into the raw stumpland came Germans, Czechs, Scandinavians, Slovaks, Croatians, Lithuanians, Poles, Russians, Serbs, and a few Irish and French with farming on their minds.)

Gunnar Gasmann had come over from Norway in 1902 (during the passage the ship steamed through waters where, ninety-three years later, the world's largest concrete drilling platform stood in the Troll offshore gas field), dragged around Wisconsin and Michigan for ten years working in the lead mines, the lumber mills, as a laborer, a hired farmhand, before the family bought the stumpland farm for fifty cents an acre. Stubborn and easily injured, Gunnar took offense if anyone had the bad manners to call him by his first name, felt patronized by a warm greeting. He thought book learning an affectation of the snotty middle class and discouraged his children from school. He had a single joke, an acid retort for those who crossed him: why don't you go back where I come from?

Under the authority of this thin-skinned man the boy Nils grew up barely literate but good with an axe, a natural for the lumber camps where he started working at fifteen. By the time he was twenty he was a tie hack in the Idaho mountains.

(His twin sister, Floretta, left the farm a month after he did. She tied up with Jack Brady's All-Girl Wild West Show for a while, switched to rodeo and became a champion trick rider and bronc rider. In 1927, at Tucumcari, New Mexico, she was thrown, landed on the back of her head, dead instantly of a broken neck.)

Nils disliked farming and returned to it reluctantly after each season's work, drinking and cursing in the polyglot camp talk of Swedish, Norwegian and English. Every summer after the river drive, suffering from squeak heel, an audible ailment of the Achilles tendon that afflicted many who drove the ties down the tumbled water of snowmelt rivers, he hitchhiked back to Old Glory where his wife, Elise, kept old Gunnar's farm going with her half-wit cousin, Freddy, a good worker who needed no pay.

But as soon as the last cutting of hay was in the barn and the corn shocked, Nils was off again for the woods camp with his chopping axe, broadaxe and peeler, hungry for tobacco, whiskey and the stink and rough company of men—the place where all of his teeth except two uppers and two lowers dead center had been pulled by Oleson, the tie pin, with a pair of oily pliers in the winter of 1936. (Oleson joined the navy in 1943, stayed in until 1947 when he was one of six hundred killed in the Texas City, Texas, explosion of a hold full of ammonium nitrate fertilizer.) Nils's mail-order dental plate was patterned from a wax impression he made with a plug of chew in his cheek. The teeth did not fit well, and because he frequently lost them during drinking bouts, he burned his initials in them with the heated tip of his knife, N.G.

"Know what that means?" said Oleson. "N.G.—No Good."

In the woods he felt at home, a fluid and tireless chopper of perfect ties seven inches by eight feet, ears cocked for the ring of the gut hammer, his imagination playing with the pleasures of the whorehouse and saloon, of fiddle and accordion tunes by moonlight with the tie hack musicians sitting on stumps in the cutover and the rest of them lurching over rough ground, treading hemlock cones into powder dancing with one another's shadows.

In 1938 Nils cut a pine; its fall sent tremors through the snow on the steep slope above, and a small avalanche, a hissing white turmoil of powder and loose boulders, raced down. He threw away his axe and ran, got far enough to escape living burial but was wedged to his knees when a small dislodged boulder, leaping and plunging, hit the side of his head so hard it laid him out senseless. When he came to in the dark, with the lantern of Oleson shining in his eyes, he did not know his name or where he was. He said, "hello, Oldsmobile," instead of "Oleson," and the men cheered. At least he was alive, and they all thought of young Som Axel snowshoeing along the railroad cut in new powder snow two years earlier, caught by an avalanche, bent and frozen in a hoop, his snowshoed feet pressed against his shoulder blades.

Nils recovered, but his memory was erratic and he came up in screaming rages over nothing, for a savage, volatile personality had been released by the erratic boulder. The logging company gave him his walking papers and there was nowhere to go but back to Old Glory and the farm.

Temper, temper

So he was there when Ivar, his second son, was born—a farmer against his will, his brain addled, while men with undented heads went off to fight the Axis powers. He came home drunk in the dawn; after bringing Elise to the hospital the night before and listening to her moans for twenty minutes, he went to a loggers' bar and drank boilermakers. As for Elise, it was a painful labor that made her shriek against her will. She sank gratefully into what the fat, cross-eyed doctor called Twilight Sleep and delivered the child, but she remembered enough to swear that Nils would never come near her again, the crazy hog.

"Ah, you'll forget. I'll see you in here next year," said the nurse.

Nils, yawning home, drunk, desperate for an hour of sleep before

starting the milking, longing for sleep in the sweet unaccustomed
silence—the other child, Conrad, was at Elise's sister's house, the half-
wit cousin burrowed in his greasy blanket still—fell into the bed and
slept for seven minutes until a hairy woodpecker roused him with a
tremendous rapping on the shingled roof. He got the shotgun and ran
outside naked but the bird flew off with a coy feminine squeak. He
cursed woodpeckers. He tumbled back into bed, the shotgun in Elise's
place, and pulled the quilt over his shoulders when the woodpecker
began again. The shattering noise was right above him. He sobbed in
fury, fired through the ceiling, deafening himself and splintering shingles, then ran outside to see the proof of his fallen enemy. The bird was
in an apple tree, working on a hole the size of a grapefruit. He dashed
inside, snatched up the gun, then back out, jumping down the porch
stairs, but again the woodpecker flew. The cows were lowing with dis-
comfort in the barn. Back into the house he went, shaking with temper,
but when he was two up the stairs the malicious hammering started
once more, and he sprang into the kitchen, incoherent, shouting male-
dictions, yanked open the red-painted drawer in the dresser where Elise
kept the matches, crumpled a ball of newspaper, ran up to the attic and
set the roof on fire directly under the rapping. His rage dropped away
in a few minutes but by then the flames had the roof. The fire department saved the lower story, and the family spent the rest of the winter
in cramped, char-stinking rooms. In the spring he rebuilt the upstairs,
but after he sawed the stringer for the staircase he found he had measured wrong, and too furious to buy more lumber and start again, he
tore the work out. From that time on, in order to use the upper rooms,
they climbed a ladder.

Ivar grew up in fear of his father's insensate rages, ricocheted from
slaps and screams in the barn to gingersnaps and cream in the kitchen.

Nils, when he was rational, gave Elise detailed commands on how to
raise children properly. His own parents had been obsessed with the
prescriptions of a book, *The Emigrant's Guide to Preserving Norwegian
Culture,* written by a homesick settler in Texas, a book that dwelt on the
merits of the Norwegian language, twice-daily prayers, Norwegian
hymns, clothes, food and, after the fortune was made, return to the
"*elskede Nord*" country. Daily they had sung "*En Udvandrers Sang,*" "*O
Norges Son*" and others. His mother wished to live in a Norwegian community where land was owned in common by all. But Gunnar shouted
for independence and his own land, purchased a mighty, star-spangled
flag. Years later, drunk, Nils could still remember one of those old
songs, "The Skeleton at the Party," with its verses about liberty and

peace across the sea: "*Bliver os Skatter, Afgifter for svær, reise vi Vest over Sø, til Mississippis Breder, o der, ja, o der i Frihed vi blegne og døe . . . ,*" but forbade his own children to learn a word of the purse-mouth tongue. Concentrate on American, he told them—Oleana, that Norwegian utopia dreamed up by Ole Bull, was a joke and Norwegians were a joke and their accent was a joke and they made themselves into jokes with stupid behavior and low comedy acts and songs, heavy with simulated farts and swollen red noses and checkered high-water pants. Norwegians were figures of fun like no others, bawling "who threw the halibut on the poop deck?" in exaggerated comic accents, playing the squeezebox through their legs, behind their ears, until you wanted to howl. And what stubborn people, unable to let go of an idea and look at another. So the birth language of old Gunnar and Margaret perished in the Gasmann family.

As an illustration of stubbornness and single-track minds, Nils told the story of how old Gunnar and the uncles began to dig a well on the farm. Seven feet down, they struck a vein of shining red-colored flakes and nuggets. Could it be copper? Perhaps. Samples of the mystery ore were wrapped up in a brown paper parcel to send off to the assay office. But in the meantime water was needed and the men dug on. For one reason or another the interesting package was never sent and in time it was lost.

"A copper mine ignored for the sake of water. We could have been millionaires," said Nils, "except for those old Norwegian fools." But he never made a motion himself to dig in the vicinity of the old well, unused for many years. There was pleasure in the thought that while stumbling about the farm chores they might be walking over a great fortune.

The Atomic Power Trailer Church

In 1951 Ivar was seven, and a traveling preacher drove into the farmhouse yard towing a plywood trailer behind a two-tone car with Tennessee plates, packed full of women, children and boxes. He knocked on the farmhouse door, said his name was Howard Poplin and asked Nils if he could set up for a few days in the lower field near the road, be glad to pay a dollar or two. Nils, frowning with his colorless eyebrows, said yes, they could stay there, no need to pay, we were all brothers in this hard world and any god-fearing Christian was welcome on his land. He didn't smile; he never smiled. After noon dinner he went down to see what they were doing—ruining something, perhaps—and called Ivar to accompany him, told Conrad to slop the hogs.

Poplin's women were off to one side going through boxes, the wife

and an older woman that must be the wife's mother, Nils decided, looking at their narrow heads and long hanks of hair, the old lady's grey, the
younger one's a yellowish brown, but the same heads, both with a great
vein bisecting their foreheads and drowsy, stunned eyes. Neither one
was much to look at.

The preacher unhitched his trailer. He and two rangy, paste-faced
girls unfolded long hinged roof sections. With a squalling scrape of raw
edge on wood they opened out side walls; the minister ducked into the
hollow structure and released the hooks that held up the floor sections
which dropped in place and rested on cinder blocks the girls had put
down.

"Son-of-a-baby, I'll be god-damn," said Nils.

"Take not the name of the Lord in vain, brother. Yep! There she is, a
traveling house, sleeps six people comfortable when she's set up. Look
inside and you'll see a good-sized living room. Got a good old kitchen,
two bedrooms. She's designed to travel, to be set down in this system of
traveling house parks right across the country, a national system, all
alike, neat as a pin, let you go off in any direction with your good little
old traveling house, with all these people traveling out to California and
New York and Florida. Hello, Sonny," he said to Ivar. "I bet you like to
cut up some, don't you? Well, I'm bad to cut up myself."

"What park system is that," said Nils. "Haven't heard a thing about
it here."

"Well, the parks ain't built yet, but they will be after Eisenhower's
road system gits finished. It come to me after prayer. The traveling
houses are going good. I got a franchise, preach the word of God, interest people in these fine little houses. There's a million need them."

The wife and the mother had gone inside with the boxes. Ivar could
hear them talking as they clattered stacks of dishes into the folding cupboards.

"We spend most of our time on the road," said Howard Poplin.
"What I predict is within ten years half the country is going to be living
in mobile housing, rolling homes. It's oppressive property taxes that's
doing it. You build you a house and settle in to raise a family and right
away they're after you with them old taxes. You are in their claws, can't
get loose, when you got a fixed house. Mean people move in next door,
shout and fight all night, their dog barks his brains out and there's not
a thing you can do. They put up a racetrack and a dance hall across the
street and you just got to take it. Plus the cost of building such a fixed
house is terrible, and the experts say that's because of the labor unions;
they've put up the cost to where it's almost ten thousand dollars to build

a simple six-room house. This little travel house is just as American as a thing can be. It's against taxation. It's *for* freedom and independence. It appeals to the pioneer instinct."

"It sounds like good sense," said Nils. Howard Poplin showed them inside. The walls were varnished plywood, wrinkled red-check curtains at the windows. The floor bounced under his feet and the whole place was echoing and dark.

"Whyn't you give Sonny here a nice cookie," Poplin said to his wife. Ivar was allowed to accept a stale raisin cookie from the woman. The pulse in her forehead beat.

"The only trouble I ever had with this travel trailer is when a big tractor truck ripped the side offn it on a narrow bridge, but being as it's only made of wood, I fixed it up again in half a hour. Now look here at this," said the man, back outside, hauling down a flat canvas bag tied to the roof of the car. He drew out a long wooden triangle and unfolded it into a three-sided shape.

"Grab ahold," he said to the girls, and they scrambled onto the roof of the house and he passed it up to them. They set it in blocks and fastened it with hooks and eyes and it became a steeple. The banner came next and Howard Poplin hung it above the front door. "ATOMIC POWER TRAILER CHURCH OF JESUS! We Believe in the Signs! We Come to You!"

"I bet that's the first traveling church *you* ever seen," he said to Ivar.

Conversion

"What time is it?" Nils asked himself in the dark. He couldn't make out the green glowing clock hands.

"Oh," he mumbled, pulling the light string, "it's—it's two A.M. And what the hell is that? Sounds like pigs being butchered." He sat up, swung his legs over the edge of the bed and began to haul on his pants. "By god, if there's hog thieves out there—"

Elise woke up, pulled the pillow off her head. "What in the world is happening?"

"It's that goddamn preacher with his folding church. I don't know what he's doing down there—listen!" There was a distant roar of voices as though a crowd were fleeing a catastrophe.

"Don't you know I had enough of this here you letting strangers set up so near? You don't know if you're going to wake up getting murdered on your pillow. You tell him to get off this here land. I wouldn't of let him on the land. Sick unto death of it. That time you let them gypsies stay down there, remember that, way they dug up all them rosebushes and carried them away after singing them funeral songs all night? They give me some sass about not pouring boiling water on ants, said ants was our friends, don't harm 'em. The tramp I caught in the kitchen scrounging around in the jars? And made like to put his hand on me? Oh, I don't know how I put up with it." She heaved back into the pillow and pulled the quilt over her head. "It was a bad mistake to marry a man who chews tobacco while he dances," she said, but Nils did not hear a word of the muffled sentence. He'd stopped hearing it four or five thousand times ago.

As he walked down the lane he could see electric lights strung up around the folding house and hear the thump of a generator. Drawing close, he made out a fringe of people swaying in front of the traveling church. Where had they come from? he wondered. Not from around here those angular women with caved-in chests and stony faces, men as gaunt as Texas longhorns, all of them rocking back and forth and watching Harold Poplin, a bible in his right hand, who stood under the raw lightbulbs, covered in rattlesnakes. Snakes twisted around his neck, up his coat sleeves and into his shirt, snakes curled up the legs of his bag-kneed pants, dripped from his fingers like frozen oil. A post with a board nailed on top of it was his altar.

"Mark sixteen eighteen!" he screamed. "They shall take up serpents and if they drink any deadly thing it shall not hurt them. They shall lay hands on the sick and they shall RECOVER. Not 'feel better by and by,' not 'show some improvement' after taking costly medicines and paying for costly X-rays and doctor bills. NO! Jesus SAID, 'they shall lay hands on the sick and they shall RE, amen, COV, amen, ER!' AMEN! THAT is what we're here to do tonight, lay hands on the sick, on the sick, so they shall RECOVER. That is why you have brought your feeble and ailing family members here tonight. Friends, I been all up and down this land with the Atomic Power Trailer Church of Jesus, traveling all over from California to Florida in this house of the Lord, laying hands on the sick so they shall RECOVER. And straight across the country and down it too, wherever I been, like a boat that leaves a white wake behind it I leave a wake of people who were sick once but have now RECOVERED. Over in Balk, Kansas, a mother brought her baby to me. That baby hadn't moved for two days, that baby was as limp and grey as an old dishrag, and I smoothed my hand—like this— up one side of that baby and down the other, and that child opened its eyes and said, 'Mama, I'm thirsty.' Yes, that's right. 'Mama, I'm thirsty.' And I watched her give that baby a sip of water, the first taste of water in TWO DAYS. My friends, that baby was on the road to RECOVERY. A man not ten miles from this very spot came up to me, an elderly man with two canes, he could hardly hobble along. 'Reverend Poplin,' he says, 'Reverend Poplin, I'm crippled with rheumatiz, I was threw from a horse as a young man, I been gnawed by the frosts of winter and lost my toes in a blizzard, an axe took my left thumb, the cataracts are dimming my eyes and I live in a state of sorrow because my wife is dead. Can you help me?' 'No, sir, I can not,' I replied, 'for you are not sick but old.' The BIBLE says, 'I have been young and now am old. It comes to all of us.' So those of you out there suffering from the effects of age, which is a different thing than being sick, accept your lot and look forward to the glory of Jesus. For nothing will make you young again. 'I have been young and now am old.' It's just common sense. But if your trouble is sickness, well, here we are. Now look at this sick young boy, he's got polio and he can't walk, but we're going to help him RECOVER with the help of ATOMIC POWER prayer and Jesus. I call it ATOMIC POWER prayer because prayer has the strength of the atom bomb, prayer can move mountains, we all know this."

With amazement Nils saw that the boy Mrs. Poplin was leading across the stage, the child shuffling uncertainly and clinging to her shoulder yet moving inexorably toward her snake-festooned husband, was his own son, seven-year-old Ivar, whom he had believed home in bed asleep.

"Ivar!" he said, but did not shout because the boy was inside Harold Poplin's embrace and snakes were coiling around his neck, slithering down his arm to drip onto the floor. Poplin held one arm over the child.

"See how white and puny this boy is? He is barely standing up, you saw how he couldn't walk without the help of my assistant, his legs are crippled, no strength, his back is twisted so's he resembles a eggbeater when he tries to walk, they give him six months to live. Think of it! Six more months of life for this precious youth who may have been destined to discover a important scientific cure and invent a process that turns grass into gold and manna. This boy needs PRAYER, ATOMIC PRAYER. InthenameofourfatherLordJesusChristhealthispoorsickafflictedboyandmakehimwellllethimRECOVERandbewelllethimgoforthandmultiplyandinventsomegreatdiscoveryorcureanddevotehislifetoJesusChristand theministryoftheatomicpowertrailerCHURCHAAAMEN. Now, son, see if you can walk." And the man collected his snakes from Ivar who took two uncertain steps, then skipped, laughing and waving his arms, to the shadows at the side.

The crowd groaned and wept, some cried out, and Harold Poplin was shouting that the collection plate was coming through, give what they could to do the work of Jesus Christ and help the traveling church get across the land.

The thrashing

Ivar was pocketing the five-dollar bill Mrs. Poplin had given him with thanks, when a demonic thing he did not at once recognize as his father burst into the circle of light and shoved the woman staggering, seized Ivar in his callused hands, and dragged him close with hissing threats, tore the bill from his pocket and threw it on the ground. He shouted at Poplin to get his filthy crook's rig off his property, promised them the sheriff within half an hour. Ivar wept and twisted and tried to escape the hard grip but that was useless. Nils was in the fury of his life.

Back at the barn, he beat Ivar with his fists, lashed him with a length of rusty cable that laid the boy's back open on the first blow and kept on until a vertebra jutted white from the bloody pulp. The shrieks and cries stopped as Ivar fell unconscious, but Nils beat on, shouting incoherently about laziness and ruin, lies and perfidy, criminal instinct, and it was his shouting that brought Elise from the house, trailing her old chenille robe in the mud. When she saw what he had done, was doing, she did not try to stop him with cries or protestations but seized the five-foot iron crowbar that stood in the corner and brought it down on his head.

She turned away from her dead husband, shaking and trembling, knelt to pick up Ivar.

"Let me help you," said a soft voice, and Howard Poplin came in, half crouching, his necktie dangling loose.

"He's dead," she mumbled. "I killed him." Poplin knelt beside the body of Nils, glanced at the great wound in the head glistening with running blood.

"You tend to the boy," said Poplin. "The boy will live. I'll stay here and pray over this man." His necktie moved and she saw it was a snake. She was numb to it; nothing could move her but the child, shuddering against her.

Howard Poplin stayed in the barn with Nils all night, praying, wrapping the snake around him, laying his papery hands on Nils's brow, and when morning came, both of them emerged from the barn, Nils staggering but with the rattlesnake twined around his arm and looping across his chest.

"I preached to him. I whirled the snake over and around him. I prayed in the name of the Father, the Son and the Holy Sperit that his life be restored. He come to and seen the Truth, reckanized his sinful past, seen he had to follow the signs, he heard me, he tooken up the snake and he is here to live and tell about it. Amen. And I ain't just whistling 'Dixie.' "

So they both lived, the boy Ivar, halting and silent, sent with his brother, Conrad, to live with Elise's sister; and Nils, converted, believing Howard Poplin had returned him to life after his wife murdered him. In a year Nils had taken to fearlessly handling hot kerosene lamp globes and picking up rattlesnakes himself, staring in their eyes, swallowing a pinch of Death to Rats with his tea, never once bitten or poisoned, because he had faith. He discarded his Lutheran upbringing as a soiled and rent shirt. He invited Poplin to stay for a year and preach, promised him he would build him a church, and when the preacher refused, saying he had to travel on, was doing the Lord's business, Nils promised to paint a message on the silo where all who passed by on the road could see it. As for his murderer, Nils bided his time. She spent each weekend at her sister's house with Ivar and Conrad, one wordless and cringing, the other a big eater, impatient and clumsy. Nils never accompanied her, behaved as though the boys were dead.

(Later Howard Poplin invested the church money in the design and manufacture of a camper vehicle he called The Conqueror and made an immense fortune. He is still alive, somewhere in Florida, but calls himself Happy Jack now.)

A little help

Nils's chance came twenty years later when a cancer grew in Elise's belly. She shriveled down to stick arms and legs, her shins covered with sores that would not heal, and between the slat ribs and jutting pelvis rose a great tumor-swollen belly, like a last grotesque pregnancy. The pain was savage, yet when Conrad telephoned on Sunday she told him in a steady voice that she was turning the corner, planning a big chicken dinner, thinking about going to Minneapolis to buy a nightgown, and was Ivar all right? When she was better, she said, she wanted to take a trip, see some of the country.

All through the dusty summer the sun rose pouring heat on the unshaded house, and as the heat filled the twisted bedsheets like some thermal gas, so the pain filled the room like rising water, just a thin shimmer across the floor, then lapping at the legs of the bedside table, rising slowly, inexorably, until it washed across her fiery bed like beach waves, growing in height and violence, long combers of pain shot through with sand and bristly kelp, flooding the bed and rising higher, up the walls, the deep weight of it weakening the walls and floor until at midday the room overflowed with it, saturating the ceiling, spurting out between the shoddy clapboards and trickling down the outside of the house to pool in the dust and runnel the driveway. Now it was impossible for her to breathe beneath the deep ocean of pain and she gasped and choked, "help! Nils, help, oh please, help, help me. Oh, help, help." And in the afternoon the pain began to boil and bubble; she was a fish dropped living into a cauldron. Her skin split open like a ripe tomato, the muscles convulsed and tightened against the bones; as the boiling liquid seeped into the marrow of her spinal column, she arched and cried until the vocal cords failed, *help, help, help, help . . .*

Nils summoned other followers of the signs to come in and pray over her. They tossed serpents to one another, sang and struck the tambourine, the anointing came over all in the room but one, Elise, and they spoke in tongues while she moaned *help, help,* but nothing worked right and a young man from the next farm died of drinking the rat poison, and it was clear Elise's time was coming. Yet how slowly.

When the phone rang on Sunday he picked up the receiver, said, she's sleeping, into Conrad's ear, and hung up.

One morning Nils felt the sun's heat when he put his hand on the bedroom wall. The house was silent in the warm morning, the heat coming up, no sound from the spare room where Elise lay. "Oh Lord," he mumbled, "let her be dead in the night, let her be taken home in the night and have it over and ended." He got up, staggered along to the bathroom where he stood in front of the toilet waiting for his water to start, but the ruined petcock wouldn't open until he turned the sink faucet to get the idea across. Still nothing from Elise. He sloughed out to the kitchen and put the kettle on. He wouldn't look in her room, wouldn't risk breaking the fine silence until he'd had the cup of tea. Oh let her be taken to the Lord in the night. The sun struck through the window over the sink. A hot square fell on the refrigerator, showing up the trails of spilled food, his greasy handprints. The water boiled and he poured it onto the tea bag in his chipped cup, waited impatiently until it went a strong reddish brown, dribbled in the milk, but the milky tan was disturbed by fine curds precipitated by the acid brew. The milk must be on the turn. Never mind, he thought, and sucked it in, hot and rank with spoiled milk. There it was. The first moan trembling behind the door cheating him of the blessed silence. "*Help. Help.*"

He wouldn't bear it any longer. Anger swelled over guilt and pity. He strode out the front door and went around to the back. *Help me.* The splitting axe was in the block by the chicken coop. He passed it by, went into the shed where his old broadaxe stood, seized the helve, felt the head to see if it was loose—a little—and went inside. "Here is your help," he said and struck.

"If I Had the Wings of an Angel"

There was blood all over the room. Elise had been full of blood, gallons of it, purple red, and it spattered, gushed, drenched. It dripped noisily and some kind of gurgling was louder than the silenced cries. Silence evaded him. So close, but not yet achieved.

He climbed up to the top of the silo on the outside ladder and sprang toward heaven, knowing that Jesus would catch him or there would be hell to pay.

The oldest son, Conrad, cried like a cloudburst when they brought the news.

"She wanted to go on an Elderhostel trip to Alaska if she went into remission," he sobbed. "She never had a chance to go anywhere. That bastard."

But Ivar only nodded and kept on scraping paint off an old table, the kind of response you'd expect from someone they said was more or less retarded.

The light of fear

Ivar's shack was dark, on the dark end of town. When he put out his light at night the place was swallowed up in darkness, the greensick leaves smoked leaden, the shadows like gigantic rolls of black wool. He could move soundlessly over his paths, knowing the stones by memory and touch, his hearing perked sharp and nostrils flared for the smell of weasel hair or fox breath, sensing without seeing the loom of posts as do the blind. And sometimes he threw himself down in the damp grass with the beetles and watched the blinking sky, always found the pleasure soured by the orange wash of streetlights from the village, the sky abuzz and streaked with planes and satellites and, too often, the gnashing clatter of a helicopter; in short, the darkness destroyed. He said what he thought to his dog, Rock, a rough-made animal with weak eyes who accepted Ivar's harangues as conversation, for the man was voluble in privacy.

"Here we got a whole country afraid of the dark, millions of people never seen the stars or sky except on TV where it's blazing rockets and comets hanging off the name of a laundry. We get born in a bright light, raised up with nightlights and headlights and streetlights and lighted signs and lighthouse lights on skyscrapers and store windows blazing all night long, lights in refrigerators and in watches, clocks that shine in the dark, headlights, airplane lights, fountain pen flashlights, keys with high beams, in the houses at night all kinds of little red and green eyes shining out of the telephone and the television and the security system and the hot water heater and the stove and the switch plate. Then comes the worst damn thing, Christmas, flashing it up in windows and on trees, on roofs, wrapped around houses, dangled all over the main street, every cheap gas station looks like the *Titanic* going down." He named safety lights and farmyard lights, walkway lights, Americans' sucking need for light, the darkness banished to space and the crazy craving for luminescence translated into burning fires all over the world, furnaces fueled with coal, wood chips, oil, gas, uranium, electricity generated by windmills and solar panels, the rise and fall of tides, turbines moved by dammed rivers and nuclear fission. Trees, fluids, gases, ores, air, sunlight, all transmuted to blades of light whetted to lance the black boil of night.

Ivar's break

Ivar's setup was this: long tables of sawhorses and planks beside the road, a display of scavenged goods, pitchers, canning jars, bits of iron-mongery, each fluttering a white tag on a white cotton string, the price marked with ballpoint pen; an easel sign that blew over in the wind announced FLEA MARKET & ANTIQUES. He turned a good dollar from the travelers and tourists and kept quiet about it. Let them think he was Crazy Ivar living on fried grasshoppers.

When Waldemar Sulk of Sulk Funerals died in 1988, his daughter came back to town to take care of things, her damp white face screwed into a pained expression. The place seemed unchanged since her child-hood; the Toole sisters might still be in the bushes ready to scream "yah yah Patty, Dead People Fatty!" and "yah yah, Sani-Flush, brush yer teeth with the toilet brush!" mortifying her out of Old Glory as soon and as far as she could get.

She walked helplessly through the musty, stinking rooms, that gag-ging smell that had seeped into the clothes and bedding, sofas and newspapers, into the kitchen cupboards, flavoring oatmeal and shred-ded wheat, rice and butter, scenting the curtains and carpets and childhood itself. Out on the sagging porch she stood in the river mist and smoked a cigarette, locked her gaze on her car as though she had never seen it before, stared at the rotting porch boards. A few cars went past, the occupants turning their heads to look at her. She could imagine them saying, who's that on Sulk's porch, must be the daughter, don't you think, pity she couldn't make it when the old man was still alive, but then she didn't make it for her mother either, hard as glass, that one.

Wacky Ivar came down the street, pushing his cart, almost empty except for a few clinking beer bottles. He sucked gently on a cherry Life Saver, a sharp little ring almost at the point of dissolution. He watched the woman run her left hand through her dyed, frizzy hair, slap dandruff from her black-suited shoulders, scrape bits of French Creme polish from her nails.

He drifted up to the porch, whistling a single note.

"What you gonna do with all the stuff in there?"

"I don't know. I don't know. It smells awful."

"That's the embalming fluid, I'd say."

She thought yes, and the cigars and the whiskey and the dirty old clothes and the yellow sheets and the rat turds and the crusty pans and the stinking old cats.

"It's a nightmare." She fingered her watch without looking at it. "The house isn't worth nothing. Who'd want to buy a stinking old house here? If it burned down, save me some trouble. Who'd buy it, smelling like it does?" She looked east—the direction of Minneapolis.

"I can take the furniture off your hands," said Ivar. "You don't think there's anything you can get for the building, donate it, donate it to the fire department for burning-down practice, you don't want it to stand empty, the kids get in there and smoke dope and get diseases, you'd get in touch with Leo Pauster, the fire chief, take the tax deduction, then you got you a nice clean lot you can realize something on."

It was good advice and the daughter took it. She signed a bill of sale to Ivar for the contents of the house, received a crumpled dollar bill and a promise of immediate action, and drove off to call the fire chief and get the hell out of Old Glory.

(During her return journey a freight train derailed near the state line, crashing from an overhead trestle onto the highway. The backed-up traffic caught her in a three-hour jam; she blamed her dead father. She began to have trouble making choices. There were too many flavors of cat food; shapes and sizes and brands of ballpoint pens; kinds and sizes of shampoo; types of canned tomatoes—whole, crushed, sauce, paste; panty hose and tights in countless shades with control tops or glitter legs, sheer or opaque, in dozens of fibers, with reinforced toes and crotches or not, petite, queen, tall, regular and irregular; brands of toothpaste; shapes and bristle grades of toothbrushes; sheets in thread counts from 180 to 320, a hundred colors, floral, striped, dotted, cartoon figured, linen, damask, Egyptian cotton, checked, satin, embroidered, monogrammed, flannelette; too many apple cultivars; soft drinks from finger sips to gallon jugs, and juices and water from uncountable pure springs; and the stores themselves, surreal, brightly lighted, cloned in extravagant malls, the source of tedious and endless choices that were no choices at all. A year to the day after her father's death, on her way to northern Michigan to see a client—she was a spirit channeler for an ice age hunter who gave advice on domestic problems through her—she suffered a panic attack on the Mackinac Bridge, stopped a third of the way across and froze, hands clenching the wheel, her head on her knuckles, terrified of seeing the hard, crenelated water below. Traffic hissed and roared around her, horns blared and she could not move. She was weeping and trembling when a middle-aged woman opened the door and nudged her into the passenger seat. "I'll drive you across," the woman said cheerfully. "I work for the bridge authority. You're not the only one, it happens all the time. Truckdrivers, even those big guys on Harleys. It's nothing to be ashamed of.")

What Ivar found

Ivar was three weeks at the dirty work of emptying the funeral home. He sold all the ancient embalming equipment and the back issues of *Today's Funeral Director* to the Museum of the Mortuary Arts in Minot, North Dakota. He climbed a rickety ladder to the attic, prowled the churned kitchen, he cracked open musty bedrooms like eggs, shuffled around the rooms dragging bureaus and chests away from the wall, lifting them, his fingers clamped, embracing each piece as though it were a wooden bride. He rented a U-Haul with cash from his secret reserve and day after day carried off the stuff: a rolltop desk, four glass-fronted bookcases crammed with first editions of the books of Jack London, six Stickley chairs in fumed oak, the soapstone sink. He took some things to his repair shop, a ground-floor room that he rented for twenty dollars a month in the abandoned woolen mill.

In Sulk's attic he found bundles of yellowed racist newspapers, *The Klansman's Kall, Pure America, White Knight,* sold them to the American Civil Liberties Union library. He spray-painted hundreds of wire hangers lime green and flashpoint red and unloaded them at local dry cleaners, a dollar per fifty, removed the old pull-chain toilet and griffin-footed bathtub which went for a good price to the Wolf Pelt Inn in Hiawatha Falls. Unusable bits he tossed into an upstairs room—cracked plastic belts, torn overshoes, broken plastic eyeglass frames, unmatched buttons, a box of fishhooks rusted into a single barbed block.

He began his examination of the undersides of the tables and bureau drawers, found a twenty-dollar bill taped under the kitchen table, more twenties pinned to the back of the chifforobe with rusty thumbtacks. The old man's reeking mattress was a cornucopia.

He emptied the house, then prised away baseboards, crawled over the floors pulling at boards, groped in unused chimney flues, steamed off wallpaper (some of the wallpaper had value to decorators needing purple plumes and deep stripes) where the wall bulged slightly. His vigor was rewarded with wads of cash totaling eight thousand dollars, a jar of Kennedy half-dollars.

By the end of 1989 Ivar had made $111,999 profit from his dollar investment. He bought the old woolen mill on the river and branched out into used furniture just as hundreds of savings and loan banks failed. From the offices and lobbies of the ruined banks came a bonanza of fine furniture: walnut desks with silver fittings, hand-rubbed cherry filing cabinets, teak customer service desks, bleached oak magazine tables, computer workstations in Finnish birch. He filled three floors with this rich stuff, which was not perfect, for many drawers were fretted where executives had clawed at the wood with their nails while listening to bad news on the telephone.

It was the foundation of his fortune. One hand of his business clenched on old Victorian houses, dismantled them and sold walnut library panels, stained-glass windows, portico columns, fretwork, balusters, and claw-footed tubs in the great house-building boom. Another picked up choice designer office furniture and garden statuary. His Out West Antiques chain, regional emporia with false fronts and hitching posts, showcases crammed with spurs, barbwire lengths for collectors, ten-gallon hats, cow skulls, he supplied through cross-country rambles to country auctions, picking through pawnshops and small-town second-hand stores. With him traveled Devil Basswood, a specialist in Americana who had once worked for Sotheby's, twenty-nine years old and dressed in Giorgio Armani pleated silk trousers, a collarless Russian shirt and white braces. A semitrailer followed them and when it was filled Devil called for another empty. (Basswood drowned in the winter when his ice-boat plunged into a lead of open water in Lake Vermilion.)

By his forty-eighth birthday Ivar owned a ranch in Montana, a beach house in Tahiti, but he looked very much the same, the long dusty ropes of hair hanging over the shoulders of his soiled linen jacket, his feet in black sneakers. He still picked up unclaimed deposit cans in his path, still took an interest in wrecked bikes. In a ragged Montana town too small to spit at he bought the contents of the Little Boy Blue Pawnshop, including an aged saddle stamped on the cantle with the maker's name, A. D. Seitzler & Co., Silver City, New Mexico, ropes and shepherds' crooks, a magazine rack with a carved bowlegged cowboy on the side, a beehive radio with speaker fabric in a honeycomb design, a basket of tarnished spoons and an old green accordion as misshapen as though a horse had stepped on it. The promising items went to his research center for identification and evaluation (in this way he recovered a lost Remington painting of a cavalry charge, and the carved magazine rack turned out to be a desirable piece by the crabby and eccentric Thomas Molesworthy). The worn spoons were good for nothing but the silver smelter, and the accordion went to the dollar bargain table in his Old Glory warehouse, open twenty-four hours, day and night, a mecca for collectors who drove hundreds of miles to see what they could find in the bins of junk.

Underground

Elise Gasmann was only one of an extraordinary number of Old Glory inhabitants diagnosed with various cancers. The town's fatigue rate was far above the national average; men slumped for long periods of time in front of their television sets, women lurched to their jobs, nodding off in the commuter vans. Alarmed health officials visited outlying farms, taking soil, water and air samples, testing the local corn and hogs. Someone thought of the limestone caves beneath the black soil. Many people had complained over the years of hearing a low-pitched hum coming from underground that in certain seasons deepened to a ceaseless grinding as if nonstop subterranean trains were rolling to hell, as members of the Pentecostal Holiness Church believed, or harsh winds were blowing through a resonating underground chamber, as the town historian conjectured. The state sent its geologist down and she in turn summoned teams of scientists who came with odd equipment and reported that indeed a low-level sound was coming from under the caves, a steady vibration of seventeen cycles per second, an accompanying harmonic of seventy cycles per second, and pulsing overtones of much higher frequencies, of unknown cause; certainly it was scientifically intriguing. In addition, there were dangerously high levels of radon gas in the caves leaking into the basements of Old Glory. The town made a rush to sell, to move out. Houses begun were never finished, their skeleton frames casting scribbled shadows, the piles of brick and sand on the sites sprouting fireweed.

Ivar's brother Conrad Gasmann

"That's why we got them damn white pheasants. The radon." Conrad Gasmann, sitting at the table in the old Gasmann farmhouse with his wife, Nancy, spit an unchewable piece of bacon rind onto his plate and tossed his head to throw back the grey curl that hung over his forehead. He had the long and bulbed nose of his father, Nils, ice-blue eyes set close enough together to give him a squirrelly look, and ears that lay close to his head. The farm had been deeded to both brothers, but Ivar, after requesting a day alone in the house, sold his share to Conrad who got rid of the land except for the four acres surrounding the house and kept on working for Rudy Henry at the gas company. (When his daughter, Vela, was small, he told her he had to work there because his name was Gasmann. Then, when they hired John Roop, he told her Roop was the name of a rare invisible gas that made birds fly.) With the house he inherited a photograph of dead Aunt Floretta in her Wild West regalia sitting on a stump in a flurry of aspen leaves, her white-blond braids descending from an enormous white cowboy hat, her gloved hand resting on a braided lariat, a little heel spur catching the light, and, in a holster on her right hip, a pearl-handled revolver supplied by the photographer.

"You know it makes me sick when you do that, spit your food out. Why do you do that?" said Nancy, breathing through her mouth, winding a curl around her index finger. "Listen at that wind. Supposed to gust to sixty, they said on the radio. Change the weather, sure enough." She threw down the folded paper. "This's the worst, a crossword puzzle that's nothing but Asian rivers and golf players from the nineteen thirties."

"Where's Vela?"

"I don't know, somewheres outside. I don't know how she can stand that wind. Why?"

Conrad's voice was as kittenish as it got. "Ah, I thought we might go up in the bedroom for a little while, lay down and take a nap." His loose, soft stomach trembled beneath his knitted shirt.

"The day you want a nap. I know you, and you don't want a nap any more than you want cancer."

"Don't get back on that subject again. I had about all the hearing about cancer I can stand. Come on, get in that bedroom." He whacked her behind. She slapped back but followed him into the dim room (it was the room where his parents had slept, redecorated by Nancy with a sparkling textured ceiling and orange striped wallpaper), the sheets and covers still snarled from the night and smelling of their bodies, and the wind whistling shrilly at the window joints.

"Of course, right at the climax, that's when our kid got her arms cut off," Nancy whispered a year later to her sister.

The Home Away

With some of Vela's insurance money they'd had insulation blown into the old house, a thousand dollars' worth of the stuff, a two-thousand-dollar oil furnace installed, storm windows upstairs, and it was still so cold in the bedroom in winter he could see his breath. Nancy had wanted to fix over the kitchen, a cramped hole with drain problems and curling linoleum, but Conrad said, better wait.

He scraped at the back window, got a look at the white corrugated fields. On the other side of the room the sun had melted the frost enough to show the spraddle of buildings and grain elevators along the road, the billboard hand-painted by the Lutheran Women's Circle showing a three-year-old child's face, golden curls and a single black tear on the cheek like a beauty mark—ABORTION STILLS A BEATING HEART—the Conoco station in the distance, the river, and on the other side, Ivar's warehouse and parking lot. There was a ruffling lump of something on the macadam, right on the yellow line. A dead raven, must of got hit picking at carrion. Dick Cude's blue pickup went by, swerved to hit the carcass, sending up a few feathers. He watched the truck, saw it slow at the diner, the Home Away.

Out of the blue he wanted a slab of cherry pie and a mug of perked coffee, not granola and instant in Nancy's arty glass cups. For years he'd had his coffee and pie at Chippewa Willy's Grill, but he could see there was a good crowd at the Home Away morning after morning.

He got mad all over again looking at the old silo as he drove past, thought for the thousandth time that he would get up there this summer and paint the damn thing out, the big peeling picture of Jesus with a snake in each hand standing in front of a house trailer. For that matter, pull the silo down. Empty for years. Snow crystals on the clumps of roadside grass like crusted salt. Past the signs OLD GLORY BELIEVES IN GOD AND AMERICA, DO YOU? and THIS IS A CHILD WATCH COMMUNITY.

He sat next to Dick Cude in the last empty place. Cude's clothes smelled of some noxious washday detergent perfume. The restaurant was full, half the farmers in town in for the breakfast they couldn't get at home, for the pleasure of ordering and getting two meaty pork chops and home fries and two over easy instead of a load of crap and whiny complaints. What the hell was wrong with Nancy that she couldn't put a decent breakfast together? She knew he loved Spanish omelets, but how often did he get one? Father's Day, and no other time. Breakfast in bed, a Spanish omelet, and a few other things. The rest of the time it was "cook it yourself." Was it just Nancy?

"Dick, what d'you get for breakfast when you eat at home?"

The man lifted his red face, the granulated complexion as though sprinkled with hot sugar.

"Frozen waffles. We got a freezer full of frozen waffles. I can have frozen waffles with margarine and corn syrup and some kind of artificial cream comes in a tub. Could be worse, could be Jell-O. How you, Mrs. Rudinger? Guess I'll have the special."

"You sure? You know there's turnip mash this morning, and not everybody likes turnip." She gave the U.P.S. man a hard look, dropped her glance to the mound of turnip on his plate.

"Sure as snow I love turnip. Gimme some fried onions too." A photograph of Mrs. Rudinger hung behind the cash register, showed her standing in front of a venetian blind holding a burning paper—the mortgage—in a pair of spaghetti tongs. Over the door the head of a six-point buck she had shot in 1986 waggled when someone came in.

"Comes with it. Liver, onions, turnip mash, two corn muffins and coffee. You want coffee?"

"I rather have milk. If I can get it." He turned to Conrad, used his sympathetic voice.

"How's your kid doing?"

"She's coming along pretty good, I guess. Goes in to the therapist twice a week, got all this equipment in the house. She spends a lot of time listening to tapes, we got her a Walkman when she was in the hospital. Seems like she wants a new tape ever other day and it gets expensive."

Two Guatemalan agricultural laborers got up, paid for their eggs and walked out. Mrs. Rudinger's new waitress came past, refilling coffee cups.

"What is she," said Dick Cude when she was out of earshot, "Chinese or Vietnamese or what?"

"I think she's Korean," said Conrad. "That's what's the matter, the country's sinking under these people—chinks and spicks, and pakis and those aye-rabs from the Middle of the East. It's not the same thing as when our grandparents come over; they were white, they had guts, a good work ethic, didn't go around blowing up buildings. These are not white people. They're swarthy, they're mongrels. It's simple—the country's filled up, there's not enough room, not enough jobs to go around."

"Well, anyway," said Dick Cude, "we got a lot of tapes at home. You know, from my sister after Russell—I could bring some of them over. It's time to let somebody else enjoy them. What kind of music she like? I hope she don't go for this here Nigro rap shit with the dirty lyrics. I won't let it in the house."

"Nah. What she likes—look, it sounds funny, but what she's going for is Lawrence Welk, all that old cornball stuff. A lot of it is on tapes now. I don't know what she sees in it, but she listens to it by the hour. That stuff was stale before I was born. That bubbly-bubbly champagne music. It's just a damn joke. Nursing home music. But that's what she likes. It's cheerful, that's why, I think. Nancy's planning to take her down to Disney World when she's strong enough, hear that Disney World polka band, they got a terrific band, lot of accordions."

"She'll grow out of it. After what the kid's been through, I guess she can listen to anything she wants. Tell you something about polka, this disc jockey in St. Paul a couple months ago said just offhand on the air that listeners could send in the names of their favorite polka bands, see? And in three days he got twenty-eight thousand postcards. Hey, we're watching old movies the other night, *Arsenic and Old Lace,* it's a special on Frank Capra movies. They said he used to play the squeezebox, showed a clip of him doing it. Jimmy Stewart, Joan Crawford, they all played. Hollywood's favorite instrument. How about Myron Floren? I got some Myron Floren. He used to play with Lawrence Welk. How about Frankie Yankovic? '*Roll out the barrel . . .*' How about Whoopee John Wilfahrt? That New Ulm stuff? There's one of them old seventy-eights of that woman accordion, Violet, Viola Turpeinin? Finnish woman. Boy, could she play. Dead now, I suppose. Beautiful stuff, some of that old Scandahoovian music, but you don't hear it much now except at them festivals, your good time there, but you don't hear it in ordinary life like when I was a kid. My dad's father could play it. He used to work with some Finns, there was a song they sang, something about a mailman. God damn, it was funny. We still got the old Hardanger fiddle, all cracked, a course. A course, that old-time music now, seems a lot of people is interested in it, you know, the Finns, the Swedes, the Croatians, all them, but you ask me, it's like pumping blood into a corpse." He wanted to say he knew something about accordions, damage and grief, but Conrad wouldn't want to hear that.

"Well, it's that sound that gets her, not no particular bunch a people. She says it makes her feel in a good mood. She told the therapist that if she got any use back in her hands she wanted to learn to play the accordion."

"Yeah? They think that's gonna happen?"

"No."

"Well. It's a miracle she's still alive. It's a miracle they could sew them back on. I mean it. The paper said only the second one they done it on. Imagine sewing all them little blood vessels back together and joining the muscles? I don't see how they done it. She's a tough, tough little kid. Somebody up there's looking out for her. I wish He could have looked out for Russell. I suppose she goes to one of them help groups, they got them for everything—Gamblers Anonymous, Overeaters Anonymous, sexaholics, shoplifters. Seems like they got to have one for blind people and maimed people, don't it?"

Conrad looked at the clock. He knew where the conversation was going, didn't want to hear anything about blind Russell, dumped out of a bus in the desert. He had twelve minutes to get down to Old Glory Gas. He hoped Pitch was around to help load the tanks on the truck. Whatever, it beat listening to Dick Cude, the big red face bunching up as if he was going to cry any minute.

"What can I say," he said. "It's light in the day and dark at night. It's cold in the winter and warm in the summer. I'll see you," he said.

Dick finished his turnip and asked for more, watching Conrad gun his truck out of the parking lot, noticing that his seat belt wasn't fastened—what a fool to take the risk. He smoked too. Something heedless about that family. Whereas his sister had taken every care of Russell and again and again terrible things had happened to him. Dick finished his glass of milk, sorry that the toast had run out before the milk. He had a thought.

"Any rice puddin?"

"Not 'til lunch, Dick. There's very few eats rice puddin for breakfast."

He left her a dime and went out, waded into the freezing wind, strung now with fine snow, toward his truck in front of the post office, eight blocks down. He always parked there. The wind in his face was unpleasant enough for him to turn his head every few steps and walk blind. It was awful cold, he thought, and his hands were freezing, even with good warm gloves. The bank's digital thermometer read eight below but the wind had to be gusting to forty. He ducked into the store—Out West Antiques—to get warm, better there than the yarn

shop or the health food store, walked around looking at the tools: beautiful old mahogany planes, a well-balanced little tack hammer, some
wrought-iron hinges. He checked the junk table; usually it wasn't
worth looking at, but once he'd found a tiny brass spirit level with
fancy engraving on it, a cabinetmaker's level. Now he discovered a small
green accordion and took joy in the find. He'd get it for Conrad's girl
even if she could never play. She could listen to tapes and look at it and
pretend. He paid his dollar and carried the old thing out to the truck.

At home he thought he'd clean it up a little—in truth, it was a dirty
piece of work—and he put it in the sink, turned on the vegetable
sprayer, hit it with a good squirt of detergent. The damn thing took on
water. It was heavy now, though clean, but when he squeezed it not a
sound came out, even when he pushed all the buttons at once. He'd just
dry it out a little. He put it on the hot air register under the window.
Sure enough, it was dry by afternoon, and it was clean in a way that
showed up how old and beat the thing was. The bellows was nearly as
stiff as wood, you could only get a few inches of squeeze out of it and a
weird, shrill chord. He sprayed it with WD-40 inside and out but it
didn't seem to make any difference. What the hell, it was only for her to
look at.

Driving down to the diner the next morning, bumping over the railroad where a track gang was taking a break, wiping their mouths with
paper napkins, dropping their empty soft drink cans and paper coffee
cups into the trash bucket on the flatcar, he switched on the radio—it
was NPR; his wife had used the truck after supper—and heard John
Townley singing "Land's End" to the accompaniment of his rare Dip-
per Shantyman concertina of West Indian cocobolo wood and goatskin,
with handmade reeds, the ends fitted with nautical engravings of stout
mermaids and cresting waves, the air button a tiny arm of polished
bone which gleamed against the dark wood like the arm of a deus ex
machina. The rich, oboelike tones set off Townley's voice, but in
midsyllable, "and the great seas ro—," Dick shut him off. Those sea
songs ended only in drowning and forsakenness.

(His nephew, Russell, had been born blind, and the family considered it a mercy when he showed an aptitude for music. He learned to
play the accordion from an Italian woman, and his first solo piece was a
Swedish version of "Life in the Finnish Woods" before its transformation into "Mockingbird Hill." She gave him good advice: "try to
develop a sound all nationalities can identify with—that way you'll
never be out of work." By age thirteen he was playing a big square
Chemnitzer concertina, studded with six hundred rhinestones, in kid-

die contests and winning them all with his version of "Cattle Call," by way of Eddy Arnold out of a tune octogenarian Old Glorians knew as "The St. Paul Waltz." His father, anxious to see the kid bring in a little money, started booking him for the Friday entertainment hour at the local summer resorts. The Lake Hideaway belonged to his friend Harvey Westhold [born Waerenskjold] who abused and ravished Russell twenty minutes before his first performance.

"Go ahead, kid, take a quick shower. You smell. Can't play for a high-class crowd all sweaty like that. Here, I'll help you get your clothes off. The shower's right over here. *Uh-uh-uh-uh.* Don't say nothing about this or I'll kill you."

By the time he was twenty-one Russell was a troublemaker. Blind or not, he'd sneak out of the house at night and stand by the road until somebody picked him up. In town he played the concertina for drink and drugs, invited tattoo artists to "do what you want." These illustrations were banal, curious, some were obscene. He worked as a street musician in Minneapolis for a year or two, then, his mind frayed by chemistry, excesses, and the longing for something more, he bought a bus ticket for Las Vegas. Forty miles out from that destination and full of multicolored pills, he got to his feet, took a pistol from his concertina case and fired it into the roof. He was quickly overpowered by two women from the University of Ohio swim team. The bus driver pulled over and asked them to put him out. They prodded him forward and down the steps, lifted him, with his instrument, over a five-strand barbwire fence and left him in the desert. Nobody heard from him again.)

Boredom

It had happened because she was bored. She'd been in the yard, swinging a broom at the swallows. There were dozens of them under the eaves of the old barn and inside, tatty nests balanced on dusty beams or stuck up under the roof and for half the summer the birds tore in and out of openings, their beaks full of beetles, ants, wasps, spiders, flies, bees, moths and darning needles.

A thunderstorm to the north was approaching, a curled lofty plume with a dark wedge at the base, tongues of wind rushing violently out from it. The wind made her feel crazy and vigorous though she kept her back to it because of the dust it stirred up. But that's all it was, wind, thunder; somewhere to the north, rain would fall. She was bored; there was nothing to do in Old Glory, nothing ever to do at home with her stupid mother and father, and Sunday was the worst, just nothing,

nothing, nothing to do when the television wasn't working and there
was nowhere to go and nothing in the refrigerator to eat except a raw
turkey breast that had been there a week and stank. So she marked the
openings the swallows used and leaped up, swatting at them, pretending they were tennis balls and she was a girl champion. The wind gusts
flared, hissing and tearing at the leaves of the tree. She heard a truck
coming, rattling like it was going to fly apart, and she spun around
gracefully with the broom racket and saw Ed Kunky's black whiskers in
the smeary windshield and beside him his son Whitey, good-looking
Whitey, a class ahead of her, who made her daydream of sitting in a
kindergarten chair so that her skirt came down around her ankles like a
bell and he came over to her with something in his hands, it was never
clear what, a bunch of flowers or a rolled-up paper or a candy bar (a
Freudian analyst clarified this years later), but he bent over her and
leaned down and kissed her on the mouth, a kiss like a mosquito dap-
ping across her lips, across her hair at night, and in the daydream she
fainted. But now she held up the broom, wrestled it against the wind,
and she was primed to smack a swallow into the middle of next week.
No swallow came, the truck drew abreast and beyond, rattling and
banging with a load of jagged-edged metal roofing and flashing from
the old Knudsen barn to the north. Three swallows dived for high holes
in the wall, a ferocious gust caught up a piece of roofing as she leaped,
swinging the broom at the swallows. The sharp metal sailed across the
yard like a silvery flying guillotine and sheared off both of her up-
stretched arms above the elbows, smashed into her face, cutting and
breaking her nose.

The Kunkys didn't even notice they'd cut her arms off, drove up the
hill, shedding metal, and out of sight. She stood there, amazed, rooted,
seeing the grain of the wood of the barn clapboards, paint jawed away
by sleet and driven sand, the unconcerned swallows darting and reap-
pearing with insects clasped in their beaks looking like mustaches, the
wind-ripped sky, the blank windows of the house, the old glass casting
blue swirled reflections at her, the fountains of blood leaping from her
stumped arms, even, in the first moment, hearing the wet thuds of her
forearms against the barn and the bright sound of the metal striking.
But she couldn't look at the ground, wouldn't see her hands down there,
still curled as if grasping the broom.

She bellowed.

From her filled-to-straining lungs poured a great pealing shout, the
defiant roar at the end of life everyone wishes to give and few manage.
It lifted her parents off the bed like a spear from the springs.

Party

Conrad formed the habit of eating breakfast at the Home Away in less than a week. The food had savor, the place was cheerful, full of news and bustle. It was a relief not to hear his wife fussing over Vela. He loved his daughter, but he couldn't stand sick people, couldn't stand seeing her scar-laddered arms and hear her whining and panting when the physical therapist, a brown-headed woman with a baby voice and a huge rump, put her through the exercises. How easily his daughter and his wife wept. The house was damp and miserable with weeping.

He enfolded a ketchup-shot egg in a slice of toast and bit into it, mashed the other egg into his corned beef hash and asked Mrs. Rudinger for two jelly doughnuts. Dick Cude came in lugging a plastic garbage bag.

"What you got, Dick—your lunch?"

"No, it's for your girl. Seen your truck out front. You said she couldn't get enough of those old tapes? There's about fifty in there and I picked up a old accordion, found it at Ivar's, y'know, thought she might get a kick out of looking at it while she plays the tapes, y'know; even if she can only look at it, least it's something. It's a miracle. She's a tough little girl. Y'know, it was criminal, hauling sheet metal in that truck without any tarp or tie-downs. I don't see how Ed Kunky can look you in the eye. Criminal. Isn't his boy in school with Vela? I suppose you seen a lawyer about it." He handed the black sack to Conrad who was belching and suffering from the first doughnut.

"You hear the one about the guy got in a plane crash and everybody's killed but him? He's in some wild place, Alaska, I don't know. So he stumbles around for a week, not a sign of human beings, he's half crazy. Then he comes to a tree and there's a rope hanging down and on the end of it is a dead nigger. Guy says, 'praise God, civilization.' Get it?"

"Yeah. That's a southern joke. I heard it about a Chippewa. But it couldn't happen. There's no place in North America farther than twenty miles from a road. Nobody can be lost for a week. It was in *National Geographic*." He ate the second doughnut, swallowed the coffee in his cup and tossed his head to get the grey curl up. He quelled the bitter rising in his throat.

"Thanks," he said and got up, a sensation of scalding itch spreading over his torso. "I'll give them to her tonight. Time to go to work and make a dollar." He was out the door and Dick Cude saw how he threw the bag into the truck cab, saw from the way he was bending over and scrabbling on the floor that the tapes must have fallen out. He'd slung in the sack hard enough to burst it. Those plastic tape cases had sharp corners. He noticed Conrad still didn't fasten his seat belt and he was smoking as he drove out of the parking lot. The way he twitched the hair off his forehead like that, he was asking for a neck injury. Dick pursed his lips.

When Conrad pulled into his driveway that evening, every window in the house shot mango-yellow light into the dusk and there were three or four cars parked out front. Oh Jesus, don't let something else have happened, he said aloud, letting the wind catch the truck door and strain the hinges, running up the steps and into the smell of oregano and yeast, from upstairs a tumult of music and feet and voices. His wife stooped over the sink whipping cream and the counter was arranged like a buffet, the blue and white plastic plates, a fan of teaspoons, celery and carrot sticks, squares of orange longhorn and two-tone olives in geometric formation, a wooden bowl bristling with potato shoestrings.

"What the hell's going on?"

"Don't tell me you forgot. I must of said it a hundred times: The *fifth*, Vela is having a *party*, her friends from *school* are coming over for a *party*. They're all upstairs now. I made strawberry shortcake. I'll never do it again; this damn dark old kitchen, it's like threading a needle in a coal mine. They're gonna eat up in her room, all the chairs are up there. We can eat in the living room. I got a card table set up in there for us. There's a couple beers for you in the icebox. What's in the bag?"

"Something for her. Dick Cude got some tapes for her, or something. Christ I'm sick of hearing him go on about the accident. It's like that's all he can talk about in that drooly voice. He kept trying to edge the conversation around to Russell."

"Russell who?"

"The nephew. Cude's goddamn nephew that's still out in the desert." The music throbbed through the floor in a steady awful beat that made him clench his jaws.

"Who's up there?"

"Audrey. Your boss's daughter. Audrey Henry and a few other girls. I'll bring it up unless you want to go up and tell them the food's ready. You want to go up?"

"No, you handle it. Maybe they can turn down the bass while we eat."

She laughed, not her normal laugh but a stagy ha-ha she had learned from television. "Oh I doubt it. It's a party."

Five girls sat on the edge of the bed or the wooden kitchen chairs. There was a line of soda cans on the windowsill. Audrey Henry held her tape player on her lap, her fingers tapping it lightly. Her silvery hair was cropped in a bowl cut, the back of her head shaved. She wore baggy army fatigues and a jewel-tone violet sweater that showed her midriff.

Nancy stood in the doorway smiling at the girls, speaking in her high party voice. "Audrey, that's a cute sweater, what is it, mohair? Cashmere! Well, it's beautiful. Anyway, the pizza and all is ready, so you gals go help yourself. And take a lot, there's more in the oven, I got it set on low. Vela, Dick Cude sent some tapes over to you."

Vela was propped against the expensive foam wedge pillow, a cola on her tray, the long glass straw protruding. Her complexion was a rash of pimples, her hair long and limp despite Nancy's work with the curling iron. Her useless hands were hidden under the art quilt Nancy had sewed, a pattern of ivy leaves she saw as elegant.

"Tapes. *All right,* tapes, what are they? It's heavy, there must be a hundred in here." Audrey poured the plastic cases onto the bed. The stiff old accordion bumped out.

"God, what's that thing!"

"It's an accordion. What a wreck." Kim, who had been playing piano accordion since the fifth grade but hated the instrument and longed to take guitar, picked it up. The stiffened bellows resisted and she quit after it panted a few thin, wailing notes like an asthmatic baby. "It doesn't play. What're the tapes? Myron Floren, who's he? 'Polka the Night Away,' 'Polka Is for Lovers'? Look at this one, look at this ugly guy."

"Hey, play one. For kicks."

"OK, here's 'Polka Maniacs.' Put it on."

They screamed with laughter, they killed themselves imitating dancers moving to the schlocky oompah, a beat that slugged with the verve of a pile driver.

Vela was mortified.

"Ma, I don't want that junk. Take it out. Just throw it in the trash. And that thing too," pointing her chin at the accordion. Audrey pressed a button on the player and the tape shot out. She dropped it in the plastic bag as if disposing of a reeking bone and slapped the booming, chanting tape in its place.

"What group is that?" said Nancy. "They sound cool."

"*Loop a troop, bazooka, the scheme . . . ,*" came the hard male voices.

"Public Enemy. I love it. Mom, that's what I want for my birthday, this tape."

"Your father says it's pretty loud."

"It's *rap!* It's got to be loud."

"Well, you gals better hit that buffet. There's strawberry shortcake with whipped cream for dessert."

"Can I squirt it out of the can, Mrs. Gasmann? I love that stuff."

"I'm sorry, Audrey—it's the kind you whip in a bowl, heavy cream."

"I'll pass. I hate that stuff. It's not sweet. I'll just eat the strawberries. You got any Tropicana?"

Nancy couldn't understand why they all started to laugh. "Vela, did you tell your friends we're going to Disney World in the spring?"

"Oh my god," said Audrey. "Disney World."

(The next year, in the darkness of early morning, Audrey flew to Boston, the first woman in her family to go to college. Below, orange-lighted towns spread across the prairie like a luminous paste, the highways traced out by long streams of headlights, workers moving down the darkness toward their jobs. The streets of cities seemed shining furrows. The sunrise broke blood-orange through sullen cloud in the east as they descended to the mass of scar tissue that was Chicago.)

Nancy and Conrad sat in the living room chairs and stared at the television, listening to the noise from upstairs.

"Who brought that jungle-bunny crap? Audrey?" He tossed back his grey curl.

"Who else? Wearing a cashmere sweater that must of cost two hundred bucks." They stared at the television.

"There's nothing on but the war," said Nancy. "It's nothing but smoke. You can't see any guns or anything."

"Yah. It's the Rackis set all the oil wells on fire."

"You want some strawberry shortcake?"

"Does a bear shit in the woods?" His pizza rinds lay on the chair arm like doughy smiles.

Trash

Old Glory and seven other towns in the county paid to send their trash to Mississippi when the state closed down the dumps and the regional landfills could hold no more. On a sun-fired March morning Whitey Kunky, working his Saturday job on the town trash truck, with red-bearded Martin H. Swan driving, heaved plastic bags and Lands' End boxes into the ass end of the compactor, occasionally finding something good and tossing it into the cab. The week before, they'd rescued some half-full bottles of gin and bourbon from the Bunnbergers' garbage and after scraping the coffee grounds and bacon grease off the bottles, drove around drinking it, and Martin made up a couple of blunts and they booted out. The job had a few perks.

"Old man Bunnberger must be going on the wagon," said Martin H. Swan, combing his beard with his fingers.

"Or his wife done it when he wasn't looking."

But today the collection was poor, a deflated basketball that perhaps could be fixed and a cracked bike frame that couldn't, a German toaster with burned English muffins protruding, and an old green accordion. He threw the toaster and the accordion into the cab.

At the end of the run they had to wait beside the loader for the semi that hauled it all away to Mississippi. Snakes, the driver, was a workout freak in a leather jacket. He wore a belt buckle stamped with a radiant cross, an award from the company for his three-year safe driving record. He leased the truck from a Christian trucking company, Covenant of God, that specialized in nationwide late-night transport of garbage, sludge and hazardous waste.

"The Snake is late."

"Yeah." Martin H. Swan chewed the nicotine gum that was supposed to ease him off cigarettes. He kept the truck running for heat against the late afternoon chill.

"He was late last week too."

"It's not him, it's the guy that works with him, that fat black jigaboo. Tapper. There's something nuts about that guy. You see the way he's always talking to himself when Snake tells him to do something?" He spat the gum out the window and took a cigarette from the pack in his shirt pocket, lit it.

"Yeah. Hey, after, let's get some beer."

"After."

"Too bad Mrs. Bunnberger didn't clean out the liquor cabinet again. There he is, down making the turn."

"It's only him. See? He hasn't got the other guy. Or else Tapper's down there giving him a blow job. You're gonna have to help him load."

"Jesus Christ, why not you? I been picking up all day."

"I got seniority. Anyway, it's all automatic. All you got to do is work the levers, pick up the spill and help Snakes get the tarp on. What's so bad about that?"

"Seniority? You can drink your fuckin beer by yourself."

"I planned to anyway, you little shit."

Getaway

Halfway through the job the hydraulic system jammed and it took twenty minutes to clear it out. It was a long, stinking job and Whitey slammed and shoveled and pitched the stuff that fell over the side. He swore aloud at Martin H. Swan who sat in the town truck reading his motorcycle magazine and every seven or eight minutes lifting his head to check on him. Snakes didn't say anything but jumped around athletically, his belt buckle winking, connecting the hydraulics, snugging down the olive drab canvas tarp.

He scraped some gluey shit off his boot, looked at Whitey and said, "hey, how'd you like to make the run to Mississippi? Tapper quit on me. I got the authority to hire a helper. But we got to get on the road. I'm running late. You want to call home or pack a suitcase, I'll give you fifteen minutes. That's all anybody needs for anything. That's my theory."

(Tapper Champagne was in Oklahoma for the funeral of his sixteen-year-old brother, Li'l Duke Champagne, sent to a Youth Leadership Academy for six months to get straightened out, learn how to eat peas, do sit-ups, mop floors and shine shoes, say yes sir and stay out of trouble. One morning he didn't get up, strangled by an asthma attack diagnosed the night before by the counselor as malingering.)

"Yeah. *Yeah,* I'll come. I'm ready now." He grabbed his jacket, the toaster and the accordion from the seat next to Martin H. Swan and climbed up into the high semi cab, into the comfortable seat, saw the rack of CDs, Dwight Yoakam and Vince Gill, and the decals from every state stuck on the headliner along with sparkly crosses and religious mottoes, and he thought, I'm getting out, it's that easy and I'm getting out. I'll never wake up here again. He called down, "hey, Martin, I wanta do this, you know? Can you call my old man?"

"Yeah," said Martin. He was chewing four pieces of nicotine gum.

It was a three-day run and they slept in the truck. The rig was one of the new computerized models that shut down after ten hours of operation forcing the driver to stop, though Snakes said he knew a way to bypass it but it wasn't worth it, and the back of the oversized cab was like a little apartment with a glass-topped stove and a counter and a TV and a fold-up sink and fancy imitation-wood paneling, but Snakes got up two hours before the computer, waiting for it to tick over, he wanted to make time, and sat eating bee pollen and drinking espresso coffee. He showed Whitey how to brew the thick stuff in a little machine on the counter, told him he'd get used to the black stuff, said Tapper put four teaspoons of sugar in his, making a thick, sweet sludge. Snakes was a good guy and he liked a laugh so Whitey mugged and did imitations and even sat on the damned accordion making it groan and loosening it up enough to squeeze some roars and farts out of it. He enjoyed Snakes's easygoing pleasantries, and on the third day, when they were coming into Mississippi, black people slouching around, Snakes said that where they were going, where the huge landfill was, was right next to some nigger houses, it shouldn't be there but it was, their wells were filled with poison.

Whitey had never thought about being a truckdriver, it had sounded like a lousy, low-down job to him in the past, but now that he was in the truck he'd changed his mind; he was out of Old Glory and seeing the rest of the world, listening to music, cracking jokes. The truck smelled good because Snakes didn't smoke and had a pine tree air freshener hanging off the rearview. Once, the talk got serious and Snakes told Whitey about his bad divorce ten years ago and beating up his ex-wife and doing some jail time because of it and getting religion, and Whitey told about the scrap metal that flew off his father's truck and cut off this girl's arms and how they never knew a thing until the girl's father came to their house and started wrestling with his father and crying and nobody could understand what he was saying until the phone rang and his mother answered it, hearing a neighbor say, you all right? I see Conrad's truck at your place and it kind of worried me considering the situation, and his mother answering, better come over quick. And he cried when he told it and was furious at this sign of childish weakness and to get back to normal again he put down the window and pitched the accordion into a wasteland of shacks and weeds.

"Yeah," said Snakes. "You know what I do now? I climb. I'm a rock climber whenever I get a break. You drive a truck, you get out of shape, you eat junk road food, you get a pear ass, you smoke, your wind is shot, you lose your strength. I started climbing a few years ago, after I found God, and it's like I was born again twice. I quit smoking, got my body back, hard as a rock, I can wear my old navy uniform now I couldn't get into since I was twenty-two. And you see some unreal places; it sets you up. You're closer to God, or something. You ought to try it, young kid like you. You'd be a natural."

"Yeah," said Whitey. "I might try it. Martin H. Swan is trying to give up smoking. He chews that nicotine gum and smokes just the same."

"That don't work. You got to do it cold turkey. You got to have faith in yourself."

(Some year or two later, Snakes, using a climbing rope with a single core in a color pattern of purple, neon pink, teal and fluorescent yellow, hung himself in the cab of his truck. A note on the seat read: "I'm not going to wear glasses.")

Your mama's got change coming

The Diamond Grocery Store stood out on the edge of the highway in the scalding sun, a quarter of a mile from two rows of shacks bisected by a mud-holed track. The store, fifteen by twenty, sported a sloping

concrete step and a three-tier false front of warped and paintless clapboard, a cracked plate-glass window mended with lightning-bolt adhesive tape. A hand-lettered sign at the top read GROCERIS, and over the
door another sign announced HOME MAD SUSAGE & HOT BOODIN.
The window was pasted up with ancient advertisements for JAX Best
Beer in Town, NEHI, Quality Ice Cream, Dental Snuff, Brown's Mule,
root beer, and Show Down, Welcome, TOP, Regal, Royal, King, Prince
and Duke's Choice chewing tobaccos. There was a single gas pump, 85
octane.

At the back of the store was a three-room ell under a corrugated
metal roof where Addie, the middle-aged daughter of Clarence Stranger
(dead since 1987 when the seat chain of a carnival swing broke and
hurled him onto a baby stroller), took care of her senile husband, thirty
years older than she, kept the store accounts, cooked heavy dinners and
painted the scenes of her childhood on square pieces of plywood, print-
ing in the margins explanatory text of the events depicted. (A tiny black
girl in a pink dress with a white cape spangled with stars ran over a
plowed-earth landscape, pursued by huge men in masks, their legs
spread like scissors, sinister bulges in their crotches. ALMOST GOT ME.
SIX YR OLD MY MOTHER TOLD ME STAY AWAY FROM FLAT TOWN
RD. I WENT THERE. MEN CHASED ME. YELLED GET OUT OF HERE
YOUR FATHER IS A B———.) She was short and thin, her face diamond-
shaped, with deep cheek dimples and eyebrows arched high like croquet
hoops.

To the left of the door was a second window, smaller than the plate
glass and with a sliding pane that let her serve customers standing outside—beer buyers. Below the sliding pane was a shelf displaying a jumble of dusty objects: two red paper rolls of caps and a toy pistol, a box
of wood screws, Smith Brothers, Vicks, and Luden's cough drops, a torn
packet of cut plug leaking brown dust, four empty glass jars, covers
askew, everything browned by sunlight, fly-specked and dusty.

Inside the store two big coolers roared, one filled with beer, the other
with soft drinks and sodas, and against the back wall stood a refrigerator with milk, bacon, eggs, a few tired heads of lettuce; from front to
back ran green painted shelves of canned goods, yams, hominy grits,
peanut butter, store bread, soap and sugar.

She leaned against the frame of the sliding window watching the
traffic pass on the highway. A white truck with Arkansas plates pulled
in, a skinny dude with three days' worth of five o'clock shadow asking
for 35-millimeter color print film; she had it. Mr. Tek walked in with
Mrs., looking for condensed milk for their chicory, looking for mar-

garine and matches; she had it all. The FedEx man, wisps of acid jazz and digital loops seeping from his earphones, swerved in, bid for a cold Co'-Cola; she had it. Cigarettes, gas, candy bars, aspirin, cold cuts, ballpoint pens, she had it, she had it.

Down by the double row of houses her glance fell on three children playing, couldn't be more than four or five years old, Tiny Faulk's twins and their baby brother, must be. One was trying to tap-dance in the dirt, copying that dancer on *Sesame Street.* Now they were jumping off the sagging step of the shack where Tiny Faulk lived, hardly more than a kid herself, thin and bad-tempered, screaming at those babies to shut up when she was home. At least she kept them, taking care of them, not like the woman in the papers up in New York, walked out of the hospital the day after she had twins, false name, no way to find her. She saw Tiny every morning walking up the road to catch the bus to World, glaring down at the road, shifting from foot to foot impatiently, had some kind of job in World, in the meat-packing plant or the laundry, maybe both. Old Mrs. Simms supposed to look after the babies for ten dollars a week, but she was half blind and three-fourths deaf and lame-legged on both sides so she sat on the porch, turned up her hearing aid and fell asleep. Couldn't hear them most of the time and Addie knew that sooner or later there'd be brakes screaming and somebody would run into the store saying, oh god, I run over a little chile.

Sure enough, the bigger ones were running up to the edge of the highway, daring each other to stand on the last safe inch, and when a car or truck came blaring by, they'd jump back, laughing. Now look at them, squatting in the dirt and raising a dust cloud. Half drowsing, she watched them wander down the row of shacks and disappear behind the outhouses. She could see them getting run over so clear it was like a painting. She might make that painting someday if it happened. She painted only after the fact for fear of making something bad come true.

It was late in the morning and she was reading the *World Journal* when the door squeaked open and the twins and baby brother came in and headed toward the beer cooler.

"What you doin?"

"We wants sodas."

"Sodas costs money. You got money?"

"Yeah."

"Well, you won't find no soda there, that's beer for mens. Other cooler got the soda." She watched them climb on the box provided for shorter customers and heave up the cover. They talked together in murmuring voices, lifting the bottles high enough from the icy water to see the contents, settled finally on a Yoo-Hoo and an Orange Crush and a Lime. The twin in the striped shirt—filthy beyond belief—handed her the money.

"What's this you given me?" She had to look and look again.

"Dollar."

"A dollar! I guess it's a dollar! Where you get it?" Her hand was almost steady.

"Found it."

"Found it! I guess you found it! Whereabouts?"

"By the road."

"Yeah. By the road." Don't that beat it, she thought. All the need in the world for money and who finds it? Three kids who want to spend it on sweet sodas, who don't even know what they got. She could keep it, let them have their sodas, and who the hell would know? Not them. Not nobody. Must of been some bank robbers or drug lords going down the road, the windas wide open and a thousand-dollar bill flyin out like a green bird. Or else a counterfeit. Probably what it was, fake money, and she was going to be out three sodas.

"You all drink your sodas," she said. She put the thousand-dollar bill in the cash register under the pullout where she put twenties when she got them. There'd never been anything bigger than a twenty in that cash drawer. She watched them stand under the ceiling fan's cool whisper, swallowing, turning their bottles around and around, tracing lines on the beaded glass.

"Right now I'm goin a take a walk by the road, see there's any more a these dollars. You all come sit out on the steps."

She walked along the road in both directions, scrutinizing the faded beer cans and cigarette packets, the muddy potato chip bags and scraps of plastic in the weeds. The sun was cruelly hot.

"There's nothin there. Must a been the onliest one." She strode back to the store, thinking she'd close up at two, go to the bank and find out was it real.

The children were sitting on the steps, down to the last inch of soda and taking tiny sips, sloshing the liquid around in the bottles for the rich wet sound.

"When your mother git home?"

"After supper. Late."

"I guess late! You all tell her come up here and see me. Tell her come to the store, she got change comin. Hear me? It's on you. You forget to tell her and it be a shame and a misery for her, she work so hard. And you all stay away from that road, you hear me?"

They put the empty bottles on the counter and straggled off toward the shack where old Mrs. Simms stood on the porch yelling, you come on here now. They kicked stones, jumped, the one in overalls saying, heyo, heyo, how you do. The smallest one's pants hung low and wet. They came abreast of the crumpled instrument in the weeds and the twin in the dirty striped shirt jumped on it again. *Waaaah,* the thing sounded, and they screamed with laughter. The one in overalls picked it up and heaved it onto the highway. A distant black dot on the shimmering road grew larger, rushed toward them.

"You all come on now," yelled Mrs. Simms.

The eighteen-wheeler moaned, slammed past them with a blast of hot air, and in its gritty wash fluttered thousand-dollar bills. Droopy-drawers bawled with an eyeful of grit.

"All right," called Mrs. Simms. "I'm gonna eat all this nice butterscotch puddin by myself. Gonna count to five and start eatin. One. Two. Three. Four." She held up a dish, gyrated a spoon above it.

"FIVE."